ONCE UPON
A BRIDGE

A TRILOGY

RICHARD LE NORMAND

The characters, situations and some of the places are entirely imaginary and bear no relation to any person, living or dead. Some of the events in this trilogy could easily have taken place as many unrecorded incidents happened during the Second World War. The author wishes to pay his respects to the French Resistance, whose enormous efforts and great sacrifice enabled the Allies to speed up the liberation of France and so shorten the War.

Book One: 'Killer at Large'
Book Two: 'Escape to Death'
Book Three: 'Play the Last Card'

First published in Australia 2014
Copyright © Richard Le Normand, 2014
This edition published 2013 by Waterwings Publishing

Cover design, typesetting: Chameleon Print Design.
Printed by Tenderprint Australia Pty Ltd.

Le Normand, Richard
Once Upon a Bridge Trilogy
ISBN: 978-0-9750000-5-2
pp476

ABOUT THE AUTHOR

Richard Le Normand was born in Jersey Channel Islands in 1927 and was educated at Victoria College Jersey 1936–1944. Richard left college early, to avoid being 'press-ganged' into the construction of German fortifications—most of the 'slave workers' having been killed off by then and labour was needed to complete their fortifications in Alderney, a sister isle.

After the Islands were liberated in 1945, Richard became a farmer, later specialising in intensive flower and tomato growing under glass. Richard then established a plastics factory to develop and produce new inventions, mainly in the horticultural field.

In 1987, Richard decided to retire and settle in Australia. He soon realised that retirement was not for him and became involved in marketing hydroponics. After spending nine interesting years working in real estate, Richard moved to the Gold Coast where he developed and patented an attachment for small boats. Finally, to pay for all his past sins, Richard started to write and publish books and short stories.

Once Upon a Bridge is a trilogy, the three parts of which have already been published separately.

The trilogy follows the journey of Marçel, firstly as a teenager, then as a young man coping with the vicissitudes and indeed, horrors of war, to its dramatic, moving and totally unexpected finale.

To dear Ruth

For all her help and support when most needed

TABLE OF CONTENTS

BOOK ONE

A Killer at Large

PROLOGUE

....

Would it ever have occurred to you that the person sitting next to you on the ten-thirty train from Brisbane to the Gold Coast could be a cold-blooded killer? No? Well, think again. The cheerful-looking and ageing gentleman in the seat next to you may be just that …

I smiled when I looked around the carriage at the four badly behaved teenage boys and wondered if given the same circumstances they would have been able over a period of three years, to quietly and efficiently slit the throats of eight men. Could they grip and hold back a man's head while sliding a knife across his throat, listen to the gasp and then the gurgle as he choked to death?

Could anything arouse in them the cold and deadly anger that had given me the power to kill?

Listening to concert music that evening and the excited chatter of the young boys on their way out of the concert hall, I pondered over the continual media coverage of an alleged Latvian war criminal of so long ago. Living in a country that has not had to face an enemy occupation brought back the memories.

I realised the time had finally come to tell my story, of the exploitation of sex coupled with violent death. It was getting on for sixty years since it all began and maybe now it was time to relive the experience that I had so successfully put out of my mind for so long.

CHAPTER 1

Walking up the stone slipway shortly after dawn that morning, I suddenly realised I had a machine gun pointing directly at me. I stood, frozen to the spot.

I had just reached the tender age of sixteen and had slipped out of the house, two hours before curfew ended. I had gone down to the beach to look at my fishing lines, which sadly only had the remains of two red mullet.

Unfortunately, the crabs had been there first ...

I decided to adopt the image of a silly dim teenager, which at the time I was anyway, quite unaware of the danger I had placed myself in, I gave the German guards a big smile and a happy wave and would have continued on my way. This was not to be and so began unimaginable events over which I would have little control and which changed me from an innocent young teenager into a cold-blooded killer.

'Halt. Kommen sie hier.'

I was grabbed by two scruffy guards who, having finished their night duty, were unshaven and had the typical German soldier sour smell that came from living off rye bread, heavy smoking, and living in cramped conditions where showers were the exception.

The gun emplacement was a machine gun located on the roof of a deserted café situated across the road opposite the top of the slipway.

From this same outpost some time later, a young man was killed trying to escape from the beach in a small boat. I was marched, or rather dragged, to the back of the café and taken into the kitchen. Although I could speak a little German, I was unable to understand what the guards were shouting to me, guessing they had been drinking on duty, but I was quite unprepared for what was to come.

They started hitting me. The blows came hard and fast. I tried to shout at them to stop but my mouth was full of blood and I was beyond speech and resistance. I was pushed down onto what must have been the kitchen table and struck in the face and body. I felt my legs being pulled apart. My vision was fading. A face with a very strange expression was the last thing I remembered before I lost consciousness.

I came to later, to the sounds of a German officer screaming at the two German guards who were then led away by two *Feldgendamerie* guards. I was told later that the two soldiers had been executed without trial for sexually assaulting a civilian.

I was still lying on the kitchen table, hurting all over. My face was swollen and very sore but the agonising pain was lower down; my bottom was on fire. I felt I had been ripped apart. I slid off the table and retrieved my pants and trousers but I could not stop myself from shaking all over. At the age of sixteen I had been brutally raped.

As well as the severe pain and aching all over my body, I was overcome with a terrible feeling of shame and disbelief at what had happened to me.

That feeling of shame was to stay with me for the rest of my life and was to turn into a deep, cold and lasting anger, which was to control my actions for many years.

The German officer walked up to me and slapped my face. 'Young English Piglet. You have flirted with two of my men and now they must die because of you. For that, I am arresting you on the charge of spying on the German coastal defences in this area. Piglet, you will be taken to the Gloucester Street prison in St Helier where you will be interrogated and then I hope that will be the end of you.'

I was pushed into the back of the waiting truck and wedged between two of the soldiers. Although it was a warm sunny day, I was still shaking badly. I could detect sympathetic if not warm glances from the two Germans who held onto me all the way to the prison, but the last thing I wanted to do was jump out of the truck.

At the prison, I was taken to a room where I was told to strip, given a piece of soap, and a hose was turned on me. The water was very cold but I was too upset to care. I was being treated like an animal and felt completely humiliated. I tried hard to wash away all that had happened to my body that morning, but mentally I was to feel dirty for a long time to come.

Still wet all over and naked I was marched down a flight of stairs along a narrow passageway and pushed into a small cell: no window, just a dim ceiling light, a wooden bed, blanket and bucket. The guard slapped my bare buttocks, pushing me roughly into the cell and locked the door on his way out. I lay on the bare boards of the bed, with the blanket as a pillow. Lying on my side with my legs drawn up was the most comfortable position for me; I was still in shock at what had happened in such a short time. My mind going around in circles, I drifted into a deep sleep.

When I woke up it must have been, I guessed, sometime in the late afternoon. I had no means of telling the time with no window in my cell; it could have been night or day but I never normally slept more than seven hours at a time. I now felt really frightened. It had all happened in such a short time. I wondered if my parents knew where I was. I forced myself to calm down and think clearly about what had happened, what my position was and what I should try to do to extricate myself from this mess.

———

My parents had sent me to the top boys' school in Jersey, though it must have been very difficult for them. The family business was having a very hard time; the factory had been destroyed when the Germans bombed the Island. I was not a very good student, being a bit lazy, and I put more energy into enjoying myself than into my studies. However, my maths master had made a lasting impression on me and I always tried to follow his logical way of resolving problems.

In 1940, soon after the terrible events of Dunkirk and the withdrawal of the Allied forces in France, a large number of people were evacuated to Britain from the Channel Islands. At this time, the Islands received several attacks from the air in preparation for the landing of the German occupying forces. They were to remain on the Islands for the next five years. I was twelve years old at that time and although frightened during the air raids, I and the other boys found it all rather exciting. Not so our parents, who realised all the dangers and shortages we were about to experience.

The shops soon became empty. All guns, cars, motorcycles and radios were handed over to the Germans. The island was put under a permanent curfew and the currency was changed from Sterling to Reich marks. The banks were emptied and the money sent to Berlin.

Sometime later when the invasion of England was called off, Hitler decided to fortify the Channel Islands, in line with the fortifications being constructed all along the French coastline. Heavy guns were brought over to the Islands to fire on any shipping entering the English Channel. To achieve this, large numbers of 'slaves' from Russia and Europe were brought to the Islands. Very many of these slaves were to die during this enormous construction of the fortifications.

Hitler was very proud to have conquered part of the United Kingdom and had special books printed for all the schoolchildren in the Islands. We were ordered to learn the German language. Although I (like all the boys at my school) tried not to learn the language, I did learn enough to be very useful in what was to happen to me in the years to come.

My first experience of slave labour came about when I, with two other boys of my age, decided to go to Fort Regent to see if we could retrieve our air pistols, which we considered quite harmless.

Inside the Fort, we happened to open a door that led into a courtyard where, to our horror, we witnessed about twenty bedraggled men running in a circle. A German with a steel whip was hitting them to make them move faster. Luckily, we had not been seen and so retreated at great speed never to go near Fort Regent again!

At another time, the boy who sat next to me at school was taken away with his father. The Germans had found them in possession of a radio set. We were told they both died in a cattle truck on the way to Germany. In those days, many stories were told of similar events.

The Gestapo were always around, their intention being to create fear and therefore discipline in the civil population. It was very successful.

———

On thinking about my experience behind the gun emplacement and all the other events leading up to this day, my fear slowly turned to a deep and cold anger that I could feel slowly rising up inside me. It took complete control of my body and brain. In a matter of minutes, I had changed from a happy young sixteen-year-old boy into what would turn out to be a cold-blooded and dangerous man. How dangerous I was soon to find out—a cold and calculating killer!

I realised that the German officer must have been told that I was flirting with the two guards and had led them into thinking I was looking for a sexual encounter. Although I was ignorant of these things at the time, I did know that a few men were homosexual and did things together, but I knew I was certainly *not* like that. Girls to me were getting very interesting but as yet, in those days, quite unobtainable. I would call for a guard to bring me my clothes and take me to the officer in charge, I would explain that it was all a terrible mistake and could they ask for my parents to come and fetch me.

The cell door opened and two guards came in. They took hold of my arms. I was still naked, but they marched me along the passage and into a large bare room. An officer and an NCO were seated at a table.

The guards moved back and I was made to stand in the centre of the room on a wire mat. The two men at the table disappeared from view as the lights were switched on. The powerful lights were directed at me and I almost lost my balance trying to shield my eyes. I was now unable to see anyone else in the room. The nightmare of finding myself naked in a room full of people no longer mattered to me. I was far too worried about my situation and was past caring about my nakedness.

'"Piglet" is the name we have here for you. Please give us your full name.' That was the last time I was to hear the word 'please'.

I gave my full name and address and tried to explain that this was all a big mistake and that all I had done was to break curfew in order to attend to my fishing lines. I asked as politely and as calmly as I could if they would call my parents and ask them to come and collect me. I heard the sound of laughter, and the officer in charge started speaking quite softly to me.

'I think the name Piglet suits you better than your given name—a pink piglet without a tail. So we will from now on, address you as Piglet.' A short silence and then in a much stronger and sharper tone: 'It is not as simple as you would like, Piglet. Your identity card gave us your name, date of birth and address. We have informed your parents that you have been arrested for spying on our gun emplacements and that you have already been sent on to our Paris Headquarters for questioning.'

As his words sank in, I had a deep feeling of fear and foreboding. I switched my mind to the events of that morning and felt the cold anger returning. *Yes, I liked the name Piglet. The Germans would rue the day they messed with Piglet.*

'When your mother became agitated, we warned her that you were very lucky to have been arrested by the *Wermacht* and not by the *Gestapo*. The *Gestapo* would have immediately arrested all your family, their close friends and your school friends also, Piglet. You also, Piglet, have been saved from a possible nasty slow death by the *Gestapo*—this is why you will be taken to Paris leaving the harbour three hours before dawn. You will be taken by train under escort to Paris where you will be interrogated. You will then be tried before a German army court. At worst you will be sentenced to death, but at least it will be quick and clean.'

Then, returning to the soft but menacing voice, 'Your parents were clearly told that if they kept quiet and just told their friends that you had been taken to Paris for questioning regarding a minor offence, there would be a good chance of them seeing you again one day. However, to complain to the local authorities could lead to disaster for them and many others. Your mother and father understand the situation and will be very quiet from now on. So, Piglet, there is now just the little matter of the complaint from *Oberleutenant* Grossman. He alleges you flirted with two of his men causing them to be summarily executed for the crime of sexual assault on a member of the local population. This *flirting* is not a charge a court would handle so we will now give you a light punishment, a taste of what is to come to you when you arrive in Paris. You will raise your hands above your head.'

My hands touched what I thought was a chain to which was attached a pair of handcuffs. The chain must have been lowered down to suit my height. The two guards stepped forward. One lifted me slightly and the other clicked on the cuffs. My feet, except for my heels, were on the wire mat.

The first blow was across my bare buttocks. I nearly lost my footing. The pain was sharp and agonising. They were using a heavy cane. The second blow was on my lower legs. I let out a scream; this was to be the only one they would get from me. I had decided that anger could overcome pain so now was the time to put it to the test. It worked. As the blows rained down and the anger in my mind took over, I forgot the pain. I was planning a vicious retribution. I would kill as many Germans as I could. I would hunt down the *Oberleutenant* and I would cut his throat. He would slowly bleed to death.

The blows stopped. I had conquered pain and fear. Well, almost. I was burning all over but I had not cried, nor would I. I was dragged to the next room and was again hosed down, I did not appear to have any cuts but I knew the next day I would have many bruises over my back and legs. When they took me back to the cell, I found my clothes on the bed. By now I had become used to being naked and had lost my sense of shame. This must have been because of the defiance and anger that I had felt.

A guard reappeared with a tin of unpleasant-looking soup and a large hunk of bread. Another tin contained water. I realised how hungry and thirsty I was—I had not eaten for twenty-four hours.

'You will be shortly receiving visitor. It is now ten o'clock. In six hours you will be taken to the harbour. After visitor, you sleep.'

The food and the thought of maybe my father coming to get me out of this situation cheered me up. It came as a shock when the cell door opened and in strode *Oberleutenant* Grossman.

I had leaped up from the bed only to find myself face to face with the person who was responsible for me being in this situation. I sank back on the edge of the bed and looked up at his face. He was smiling at me. I was not sure what to expect from him. I was reminded of the expression on the face of my headmaster at prep school just before I was to receive a heavy caning.

'So, my Piglet, you have a sore arse, huh? That is good, a small compensation for me. However, you have stirred up certain feelings within me, which, I have decided, will make me more lenient towards you. I also will travel to Paris. I travel on behalf of the prosecution; I hold your life in my hands. On the other hand, for certain small favours … I could help you.'

I was shocked, but then it all fell into place. This Grossman was a homosexual and he was going to take control of me. My mind was racing: do I go along with this and then go back to face my family, or was I prepared to face more beatings and then finally be executed?

I knew that if I did what this swine expected, I could never go back to my family without feeling a terrible shame that would be with me forever. I could not face that.

My eyes were about level with his waist. I looked at his revolver and wondered if I could snatch it from its holster. Impossible.

Then it dawned on me that maybe Grossman had handed me a different and perhaps, very powerful weapon that I could use to my advantage, but not at this moment.

I decided to take a risk.

I looked up at his face with an innocent smile, '*Herr Oberleutenant*, what am I expected to do and how are you able to help me?'

Grossman roared with laughter, turned on his heel and walked out of the cell. I was puzzled at first and then on reflection began to feel rather stupid.

The *Oberleutenant* called the guard as he left the cell, the guard looked back and smiled.

Within minutes, I was fast asleep.

CHAPTER 2

'Wake up, Piglet.' The guard was leaning over me. It took several seconds for me to realise where I was. 'We leave in ten minutes.' He had placed a tin of liquid porridge and a tin of water by the door and on the bed—a grubby-looking jacket. I was still dressed in my fishing clothes—just shirt, pants and trousers so the jacket was very welcome to me at this time of night.

I washed my face with some of the water and ate the porridge, or rather drank it and painfully moved around the room until I was able to rid myself of the stiffness from the beating of the evening before.

Two guards came in and I was marched out of the cell along the passages and out through the large studded door of the prison. It was pitch dark and quite cold. We walked the length of the esplanade and then all the way down to the end of the jetty past several converted river barges that were used to bring troops, slaves and supplies to the island. We went down a steep gangway onto the deck of a German patrol boat.

This rather surprised me as I expected to be taken to France on one of those converted barges. I realised the reason for the patrol boat was that neither the army nor the navy wanted the *Gestapo* involved in my arrest.

Long and deep investigation by the *Gestapo* often revealed matters that also involved members of the armed services and so for their own sakes they were determined to get me to their Paris headquarters as quietly and as quickly as possible.

Not being a good sailor, I was pleased that we were travelling on a fast and therefore a much safer boat across the thirty-odd miles of water to France. Maybe we would get to our destination before daylight and avoid being attacked from the air.

We were taken to the stern of the boat where I was then handcuffed to one of the guards. I carefully noted into which pocket he put the key.

The other guard laughed and saluted his friend. 'Some people get all the luck; have a good time in Paris.' He turned on his heel and marched up the gangway and into the night.

We sat on a pile of rope between the depth charges and I wondered what would happen if they decided to fire them. When I asked, the time by the guard's watch (stolen I expect from some unfortunate prisoner) was three-thirty am.

Although the deep anger was still with me, because of my age I expect, I had a slight feeling of excitement and adventure and my spirits lifted a little. It was time to plan how I was going to escape. I had no intention of going to Paris and perhaps facing a firing squad. If I was going to die, it would be at *my* time and place and I would try to take a German with me. Such is the optimism of youth.

I knew we had a choice of two ports: St Malo or Granville. Granville was the nearer and had a better train link with Paris. However, we went to St Malo. It took us five hours. That suited the plan that was starting to form in my mind. My father had mentioned at some time that it used to be a slow train from St Servant to Rennes via Dol, where you then changed to a faster train for Paris.

However, that was before the war so things might have changed a lot since then. Grossman had given me a very useful tool that I intended to use on the guard and which would give me a good opportunity to escape—sex.

The guard's name was Heinrig, but I decided to call him Henry. He was of medium height, a little on the fat side and to me quite old, at least thirty. He came from Austria and was married. I noticed he kept looking down at me and when he accidentally brushed his hand against my leg, I looked up and smiled at him. I had started the process that could lead to my escape. Henry did not have a heavy coat or helmet. He carried a light bag and was armed with a revolver and a bayonet. It was this that interested me, not the revolver. I had a plan that would depend mainly on the time that we left St Malo for Paris, for I would need the cover of darkness to make my plan work.

A sailor appeared with two mugs of *ersatz* coffee and two large hunks of bread filled with a very tasty sausage—a real 'hot dog'. This was the best food I had tasted for a long time and was also the last good food I was to get for quite some time.

We left Jersey at low tide so that we could enter the St Malo basin at high tide and avoid using the damaged lock gates. As it took five hours to reach St Malo, we must have gone the long way around the large reef that ran between Jersey and St Malo. It was a bright sunny day when we arrived and we had not been attacked by Allied planes. Several barges carrying supplies, including food for the civilian population, to the islands had been sunk recently. There was a whole lot of activity on the dockside.

Barges were being loaded for the Channel Islands with food for the local and German population, guns and ammunition. The islands were not liberated until well after the French ports were retaken by the Americans, which meant the Germans were cut off from their supplies and were facing starvation by the time the war ended. The civilian population by then was receiving Red Cross parcels.

The lock gates to the harbour basin had been badly damaged when the British forces had evacuated in 1940, but they had been repaired sufficiently for us to enter the basin and tie up close to the old city wall. St Malo was a very fine walled-in city and was later to be flattened by the Americans. After the war, St Malo, with the aid of America, was restored stone by stone.

We disembarked, crossed the road and entered the old city through an archway. Henry marched me to an office which was a converted bar in the old city wall, a part that later survived the bombing that destroyed the town. The handcuffs were removed and I was told to sit on a bench while my guard completed all the paperwork and was given the train passes. Our train was to leave St Servan at eleven am; it was now nine-thirty am.

We were told we would have to walk to the station at St Servan, which was, I think, about two miles from where we were. I liked the idea of walking as I needed the exercise both for body and mind. The handcuffs had been put back on so I was securely attached to Henry. I think he liked having me attached to him.

I was a bit disappointed that the train was leaving so early, as my plan would have a better chance of success after dark and that meant delaying my move until we were almost in Paris. But I was about to get a little help from above.

We were about halfway to the station, in open ground with the water on one side and wooden sheds on the other. It looked like a holding place for slave workers. We heard the sound of aeroplane engines, which quickly turned to a roar. Henry pulled me down into a ditch that was filled with filthy water and then all hell was let loose as three *Spitfires* skimmed overhead, followed by the roar of exploding bombs.

In the silence that followed this lightning attack, we picked ourselves up, soaked from the very dirty water we had fallen into, but otherwise both unharmed. We could see a cloud of black smoke rising from the station and when we reached there the train was no more. The engine and two carriages had been destroyed and First Aid workers and police were pulling out the dead and wounded. This was my first experience of death at close range. Forty-eight hours ago I would have been shocked, instead I found myself smiling. This was not the innocent boy of yesterday. I was now a man and was soon to be a vicious killer.

We eventually found the station master who directed us to a truck that was going to Dol from where we were to get a train to Rennes if the lines were open. The journey to Dol was very uncomfortable. The road must have been damaged in several places by the Allied bombing and at times it felt as if we were not even on the road it was so bumpy. Henry had undone the handcuffs so that we could keep our balance, as the truck had to swing from side to side in order to dodge the worst of the damaged road. We were one of several armed trucks, I presumed because of possible attack from the French Resistance. Safety in numbers, but I just hoped we would not be strafed by another RAF patrol; it would be a shame to be killed that way and by our own side.

The railway yards were very busy at Dol as this was the crossroads to Mont St Michel, Granville and Cherbourg to the East and North, while to the West were St Malo, Dinan, St Brieuc, Morlaix and Brest.

The damage from bombing was everywhere but despite the Allied bombing, there was still a lot of activity transferring supplies from railway trucks to a string of waiting army trucks. I guessed most of the train movements must have taken place at night. I did notice that the trucks were being loaded and unloaded by slave workers heavily guarded by armed soldiers.

Henry clicked on the handcuffs and we both carefully lowered ourselves from the truck. It was now one-forty-five pm according to an ancient railway clock on the departure platform. We entered the cigarette smoke-filled army station master's office and an officer told Henry that we would board a train that was passing through at seven that evening or thereabouts. We were to report to his office at six-thirty. In the meantime, he gave us an address in the town where friendly locals and collaborators would feed us and we would be able to rest there until it was time to return to the station.

Henry was on no account to release me from the handcuffs and he was told that he was entirely responsible for my safe delivery to the headquarters in Paris.

We found the café, which was down a side street just off the main square; we went down two steps into a dingy room with lots of wooden tables and benches. There were several soldiers and navy men sitting around eating and drinking, all I presume waiting for trains that were going in different directions that evening.

The *patron* was expecting us and we were taken to a small room up some stairs. It had a table, chairs and a bed. There was no door to the room and just a very small window. The *patron* returned with two bowls of vegetable soup, a camembert cheese, tomatoes, an onion and a small loaf of German rye bread. This to me was an absolute feast. He returned a few minutes later with a bottle of local cider, a carafe of water and two grimy glasses. Henry slipped two English pound notes, stolen in Jersey no doubt, into the *patron's* pocket. He must have been here before. Between us we polished off all the food, but one taste of the cider was enough for me, I stuck to the water. I would need a very clear head for the next few hours.

We moved across to the bed, still handcuffed and lay alongside each other. Henry's free hand came across and touched my thigh. I gave him a sweet, innocent smile and luckily for me, the cider took effect. Henry fell asleep.

I had made this train journey five years ago with my dad; it was about thirty-four miles from Dol to Rennes, between the villages of Comburg and St Germain and a little before St Germain, there were two bridges fairly close together in wooded countryside. This would be the best place to jump. Hopefully the train would stop at some of these small stations or would be slow enough for me to at least see their names. I had a vague idea of how to deal with Henry. He was a substantially built man and I felt sure that he must be very fit. I was certainly not strong enough to overpower a person like him; I would have to be very agile, cunning and fast moving.

We arrived back at the station master's office sharp at six-thirty and were directed to a waiting room where there were a number of other people—civilians, army and navy personnel. At seven-forty-five our train arrived; two passenger carriages and a whole string of goods wagons. We were escorted to the rear of the second carriage by the station master's assistant. I had the window seat on the right-hand side, which was to prove very useful when it came to making my move.

The carriage was about half full and once we got under way, I noticed that most of the passengers were either sleeping or looking as if they would be asleep soon. Being late summer, the days were still quite long. It was after eight by Henry's watch and the light was beginning to fade. Another hour and it would be dark.

The train was moving very slowly, I thought about fifteen miles per hour, a good running speed. If Rennes was thirty-four miles, then I reckoned that it would be about a two and a half hour journey and I should therefore be ready to move just after nine—by Henry's watch in about forty-five minutes' time.

Henry had been a bit quiet since leaving the café. I think it must have been the effects of the cider so I moved our attached hands between his legs and wriggled up closer to him. When he looked down at me I gave him my sweet innocent smile. I would exploit the situation. I had a feeling of excitement, fear, and deep anger as I thought of my rape by the two guards. I continued to tease this German; it was going to be his last bit of pleasure in life.

We halted at Comburg and two civilians got off the train. Our next stop was Montreuil where just one person left the train. Time to move; it was getting pretty dark and we were moving through what appeared to be woodland.

'Henry, I badly need to go to the toilet.'

I gave him my warmest smile. 'Will you take me?' I held his hand.

He got the meaning and started to move. Out of the window I could see water; we were travelling alongside the Rance which ran from St Malo to Rennes. Perfect.

The toilet was very close to us at the rear of the carriage. We squashed in and Henry locked the door. He took off the handcuffs and laid his belt with his revolver and bayonet on the toilet seat.

Henry sank to his knees and lowered my trousers. What he did next roused me from my anger to a cold and clear-minded rage …

I slowly withdrew his bayonet and with a hand at each end, I brought it down with all my strength to the back of his neck. Henry collapsed in a heap. I think he was already dead but I held back his head and slashed his throat to make sure. The train rattled as it crossed the second bridge.

Henry was dead.

There was blood everywhere. I picked up the bayonet and wiped it on Henry's jacket. I removed his watch, placed the revolver and bayonet in his shoulder bag, pulled his body to one side of the toilet and with his bag over my arm, slowly opened the door. All was clear.

I crossed to the carriage door and looking out of the window, saw that the moon had come out. We were travelling alongside the Rance. The railway line was very near the riverbank, which was covered with grass and tall weeds. Perfect.

I opened the door and clutching the bag, leaped out as far as I could from the train. I hit the bank hard and allowed myself to keep rolling until I fell into the water. I scrambled back onto the bank, removed my shoes and jacket and squeezed them into the bag. The river, which was really a canal, was not very wide and I was a very good swimmer. I re-entered the water and lying on my back holding the bag with one hand, managed to slowly make my way across the canal.

I reached the bank on the opposite side, climbed out of the water, crossed the footpath and moved into the woodland. I found a spot amongst some bushes and sat down.

It was time to savour my escape and assess my situation.

—

I felt bruised and battered but was otherwise quite intact, except for a light cut on my left hand from holding the bayonet at both ends when I delivered my first blow to Henry. The rage had subsided and I was elated at what I had achieved. I felt no remorse or horror at what I had done—Henry had got what he deserved. I had killed my first German and it had been easy. Now there were three dead because of me in two days. Not bad.

So my position was this: Henry's body would be discovered at Rennes, or before if someone used the toilet, but I had all the documents regarding my arrest so it would take some time for the authorities to know who to look for and where to start looking. They may not even bother to do that, as so many Germans were being killed by the Resistance at this time and it might be simpler to just cover up the loss of one more soldier. However, I knew that I had to get as far away as possible from this railway line. I decided to become absorbed into the French way of life, perhaps on a farm, and keep a very low profile until the end of the war when I could return to Jersey.

Fate was to decide otherwise ...

CHAPTER 3

I decided to move on and find a place where I could dispose of the documents, the shoulder bag and all traces of Henry. I moved on through the woods up a steep slope, along a ridge and down a grass field to a road that I followed, keeping well to the side in case I had to dive for cover if any Germans were to appear.

I realised I would need certain things if I was going to survive—food, a map, a compass, a strong pair of shoes. I would also need some kind of bag as I could not, for obvious reasons, keep Henry's bag.

I noticed a large pond a little way off the road so went across to look at it. At one end of the pond there was a dilapidated hut surrounded by reeds, no doubt used for duck shooting. Inside the hut, I placed Henry's bag on a bench.

The first thing I found in the bag was a small flat German army torch, two boxes of matches and four packets of cigarettes of no use to me but they could be used perhaps as currency for food. There was a bag of toilet things (I might find the razor useful later to shave the few whiskers that were starting to grow on my face), a grubby pair of underpants and a vest. Henry had not intended to stay long in Paris I guessed. There were several documents that referred to me, including the passes to take us to our destination. These I burned using Henry's matches and I hid the ashes amongst the reeds. To my delight at the bottom of the bag I found a small army compass; this was the best thing that I found in the bag and was to prove very useful to me in the future.

Henry's toilet bag was quite big. It was a cloth bag that had a strong tape for closing it up. I expect Henry's wife must have made it for him. I put the razor, toothpaste, soap, cigarettes, matches and torch back into the toilet bag. After washing off the blood, I attached the bayonet to my belt and slipped it on the inside of my trousers. This was a bit uncomfortable but necessary. The compass I kept in my pocket. The rest of the things, including the revolver, I put in Henry's bag. I found a large stone which I also put in the bag and then waded into the pond up to my waist and lowered Henry's bag deep into the mud. I checked to see if I had left anything in the hut and clutching Henry's toilet bag walked back to the road.

———

Although the sky was now overcast, it was still light enough for me to see where I was going. According to the compass, the road was heading north. I found myself once again following the canal; I kept well clear of a series of locks, which must have been close to Hédé. Several hours later, I passed some houses and a battered sign by the side of the road that said 'Tinteniac'.

I walked cautiously along the village street past a few shops, but there were no locals about as it was long past curfew. There were a few cottages on the far side of the village.

I suddenly froze.

Just a few yards in front of me, I could see a German guard; he was standing on a stone bridge, lighting a cigarette.

I sank down to my hands and knees and slowly backed away, slipping into some low bushes. I was in the garden of the last cottage. Two motorcycles with sidecars were parked outside. The Germans who were guarding the bridge must have been based there. I kept slowly moving backwards until I came up against a low fence, slipped over the fence and landed in a duck pen. I decided to get to the back of the cottages where there must be better cover.

I found a lane that ran behind the cottages. At the end of the lane there was a narrow river, and close by, a smart-looking house with a large garden in front. At the side of the house was a double garage. This would be my target, hopefully I would get an opportunity to get inside, steal some food and perhaps find some more suitable clothes.

I found a small unlocked shed in the garden that was almost hidden by an overgrown magnolia bush from which I was able to clearly see the front of the house. I lay down on the bare boards inside the shed and fell asleep, oblivious to the sound of an arriving motor cycle, the slamming of a garage door and the opening and closing of the front door.

The sound of dogs barking woke me up. The front door of the house was open; two small dogs were dashing around the garden, chased by an attractive woman in a dressing gown. After a while, the woman and the dogs disappeared into the house and the door closed.

It was a fine summer day and it would soon become very warm inside the shed. I was hungry and thirsty but I was going to have to wait until the house was empty before I could leave the shed. I would have to reconsider my plan if the people remained in the house. It was more than likely that on a lovely summer's day like this the house would be unoccupied for a short while at least and I would be able to slip in and steal what I needed.

I looked at Henry's watch, seven-thirty am.

An hour later, a man came out of the front door. He was well dressed, wearing a dark suit, and carried a large briefcase. He crossed to the garage and backed out a small Renault motor car. The woman, also smartly dressed, followed by the two dogs and carrying a small suitcase, came out of the house slamming the door behind her. She ran across the garden to the waiting car. The dogs scrambled into the back of the car and the woman got into the front. The car turned on the gravel driveway and, travelling fast, disappeared up the lane.

At least my problem with the dogs was solved. I moved over to the house, which had French windows either side of the front door.

———

I decided to explore the back of the house first as it might have an open window; also I might have to make a quick getaway if the owners returned. More French windows opened onto a large lawn that had several laden apple trees. At the far end of the lawn I could see a vegetable garden and behind that, the river with trees growing right down to the water on both sides. I thought I would leave that way, crossing the river into the woodland that would provide cover for me all the way to the hillside, which I could see in the distance.

The kitchen door was at the far end of the house close to the garage. Using the bayonet, I forced open the door and entered the passageway that led into the kitchen. On one side of the passage, there was a washing machine and several cupboards, on the other side a row of hooks with waterproof jackets and raincoats, underneath a row of boots and shoes. I spotted a dark green backpack under one of the jackets. This was perfect; I took it down and carried it into the kitchen. It was a large bright kitchen with a solid table and chairs in the middle. I went straight to the fridge and found to my delight a jug of milk and some pastries that I quickly devoured. I filled the bag with bread, cheese, a large piece of ham and a few tomatoes. I also found a large unopened packet of biscuits and a bottle of mineral water; this almost filled the backpack. I selected a sharp medium-sized kitchen knife and slipped it into the bag. The kitchen dresser had several books and magazines and there among the books I found a Michelin road map that I slipped into the bag with a plate, cup, some cutlery and a small saucepan. This was all I could fit into the backpack.

I left the bag on the table and went through to the dining room, which had some fine Breton carved furniture. I noticed several silver framed photos, one of which was a group of German officers and civilians.

I should have taken more notice of this …

At the top of the stairs there were four doors. I walked through one that was open and which happened to be the main bedroom. It was a lovely room with fine dark wood furniture and brightly coloured bed covers. The owners of this home had good taste and must have been wealthy so I guessed they would not miss one or two modest items. I started to look at the man's clothes in the walk-in wardrobe. They were all much too large for me but I found a pair of strong walking shoes and was packing the toes with socks so that they would fit me, when I received a blow to my head.

———

I opened my eyes some time later; a familiar face was staring down at me.

'So, Piglet, we meet again.'

It took me several seconds to realise I was looking up at the smiling face of *Oberleutenant* Grossman.

'How strange you should have found yourself at my sister's house tucked away in the middle of the French countryside. Fate has decided that we should meet again.'

He was smiling down at me but I seemed to detect a slight change in his appearance; he looked far less arrogant.

I was tied to a small bed with my hands and legs tightly fastened with leather bootlaces. There was a large bed on the other side of the room and I noticed Grossman's hat and jacket on an armchair and an open case on the floor. This must be his bedroom. How did he get here? How on earth did he find me? I wondered what sort of treatment I would receive after my last encounter with him.

'I could not have imagined the chaos that would arise from your arrest. What I thought was an over-sexed young local boy has turned out to be something quite different. That innocent smiling boy turned out to be a young psychopath. I completely misjudged you, Piglet: that you should calmly accept the beating in prison and then go on to commit the savage murder of one of our men is not what I would have expected from a normal teenage boy.'

Grossman crossed the room and moving his hat and jacket, sat in the armchair staring at me for several minutes.

'Your score so far: three German soldiers dead and thanks to you, one German army officer now on the run. All this in forty-eight hours; not bad for a sixteen year old.'

Grossman paused to light himself a cigarette. He seemed very calm and quite different to the person that had visited me in my cell after my beating.

'As stated before, Piglet, I find it quite extraordinary that you should turn up here at my sister's home,' he continued. 'The guard found the soldier's body on the train on which I also was travelling, I did not realise at the time that your train had been destroyed at St Servan and that you were on the same train as me. After the discovery of the body, the train was diverted to a siding at Renne; the *Gestapo* arrived and took charge. Everyone on the train was interrogated. They must have contacted headquarters in Jersey, because by the time they got to me they knew all about your case, my involvement as arresting officer and even my visit to you in prison. I knew by then they had figured out that I was somehow involved in the murder and with your disappearance.'

Grossman paced the room, and finally looked down at me and slowly continued. 'We were all allowed to leave the train. It was well after midnight but I was told to report to the Renne *Gestapo* headquarters at ten am. I knew that I was already under suspicion by the *Gestapo*. They had found out that I had a sister somewhere in France and that her husband was known to be sympathetic to the Allies. I realised that now they would make every effort to track her down and use her to break me.' Grossman returned to the chair and lit another cigarette.

'After the *Gestapo* left I walked across to the army depot; as an army officer I had no problem in commandeering a motorcycle. It took me less than two hours to get here to warn Gerda and her husband Pierre of their danger. Pierre is a well-known lawyer with contacts all over France. They will drive to the south where their friends in the Maque will guide them across the Pyrenees and into Spain where they should be safe for the rest of the war. So, my little Piglet, we are now both in deep trouble.'

If Grossman was looking for sympathy he was mistaken—I was getting a great deal of pleasure from his predicament. I waited for him to continue.

'Anytime now the *Gestapo* will arrive here and we will both be arrested and I have no doubt that we will, for different reasons, both die. I have two options—if I run I will probably be picked up by the Resistance and they will show no mercy towards an officer of the *Wermacht*. I'm sure it will not be a pleasant death. Unlike my brother-in-law, I do not have any contacts in France and I would have very little chance of reaching Spain.' Grossman paused for a moment.

'My other option is to surrender myself to the *Gestapo* and face disgrace and probably be executed for murder and treason. Some choice!' Grossman seemed lost in thought for some time. I remained silent. At last he came over and looked down at me still tied up and lying on the bed. I was beginning to lose the feeling in my wrists and ankles and also needed to relieve myself.

'For you, little Piglet, the situation is slightly different. I must admit I admire your resourcefulness, to have gone so far. But for the sheer coincidence and your bad luck in finding me here, you would have been well on your way by now. Piglet, you still stand a very good chance of saving yourself. I know the locals would help you to hide and you would probably eventually get to England.'

The *Oberleutenant* picked up his revolver, clicked back the safety catch and pointed it at my head.

I closed my eyes and allowed my anger to take over.

I would not cry out.

Instead, I wet my trousers.

———

'I shall play a little game with you, Piglet. You must have, like me, played the game of hide-and-seek when you were a child. I shall untie you and I will count to thirty and then come after you. If I find you after that, I will kill you. I shall be interested to see how fast you can run. If you get away from me, maybe when the war is over you might return to this house and meet my sister.'

Still pointing the revolver at me, with one hand Grossman untied the bootlaces. He moved back and sat in the chair. I rubbed my wrists and ankles and stood up.

I noticed a slight smile on his face. 'Good luck, little Piglet. *Ein, zwie, drie …*'

I turned and ran down the stairs and into the kitchen. The backpack was still on the table; I grabbed it and flew out into the back garden. I was halfway across the lawn when I heard a gunshot. I stopped dead. I had to go back, I walked slowly back to the house, through the kitchen and up the stairs.

Grossman was still sitting in the armchair—dead.

I was about to relieve him of his wallet and revolver, but it occurred to me that when the *Gestapo* arrived and found Grossman had been killed and robbed, they might guess it was me and the whole area would be searched until I was found.

I retrieved the bootlaces and tidied the bed where I had been tied up and left Grossman still clutching his revolver.

On the way downstairs, I slipped on the shoes I had been looking at when I had been hit on the head. I was careful not to leave any traces of my visit in the kitchen. Leaving the backpack outside, I covered with mud the marks on the door that I had made when I opened it with the bayonet. I locked the door from the inside again being careful to leave everything undisturbed. I slipped out of the kitchen window, closing it behind me.

Picking up the backpack, I walked slowly back across the grass to the river and waded downstream for some time before crossing and climbing up the opposite bank.

I very soon disappeared into the woods.

CHAPTER 4

With no one in sight, I crossed a road that happened to be the main road from Renne to St Malo. I found a track that took me through the forest shaded from the afternoon sun by tall trees. The track wound its way up the side of the hill and I soon reached the top. I had been walking for about forty-five minutes when I decided to have a rest.

I found a clearing a little way off the track and right on top of the ridge. From there I had a wonderful view of the countryside both to the north and to the south. France on a warm summer's day was really quite something. It was hard to believe that there was a war going on.

I had come from the southeast and behind me I could see the house that I had just left with the stream at the bottom of the garden. The stream joined the river, which then curved around to the west where it disappeared behind the hill where I stood. The village behind the house was quite small. A stone bridge crossed the stream at the end of the village where I had seen the guard the night before and which was some way beyond the house. In the distance behind the village, I could see the main river and a much larger village with a series of locks and the lockkeeper's house close by. I could just see two barges passing through them; I expected that they were carrying German supplies.

Looking to the north I saw the river reappearing from behind the hill; the road I had just crossed ran through another small village to a bridge that crossed the main river. The road continued to the north until it disappeared from sight. The river flowed to the west, then curved again quite sharply and disappeared to the north where it eventually finished up at St Malo and the open sea.

On the bend to the north, there was a branch that ran to the southwest for about four miles; it then became a large area of high reeds. Amongst the reeds I spotted what looked like a small shed.

I decided I would go there as it would certainly be out of sight from a lower level and might make a suitable shelter for me.

An hour later, I arrived at the spot where I had seen the shed.

I walked around the reeds until I found a muddy path that took me to the water's edge. I waded through the reeds and when I got to some open water, to my surprise, I found three derelict river barges. By the time I reached them I was up to my waist in water but managed to climb up the side of the nearest one.

The barges were very badly damaged and two of them had been burned out completely—victims of allied bombing. They were tied together and seemed firmly stuck on the riverbed so I could step from one to the other. They must have been towed to this spot and then flooded. The third boat had the bow completely wrecked; it looked as if the back was broken as both bow and stern were lower than the middle section. The bridge and stern accommodation of this barge appeared to be undamaged. This was the 'shed' I had seen from the top of the hill. All the glass had been blown out of the bridge section. I entered through a door that was still intact; the inside had been stripped of all fittings including the steering wheel. A broken door led down two steps to the living area, which had also been stripped of everything except for a large wooden table in the centre. On one side of the cabin was an iron stove with a chimney that went out through the roof. The portholes still had glass in them, and set into both of the side walls of the cabin were four bunks.

At the rear end of the cabin, steps led up to the stern deck and another set of steps led down into the engine room. Although there was some water, I could see the engine and all the controls had been removed so I closed the hatch that led down to that section and climbed up onto the rear deck.

—

It was a lovely summer evening and I was standing on the small deck of my new home, with tall reeds and water all around me. This was an ideal hiding place, unlikely to be visited by anyone. I could easily escape into the reeds if any Germans were to appear and there would be no give-away footprints around the barge to show that I was living here.

I sat on the roof of the cabin and ate some of the food I had stolen, pleased that I had brought the bottle of water as I did not fancy drinking unboiled water from the lake.

On reflection, I realised I could not return to Jersey until the war was over and even then, I could not imagine having to go back and explain to my parents the events that had happened to me in the last few days. So I decided I would start a new life; I now had a home. I would try to make contact with the French Resistance Movement and in the meantime, I would start my own little war with Germany. First I would have to get myself very fit. That would mean good food and some hard training. I would start right now. It was at this point that I decided to change my name to Marçel Beaumont.

—

After a good rest I packed the contents of the backpack into one of the several cupboards in the living room, tucked the bayonet into my trousers and wearing the empty backpack, set off back to the house. It had taken me three hours to get here so it should take two and a half hours to get back. If the house was still empty I would collect some bedding and as much food as I could carry.

The journey back was easy; I used the compass to take bearings to help me find my way back to the barges. It was quite dark when I arrived at the stream. I took off my shoes and stripped down to my pants and swam across to the garden. In my bare feet, I crept slowly up to the house. No lights were visible so I circled the house. There was no sign of life and no vehicles parked outside. I entered the garage from the side door and shone Henry's torch around.

There was very little in the garage: a bench at one end with tools neatly fastened to the wall and in one corner all the gardening tools including a lawn mower. I flashed the torch upwards and to my delight, I saw an Indian-type canoe suspended from the rafters. I managed to lower it down to the floor. It had two paddles inside and looked in very good condition. I put an assortment of tools, nails and a length of rope inside and very carefully dragged it down to the water's edge making sure not to leave any tracks behind.

Returning to the house, I was able to enter by the same kitchen window that I had used earlier that afternoon. The kitchen was in a mess; all the cupboards and drawers had been emptied but the food, to my surprise, was still there. In the dining room the same thing, I noticed the photos and all the silver had been taken. Upstairs, Grossman had been removed and apart from bloodstains on the armchair, there was no sign of his having been in the house.

Amongst the chaos in the main bedroom, I spread out a sheet onto which I piled an assortment of bedding. I found a pair of Gerda's slacks that fitted me quite well so I put them onto the pile along with one of her sweaters, adding two towels and some of Pierre's socks and underpants.

———

I pulled the four corners of the sheet together and tied them in a knot; it now looked like a very large Christmas pudding, which fitted nicely into the centre of the canoe. Going back to the kitchen I loaded all the food I could find into the backpack, closed the kitchen door and returned to the canoe, which I slid into the water. I climbed into the rear end and paddled across to where I had left my clothes.

This, I thought, was the start of another great adventure. With the tools and bedding in the bow end, the canoe was well balanced and slid nicely through the water. I reckoned after joining the main river I should arrive at the turning point, where the barges were, by dawn—say five hours. I then remembered I had to pass under the stone bridge that was guarded by a German soldier and later, the larger road bridge crossing the main river.

———

I pulled into the bank on the opposite side of the stream and spent a few minutes thinking how I could get rid of the guard. Just to slit his throat and leave him would alert the *Gestapo* that I was in this area and so a search would probably reveal my new home. A plan was forming in my mind, which was again going to entail some very good timing and a lot of luck.

I moved slowly to the bridge and crouched below the end of the bridge wall. I could see the guard at the other end of the bridge leaning on it, smoking. I slipped out and placed Henry's torch upside down three feet beyond the end of the wall. When I turned it on, it gave just a glimmer of light. I slipped back behind the wall and started throwing stones as far as I could down the track from the bridge. The guard heard the noise and moved slowly across the bridge. I stopped throwing the stones. He walked past me on the other side of the wall and noticed the faint light on the road. As he bent down to look at the torch, I stepped forward and with the bayonet held with both hands above my head, brought it down across the back of his neck just below his helmet. It was instant death.

I picked up the torch and ran back to the canoe, paddled under the bridge and twenty yards past the bridge, I jumped back onto the bank and ran back to the guard. He had four hand grenades attached to his belt; I pulled out the pins on two of them and ran as fast as I could back to the canoe.

I had barely made it when the grenades went off. I leaped into the canoe and paddled like mad until I reached the main river. Now I was well out of sight. Hopefully the other guards would assume this German had taken his own life. I felt strangely elated. I had just enjoyed another killing …

——

I paddled on for the next four hours keeping close to the riverbank. It was just beginning to get light when I spotted the road bridge. I waited until I heard some trucks approaching the bridge; then keeping close to the river bank, I quietly slipped past. The guards were watching the trucks. I was very lucky. I reached the entrance to the turnoff where the barges were. If I had not known it was there, I could easily have gone straight past—another good reason for making it my home.

I tied up the canoe at the stern end of my barge, keeping it well under the stern and between the two barges; it was almost out of sight. I carried the Christmas pudding down the hatch and dropped it on the floor.

It was then the gun went off. I threw myself onto the Christmas pudding—I had not been hit.

'Stand up slowly, dear boy, with your hands above your head.' An English voice—who the hell was this? I was shocked. He had tried to kill me. 'Now slowly turn around and keep your hands up.'

I turned to see two faces peering over the engine room hatch and a revolver pointing straight at me.

'Bonjour mon petit cochon, quel méchant voleur.' A man with a pencil-line moustache stepped out and checked to see if I had a gun. He was admiring my blood-stained bayonet when the other man came across and dropped his gun on the table.

'Just testing your reaction, dear boy. You will have to learn to move faster than that if you want to survive around here. My name is Pete and my friend here is Pierre, easy to remember, and you, dear boy, I gather are the famous "Piglet".'

Pete smiled at me. 'Pierre has a bone or two to pick with you, killing his brother-in-law and robbing his house. Naughty boy.'

'I thought Pierre had gone to Spain with his wife. I don't understand what is going on. What are you doing here?' I was still recovering from the gunshot and was confused at the sudden appearance of the two men.

Pierre looked down at me; he was no longer wearing his smart suit, just open shirt and trousers.

'What have you stolen from me this time, Piglet?' His English was perfect. 'Did you enjoy killing my wife's brother?' I noticed he was also smiling and did not seem to be too bothered about his brother-in-law's death.

'The *Oberleutenant* took his own life after letting me escape. He also told me that you and your wife Gerda had gone to Spain.'

'Yes, Gerda has gone to Spain but Pete decided that I had work to do here. Klaus, my brother-in-law, told us all about you and how you had got him into so much trouble. He had no alternative but to do what he did. It would have come to that sooner or later anyway. He knew too much about our involvement with the Resistance and would have cracked under *Gestapo* questioning. Klaus even suggested you might be of some use to us. I am very sorry; he was a good man caught up in an impossible situation.'

Pete gave me a friendly punch in the chest. 'There ain't much of you there, young Piglet. We have followed your every move since you first left Pierre's house. We followed you here and we followed you back to the house. We saw how you dealt with the guard. I must say I was most impressed by the way you pulled out the pins of the hand grenades to cover your tracks.' He paused. 'I don't suppose you brought any wine from the house, Piglet?'

'I'm afraid not. I don't drink myself but I like to see Germans drink. It makes them more vulnerable and easier to kill.'

'So far, Piglet, you have passed all the tests. We believe you might be of some use to us, King and country and all that. You seem to be quite good at killing Germans, but that is only a small part of what we do. Gathering information is our primary aim. Because of your size and your ability to improvise and kill when necessary, you could be very useful to us. There is no glory in what we do; we are the lowest of the low and very dispensable.'

Pete grabbed me by the shoulders. His face was almost touching mine and he seemed to be searching my soul. I saw so much power in his eyes: I knew then that I would walk through fire for this man.

'When any of our people are taken by the *Gestapo*, they are tortured until they divulge all they know. Afterwards the *Gestapo* kill off what little life is left in them. So if you join our little party, you will only be told about the jobs you do. You will have no direct contact with anyone except Pierre. So, dear boy, are you with us or not?'

I remained silent for several moments.

'Do I get paid?'

They both laughed, 'Definitely NO. You will be supplied with the tools of the trade and possibly an allowance to purchase food but only at specified times and places.'

'I had already decided to start my new life here and to devote my time to killing Germans. It would seem I would be able to kill a lot more by working with you. So I'm with you all the way!'

'A wise decision, dear boy. By the way, we would have killed you if you had said no. So let's have some of Pierre's food and later when it gets dusk, you can take us for a ride in your new canoe. I hate getting my feet wet.'

We unloaded the canoe and sat on the cabin roof eating tinned asparagus, sardines and rather stale bread. We shared the last of the water.

'I'm returning to London soon. You must forget you have ever seen me. Pierre will keep in contact with you. Remember, if you are caught you know no one and we certainly will not be able give you any help. Find a good hiding spot on the barge and put everything there when you are away for any time. Today you will have learned to check very carefully before coming back on board.'

Pete handed me a small pad and pencil. 'I want you to get yourself very fit, especially when using the canoe. One day you might need to travel far and fast; in the meantime your job is to watch the railway bridges. We want to know the times and number of trains passing these bridges at night.'

'Don't try to kill too many guards! If you do, make sure you safely dispose of the bodies. Too many missing guards in this area will lead to widespread searches and one day you will be caught.'

We cleaned out the bunks, shared the bedding and rested until dusk. I paddled my passengers through the reeds to the bank of the river. Pierre shook my hand.

'I will bring you food in two days' time; find yourself a stream with fresh water. And no fires at any time.'

I returned to the barge feeling quite elated. I had joined the Resistance. I was now fighting for my King and country. I would become a hero and be presented with medals at Buckingham Palace after the war. Sweet dreams.

Lying in the bunk I could hear rifle shots in the distance. The French Resistance was at work. I hoped it was not Pierre and Pete. Sleep overtook me.

CHAPTER 5

The next morning I woke up to find the sun shining into the cabin. It had been my first good sleep since leaving home to go fishing. In less than a week so much had happened; I had entered a scary new world. My life and my personality had changed forever.

I jumped into the canoe and went looking for clean drinking water. I found a very small stream that flowed into the reeds, the water tasted good and was clean so I filled my bottle and returned to the barge.

I had a swim off the barge and was ready for my French breakfast of biscuits and water. I found a good dry hiding spot, a cupboard at the back of the engine room where I could keep all my bedding and foodstuffs safely out of sight, but I knew it would not stand up to a thorough search of the boat. I decided not to clean up the cabin, as this would just raise the suspicions of any intruder.

Deciding to use the canoe to explore the backwater, and keeping to one side and close to the reeds, I paddled to the junction with the main river. I pulled into the reeds where I could watch the traffic going up and down the river. I could just see the road bridge and part of the village that I had slipped past the night before; it was only about a mile away.

I was surprised how many barges were travelling up and down. Most had one Frenchman as helmsman and a deckhand. There were German soldiers on some of the barges, no doubt carrying supplies to and from St Malo. This would be a slow but very cheap and safe way of transporting less urgent things like building materials and heavy equipment.

Later, when I returned to the barge, I fished out the road map that I had taken from Pierre's kitchen. The railway bridges were at least eighteen miles from here by water and about sixteen if travelled overland. The trouble was I had to pass under the road bridge both ways and somehow get past the row of locks near Hédé. Either way, I would find it impossible to get back in one night if I was going to count the number of trains passing over the bridges after daylight. I thought a German soldier's uniform would be a great help. It would have to be from a little fellow to fit me. Where to find a small German soldier at night? Not in a bar, but maybe in a toilet outside a bar or perhaps just in a public toilet.

—

I decided to rest until dark and opened a tin of suspicious-looking meat—it was probably dog food—and finished the rather stale bread. You learned not to be too fussy in the occupation. I dusted the table with Gerda's slacks to give them a much-used look. They fitted quite well; I slipped my precious bayonet inside them and wore my very grubby shirt on the outside. I then ruffled my hair and set off in the canoe.

It was now quite dark and I carefully concealed the canoe amongst the reeds close to the village; where I would be able, if necessary, to make a quick getaway.

I walked down the main street of the village keeping a good distance between myself and the few people still about. I arrived at the village centre, a large tree-lined Square surrounded by buildings, which included two cafés and a small hotel. Several army trucks were parked in the centre of the Square between two rows of trees. Near to the trees, there was the typical French circular toilet that exposed both your head and feet. Quite a lot of Germans were sitting at the tables outside the cafés. This must be a resting place for the truck drivers on their way to and from Renne. I found a spot a little way from the trucks and leaned up against one of the trees. It was now quite dark. I stood there for some time watching the trucks come and go.

My problem as usual was how to dispose of the body. The discovery of a dead German in this situation would probably lead to the whole village being punished. The *Wermacht* showed no mercy in these cases.

Most of the trucks carried several soldiers in the back. They all jumped out, heading straight to the toilet and then drifted across to the cafés. After a time the number of trucks started to dwindle until only three trucks remained. Then a truck came in with just two men in the front and one in the back. He looked fairly short.

The three of them went straight to the café and sat down.

With no clear idea of what I intended to do, I quietly climbed into the back of this truck. There were several cases on the floor. I undid the catches of one and felt inside with my hand. I had struck gold; the case contained hand grenades. I clipped two onto my belt and leaned forward to get two more and at the same time I felt an arm around my neck. *'Que fait tu, Cherie?'*

I jerked around. 'Oh, my God.'

'*Zut*. You are English pig. I call my friends.'

I held my hand across her mouth as we fell across the case of grenades. I was on top of her and I pushed her head back, pulled out the bayonet with the other hand and brought it down across her throat.

It was all over very quickly and without a sound. I carefully undid the front buttons of her dress turned her over and slipped it off before it got too much blood on it. I felt around until I found her shoes and shoulder bag, grabbed two more grenades, wrapped them all in the dress and slipped out of the truck.

The Germans were still sitting outside the café. I crept slowly down behind the trees until I reached the far end of the square and crossing over to the buildings on the opposite side of the café. I quietly slipped down a side lane and was soon out of the village.

I had killed my first woman. It was so easy. I was getting quite good at the job; far less blood this time. It was not so much strength as technique.

In future I must train myself to think in French. I had given myself away too easily. The girl was a 'Jerry Bag'—a name given to female collaborators. Her death would be an example to the other girls in the village. A certain German soldier would now have a lot of explaining to do. He most certainly would have to die for this murder. Two for the price of one.

———

Back on board the barge, I placed the grenades at the foot of my bunk, hoping I wouldn't kick them in the night! With the aid of the torch, I tried on the dress. It was quite a good fit. The shoes, slip-ons, were a bit tight but wearable. I suppose at sixteen I still had a bit of a girlie figure and my hair was now quite long. The shoulder bag contained lipstick and other cosmetics, a small mirror, a handful of Reich marks and an identity card. This could be even better than a German uniform. I would now be a 'Jerry Bag'. I took off the shoes and climbed into my bunk and was soon dead to the world.

———

Something cold was pressing on my nose. I slowly opened one eye to find a grenade resting against my face. I carefully slipped my hand under the pillow until I had hold of the bayonet. I sat up sharply swinging my feet to the ground, hitting my head on the top of the bunk.

'*Zut merd!*' My French was improving.

34

Pierre sat on the edge of the table, a big smile on his face. 'Not a bad reaction, Piglet! Try not to hit your head next time and I would suggest you throw the grenade away first.'

Standing up, Pierre shook my hand and pointed to a bag on the table. 'I've brought your breakfast, fresh bread and a jar of confiture. So where is the girlfriend? I don't think much of her dress but then she won't be needing it now, will she, Piglet?'

I attacked the bread, spreading a large amount of strawberry jam on it and then slipped on my trousers and slipped out of the dress.

'I thought this could be a very useful disguise when I go to watch the bridges. The girl had a bit of an accident last night.'

Pierre laughed. 'I heard all about your visit to the village last night. I feel a little sorry for the poor soldier taking the blame for your bit of pleasure. Anyway I have news for you. I have other men taking care of the bridges so you will not be needed there now. However, we have something which will be much more fun for you.'

I finished eating the bread and washed it down with some water.

'As you might have noticed there is quite a lot of traffic on this canal and river system. At first the Germans were just using it for transporting small amounts of building materials and some farm produce. The situation is changing due to the Allied bombing of trains and the beginning of a fuel shortage. Most of their resources are now being directed to Russia.'

I noticed Pierre was now talking to me as an equal and not a teenager—I had graduated.

'We have noticed that the Germans are now using the French canal system to transport heavy equipment, large guns, ammunition, large quantities of cement and other building materials,' he continued.

'There is a canal and river system all the way from northern France to the ports like Brest, Lorient and St Nazaire where the Germans have their U-boat bases.'

I wondered where I was to fit in to all this and what sort of fun to expect.

'Due to an unfortunate accident of a friend and his nephew, I am now the proud owner of a barge and you, young Piglet, are my crew. He had only just bought this barge when they were both killed by the French Resistance for being too cooperative with the Germans. Their Identity cards have been altered slightly to suit you and me; your name is now Marçel and I am Pierre La Valle. We are to be picked up later today by another barge and will travel to Renne where our new home is waiting for us. The barge has been completely overhauled; it has been repainted and has a new engine with all new fittings. We have an agent in Renne and will be able to accept our first cargo as soon as we take over the barge. We must dispose of everything here, so let's get started.'

We spread the sheet out in the canoe and piled the bedding and all my worldly goods onto the sheet, except for my bayonet, the torch and the compass, which I kept. We decided not to keep the girl's clothes and shoes or Gerda's slacks. We put the stones on top of the pile and I tied up my Christmas pudding.

As no one was about, we paddled to the centre of the river and heaved the large parcel over the side and because of its size, nearly followed it in. It was not safe to take the hand grenades with us so we concealed them by lifting a board under one of the bunks and carefully replacing it afterwards.

I was sorry to part with the canoe. We found a spot amongst the reeds where we filled it with water and some more stones. It sank out of sight; we would come and collect it at a later date.

We had a swim off the barge and lay on the deck in the sun. Pierre, unlike his boss Pete, was of medium height, quite thin with dark hair and a pencil-line moustache. He was a typical Frenchman. In his late twenties, I could see he was very fit and I was looking forward to working with him.

Later that afternoon we finished all the food that was left, disposed of the rubbish and waded across to the riverbank.

'Marçel, when we get to the barge you will change into more suitable clothes, and remember you are now a French boy. Because your language is limited, you will act like a retarded youth. Just nod your head and mumble a few words.'

We walked to the junction of the main river and sat and waited until dusk when the barge was due.

'By the time I have finished with you, Marçel, you will be able to speak fluent French.'

TOP LEVEL

A secret cabinet meeting was held deep in a London bunker. Present—the Prime Minister, five senior Cabinet Ministers, Head of British Armed Services, Head of American Armed Services, Chief of British Intelligence MI5 and his American counterpart from the CIA.

'This, gentlemen, is a special one-off meeting. No record will be kept of this meeting and we have only one item to discuss. Except for two members present, all memories of the discussion and decisions made here must be erased from your minds. No one, I repeat no one must ever hear of our gathering and the decision made by us today.'

The Prime Minister continued, 'The war with Germany will eventually come to an end. There will be an enormous clean-up operation and many top Nazis will be killed or captured but gentlemen, there are thousands of evil men who will endeavour to escape our net. When final victory is achieved, the British public will be pleased to put the war years behind them and rebuild their lives. They will want to see a few top men tried and punished, but will not tolerate a witch-hunt where many more Germans would be killed.

'It is quite likely my government will be replaced by the Labour Party and they will be more interested in the rebuilding of the country than wasting time hunting down the men responsible for all the atrocities committed during the war years. I therefore propose we set up a covert operation that will help certain high profile Germans to escape from their country. In the confidence of reaching a safe haven, they will fall into the pit that we shall dig for them and die quietly, unknown and forgotten.

'Gentlemen, the meeting is open for a short discussion. We all have many things to do.'

―――

Fifteen minutes later a unanimous decision was made. The two heads of the Secret Services, MI5 and the CIA were given a free hand to jointly draw up a plan that would aid escaping Nazis and which would lead to their eventual elimination. *The plan was to be put into operation as soon as possible and to continue for at least five years after the end of the war. The operation was to receive generous funding from the large amounts of money and treasures that would be recovered from the fleeing men.*

'Thank you, gentlemen. This operation will now go ahead in the hands of the two organisations here tonight. No doubt there will be mistakes made but we will know nothing of this.' The Prime Minister gave the hint of a smile.

'Bear in mind that if any one of us here tonight were unable to forget this meeting and happened at some time to be indiscreet, their name would automatically be added to the list of escapees. Good night, gentlemen.'

CHAPTER 6

It was dark when at last a barge appeared from the north. As it got closer, the engine stopped and it drifted slowly towards us. There was no one in sight except the man steering the barge. We swam out and quickly climbed the short rope ladder hanging over the side. The engine restarted and the barge picked up speed. We were on our way.

The man in the wheelhouse was bare-chested, with dark trousers and a peaked cap. After he had spoken a few words to Pierre, we made our way down into the cabin. We found a pile of grubby-looking clothes on the table. Pierre slipped into some old navy blue trousers, a grey shirt, an old jacket with brass buttons and a peaked cap. I found a pair of heavy black trousers, an off-white T-shirt, an old windcheater and a peaked cap, without gold braid. We put all our old clothes in a weighted bag and threw them overboard. I was now Marçel with the nodding head, a fixed smile and an unintelligible mumble.

We passed under the road bridge and arrived at a stone jetty, where we tied up for the night. Later we sat around the table in the cabin drinking real coffee—black market no doubt—and eating large hunks of bread and cheese, with just a sharp knife for cutlery.

This was also my introduction to *Calvados*, a powerful alcohol made from distilled cider. Jean, our host, handed me a half-filled mug and insisted I finish it off. I took small sips at first and gradually got used to the strong cider taste and quite enjoyed the second mug, but soon after, things started to spin around and I was unable to stand up.

The next morning, I woke up in one of the bunks with a splitting headache and feeling very sorry for myself. Pierre was at the table, dipping bread into a bowl of black coffee. I went on deck.

Later, Pierre joined me. 'We will shortly be passing through the locks at Hédé; all our papers are in order. Here is an identity card for you. The photo is a bit smudged but don't worry it's near enough. Just watch me and Jean and do what you can to help us when we go through the locks. Try not to look like a novice and don't talk in English.'

We entered the first lock with another barge. When the gates closed behind us the water level in our lock rose up to the level of the lock in front. There was quite a lot of turbulence as the water poured in and we had to use poles to push ourselves off the walls. I was standing in the bow when we passed under the two railway bridges where I had killed Henry. I could not resist making a rude sign to the guard standing on the bridge. He pointed his gun at me, but he was smiling, I think.

'Don't push it, Marçel!' I could see Pierre was enjoying the journey to Renne. His responsibilities would start once we got to our own barge. 'We should arrive at the commercial docks at about nine tomorrow morning, Marçel. I will go to our agent's office, collect the keys and see if we have a cargo waiting for us.'

'D'accord monsieur le capitaine.'

Pierre winced. 'Oh, God. Spoken like a true Englishman.'

We tied up near St Germain for the night, found a small bar and tucked into bowls of soup d'onion with lots of vin ordinaire. I was pretty exhausted by then, not yet used to working all those lock gates. I was pleased when we passed out of the last of the thirty-eight locks and arrived at Renne. We tied up at Renne's very busy commercial wharf. A number of barges were being loaded and unloaded, mostly by Frenchmen, and there were quite a few Germans who appeared to be supervising the work.

Pierre went off to the office while I sat on the edge of the jetty. I was gazing at all the barges when I felt a tap on my shoulder. Two German 'Feldgendamerie' were standing over me, the silver plates that they wore on their chests shining in the sunlight. I stood up grinning and nodding my head. I mumbled some rubbish, hoping I was not overacting.

'Carte.'

I handed over my identity card. One of them gave me a push and I fell into the filthy canal water. When I climbed out, a small group had gathered around and were having a good laugh. With quite an effort, I maintained my silly grin. I was handed back my identity card and the Feldgendamerie moved on.

Pierre hurried over; more concerned than I, in case I lost my temper. 'Stay cool, Marçel. You will get your chance one day. In the meantime, let's go and find our barge. Our barge is the fourth one out, at the end of this pontoon. We have our first job in the morning. We go back to Montreuil-sur-Ille where we will load sixty carboys of distilled water. We are to deliver them to La Roche-Bernard on the west coast. I think they will go on from there by road to St Nazaire where there is a U-boat base.'

We stepped across three barges, all manned, with some delicious smells coming up from their cabins, and arrived at our own freshly-painted barge. Pierre unlocked the wheelhouse door and we stepped inside what was to be home, for some time to come. Our barge was similar to the one we had just left, although a much newer version. The varnished wheelhouse was well equipped with a large steering wheel, brass engine controls, compass, a chart table, signalling lamp and various other bits of safety equipment.

The cabin was very smart. It had a gas cooker, a refrigerator and a good-sized wood burning stove. I opened the fridge door and looked into the cupboards. We had a fully equipped kitchen and someone had also made sure that we were well stocked with food and wine. At the far end, a small section had been panelled off and we had the luxury of a pump-out toilet, a shower and washbasin.

'Bring your torch, Marçel. I have something interesting to show you.' We went down into the engine room. There was a large and powerful-looking diesel engine, on one side of it a generator, complete with batteries, and on the other side, a good-sized electric powered bilge pump. The control panel was on the forward bulkhead, and alongside, attached to the bulkhead, rows of spanners and other tools. It all looked spotless; I intended to keep it that way.

At floor level, Pierre ducked under a small door. 'Follow me, Marçel.'

We crawled under the cabin floor and came to a higher section that was under the raised bridge. On either side were two tanks. The one on the right side was the fuel tank, and on the left side, a much newer tank had been placed on top of the old water tank.

Some oil drums were stacked in the gap between the tanks and the far bulkhead. Pierre moved some empty drums at the end of the old water tank and revealed a rusted panel.

'Slip inside this water tank, Marçel!'

I removed the panel and crawled inside the tank. I switched on my torch and was surprised to see that the inside had been painted white. On a slightly raised wooden floor there was a large mattress complete with pillows and blanket. Alongside there was a bucket and several large tins, one containing a torch, a mug, packets of biscuits and several bars of *Suchard* chocolate and in another tin there was a portable radio transmitter.

A third tin contained handguns and grenades. A small tap in the ceiling with a length of hose ensured an ample supply of water. I noticed a small amount of light coming from the bottom edge of the tank. The inside of the tank was about eight foot long, six feet wide and four feet high. Once someone was inside, the panel was clamped in place and it could not be opened from outside. I backed out of the tank, closed the panel and replaced the empty oil drums.

'Our little secret, Marçel. If anyone happened to be inside the tank when a search was on, they would open the water tap and allow a small amount of water to seep out of the cracks in the side of the tank. This should convince the searchers that the tank is not a hiding place.'

Back in the engine room, Pierre explained the workings of all the equipment; I was shown how to start and stop the large diesel engine and to make sure the batteries were always fully charged.

'Our masters have equipped this barge especially for us. As you see it has a few hidden extras. Providing we are discreet and don't draw attention to ourselves, we have the potential to do a lot of damage to the Germans.'

Back in the cabin, Pierre had cooked potatoes and was frying up some steak, probably horsemeat, but it smelt delicious. 'Boat people eat very well. They are able to trade with the farmers and the townsfolk and often get access to stolen German supplies.'

I opened a bottle of *vin rouge* and we tucked into our first good meal in a long time. I thanked my parents for introducing me to wines at an early age; this was one item we would not be short of.

'Marçel, I have to meet someone at a café near the docks. I will be some time so just keep an eye on things until I get back.'

I washed the dishes and tidied up, determined to keep this cabin neat and clean. The bunks had clean linen, towels, pillows and blankets and the drawers under the bunks had an assortment of clothes to fit us both. I went onto the roof of the cabin and admired the star-filled sky. It concerned me a little that we were taking supplies for the German U-boats. This is not what I had planned to do—I just wanted to kill Germans.

When Pierre returned, I followed him back down into the cabin; he placed a large vet's syringe and a bottle of clear liquid on the table.

'A very small dilution of this liquid in the distilled water should, over a period of time, destroy the batteries of some of the U-boats. I'm putting this down into the old water tank until I get the opportunity to use it.'

Pierre returned from the engine room. 'Let's hope they don't send a German guard with us. In the morning, Marçel, we set off at dawn so get some sleep. We have a hard day in front of us tomorrow.'

I was soon asleep lying in the very comfortable bunk.

'Wake up you land lubber; we are moving out.'

I slipped on my clothes and climbed out on deck. It looked chaotic: the barges on our outside had already left, and the skipper on our inside was shouting at us to take in our ropes. Our engine roared into life and Pierre came up on deck.

'*Prenez les cordes vite, Marçel.*'

I pulled in the ropes and laid them out on the deck as I had seen Jean do the day before. Pierre put the engine into reverse and we slipped out of the line of barges. When we were well clear, Pierre gave the engine full speed ahead, the barge slowly swung around and we were heading down the canal. I went below and put on the coffee.

It was a glorious morning and Pierre let me take the wheel. It was not as easy as I thought—I kept overcorrecting and it took me some time before I was able to steer a straight course. We were heading north at about five miles per hour and had twenty miles and seventeen locks ahead of us. Allowing for a lunch stop at Saint-sur-Ille, we should arrive at Montreuil-sur-Ille at three pm.

Pierre decided to give me a French lesson. He started by teaching me the phrases we would be using when working the barge, although I already knew most of the swear words!

At midday, we stopped at Saint-Médard. We tied up to the jetty just behind another barge and Pierre went off to telephone our time of arrival at Montreuil. He returned with loaves of fresh bread and a dish of *Pate de Campagne*. We washed this down with red wine and after a short siesta, leisurely cast off and headed for Montreuil-sur-Ille.

—

There were four trucks waiting at the jetty when we arrived. We tied up and Pierre started up the winch that pulled back the hold cover. This was done by a series of cables attached to the winch and saved us a lot of manual work. The trucks backed up to the barge and a group of soldiers passed the carboys of distilled water into the hold. Down in the hold, Pierre showed me how to place them close together so that they would not fall over and break. When they were all in place, we ran a rope through the front row of the frames of the carboys and then attached the ropes to the sides of the hold.

Pierre closed up the hold cover. Back in the wheelhouse, a German NCO was waiting for Pierre to sign the paperwork.

'My name is Klaus. I shall travel with you to make sure you do not steal from the *Führer*. I'm sure you will make me very comfortable on this voyage.'

Pierre gave a grunt of disapproval. 'I will show you a berth as soon as we finish the paperwork.'

There were sixty carboys written in on the consignment note; we had taken seventy on board. 'We have ten more carboys on board than you have put down on the paperwork. Why is this?' Pierre demanded.

'A poor soldier's perks! Don't worry; I will pay you for the extra transport cost.'

Pierre grabbed the German by his shoulders. 'I will carry your perks on one condition only, soldier. You will give me five hundred Reich marks for the transport cost and you will also give me a signed receipt for this transaction.'

Klaus gave Pierre a sly smile. 'Why not? You would never have the nerve to use the receipt. My word as a German will always stand up against yours, Captain.'

Klaus gave Pierre the five hundred Reich marks and Pierre wrote out an account to Klaus for the delivery of the extra ten carboys. Klaus was not pleased when I added my name to the delivery note, and would have been even less pleased if he had realised that he had just signed his own death warrant.

Although it was a little late to set off that evening, Klaus insisted that we start on our way. It was dark when we tied up at Saint-Medard-sur-Ille and Klaus went off to the local café. We stayed on board and cooked a light meal.

'You realise Klaus has created a situation where we are now able to dispose of him once he delivers his ten carboys to his accomplices. We now have his signed note, which I can give to the *Feldgendamerie*. They will believe him to be a thief and deserter.'

I chuckled. 'I will be delighted to play my part when the time is right, Pierre. In fact I might even sharpen my bayonet in anticipation!'

It had been a long day; we were both tired so we turned in. Sometime later, I heard Klaus scraping along the deck. He sounded drunk. He came down the steps, threw himself on his bunk and started snoring like the pig he was.

We set off at dawn the next morning, another bright sunny day. I was finding it hard not to talk in English, so I kept well away from Klaus and Pierre. I felt sure I had convinced Klaus that I was quite mad and perfectly harmless.

We reached Renne about nine am; Pierre decided not to stop as we had plenty of fuel on board to get to our destination. I went below to make some sandwiches; Klaus followed me down. I was standing at the table cutting bread when Klaus moved up behind me; he pressed himself against my back and his hands came around and he started to feel my private parts.

'Does that feel nice, dumb boy?'

I realised sixteen-year-old boys are just as much at risk of being molested as girls. I quickly moved to the fridge to get some ham for the sandwiches. I gave Klaus my innocent smile, finished making our lunch and moved quickly up on deck. Klaus followed close behind me. I gave Pierre a quick sign. He guessed something was going on and knew that Klaus was in for a very nasty shock.

Klaus shared our lunch and had his fill of wine—I was thinking of the condemned man and his last meal.

'You will stop at Messac. I will discharge my ten carboys there.' Klaus looked at the map on the chart table. 'We should be there late this afternoon. That is good.'

We were travelling at a steady six miles per hour, which was a reasonable speed on the Villane River and we arrived at Messac at six pm. Klaus disappeared and returned some time later with a truck and three men.

Pierre opened the hold so that Klaus and the three men could load the truck. There was no one about when they finished and the truck drove off with the carboys and the three men.

'We go,' Klaus ordered. He was looking very pleased with himself and we were happy to get going so quickly. We cast off and continued on our way.

Klaus went down into the cabin. Pierre turned to me. 'Marçel I think it would be a good time now for you to go and do your job. Are you quite sure you want to?'

I could feel my heart beating faster with excitement, fear and anticipation. 'Just try and stop me, Pierre.' He gave me a funny look. Just for a moment I felt superior; I knew he was not capable of doing what I was about to do.

To me Klaus was just a pig to be slaughtered and I went eagerly down the steps to the cabin.

Klaus was sitting at the table counting money; I slowly brushed passed him and moved over to my berth. I leaned over and felt for my bayonet, which I kept under my pillow. Klaus was right behind me.

I smelt his foul breath; he was breathing heavily as he put his arms around me. I allowed my rage to take control, I swung around but Klaus stepped back and I was only able to graze his neck. He ran back to the table, picked up the bread knife and came straight for me. I moved away from the bunk—we stared at each other for a few seconds. Then Klaus lunged at me with the knife. I stepped back, Klaus launched himself at me. As he came forward, I ducked and Klaus was off balance—he had taken a step too far. I stood up inside his arm that held the knife, slipped one arm around Klaus's waist and with the other, slit his throat. Klaus literally died in my arms.

Pierre appeared from the wheelhouse. 'Marçel, did you have to make such a mess?' He went back to the steering wheel.

I lifted Klaus onto a large sack and cleaned up most of the blood. I was a little puzzled as to why I always felt so elated after a killing. Maybe the rape had made me a little unbalanced. Klaus had made sexual advances to me but that was not always the reason I killed. I joined Pierre in the wheelhouse.

'As soon as it's dark enough we will get him on deck, lash him carefully to that crowbar next to the winch and then dispose of him.' Pierre was laughing. 'We really must get some heavy weights and a few large sacks on board if you are going to make a habit of killing our passengers, Marçel.'

Pierre allowed the barge to slow down until we were just drifting. Between us we dragged Klaus up to the wheelhouse. I took the wheel and brought the barge back on course while Pierre carefully lashed Klaus to the heavy crowbar.

It was now getting dark and we were going through an area with woodland on both sides of the river. We moved to the centre of the river and stopped the engine. There was no one in sight so we carefully rolled Klaus over the side. He sank immediately. Pierre crossed himself. We started the engine and were on our way.

I spent the next two hours scrubbing and cleaning the cabin; every trace of Klaus was removed. It was not easy finding our way in the dark but we finally arrived at Redon.

The Redon commercial area was much larger than at Renne. Redon was the junction for several canals and rivers. We found a vacant berth at one of the jetties. Pierre decided he would report to the *Feldgendamerie* first thing in the morning. We both found it hard to sleep that night.

———

Early next morning Pierre nipped ashore and returned with an armful of freshly baked *baguettes*; I don't know how he managed to get hold of this fresh bread when everything was in such short supply.

Pierre set off to the *Feldgendamerie* to report the missing Klaus. He used all his skills as a lawyer to explain how Klaus had forced us to carry his stolen cargo and to deliver it to his friends at Messac. He had then gone off with his friends in their truck and we presumed he had deserted the army. Pierre stated that he felt it his duty to report Klaus to the *Feldgendamerie* as Klaus was both a thief and a deserter, and whatever his nationality, he should be punished. Pierre also produced the signed delivery note as proof that Klaus had stolen the ten carboys from the *Wermacht*, and that we had done everything possible to help the *Feldgendamerie*.

Pierre had done such a good job that the Germans actually thanked him for all his help. They came back with him to check our cargo, and all our papers and identity cards. We were told we had to stay where we were until they had spoken to their counterparts in Renne. Later in the afternoon, they returned to tell us we could continue on our way. The Renne *Feldgendamerie* had been watching Klaus for some time and had hoped to catch him stealing army supplies. They thanked us again for our help.

We decided to make it a complete rest day and to leave for La Roche-Bernard early the next morning, so we spent the rest of the day topping up the fuel tank, washing the decks and generally tidying up the cabin and wheelhouse.

Pierre went below to prepare a special meal in honour of our departed guest Klaus.

I stayed on deck.

Chapter 7

A very smart barge with several Germans on board was approaching us. As it brought its stern close in to us, I noticed a very attractive young girl standing on the deck, waiting to throw the ropes across.

'*Prenez les cordes, garçon.*'

I slipped the loop over a bollard and we both ran to our barge bows.

'*Alors, prenez.*'

As I caught her rope she gave it a sharp tug; caught off balance, I fell straight into the river. When I surfaced I could hear shrieks of laughter coming from the newly arrived barge but I don't think the Germans appreciated the joke. The girl dangled the rope over the side and I swam over and pulled myself on board. By then Pierre was on deck and took the rope from the girl and made fast.

I was very wet and quite speechless at seeing such a pretty girl. She had long black hair, with a gypsy look about her, and a lovely smiling face. This was a girl of my dreams.

'*Je suis navrée, m'sieur. Je m'appelle Simone, et vous?*'

I put on my best French accent, '*Je vous en prie, Simone. Je m'appelle Marçel.*' I certainly had no problem accepting her apology.

One of the Germans waved to me to get off their barge. I noticed through a partly open hatch they were carrying torpedoes, which would account for the Germans on board.

'*Plus tard, Marçel.*' Neither had I a problem with that.

Pierre and I tucked into grilled trout washed down with a great wine from Saumur on the Loire River. As soon as we finished clearing up, I went on deck in the hope of seeing Simone. A few minutes later there was a thump as she jumped onto our deck.

'*Venez avec moi, Marçel.*'

I followed her onto the jetty and we both ran up the main street until we came to a park. The moon was out, and for a while I became a boy again. We found some swings and pushed each other so hard that the swings began to rock dangerously. We ran wild around the park, unleashing all the pent-up energy we had stored up from living in the confines of our barges. At last totally exhausted, we returned slowly to the jetty. Simone had talked a lot. I understood very little of what was said and I replied when I could, but mainly with just the odd grunt here and there.

Back on board, we stood together on the stern deck, both staring at the bright full moon and the star-filled sky. The only sounds on this magic summer night were the frogs calling to each other, and the occasional splash of a fish jumping out of the water.

Simone touched my hand lightly. It was like a small electric shock that made my fingers tingle. I took her hand in mine and wanted to say something, but again I was lost for words.

'I think you are English boy, Marçel! Don't worry; I will not give you away. I am a true French girl and will do anything to save my country.'

I was not surprised. 'You are quite right, Simone, but that seems a long time ago. The *Gestapo* are looking for me; but I have found safety here on the barges and I think I shall be able to help, in a very small way, in the liberation of your lovely France from the evil Germans.'

'You are one of us, Marçel, and I know we will always protect each other. My father and I do what we can and sometimes we are able to pass back useful information to the Resistance.'

I turned towards Simone and she moved closer to me. I looked down at those lovely shining eyes, I was mesmerised by her beautiful oval-shaped face, and her little turned-up nose and lips that I so badly wanted to kiss. Simone leaned forward and her lips gently touched mine. I was overcome with warmth, joy and excitement. I took her face in my two hands and kissed her lips with just the lightest of contact. I felt myself shaking. I was floating on air. Suddenly our kisses became stronger and wilder and then just as suddenly we both pulled back, so as not to break the magic of our new bond.

The kiss had sealed our two hearts together and we both knew that we were in love and that nothing could ever change that. We laughed and cried together, hugged and then we parted. Simone returned to her barge and I went slowly down the cabin steps and collapsed onto my bunk. I had never felt so much joy in all my life.

—

I woke up the next morning to the sound of our engine running. Pierre was casting off by the time I got on deck. I could see Simone's barge moving away in the distance.

Anti-aircraft guns were firing and were leaving puffs of black smoke in the sky. Several aircraft passed very low overhead and then there was a terrible explosion.

To my horror, a flash of fire erupted from Simone's barge. The barge lifted and then disappeared into an enormous cloud of black smoke. When the smoke eventually cleared, there was nothing left but a few bits of debris floating on the water.

I stood in the silence that followed, completely stunned. On this fine summer's day, my world had been blown apart.

I started to cry. I fell onto my knees, weeping, howling like a dog and shaking all over—I wept for all the things that had happened to me in the past few days. I don't know how long I cried. At last I felt a hand on my shoulder.

'So you really are human after all, Marçel. You know of course Simone would have known nothing; it all happened so fast. Maybe better she died that way than perhaps killed sometime later at the hands of the *Gestapo*.'

I slowly got to my feet, completely emptied of all feeling. Was this a punishment for all the terrible things I had been doing in the last few days?

Pierre put his arm around my shoulder. 'Come, Piglet, we have much to do.' He restarted the engine. 'Take the wheel, Marçel; we must continue on to La Roche-Bernard. Study the map, the river is much wider from now on and it gets quite tricky in places.' I could see Pierre was also very upset.

'You know, Marçel, Simone's father was one of us. He had informed the Resistance that a large consignment of arms was due to be sent through by this route to St Nazaire; he could not have known it was to be on his barge, and that he would die for passing on this information.'

'Pierre, how could the RAF have possibly known which barge to attack?' I was crying again.

'Come on, Marçel. This is where you prove that you are a man. This is a very dirty business we are in. A member of the Resistance must have managed to paint a large sign on the roof of the wheelhouse at some stage. They would have radioed London last night to say the barge with the sign on the roof was leaving Redon at first light.'

I couldn't believe what I was hearing. 'We are going past now, Marçel; keep well to the far side of the river and just keep looking ahead.'

———

The banks on both sides of the river were badly scorched. I found myself staring at the water although I knew there could be no remains left after such an enormous explosion.

Oh, Simone, why couldn't I have been with you?

We passed over her grave and continued down the river. It was some time before I finally stopped sobbing.

I have never cried much since.

———

The river was quite tricky at this point. I had to take care to keep within the marker buoys. I very nearly took the wrong turn, which would have taken us to Nantes and the River Loire. Because the river was flowing strongly at this point, I had to keep the barge at full speed in order to maintain steering control.

Pierre appeared with some enormous sandwiches and a bottle of wine. He took over the wheel and I tucked into the meal. I had a deep feeling of sadness and the wine helped to dull the pain.

The memory of Simone has always remained with me. I have not met anyone like her since.

Nor would I ever want to …

Chapter 8

Ashmore Manor

Peter Lonsdale passed through the front door of Ashmore Manor shortly after lunch. It was a warm summer's afternoon in 1943. Pete was old at twenty-three, slightly built, just over six feet tall and very fit. He had a mop of fair hair, a well-shaped face and a sunny disposition.

An only child with a strict father and a doting mother, Pete's father would beat him for the slightest misdemeanour when he was just a child. His mother, being helpless to intervene, would often retire weeping to her room. Pete's father died of a heart attack when he was fifteen years old and life for Pete and his mother from then on changed for the better. Mr Lonsdale senior had left his wife and Pete quite well-off financially. So when he finished school at seventeen, they spent the next two years touring France and Germany where Pete became fluent in both languages.

When war started, Pete volunteered for the army and because of his fluency in French and German, he was posted to a special service section that operated from this manor house in Somerset.

In November 1940, Pete went to visit his mother in London to find his house had just been destroyed and his mother killed in an air raid. He watched as the fierce fire continued to destroy all the houses in his street. This was to change Pete forever. That night he declared his own war on Germany.

His red Triumph sports car looked a little out of place amongst all the camouflaged army trucks and jeeps parked on the gravel drive. Pete was also the only person wearing civilian clothes.

Having identified himself at the reception desk, Pete was escorted to a waiting room where he sat for a short while before being invited into the plush office of the Head of Operations.

'So you made it back safely, Pete.' The person addressing Pete was also in 'civvies'. Stephen Harvey had spent many years in the diplomatic service and refused to wear a uniform. Because he was dealing with senior officers of the three Services, Stephen had been given the rank of Air Vice Marshal, a rank he preferred not to use.

'You have done excellent work in northern France helping to organise Resistance groups, and your barge on the canals has already started to show us some good results.' Stephen invited Pete to sit down and then offered him a cigar, which Pete refused.

'It's progressing well. We have some very good men in the field now, but as the Germans become more organised, we are bound to have heavy losses in the next twelve months. Stephen, I expect you know all about my sixteen-year-old boy from the Channel Islands.'

'Indeed I do. I think you should handle that boy very carefully. He seems to have psychopathic tendencies, which is useful to us at present but could prove a problem to you at a later date. Pete, you have been summoned here today because of a very unusual request that I have received from our lords and masters. We have been requested to set up an organisation, with absolutely no links to any of the existing Government or service departments.'

Stephen continued, 'I believe you are the best person to set up this "business venture". Although you will not have any help from us to organise and run this venture, you will have the blessing of both the British and American Governments and perhaps at times a certain amount of protection. We want it operating as soon as the Germans realise the war is coming to an end, which should be sometime next year and we also expect your business venture to continue for at least five years after the war has ended.'

Pete was intrigued. 'This sounds interesting, Stephen, but what sort of business? And who pays all the bills?'

'You stand to make a large amount of money in the next few years, Pete. We want you to set up an underground line of escape for minor Nazi war criminals. They will come to you in Germany, in the belief that you will deliver them through France and Spain to Portugal, where a waiting ship will convey them to South America. We will supply the ship, and you will man it. Their journey will end somewhere in the Atlantic.'

Stephen sat back, a wicked smile on his face. 'None of this evil scum will be able to warn their colleagues of this 'journey to the death'. They will be changing their identity and will be expecting to start a new life in South America so no one will ever know of their fate. We owe this "payback" to the thousands of Jews who we believe are being transported to the death camps in Germany. Every day thousands of men, women and children are dying in the gas chambers and at present we are unable to help them. As to costs and your payment, dear boy—these scums of the earth will be loaded with gold and precious artefacts, stolen from the Jews. As you are running a private business, we will turn a blind eye to the stolen gold, but we would expect, at some time in the future, the artefacts to mysteriously arrive at the British Museum, from where they might eventually be returned to the surviving Jews.'

Pete was intrigued with the idea and realised the enormous financial gain to be had from such a plan. 'So is this to be my retirement pension?'

Stephen was smiling again. 'As a matter of fact, yes. I would suggest you bring your 'Piglet' back here for some intensive training. He could make a very useful partner for you, especially in disposing of any difficult customers on the way. When you are ready to start this enterprise, you will both return to France. At a suitable time you will both have to be officially eliminated by us. I think you might be burned to death in a barge somewhere. I'm sure the French Resistance would cooperate in this matter, especially if they knew you were transporting guns and ammunition to St Nazaire for the Germans. All we need is just a couple of charred bodies!'

'I like the whole idea, Stephen. Two of us would certainly be enough to carry out this scheme. We will set up a series of safe stopovers all the way to Portugal. There we can operate our ship from a quiet part of the coast.'

'We will have another agent who will find and direct clients to you. How you organise yourself is entirely up to you, Pete. We just want to know that the Nazis trying to escape the net are being quietly eliminated. We have decided to write off the barge—it will be your property from now on. You will no doubt be able to use it as a base. If you can get a cargo of ammunition, then blow the bloody thing up.'

They stood up and shook hands.

'I must say I like the young 'Piglet', Stephen. He has guts and with some of your intensive training, he and I will make a good team. I also appreciate that 'Piglet' and I could become very rich in the process!'

'If you stay alive that long, Pete. No one will realise quite what you are doing. You will be in danger from all sides. I understand you return to France tonight. Good luck. We are bringing back two RAF boys on your plane. When you rejoin the barge, you will drop Pierre off at Pontivy. He is needed by the group that are operating near Brest.'

———

Pete drove down to the village pub, his thoughts on the serious implications of the meeting. It meant going underground for the next six years or even longer. It also meant the killing would go on long after the war was over. What sort of life could one lead after so much slaughter? Would he and 'Piglet' be able to retain their hatred of Germans for all that time?

Pete entered the pub.

He had time for a couple of pints and a game of darts.

Chapter 9

I took over while Pierre went down below, reappearing with the syringe and the bottle of clear liquid. 'I'm going down into the hold, Marçel, so keep a good lookout and call me if you have a problem.' Pierre eased back the throttle until we were travelling at half speed and then disappeared into the hold.

Sometime later he joined me in the wheelhouse holding the empty bottle. 'I managed, with great difficulty, to inject a small amount of this special liquid through the corks of ten random carboys. Over a period of time, when this distilled water is used to top up the battery systems in the U-boats, the batteries will become contaminated and if the U-boats are at sea, they will become disabled. This liquid is undetectable in the carboys and there is no trace of damage to the corks where I used the syringe.'

One hour later, Pierre took the barge up a small side river called the Trevelo. When we were well out of sight, we pulled in to the bank. I went below and fetched the radio transmitter and Pierre went off with it into the surrounding woodland. I didn't question him when he came back later, but I knew he had gone to send and receive messages to England. I guessed they would only be interested in the success of the air raid and the contaminated distilled water, but not in the death of Simone and her father.

We returned to the main river and continued on our way, arriving at our destination La Roche-Bernard, quite a small port that was crawling with German sailors. There were several patrol boats anchored near the small jetty. Our cargo was quickly discharged and loaded onto trucks where it would go on by road to St Nazaire.

The paperwork completed, we were told to move out as several barges were waiting to unload. As there were no locks to negotiate on this trip, we set off and headed straight back to Redon.

It was dark when we arrived. Pierre had sent me down to the cabin to prepare our evening meal so that I would not see the place where the barge had been destroyed that morning.

We tucked into an enormous meal of stewed lamb and potatoes and lots of red wine. We both got very drunk and I only vaguely remember Pierre helping me into my bunk.

The next morning, I woke up with a splitting headache. Pierre had just returned from our agent and was making coffee. 'We are to take a large consignment of produce containers to Pontivy. This is a rich farming area. On the way, Marçel, we have a very interesting job to do for our masters. We head north up the Oust River, to a point where the River Aff joins the Oust. There we pick up two passengers and take them to a remote place near the Lanouee Forest. We then meet up with another French Resistance group. They specialise in organising landing strips and the handling of 'Airdrops'; our two guests will be picked up by an aeroplane and flown back to England.'

We moved the barge farther up the jetty until we were opposite a very large stack of assorted crates and boxes. Pierre opened up the hold, and a group of men came over and started to load the hold with the crates, boxes and tubs. When the hold was full, the men carried on stacking the crates on the deck, until Pierre had to stop them from completely blocking out our forward vision from the wheelhouse.

'We should do very well out of this cargo, Marçel.' Pierre was smiling. 'We are dealing with French farmers and will barely cover our fuel costs on this run, but we should make it up on the way back with a load of their produce.'

We set off late that afternoon after refuelling and topping up the water tank. One of Pierre's black market friends had delivered a large crate of supplies earlier that afternoon. It was starting to rain. I cast off the bow rope and because of the deck cargo, had to run down the jetty to get to the stern end of the barge.

—

This time we headed northwest and on the River Oust, part of the Brest-St Nazaire canal. I was glad not to be passing the place where Simone had died—I now had even more reason to want to kill Germans. We travelled quite slowly up this lovely part of the country, as Pierre wanted to arrive at our meeting place at dusk. The rain had stopped and the sun was out so I had a sleep on the cabin roof until I heard the engine slow down.

Pierre took the barge up the small side river, and then carefully turned around so that we were pointing the way we had come.

'If anyone was watching they would think we had made the wrong turn. Just keep your eyes on both sides of the river, Marçel, and tell me if you see any signs of life.'

I could tell Pierre was a little nervous; he was holding our signalling lamp and staring into the reeds on the riverbanks. 'Our guests will signal to us with a mirror or a torch. We must be absolutely sure that no one else is in sight before signalling them to come out to us.'

At last, just as it was getting dark, we saw a slight flash of light coming from the reeds. Having made sure no one else was around, Pierre signalled them to come out. A small rowing boat emerged from the reeds and two scruffy men in very dirty RAF uniforms climbed onto the deck. The third man immediately turned the little boat around, rowed back and disappeared into the reeds.

'Marçel, take our guests straight down to the cabin.' He turned to the two men. 'You must stay down below out of sight until I tell you to come up. You must only come on deck when either Marçel or I tell you.'

I took the men below and Pierre started the engine. He headed down to the junction of the rivers and then turned the barge until we were once again heading up the main river.

The two airmen, Geoff and Anthony, had been shot down in northern France during a daylight raid two weeks earlier. Their *Beau* fighter-bomber had been hit by anti-aircraft fire but they had both been able to parachute safely to the ground. They had hidden in a forest until they were found by an old couple, who took them to their cottage. The old people were in contact with the local Resistance and each night they had been passed on from one safe house to another until finally they were delivered to us.

Pierre called down, 'Marçel, show these gentlemen their sleeping quarters and make sure they know how to access the water.'

I took them through the engine room to where the storage tanks were, and showed them how to open the cover leading into the old water tank.

They crawled into the tank and I was just able to follow them in; it was a very tight squeeze. There was ample room on the mattress for both of them and I showed them how to get water by using the tap above their heads. I also showed them how to allow water to flood the floor of the tank, and thus allow a little water to seep out of the cracks in the old tank. This would indicate to anyone searching that the water tank was quite unusable. I could see they were not impressed with their sleeping arrangements but too bad, they would be very safe there if the barge were searched. I warned them not to talk or make any sound if the Germans came aboard to search the vessel.

I had survived so far by keeping my wits about me and I was not going to let anyone place our 'ideal set-up' at risk. I decided I was even prepared to kill our own people if they were at any time to endanger our enterprise. Pierre and I had created, with the use of our barge, great potential for doing a lot of damage to the Germans—with the radio, we were in an ideal situation for passing valuable information on to the Allies.

Back in the cabin Pierre put his head down the hatch. 'Marçel, come and take over for a while. We will tie up to the bank before dark.'

Up in the wheelhouse, I had to concentrate on the steering as the light was fading. A hand came up holding a mug of red wine but I was not in a celebratory mood. In fact, I was consumed with sadness and anger. I had no wish to talk to the two airmen; one of their planes could easily have killed Simone.

We found a suitable place where we were able to tie up and made fast to some convenient trees. It looked very quiet with no houses in sight. Sociable Pierre was well away and he and our guests were soon into their second bottle of Merlot. I cooked some eggs with slices of ham and tomatoes. After we finished our meal I cleared up.

'Pierre, I think you chaps should keep the sound down.' I poured myself a mug of wine and went and sat quietly on deck. It was another still summer's night, the sky clear and filled with millions of stars. It was like the sky two nights before, only this time I was alone.

Pierre came noisily up the steps. 'What are you doing up there, Marçel; come and join the party. It's not often we have guests.' I was looking at the riverbank. It must have been a bird that moved, but it was enough to make me very aware of our situation.

'Pierre, I have never been a party person. Anyway I think we should keep a watch while we have these airmen on board.'

Pierre grunted. 'I also think our guests are making far too much noise; sound travels a long way over the water especially on a night like this.'

Geoff and Anthony came up on deck. I was starting to get angry; this was too much. 'I think you two chaps should stay below especially when we are travelling in daylight tomorrow morning. I also think we should each do a four-hour watch on deck tonight, starting from now. Only one person should be on deck at a time.'

Pierre was looking at me; I could tell he was impressed. 'Marçel is quite right. Geoff, you take the next four hours, then Anthony will relieve you. Marçel and I will then take over. If you hear or see anything, wake Marçel and me and then you must both go quickly down to the water tank. As for tomorrow, you will have to stay below in the cabin. If it becomes necessary, you will have to go down into the tank.'

We left Geoff on deck and went below. I checked to make sure there was nothing to show that more than two people occupied the cabin and shortly after, we turned in. Still on edge, I decided not to undress. I was worried that Geoff and Anthony were on different wavelengths to us. Our life was all about survival, kill or be killed. We were always on the alert, never sure when we might be arrested and killed by the *Gestapo*.

I was just drifting off when I heard the sound of engines. I flew up the steps. 'Quickly! Get down below, Geoff.' As I followed him down, a German patrol boat flashed its searchlight directly on to the barge. I grabbed an empty bottle of wine and scrambled back on deck. The patrol boat slowed down and stopped just a few yards from us.

'Attention. Qu'est-ce qu'ily a?'

I lurched forward and replied in my best drunken French, 'C'est le capitaine, m'sieur. Il est soul encore.'

I felt a tug at my trousers. 'I'm certainly not drunk now,' whispered Pierre. The patrol boat's engine restarted and to our relief continued up the river.

———

Pierre and I were up at first light. As it would take at least ten hours to reach our destination (it was only about twenty miles, but we had to pass through twenty or more locks), we decided to take it slowly.

We needed to meet our contacts at dusk as there was some distance for our two airmen to travel to the arranged landing strip. I was to go with them to the aircraft in case anything went wrong with the pick-up and I would be forced to bring the two men back to the barge. Pierre would stay on the barge and be ready to move off if things got out of control.

Geoff and Anthony were sound asleep. I wished they would stay that way all day. We decided to give our guests a special treat—when they finally came to, we gave them *ersatz* coffee and some rather stale German rye bread for their breakfast. I hoped they would appreciate our occupation fare.

We travelled slowly up the river, the sky was overcast and it was raining quite heavily. Most of the locks were between the attractive towns of Malestroilt and Josselin. The castle at Josselin is quite imposing. Geoff and Anthony stayed in the old water tank. A pack of cards and a bottle of wine kept our guests occupied while Pierre gave me a French lesson in the wheelhouse.

Once past Josselin, as there was very little traffic on this part of the river, we were able to tie up to a deserted jetty and have a very late lunch. This time we made up for the skimpy breakfast and gave our guests fairly fresh French bread, ham, *saucisson* and an assortment of cheeses.

Just after seven pm, we turned off the main river and into the entrance of the Lie River. We pulled into the bank and were partly concealed by tall reeds and overhanging branches. I looped the ropes around two tree trunks so that we would be able to make a quick getaway if necessary.

The light was starting to fade; the rain had stopped and the clouds had lifted. It would be ideal for night flying. The small village of Les Forges was in the distance and beyond it a large dark area, the Forest de Lanouee.

After a while, we saw a man standing on the bank. He signalled to us to come over. I went below and told Geoff and Anthony that we were ready to go and to follow me. I told them to move as quietly as possible and not to talk. I had the compass and small torch in my pocket and slipped the bayonet into my belt. We dropped into the water and waded ashore. Our guide signalled us to follow him. When we reached the top of the bank, I took a compass bearing on the opposite riverbank, where we had entered this part of the river. This would guide me back to where the barge was tied up.

We climbed up through rough scrub until we came to a road at the top of the bank. Our guide paused to make sure there were no Germans on the road, we slipped quietly across and were soon moving through the forest on level ground. I noted that we were still more or less on the same compass bearing; this would make it easy for the return journey.

About thirty minutes later, we came to a large clearing in the forest. We were led to the remains of a building—just four walls and no roof. The floor was covered with tall weeds and rubbish. We sat up against one of the walls and waited.

With my limited French, I managed to talk quietly to our nameless guide. We were at a derelict World War I training aerodrome that the Germans had not yet put to use. His Resistance group had cleared a short landing strip, which they had then disguised by placing on it rubbish, tree branches and oil drums. When an Allied aircraft was due to land, they cleared the strip and then replaced the rubbish after the plane left.

He told me the aeroplane tonight would stop very close to where we were. I was to tell Geoff and Anthony to run out as soon as they saw it starting to turn around. They had to move very fast as the plane would not stop for more than a few seconds. I explained this to them and I knew they would not waste a second in dashing across to the aeroplane. In the distance we could hear the sound of heavy bombing. We could see a large red glow to the northwest. This would give the cover and protection needed for our light aircraft.

It would be here soon. After picking up the two men, it would join up with other aircraft and would receive protection for the return journey to England. It did not occur to me that I could have joined the two airmen and escaped to England.

We heard the approach of a small aircraft. Our guide disappeared.

Standing near the entrance of our building, I saw two figures running down the landing strip placing a row of torches as they ran. As they got to the end of the strip, I saw the aeroplane coming in to land. The plane was coming straight towards us. It slowed down and started to turn. Geoff and Anthony ran off towards it and I wished them good luck.

They reached the aeroplane before it had completed its turn. I think it was a 'Lysander' Aircraft. A figure jumped out and I saw our two airmen get in. Suddenly I heard the gunshots, the Lysander lifted off, started to climb and then hit the ground in a ball of fire. In the glaring light I saw two Resistance men run along the landing strip and collapse to the ground. The figure that had left the Lysander was coming straight towards me. Just before he reached me, a German soldier appeared from nowhere and leaped on him. They were both on the ground.

I reacted instantly; I sprang forward and launched myself at the dark figures. Holding my bayonet in both hands, I landed on top of them and my bayonet went right through the German's throat and into the ground. My face was covered in blood; German blood.

The body underneath wriggled out from under the German. 'Not bad at all, Piglet.' I recognised the voice.

We ran into the forest. I could still hear gunshots behind us. The French boys were keeping the Germans occupied. I hoped they would have the opportunity to slip away as well. As soon as we were sure we were not being followed, we stopped to catch our breath. Pete put his arms around me and we gave each other a powerful hug.

Pete gripped my shoulder speaking quietly. 'Am I pleased to see you, Piglet! Looks like I might owe you one.' I was very pleased to see Pete again. I felt a strong bond had now been established between us.

We moved on silently through the woods until we reached the road. An army truck was parked a little way farther up the road. We had been very unlucky; a passing truckload of German soldiers had seen the small aircraft coming in. They arrived at the landing strip just as the aircraft was taking off and a lucky shot must have hit the fuel tank. We heard later that they had been pinned down by the Resistance and had all been killed. Three Frenchmen also died that night.

We moved farther down the road. I followed Pete as he wriggled to the opposite side. Later I would be trained to do this properly and not graze my hands and knees as I did that night. When we were safely across the road, I took a compass bearing. We headed to the right for about one hundred yards, I took another bearing and we were then on course to the barge. We slipped down the bank and arrived at the spot where I had left it.

No barge.

'I think Pierre might have moved back onto the main river when he heard the gunshots, Pete. If we walk to the mouth of the river we might just spot him.'

We got to the bend and waded through the reeds until we could see up and down the main river. Pete spotted the barge on the far bank about two hundred yards downstream.

'Race you across, Pete! I need to wash the German blood off my face and you smell of deodorant! You're not in London now!'

I sat on the opposite bank waiting for Pete. Pierre had the engine running by the time we clambered aboard and we moved off slowly heading up the river.

After drying out, I took over the steering wheel, while Pete and Pierre went below to discuss the events of the evening. With the engine running slowly, we crept up the river until we were well past the branch of the river where we had landed earlier that evening. After another two miles, we reached a place where we were able to bring the barge into a small side turning, out of sight of the main river. We tied up to the grass bank, again with the help of two convenient trees.

We were all feeling a bit subdued by now. The loss of the aircraft, the pilot and the two English airmen we had tried to help. Also, we did not know how many Frenchmen had died in the fighting.

'So just when I was beginning to enjoy life on the canals, I have now been ordered to move up to Brest. You don't have to worry, Marçel. Pete knows the canals far better than I. He has just as many contacts as I have, so you certainly won't starve.'

Pete got up and gave Pierre a friendly slap on the back. 'Pierre, you know, with your talents you really are wasted here on the barge. Anyway you will meet lots of girls when you get to Brest and you will be able catch up with some of your old friends.'

Pete continued. 'I'll leave the barge early in the morning and will rejoin you when you get to Pontivy, the day after tomorrow; that's when I officially take over the barge. In the meantime, I'm going to get some sleep in the water tank, just in case we have visitors in the night.'

Pete disappeared into the engine room and Pierre and I turned in. I lay in my bunk thinking of the two RAF men. I had been the last person to speak to them; I had wished them 'good luck'.

Chapter 10

We set off at daybreak. Pete had slipped ashore before it grew light and was now on his way to meet us at Pontivy. We only had twenty-four miles to travel but we had a staggering sixty-four locks to pass through on the way, so we expected to reach Pontivy about lunchtime the following day.

The journey to Pontivy was uneventful, apart from working our way through the locks and in places, finding the river quite narrow. We spent that night in one of the locks. The next morning we eventually came to a road and a railway bridge and finally arrived at Pontivy.

A group of Germans were standing on the jetty. They jumped aboard and immediately started to search our barge. The patrol boat that had stopped to look at us three nights before was tied up at the end of the jetty. Pierre, guessing what was happening, went down into the engine room to turn off the engine; he reappeared wiping grease from his hands.

The officer, the captain of the patrol boat, approached Pierre. 'Why has it taken you so long to get to Pontivy? What have you been doing all this time?'

Pierre showed the officer his greasy hands. 'Water in the fuel lines, *Herr Capitaine*. The fuel today is of such poor quality! I spent hours cleaning the filters and fuel lines.'

The search not having revealed anything, the German captain ordered his men off the barge. As he was about to leave he turned to Pierre. 'Did you hear any gunfire the night before last?'

Pierre replied eagerly, 'But yes, *Herr Capitaine*. We guessed you Germans were out hunting in the forest. There are plenty of deer in the forest.'

Shortly after, the patrol boat and the Germans set off down the river. Pierre gave them a friendly wave as they passed. The *Capitaine* returned a frosty salute.

The local farmers arrived and started to unload and sort the crates and boxes. After we finished our lunch, Pierre decided not to wait for Pete as he thought we might be getting another visit from the Germans, this time from the *Gestapo*, regarding our presence near the shooting two nights ago.

'They won't bother with you, Marçel, as long as you act the dumb boy. If Pete gets back when they are here, he can easily explain that he has just arrived to take over the barge.' Pierre packed a few things in a bag, warmly shook my hand and left. I was sorry to see him go, and did not wish him good luck.

The hold was almost empty by now so I went down and started to sweep it out. The crates had left quite a mess and our next cargo was to be farm produce. I found an old dustbin and carried all the rubbish and dumped it at the rubbish area, which was just behind the jetty.

I was about to return when a car pulled up at the jetty and four Germans in civvies, *Gestapo* men, jumped out and headed straight for the barge. I dropped down behind the pile of rubbish and backed away until I was able to hide behind some bushes. Dumb boy or not I was not going to take the chance of being recognised as the 'Piglet'.

I could see one of the *Gestapo* men talking to the last of the farmers, who was tying up his load of crates. The farmer pointed in my direction. I was going to have to bluff my way out of this, so I slid back to the rubbish heap, picked up the old dustbin and started walking back to the barge. I forced myself to grin, tried very hard to whistle, but very little sound came out.

As I stepped onto the barge, I was grabbed by the collar and forced down into the cabin. One man had stayed on deck. Two held onto me, and the other, who was in charge, hit me hard across the face. I was trying to keep my silly grin, and started to nod my head. For this I received two more blows to the head. My nose started to bleed.

'*Ou est le capitaine, garçon?*' he demanded.

'*Le capitaine il est parti m'sieur. Le nouveau capitaine arrive bientôt.*'

I received one more blow for luck, then they let go of me and I slipped to the floor half stunned.

The four *Gestapo* men were on the jetty when Pete arrived, carrying an old kit bag on his back. After lots of shouting and arm waving the *Gestapo* men got in their car and drove away.

I was standing by the table trying to stop my nosebleed when Pete came down into the cabin. 'Looks like you came off worst this time, Marçel. Never mind, you are now my "First Mate" and from now on "Mate", you and I are going to create absolute havoc amongst the Germans.' Pete threw his kit bag at me. I caught it and nearly collapsed with the weight. 'Have a look in there, my boy; I'm glad you didn't drop it.'

The bag was filled with detonators and explosives, two revolvers and two Sten guns (light machine guns) with a quantity of ammunition. 'I must say,' Pete was grinning, 'I was a little concerned when I saw your friends on the jetty. However a little friendly chatter and all is now well.' Pete produced a flask from his pocket. 'Let's celebrate our new start and afterwards you can cook me my first meal, God help me!'

'Pierre thought it smarter to set off early and so avoid meeting the *Gestapo*. A wise move as it turned out,' I said as I passed some papers to Pete. 'He told me to make sure you looked at all the paperwork, and to check all our permits. We will be getting a load of farm produce in the morning which we are to take back to Renne.'

'That sounds good, Marçel. We will have to make a fast run to Renne as it will be perishable cargo. I need to see some contacts in Renne anyway. By the way, I thought we might blow up the railway bridge, which is farther down the river. We could do it on our way back to Renne.'

The next morning at daylight the farmers started to arrive with their produce—a mixture of cauliflowers, cabbages, carrots, potatoes and other vegetables. An agent for the farmers was writing out consignment notes. I was given the job of double-checking the number of packages for each consignment.

They arrived mostly by horse and cart and just a few came with their tractors and trailers. The farmers organised the loading and I must say the produce was all carefully stacked in the hold, with gaps to allow air circulation.

Pete had gone into the village to see his friends and reappeared just when I was checking the last load of cauliflowers. By the time we finished the paperwork, the farmers had all disappeared into the village bar. It was after twelve pm so we decided to get going straight away. I worked the winch and closed up the hold, careful to leave a gap for air circulation.

Twenty locks after we left Pontivy we saw the railway bridge in front of us. I took the wheel and Pete carefully studied the underside of the bridge. There was a guard standing at each end and we could see that the guardhouse was on the opposite side of the river.

The locks were all hand operated so I had to help the '*éclusier*' (lock keeper) each time to open and close the gates. Because the locks were so close together, by running ahead and opening the next lock we were able pass through a lock in less than ten minutes.

It was dusk when we passed the village of Gueltas and shortly after we found a secluded inlet. Pete made some coffee and produced some large pieces of *gateaux* he had brought back from the village. Pete went down to the 'water tank' and returned with a bag of explosives and detonators. 'My friends have supplied us with transport. We can be at the bridge and back here before dawn. There will be no connection between us and the sabotage to the bridge as we should be well down the river by then. I will use a timing device which will enable us to be well clear when the bridge blows.'

We set off along the riverside track at two am. A few minutes later, we saw the remains of an old barge on the riverbank. Pete disappeared into some bushes and returned wheeling two bicycles.

Keeping to the riverside we soon slipped past Gueltas and followed the dirt road. We arrived at the main road and the river bridge, quite close to the railway bridge, our target.

We concealed our bikes in some bushes, carefully crossed the road and slipped down to the riverbank moving cautiously along the bank until we arrived at a sharp bend in the river.

Once around the bend we had a good clear view of the bridge and could see the red glow of a cigarette coming from where the guard was standing right at the end of the bridge. I wondered how many guards had been killed just by having a lighted cigarette in the mouth—such an easy target.

We waited patiently for at least forty minutes when at last we heard the slow approach of a train. As it got close to the bridge, Pete moved forward and climbed the bank until he was just under the bridge. I crept up behind Pete until I was close to where the guard was standing. The guard was watching the train.

As the train came by us, the guard stepped back and I stepped forward. My bayonet gained itself another notch. I quickly pulled the dead guard off the bridge and joined Pete.

'Pass up the explosives, Marçel.' The longest ten minutes of my life then followed as Pete finished his task and set the time clock. We had a thirty-minute start before the bridge blew. We hoped the guard at the other end would not decide to walk across the bridge to see his mate.

We crept back along the bank and up to the road, crossed over, retrieved our bicycles and rode like mad down the dirt track. We had just passed

Gueltas when we heard a rumble and saw an orange glow behind us. We kept going and soon arrived at the place where we had picked up the bicycles. We hid them in the bushes and ran back to the barge.

Pete started the engine and I pulled in the ropes. It was five am with just enough light to see our way. As soon as we were able, we ran the engine at full speed. We were now far away from the bridge and would not to be connected to the sabotage.

Our breakfast of coffee, bread and cheese never tasted so good; Pete and I were still riding high. 'You really have become an expert killer, Marçel, I would not like to be your enemy!' I leaned across and gripped Pete's hand. 'Don't worry, Pete, you are quite safe with me ... at present.' Our high spirits were soon to become overtaken by tiredness. It had been a long and busy twenty-four hours.

Chapter 11

We kept the engine running at full speed most of the next day, except for when we passed through the locks. We wanted to get the farm produce to its destination as quickly as possible, especially as it was such warm weather.

It was almost dark when we tied up at Redon. We went ashore and found a café still open and had a good meal of river perch and *pommes frites*, washed down with a carafe of *vin du pays blanc*.

We made an early start the next morning and were due to arrive at Renne in the afternoon. Before leaving, Pete had telephoned the office at Renne and given our expected arrival time.

Pete insisted we speak only in French and I soon found I was starting to think in French. I was quite enjoying myself and took every opportunity to talk to people as we passed through the locks or tied up at a jetty.

'Have you thought about your future, Marçel?'

I was standing next to Pete in the wheelhouse while he negotiated our way past two extra-large barges. 'I could never go back to my family now, Pete. I've moved into a completely different world and I have so much blood on my hands. I have to make my own life now; it might not be so easy for me to stop killing people.'

I thought about it for a few moments. 'After the war Pete, I think I would like to stay here and become a *batelier*, and have my own barge. At least I wouldn't have to pass any exams to qualify!'

'It is quite possible, Marçel, that you could be employed in some undercover work which could last for a few years and continue well after the end of the war. It might not mean living on the barges, but you could be travelling on canals in different parts of France; you might even make a lot of money. Would this interest you?'

'Tell me more, Pete. Would I be working for you?' I certainly was interested—I might even be able to kill a few more Germans.

'If you were to take this path, Marçel, you would be working with me, not for me. We would be running our own business in Europe with the doubtful blessing of Her Majesty's Government.'

I took over the steering from Pete; this was getting very interesting. 'Just think very carefully about what I am proposing before you make any decision, Marçel. If you decide to join me in this enterprise, you will have to fly back to England fairly soon. In England you will go through some very special and intensive training. This will be extremely hard for you, but I've no doubt you will survive the course and you will certainly become very fit and will learn the essential principals of self-preservation and of course improve your killing skills!'

I had not seen Pete in such a serious mood. He seemed to be making a difficult decision himself.

'Once you return to France, Marçel, until the work we are undertaking is finished, the only "let out" for you is your demise; we will be involved in something far more dangerous than anything you have done so far. You will see, and take part in, the killing of a lot of very evil men and women. You will be meeting people who have been involved in the deaths of thousands of innocent men, women and children. So just think very carefully before you come to a decision.'

Pete strode off to the bow; he just stood there for a while and I could sense his deep-felt anger. I knew that Pete was referring to certain things that were happening in Germany and I also knew Pete would show no mercy to the people involved in the running of the death camps. We had heard rumours of the mass killing of the Jews in Europe, but we still had no idea of the full horror that was to be revealed to the world in 1945.

I did realise that once I became involved in this 'business venture', I would be unable to retract, as with my knowledge of the plans to punish these people, I could endanger the lives of those still involved; they would probably have to kill me. Pete and I had the same mentality: if killing was justified, then we could both kill in cold blood and feel no remorse, almost a feeling of satisfaction, if not pleasure. I knew we could work well together. I liked the idea that we would be involved with the people trying to escape their punishment at the end of the War. Even better, we would be paid for it.

The agent and several men were waiting at the jetty when we arrived at Renne. As soon as we tied up, the agent took all the paperwork and set up a makeshift desk on the jetty. I opened up the hold and the gang of men started to unload the produce. Pete and I did our best to separate all the consignments. It was a complete waste of time; the wholesale merchant mixed everything up again when he came to load up his trucks.

When the last of the cargo had gone, we swept up the rubbish in the hold, moved the barge across to a pontoon and joined a row of empty barges.

'I might be away for a few days, Marçel. If I am more than a week, go across to our agent's office. Joseph will tell you what to do. In the meantime have a rest, work on your French and keep out of trouble.'

Pete went ashore to see the agent. Afterwards he went off to meet his 'friends'. I tidied up the deck and had a sleep on the roof of the cabin.

—

The next four days seemed endless. I spent a lot of the time studying the French books that Pierre had given me. I talked a little to one or two of the *bateliers* on the barges nearby, but I still had to be very careful with my accent. One woman tried speaking to me in English. I gave her a blank look. It worked.

I found some paint and went around the deck touching up any small patches of rust I could find. We had plenty of food on board so I had no reason to go ashore.

Occasionally a barge would move off to pick up a cargo and another empty barge would arrive to take its place. Life on the barges in summer was good. There were whole families on some of the barges; they seemed to be generally quite a happy bunch of people.

I had plenty of time to seriously consider Pete's offer to join him in his future plans; I liked the idea. I had started a new life and was enjoying the excitement. The boy had become a strong, ruthless and determined man. I would continue this life for the next few years and I hoped to make a lot of money. If I turned this proposal down now, Pete might have to eliminate me as I already knew too much of his plans. Maybe one day I might even have to eliminate Pete.

A very scruffy-looking Pete returned on the third evening. Much to my relief, he looked very pleased with himself. I grilled the large piece of steak that he had brought with him and over the second bottle of *vin rouge* he told me just a little of what he had been doing.

'I have been in contact with the French Resistance boys who take care of the secret landing strips. They lost three men the night I came in, and killed all the Germans that attacked us that night. They took the bodies and the truck to another location, well away from there, and blew up the truck. They made sure all the German bodies were destroyed in the fire.'

I refilled Pete's glass and he continued. 'They went back to the landing strip to clean up, removed the remains of the *Lysander*, buried the three English men in the forest and covered up the remains of the fire with debris and old bits of burnt timber. The Resistance boys are convinced the Germans still have no idea of the existence of our landing strip. They are keeping a man close by to see if anyone comes by there in the next two weeks. After that they believe we can use the landing strip again. In the meantime, Marçel, we have a cargo of fertiliser to take to Redon, and then on to Pontivy, which means another return cargo of farm produce.'

'I shall be pleased to get moving again, Pete. By the way, I accept your offer of a partnership in the human "dust cart" business. I am prepared to go all the way with you in eliminating the scum.'

'Pleased to hear that, dear boy. I was going to eliminate you if you had said no but I was pretty sure that would be your answer, Marçel, so I took the liberty of organising your return to England and a six-month training course for you when you get there. I shall join you much later in England. We are expecting the invasion of France next year and I still have much to do over here.'

It took a third bottle of wine before we were both ready to turn in. We drank to our future partnership. We both knew our friendship would be strong enough to see us through the times ahead.

The next morning we moved over to the jetty. We were loaded with an assortment of fertilisers, which were to be delivered to Redon and Pontivy. This time the barge was low in the water, weighed down with its heavy cargo. We would have to be careful not to become stuck in shallow water.

It was midday before we left Renne. We kept up a steady speed down the Villane River but it was almost dark when we arrived at Redon. I did not go ashore this time.

An agent with his gang of unloaders appeared soon after daylight. While they were unloading part of the cargo, Pete went ashore and returned with fresh food, wine and several freshly baked *baguettes*.

'Marçel, we will be receiving another guest tonight; a surprise for you, someone you have seen before.'

I was puzzled, I had met so few people and they were mostly Germans.

'I hope this is not going to be another air disaster Pete. I'm already trying to face up to flying across to England.'

—

We set off again later that morning and headed up the Oust River to Pontivy. It was another fine summer's day. We had to pass through all the locks again, which made the journey interesting, but hard work.

Late afternoon we passed the small town of Malestroit. Further up the river we pulled in to an old jetty and tied up for the night. The town was quite deserted. There were several derelict cottages and a tumbled-down barn that must have been abandoned a long time ago.

After a light meal and lots of freshly made coffee, Pete went below to the old water tank and returned with the two Sten guns. 'I can't let you practise firing this gun, Marçel, but I can at least show you how to hold it and fire it. I'll also show you how to strip it down and reassemble it.' After several attempts, I was able to strip and reassemble the gun and felt quite confident that I would be able to use it, if necessary.

It was now close to midnight. 'Time for us to head off to the pickup point. It won't be landing this time, Marçel. Our guest will, with luck, be landing by parachute. There should be just sufficient light to spot the white parachute.'

I slipped my good friend, the bayonet, in my belt, put the torch and compass in my pockets and joined Pete on the deck. The two Sten guns had shoulder straps, which left our hands free so that we could climb up and over the old jetty.

We followed a dirt track that ran past the cottages and directly away from the river. I took a compass bearing of the barge. This amused Pete, but I was not taking any chances in case I had to return to the barge alone. The track was overgrown as it had not been used for a long time. We eventually came out of the trees and passed through some rough scrubland, which gradually turned to grassland. I could smell cattle and heard the lowering of a cow not too far away. In the distance ahead, we could see another line of trees.

There was just enough light from the new moon to show up the track to the pilot of the aircraft. We stood and waited.

'I will need your torch, Marçel; I just hope we are alone here tonight.'

It seemed ages before we heard the sound of aeroplane engines. There were a large number of them and they were flying very high up. 'On their way to bomb St Nazaire tonight, Marçel.'

Another aircraft was approaching. It was flying much lower and it had a much quieter engine. As it got nearer, Pete pointed the torch in its direction and signalled VE in Morse code. The aircraft flew overhead and disappeared, following the other aircraft. About ten minutes later, we heard it coming back towards us. Pete repeated the signal. The plane passed overhead and continued on its way.

We were both searching the sky. 'There it is, Marçel, about two hundred yards ahead.' We started to run towards the white patch. Halfway there, Pete grabbed me. We stopped, stood still and listened. Except for the distant rumbling, all was quiet. We ran up to the figure rolling up the parachute and bent down to help. 'Bon soir, mes enfants,' said a woman's voice.

'Welcome back, Gerda. We will talk later but now we must get back to the barge as quickly as possible.' Pete took hold of the parachute and we quickly made our way back to the cottages. Pete gave me the parachute while he went ahead to make sure it was safe to return to the barge. Once on board, we cast off and continued up the river with the engine running as quietly as possible. It was just becoming light.

Our first job was to pack the parachute in a strong bag. (Pierre had laughingly brought some large bran bags that he called 'body bags' when last in Redon. 'These are especially for your use Marçel,' he had joked.) We placed some heavy weights in the bag and then dropped it over the side, making sure we were in the centre of the canal.

———

By the time we reached the first lock it was daylight; we had to wait for the *éclusier* to open the lock.

I was in the cabin making coffee when Gerda joined me. 'So, Marçel, you are the famous boy who witnessed my brother's death.' Gerda's French was far better than her English. 'Klaus was a good man and I loved him very much. He was so unlucky to have a sister on the opposite side. I do not blame you, Marçel; the *Gestapo* were on to Klaus long before you arrived on the scene. I'm glad he died as he did, and not at the hands of the *Gestapo*.' Gerda moved across to me and kissed me lightly on the forehead. 'So, we are friends now, Marçel?'

I stood there recovering from the kiss. Gerda was a tall, slim and very attractive blonde, I guessed in her early twenties. I had not noticed this on our first encounter. She looked very fit and had small, lovely breasts.

I was starting to blush. 'Why yes, sure. I think you're lovely. I mean yes, yes let's be friends.' To add to my confusion Gerda started to undress. She removed her flying overalls and stood in front of me, in her pants and bra. Gerda was laughing at me as she slipped on some old clothes, let her hair down and put on a pair of worn shoes.

I was smitten. *Lucky Pierre.* I had to turn my back on Gerda for a few minutes. 'The little boy is shy, yes? You will have to get used to living with an old woman for the next few days.'

Pete came down the steps; Gerda put her arm around me. 'I think I embarrassed the boy, Pete. We are good friends now—he is lovely.'

We sat around the table enjoying our coffee. Gerda explained her reason for being with us. 'I am to go to Paris to work there until the invasion of France which hopefully is next year. I am to help prepare lists of war criminals who will be dealt with by the Allies, both in France and in Germany. As soon as the Allies start moving into Germany, I am to follow them and work with British Intelligence in Germany. Pete, when the time comes I will be able to furnish you with a separate, detailed list of minor criminals. My condition for taking on this job was that I could spend a few days here with Pierre before going on to Paris.'

Gerda took Pete's hand. 'I was told you could arrange that for me, Pete. By the way, for my cover I am your wife having a short break on the barge. I have the necessary papers for that.'

Pete had a wicked smile on his face. 'That, Gerda, is your bunk over there, and the one on the other side is only, and I mean *only*, for me.'

'You flatter yourself, Pete; I would much rather share with Marçel—I like them young!'

The *éclusier* was shouting and the lock gates were opening. We started the engine and moved into the lock waiting for the water to rise before the other gates could open. Apparently, the Germans had not spotted the parachute descending the night before.

By eight that evening we had reached Gueltas, having had an uneventful trip. We ate lunch on the deck, taking advantage of the warm sun and enjoying the superb countryside. I found it difficult to take my eyes off Gerda, who kept us laughing all the way. After having an hilarious and slightly drunken evening tied up in one of the many locks, we retired for the night, making a late start the next morning for the rest of the journey to Pontivy.

We tied up to the jetty at Pontivy and the agent came aboard. Over a bottle of *vin rouge*, Pete introduced his wife, Gerda. The agent told us he would unload the fertilisers the next day and arrange to load the produce for Renne the day after.

Pete went off with the agent to meet his contacts in the town. Gerda went off to get eggs for the evening meal. I set about tidying up the cabin.

Gerda was soon back but it was quite late when Pete returned. Gerda cooked us a beautiful omelette with lots of French fries and a well-dressed salad.

'I have made contact with the group from Brest. We have set up a meeting for tomorrow night. Pierre will be coming back with us, so we need to take an extra bicycle. Our bicycle friend is going to borrow the extra bikes for us.' Pete was looking thoughtful. 'Maybe you should stay here, Gerda. I don't have a good feeling about this meeting.'

'Just you try and stop me, Pete. Anyway you need me; I'm very good with a gun.'

Pete gave Gerda a thoughtful stare. 'It may very well come to that. Tomorrow night we will travel for about ten miles along a dirt road and through a forest until we come to Lake Guerledan. There is a deserted cottage on the edge of the lake.'

——

The next day the farmers arrived to unload and collect their fertilisers for the following season. When they finished, we had the task of cleaning out the hold as the smell of the fertilisers would contaminate the fresh produce. In the end we washed down the sides and then had to pump out the water.

We ate very little that evening; I think Pete and I were thinking of our disaster at the airstrip. I also worried about taking Gerda with us. We decided to leave at ten pm so that we could arrive at the meeting point at midnight.

We found the bicycles at the back of the rubbish dump and set off down the dirt road heading north. Pete and Gerda each had a Sten gun slung over their shoulders and I had one of the revolvers and my trusty bayonet, tucked in my belt. As usual, I had my torch and compass. We took it in turn to hold the spare bicycle; this slowed us down a little. The track ran into the forest just past a crossroad.

'We'll leave the bikes here and walk the rest of the way, chaps.' I could see by now Pete was very alert and ready for anything. We concealed the bicycles in the bushes.

'I want you to spread out. I will lead, Gerda, follow about ten paces behind me, and you, Marçel, keep well behind to cover our rear. If you see Germans coming up behind us, it means we have walked into a trap. Fire your revolver to warn us and get the hell out of here. Make a large circle back to the bicycles and wait.'

We moved slowly and silently amongst the tall trees until the old cottage came in sight. Pete had stopped dead; he was staring at what looked like a decorated Christmas tree. Gerda ran up to him. 'Oh no—my God! It can't be.' She ran forward.

'Come back, Gerda.' Pete tried to grab her but it was too late.

Four French Resistance boys were hanging from the tree. One of them was Pierre.

Gerda screamed and all hell broke loose.

Germans ran out of the cottage firing their guns as they ran towards Gerda. She stood still, firing her Sten gun, sweeping her fire back and forth. Gerda fell to the ground. Pete moved forward, firing as he went. He took Gerda's arm and dragged her back to the bushes.

I fired my revolver at the Germans, then ran ten yards to the left and fired again. I fired and ran again. It was enough to distract the firing from Pete; to give him time to lift Gerda onto his shoulders and dash deep into the forest.

The Germans were heading in my direction. I decided discretion was the better part of valour and retreated up the track. As soon as I thought I was far enough away, I turned sharply to the right and into the forest. I started to make a large circle that I knew would take me back to the bicycles.

I heard someone coming up behind me and slipped behind a tree trunk. It was Pete, carrying Gerda. Some sort of instinct made me hold back. I let them pass and waited behind the tree. I heard a rustle of dead leaves by my tree. I stepped out. The look of surprise, which quickly turned to horror on the German's face as I slit his throat, gave me some satisfaction after having seen Pierre hanging from the tree. Perfect timing, I thought, as the German crumpled to the ground.

I could still hear gunshots. I quickly caught up with Pete and Gerda, who had partly regained consciousness. She had been hit in her arm and her leg and was in shock. We reached the bicycles—four bicycles and two riders.

We managed to get Gerda wedged onto the crossbar of Pete's bike, with her top half draped across the handlebars. 'You keep going, Pete. I'm going to try and hide these bicycles so that our Pontivy friends can retrieve them later.'

Pete gave me Gerda's Sten gun; I gave him a push start and he was away. 'I'll catch up with you later.' After a very shaky start, Pete managed to control the bike sufficiently and set off to Pontivy.

I wondered why I could still hear shots coming from the cottage. I guessed I had not seen the last of the Germans. I found a suitable spot deep inside some bushes where I concealed the two bicycles. It was the best I could do but would not stand up to a thorough search. I hopped on the remaining bike and rode as fast as I could to catch up with the others.

I was about halfway to Pontivy when I heard the motorcycle coming behind me. I knew what to do. I left the bicycle at the side of the road and stood behind a tree, close to the road. The motorcycle and side car came bumping down the road. It slowed down when the two Germans saw the bicycle and before it stopped, I stepped out and fired the Sten gun until it ran out of bullets. After checking that they were both dead, I rode like hell until I reached Pontivy and left the bicycle by the rubbish heap. I saw a figure come over to collect it.

—

There was no sign of life on the barge. I made some coffee and waited in the wheelhouse. A little later two men appeared, pushing a wheelbarrow. Pete and the other man gently lifted Gerda on to the barge and brought her through the wheelhouse and down into the cabin. Pete thanked the man, who then set off back to the village pushing the wheelbarrow. 'Gerda has been very lucky, Marçel, She has two bad flesh wounds but no serious damage. I'm afraid, Gerda, we will have to hide you in the old tank. With those wounds you will be a dead giveaway when the Germans come to search us.'

We managed to get Gerda down below. I got into the tank first and carefully pulled her in and onto the mattress. The local midwife had managed to dress Gerda's wounds and had given her some sort of homemade knockout drug.

Pete poked his head into the tank. 'I think you should stay with Gerda until she becomes fully conscious, Marçel. Gerda is going to need someone to calm her when she comes to and remembers exactly what happened.'

I was more than happy to stay with Gerda. I guessed she would need someone to talk to—waking up in the tank would be very scary.

'That's fine by me, Pete, as long as you bring down some hot coffee.' I covered Gerda with the blanket, arranged her pillow, sat by her and gently stroked her head. I felt so sorry for Gerda; she had lost both her brother and her husband in such a short time.

Sometime later I realised she was awake. She was lying very still, tears running down her face. She began to sob, first quietly and then her whole body started shaking, I held her tightly. Our faces were touching and my tears joined hers. I had nothing to say to comfort her.

After a while, Gerda stopped sobbing but still clung to me. We stayed like that for a long time. Finally, she released herself, took my head with both hands and gave me a long but gentle kiss on the lips. 'Thank you, Marçel. You don't realise how much you have helped by holding me and sharing my grief.'

Sitting up, she pulled back her hair, brushed herself down and gave me a big smile. 'So now we both have a mission. One day I will avenge Pierre's death and help to kill many of the vermin that are living amongst my people. You will come and visit me in Paris, Marçel. We will share a real bed next time.'

I slipped out of the tank and joined Pete on deck. It was just starting to get light. 'Gerda will be all right now, Pete. She's had a good cry and is ready to carry on.' Pete raised his eyebrows and gave me a knowing smile. 'Pete, she just needed a shoulder to cry on.' I was not amused.

'We had better be ready. We will be searched any time now. Take everything of Gerda's down to the tank, Marçel.'

I cleared Gerda's bunk and took down all her gear, with a mug of coffee and some sandwiches.

———

At first light a very agitated agent appeared. 'All hell has broken loose in the district, Pete. We are expecting the Germans to search the town any moment. Luckily the local Resistance followed you to your rendezvous last night. They saw what had happened at the cottage and when the firing started, they attacked the Germans from the other side of the cottage and gradually withdrew to the west. The Germans followed, believing it was an attack by the same group from the northwest. Later some of our other men found the motorcycle that they dumped into the river. They cleaned up the scene of the killing and disposed of the two dead Germans.' The agent paused for breath.

'Where is the woman, Pete?' Pete was smiling. He appeared to be quite unruffled by the situation. 'Don't worry my friend. Once again your boys have done an excellent job. "The woman" is well hidden. The Germans will never find her. Our worry is that we have an informer somewhere in our midst. We must find him and kill him.'

'I have a good idea who he is, Pete. One of our farmers had a grudge against Pierre from a court case before the war. Tonight he will die slowly— and very painfully. Now we must start loading your barge. The farmers are arriving. We know nothing of any shooting last night.'

We were all busy loading the farm produce when the Germans arrived. We were immediately forced to stop work and were all lined up on the jetty while the barge was carefully searched.

The farmers and workers chatted and laughed amongst themselves. I realised this was all part of the cover; the French were experts at fooling the Germans, especially when they had something to hide. I noticed Pete was having a friendly chat to an officer standing on the jetty.

Every inch of the barge was carefully searched, but the water tank remained undiscovered. At last, the Germans clambered off the barge, looked underneath the jetty and searched all around the area.

There was a lot of shouting and door banging coming from the town. A house-to-house search was in progress—no Resistance men would be at home and certainly no weapons would be left in any of the houses.

Finally, the officer in charge waved to the farmers to carry on loading. The Germans climbed into their trucks and headed off to join the soldiers searching the town.

'We were very lucky this time, Marçel. That officer told me that a good part of the produce goes to the German forces; because of that they have been ordered to go easy on this town and the local farmers. In other places a lot of good, innocent people would have been shot today.'

We kept on loading until the last of the produce was stacked in the hold. It was quite possible the Germans would return and carry out another search. When all the paperwork was completed, I slipped down to see how Gerda was. She said she had slept most of the time but was a bit worried when a German started tapping on the tank. They missed the well-disguised panel at the end of the tank.

The agent shook our hands and wished us well; he was pleased to see the back of us this time. He untied the ropes and we started the engine and with great relief we pulled away from the jetty. I got the winch working, pulled the cover over the hold and took over the steering from Pete. He went below and helped Gerda out of the tank and up to the cabin. I could soon smell coffee. It was midday and we had not eaten since yesterday.

'This will keep you alive until tonight.' Pete passed me up a mug of coffee and a hunk of bread and sausage. 'Keep a careful lookout all around in case that patrol boat appears. If you spot any Germans at the lock gates we will have to quickly get Gerda back into the tank.'

We passed under the bridge that we had tried to destroy on our last trip to Pontivy. A number of workmen were busy repairing the damage and unfortunately, it would soon be back in use. At least it would have been out of action for a while. 'I should have climbed out to the centre of the bridge. The damage would have been far greater and it would have been much more difficult to repair.'

Pete went down to the cabin. All these minor damages of the railway system by the Resistance kept the Germans on their toes and tied up a very large number of their fighting men.

We were kept busy opening and closing the endless number of locks. Pete was fending off while I helped the *éclusier* but there was no sign of Germans at any of the locks. At dusk we pulled into a quiet part of the river and tied up for the night.

In contrast to our lively evening on the way to Pontivy, we had a very quiet and sombre meal of pork chops and fresh vegetables, supplied by the farmers. Gerda was feeling much better physically and decided to go back to the safety of the tank for the night. This meant we could all have a good night's sleep.

The next morning it was raining when we set off. We decided to leave Gerda in the tank as Pete was going to make contact with 'his friends in Rohan'. At Rohan, we tied up to the jetty and Pete disappeared into the village, returning an hour later laden with supplies, including some fresh bread.

I had the engine running and we immediately cast off. Much later, we passed the small side river, which was near the landing strip. I wondered when I would be flying to England; it could be from this same landing strip.

Pete brought Gerda up to the cabin. It had been arranged that Gerda would be met at a point north of Redon. She would have to take the slow route, being passed down a line of safe homes until she eventually reached Paris. Gerda would have to avoid Renne, where she was well known. She would go southeast past Angers, Orleans and Fontainebleau and then on to Paris.

Gerda's wounds, although painful, did not restrict her movements and she was now able to walk. It would take a long time for her to get over the shock of seeing Pierre hanging from the tree. Pierre's death had cast a deep shadow over the three of us. These events just strengthened our determination to do everything possible to help destroy the enemy.

I spent most of the day at the wheel while Pete stayed with Gerda. In the late afternoon, we passed the old castle at Josselin and tied up for the night at Roc-Saint-Andre; it was to be the last meal we would have together for some time. We drank a lot of wine that night, especially Gerda, who shakily stood up to make a slurred thank-you speech.

'I will never forget how you helped me get through those first few hours, Marçel. Pierre and I were devoted to each other—life will never be the same again—but with so much fear and hate around us, it will not be too difficult to move on. There is so much to do. We have to end this terrible war, punish those responsible and try to re-rebuild Europe. You, Pete and I will do our small parts but I know that what we will be doing will play an important part in the future.'

Gerda took my hand. 'Sometime in the future, you come to Paris to stay with me. By then, Paris will be free and maybe you make love to me; that I would like.'

I was lost for words again, I just said a feeble, 'Me too.' I wanted to make love to her then and there—but Gerda passed out.

It was to be a long time before we eventually met up in Paris. I often wondered if she would ever remember that invitation ...

—

I had the engine running and took in the ropes at first light. Pete and Gerda slept on. It was a very sheepish Gerda who appeared later. 'I think I must have talked too much last night, Marçel. I don't remember going to bed and getting undressed.'

I gave Gerda my innocent smile. 'I do, Gerda.'

We passed through the locks at Redon after lunch and headed on up the Villane River to Messac where Gerda would be leaving us. We would continue on to Renne the next day to unload the produce. There were several Germans wandering up and down the waterfront.

Pete went into the town to make contact with the Resistance and came back at dusk with two girls. The two young girls came on board and after a few glasses of wine, we were soon enjoying swapping our rather smutty jokes. Later, Pete went off with Gerda and one of the girls. Gerda gave me hug and a kiss that turned my legs to jelly.

I chatted to the other girl until Pete came back to take her home. Gerda was now safely on her way.

Chapter 12

We arrived back at Renne at lunchtime the next day. Our cargo of vegetables was immediately unloaded. We swept out the hold and moved over to join the waiting barges where we spent the next few days waiting for our next job. Pete and I spent hours down in the empty hold doing body-building exercises and playing football and cricket.

One morning a German Navy *Leutenant zur See* and an *Obermaat* (NCO) came aboard. 'I wish to inspect your barge to see if it is suitable to take to sea.'

The *Leutenant* spent the next hour carefully going over the barge, looking at the anchor and chain, the hold cover and the state of the hull and he spent some time in the engine room looking at our fairly new and powerful engine. 'You have a fine barge here. I shall make my report. It is possible we will use you for a special trip across to the Channel Islands.'

Two days later the *Leutenant* turned up with an official document. 'Your barge has been commandeered by the German Navy. You will both be retained as crew. I am *Lieutenant zur See* Hans Shrider and I am taking command of this barge. If you do not cooperate with me entirely you will be removed from the barge. However, if you are cooperative, when this voyage is over, your barge will be returned to you and you will receive one thousand deutschmarks.'

'I see we have little choice, *Herr Leutenant.*'

Pete gave his hand to the Lieutenant. 'If you are reasonable and I must add, good at your job, we will be happy to allow you to run our barge for this trip. My name is Pete and my mate's name is Marçel. You may have a bunk in our cabin.'

'*Sehr goot.* I think you may call me Hans as this is a non-combatant vessel. We will now move over to the main jetty—I will prove to you that I am capable of handling your barge.'

We started the engine, cast off and waited to see what would happen. To our surprise and disappointment, Hans handled the barge superbly and brought it alongside the jetty. Two trucks were already there and the *Obermaat* and three sailors were standing to attention.

'Open the hatch cover. We will start work immediately,' Hans called as he jumped ashore. He dismissed the men, the *Obermaat* carried the Lieutenant's kit bag down to the cabin and the three other men started to unload the trucks. I started the winch and pulled back the hatch cover. The Germans passed wooden planks into the hold and began work building a number of partitions. The *Obermaat* was attaching a frame to the bow deck. Later, he fixed a machine gun to the frame.

Another truck arrived with a life raft and a pile of life jackets, which we put on the wheelhouse roof. They erected an aerial on the roof and installed a small transmitter in the wheelhouse. To my disgust, a German Navy flag was hung from the stern of the barge.

By late afternoon, the noise died down. Thirteen stalls had been built at the rear end of the hold. So we were to carry livestock. The Germans and their trucks drove off. 'We stay here tonight. In the morning we move to the jetty where the crane will load our cargo. So tonight, my friends, we have a banquet.'

Hans disappeared ashore and returned much later, his *Obermaat* pulling a laden handcart. *Leutenant* Hans stepped aboard laughing. 'Navy supplies, my friends. We will certainly not go hungry! Tonight we celebrate my first command in two years. We have plenty of officers but few ships. Karl here will cook us a very good meal tonight. In the meantime …' Hans slapped a bottle of Calvados on the table—and so started a very wild night.

Strangely enough, I felt little animosity towards Hans; he seemed a different breed. Perhaps being a navy man and having such a great sense of humour made the difference. As the evening progressed we realised how much he hated the present regime and longed to get back to a peaceful world.

We woke up to find the cabin amazingly clean. Karl had cleaned up and returned to his quarters in the town. After a brew of fresh coffee, Hans moved the barge over to the jetty, which had a small crane.

I thought for a moment we had arrived in the 'Wild West'—six covered wagons were lined up on the jetty, each one pulled by two horses.

Hans was standing next to me. 'It is not a circus, Marçel. The German army is running out of fuel and this is an ideal form of transport for the islands.'

'We could use two of those to pull us down to St Malo and save fuel,' I replied.

'Some fine horse flesh there, Hans. Maybe we could stage an accident and fill up our refrigerator,' Pete said laughingly.

The horses were unhitched and taken up the track to a patch of grass. The wagons were loaded with sacks of flour and cartons of foodstuffs. The wheels and covers were removed from the wagons and the crane carefully placed the wagons in the hold, followed by the wheels and covers. Two trucks arrived laden with sacks of flour which were carefully stacked in the hold. The stalls were filled with hay and straw. The horses were brought back and the crane lifted them one by one into the stalls. Karl and his two horse minders put their gear into the last stall. I pulled the hatch cover most of the way over the hold. We had filled up with fuel and water after unloading our last cargo of produce. We were ready to go.

This was a test for all of us, especially for the barge, which had never been to sea. I had very mixed feelings returning to my island homeland. I would not be able to make any form of contact with friends or family.

Chapter 13

Shortly after ten on a fine September morning we motored down the Rance. I was steering the barge, we were flying the German Navy flag, carrying German supplies back to my home island, and with a German in command that I could not help liking. Bloody hell!

My hate for the Germans was just as strong and my desire to kill and disrupt was still burning me up. How could we destroy this cargo and these Germans? We were now employed by the enemy.

I would be reluctant to destroy our barge, I would certainly not want to harm all those horses down in the hold and I would be quite sorry to have to kill Hans. I had no desire to contact my family or friends in Jersey; in any case I would be putting them in great danger. For my own safety, I would have to keep out of sight while on the island.

Pete joined me in the wheelhouse and for a few minutes we were alone. 'One of fate's little tricks, Marçel. We just have to go along with this for now. Keep your head down when we are in Jersey. You will have to stay on the barge for your own safety. I will take the opportunity of gathering as much information on the island defences as possible.'

'I just hope I can control my frustration without going crazy,' I replied. 'We might get the chance to do something on the way back, Marçel, so just enjoy the trip. You never know, we might even see the RAF boys on the way.'

Pete was quite right so I decided to enjoy the trip; it would be interesting taking our barge across to the island at night.

We were travelling at a steady six knots but because of all the locks we had to pass through, it would take us two days to get to St Malo.

It was dark when we arrived at Hédé. Pete and I decided not to go with the Germans to the café in the village. Instead, we stayed and kept an eye on the horses.

We were expected to rendezvous with other barges at St Malo the next evening and we had a long run the next day. We passed the town where I had killed the girl in the back of the truck and which was a short distance from the damaged barges where I had first met Pete and Pierre. In the afternoon, we passed the old town of Dinan and continued down the estuary arriving at Dinard, which is just across the river from St Malo, by evening.

A launch came alongside of us and we were told to tie up to a jetty and be ready to join the other ships at ten pm. At nine, Hans got a message on the radio. We were to move into the centre of the channel where we would be joined by two other barges and a patrol boat. This was a little tricky as there was a strong ebb tide, so we faced the barge upstream with the engine ticking over, in order to remain in the centre of the channel.

At last we saw lights flashing. The patrol boat appeared, followed by two barges. There was just enough light from a half-moon to see the outline of the three other craft. The radio crackled and we were ordered to follow behind the patrol boat ahead of the two other barges. Hans turned our barge around and with full power, we quickly positioned ourselves. This was to be one of the last convoys of barges as so many barges had been sunk between St Malo and the Channel Islands.

There is a reef about twenty miles long between St Malo and Jersey called des Minquiers. This meant we had to travel a distance of fifty-one nautical miles with a speed of just over six knots. We also had to allow for strong tidal runs and at our speed, it was going to take us at least eight hours to get there.

The sea was relatively calm that night but the Germans were still kept busy calming the horses. The barges were not designed to travel in rough seas and several had already been lost in storms.

We took two-hour turns at the wheel. Halfway across we got into a swell and it was extremely difficult to keep the barge on a straight course. I had to close the hold completely as the spray was blowing right over the hull. At one stage we lost sight of the patrol boat just at the time we were due to change course. We had left St Malo and were heading northwest. After passing des Minquiers we had to head northeast. Luckily, the patrol boat turned back to find us.

At six the next morning we could see the outline of Jersey. We were now vulnerable to an attack from the air so Karl stood by the machine gun. Twenty minutes later they arrived. Two low-flying aircraft were coming straight for us from astern, firing their guns as they came. The patrol boat and our gun were firing back—Hans spun the wheel and the barge started to turn as one plane flew over us. There were several loud explosions and

Pete and I were thrown to the deck—I felt the barge shudder and we were showered with spray. Hans was spinning the wheel again. And then they were gone.

Maybe they were short on fuel. Thanks to Hans and his brilliant timing, we had escaped with just a shower. But the last barge was not so lucky—we could see it sinking, its bow low down in the water.

A message came over the radio. We were to maintain our course and speed while the patrol boat picked up the survivors of the sinking barge. We watched the barge disappear under the waves while the patrol boat picked up all the survivors.

We followed close behind the patrol boat for the rest of the way. If there were any stray mines, the patrol boat would be hit first!

With Elizabeth Castle on our left and a reef on our right, we approached the harbour entrance. There were guns pointing from every direction both seaward and skyward and I wondered how close we had passed to mines. I had a funny feeling entering the harbour. Except for the *SS Vega*, a Red Cross ship delivering food parcels to the locals, the harbour seemed deserted. I remembered the times I had played with other kids in small boats and the many gang fights, when we had all finished up wet, tired and happy.

We tied up to the high granite wall of the harbour and Hans and Karl went ashore with the paperwork. I opened up the hold and a crane moved into place. Soon the first of the horses was being lifted out of the hold. Despite the sudden twisting and turning of the barge during the air attack, all the horses had arrived uninjured.

Hans returned with an old camouflaged Morris Minor. 'When we have finished discharging the cargo I will take you around the island in this car.'

I had no inclination to go ashore. 'Hans, I am quite happy to stay here and watch the unloading and then clean up the hold. Why not go off now with Pete? There is so much for you to see.' I could have bitten off my tongue.

Hans looked at me. 'You have been here before?'

I turned away to hide my face. 'No, Hans, but I have read a lot about the island.'

'Let's get going now, Hans. Marçel is right; we have a lot to see.' I knew what he meant. This was a golden opportunity for Pete to gather a lot of information which he would be able to send to London when we arrived back in France. They set off with Karl sitting in the back; I wondered if he was there for a purpose.

The wagons, the flour and food cartons were unloaded and the German sailors, who must have had a very unpleasant journey in the hold (especially when we were attacked from the air), dismantled all the wooden stalls. I got the crane driver to lower a large wooden container, which we filled with all the old straw and horse droppings.

After the last of the Germans had left, I swept out the hold and we were now ready for the next cargo. I had a shower and decided to catch up on some sleep.

I awoke to crashing and banging as the three returned to the barge.

'Wakey, wakey, young Marçel. We are moving across the harbour to a much larger crane. We are to load three army trucks and will return to St Malo tonight. A very interesting tour today, my boy.' Pete had a very satisfied look on his face.

It was after six pm. We moved to the heavy crane and loaded the three trucks and four motorcycles. They completely filled our hold and we were unable to cover the hold as the truck covers were much too high; I just hoped it would be a calm night. The three Germans settled themselves in the rear of one of the trucks.

The second barge, which had carried ammunition, had unloaded and was now loaded with trucks and ready to leave. At nine pm the patrol boat came alongside. We were told to follow close behind the other barge until we were well clear of the island. We would then receive a signal to split up.

The patrol boat was to escort the other barge to the port of Granville and we were to find our own way back to St Malo. Hans was quite happy about this; he had done this trip several times before. He said he knew where the minefields were as he had helped to lay them. I hoped he had a good memory! It was unlikely we would be attacked at night and the weather was good.

———

We were all standing in the wheelhouse heading for the turning point west of des Minquiers. Hans was at the wheel. 'This war will be soon over, my friends. We have some very stupid men in Germany running this war. We have just left the islands bristling with guns and thousands of our troops manning them. The British will never invade these islands. The local population has its Red Cross food parcels but eventually the Germans will starve. The occupying forces will never harm the locals because they know that one day they will have to surrender to the Allies. The British are laughing because they have thousands of prisoners here and they don't have to feed them.'

'So where does that leave you, Hans?' I wondered if Pete was thinking of taking the barge across to England.

'My friends, I am a German. Because of the heavy losses, boats will no longer be going to the islands. I expect I shall be transferred to the army when the invasion starts and will probably die fighting on land for my doomed country.'

Pete produced the bottle of *Calvados*, grinning. 'Cheers, boys—let's drink to that!' We all enjoyed the joke and the *Calvados*.

By the time we reached the turning point to head towards St Malo, the sea had become rough and we were taking a lot of spray on board. Water was starting to build up in the open hold. I went below and started up the bilge pump.

A short time later, the sea calmed down and I was able to stop the pump and I took over the wheel to head south-southeast. Pete and Hans went down into the cabin to brew coffee.

Although it was still dark, I could see a red glow starting to build up in front of us. I called Hans and Pete to come and see. 'My God, St Malo is getting it tonight. I just hope it is all over before daylight as we will be a perfect target for any leftover bombs.'

Hans did not seem too bothered. 'At least the glow will help us find our way up the channel.'

It was just starting to become light when we came abreast of the island of Cezembre—a small island just outside St Malo. It was heavily fortified and with a madman in command, who refused to surrender when St Malo was finally liberated. The island was completely destroyed by Allied bombing.

Fires were burning in several places at St Malo. A launch came out to meet us in the estuary and two officers came aboard. The lock into the basin had been damaged again and we were unable to enter to use the cranes.

This presented a big problem. We would have to wait before we could enter the basin, possibly weeks. As there were no heavy cranes at Dinan or Renne capable of lifting the trucks, we would have to go all the way down to Redon or possibly on to Roche Bernard on the Villane River. It was decided that we would probably be attacked if we stayed here so we were told to make the long trip to Redon. The two sailors went off with the launch and Hans and Kurt remained with us, no doubt to make sure we didn't steal the trucks!

———

Late the second day we arrived back at Renne and the following morning set off for Redon. Still unable to unload the trucks at Redon, we continued the next day to Roche Bernard where we were sure there were heavy lifting cranes. This was a crazy situation and demonstrated how inefficient and disorganised the Germans were becoming.

We finally discharged the trucks and Hans and Kurt, to our relief, reluctantly left us while they reported to their headquarters. We had the barge back to ourselves. Unable to destroy or sabotage the trucks, the only benefit from this trip was that later Pete was able to radio a lot of information regarding defences, the health and general state of the Jersey population.

Chapter 14

Pete had received word that the Resistance had an RAF pilot waiting to be flown back to England. His plane had been shot down during an air raid on St Nazaire and he was the sole survivor. The Resistance had watched his parachute descend and had got to him just before the Germans arrived on the scene. He had been taken to a safe house a few miles north of Nantes and was now waiting to be collected.

Our agent had told us we would have to wait a few days before a cargo of produce would be ready for collection at Pontivy. In the meantime he had a load of empty wine casks for us to deliver to Nantes on the Loire River. We loaded up the empty casks and set off for Nantes. On the way we would make our contact with England regarding the pick-up of this RAF man.

Due to German infiltration into the Resistance, it was found to be too dangerous for one Resistance group to make direct contact with another, so we acted as a go-between and delivered the airmen to the group that organised the landing strips.

At Redon we entered the canal that ran alongside the Villane River and then headed up the canalised River Isac. It was fifty-seven miles and eighteen locks to Nantes. As soon as we found a quiet spot, we pulled in and Pete went off with the radio, returning two hours later. He had made contact with London and after decoding their reply came up with some surprising news. 'Marçel, the landing point is different this time; in fact it's only a little way ahead from where we are now. Tomorrow night at ten pm we will meet the Resistance two hundred yards east of a road bridge. The road leads on to Plesse, which is close to the Foret du Govre. A replacement for you is arriving and you will return to England with the RAF man.'

I thought about this for a minute. I was reluctant to leave this ideal situation behind but I knew that I needed the training in weapon handling and hand-to-hand fighting; this would enable me to destroy more Germans and be of much more use to Pete.

'That's fine by me, Pete. Just keep this old tub afloat until I get back or else, with all this extra training, I'll beat the hell out of you.' We moved off and fourteen locks later joined the wide and attractive river Erdre. At dusk we finally arrived at Nantes. Nantes is at the lower end of the Loire River and it was extremely busy with many barges of all sizes. We arrived at the jetty where we tied up three abreast. In the morning we would move over to the jetty where we would be unloaded.

'I am going to introduce you to the low life of Nantes tonight, Marçel,' Pete promised.

———

We crossed over two barges and walked across the road to the café where all the barge men met up with their friends and enemies. They also caught up with their drinking.

We pushed our way through the smoke-filled room to the bar. The noise was incredible. At last the *patron* came over to us and gave Pete a warm handshake. They exchanged a few words and he produced two glasses of red wine and nodded his head in the direction of the table at the end of the bar. We pushed and shoved our way over to the table and sat down with the two men sitting there. One man got up and left. Pete leaned over and spoke quietly to the other man. *'Comment vous appelez vous?'*

The pale-faced man looked very out of place amongst all us weather-beaten barge men. He whispered, 'Flying Officer John McDonald at your service, sir, and already to go, old boy.' I thought it was hardly the time to be so flippant.

As we started to get up, the doors of the café flew open and several *Feldgendamerie* burst in. The café was suddenly silent. The Germans moved forward, examining identity cards.

I noticed the *patron* give a signal to a large rough-looking man leaning on the bar. This man picked up his glass and threw it at Pete hitting him on the side of his head. Pete picked up a bottle from the table, smashed the end off and rushed at the man at the bar—and then all hell was let loose.

A fight to end all fights started while the Germans stood stunned. They backed away to the door and watched as we tried to beat hell out of each other—chairs, glasses and bottles were flying in all directions, the screams and shouts must have been heard for miles around as old scores were settled.

I dragged myself off the floor with the taste of blood in my mouth and was grabbed by the *patron* who had come around the bar. He pushed me and John McDonald through the door to the toilets; at the end of the passage way he unlocked a door and shoved us both out into a side alley. The door slammed behind us.

I had to get the flying officer back to our barge and the safety of the tank. We crept to the end of the lane. I told John to keep close behind me. Truckloads of Germans were arriving. We crept along the side of the building and away from the café. I could see a stack of empty crates on the jetty a little way ahead. We slipped across the road and got behind the crates. The *Feldgendamerie* were bringing the now-subdued customers out of the café and loading them into the trucks. I wondered where Pete was; if he had been arrested I would have to take command and deliver John to the aircraft. I realised I would have to stay behind to take charge of the barge and not fly to England.

Germans started moving in our direction. 'Follow me, John. I hope you can swim. This is our only way back to the barge.'

He seemed to be enjoying himself. 'Like a fish, old boy. Lead on!'

I was not in the mood for his frivolous humour, 'Just shut up, John, and follow me.'

We jumped down onto the deck of the barge in front of us and quietly stepped across the other two. 'Take off your boots and jacket and follow me.'

We dropped into the water on the outer side of the barge and swam until we arrived at the next line of barges. I was pretty sure our barge was in the next line. When we got to our barge we could hear voices and there were lights flashing inside the cabin. Our barge was being searched.

We moved right under the stern and clung to the rudder. After a while, the Germans moved on. We waited a few minutes and then climbed aboard. I gave John some dry clothes. He dried himself while I made some hot coffee. I took him as well as all the wet clothes down to the tank. I showed him where everything was and told him to fasten the tank entrance plate once he was in and not to make any noise. Back on deck the Germans were still searching barges. I wondered how many of the barge men had been taken to prison. There was nothing I could do, so I climbed into my bunk and eventually fell asleep.

When I woke at first light, there was no sign of Pete. He had shown me where we were expected to unload our cargo, so I decided to move the barge across on my own. I started the engine, untied the ropes and carefully reversed out into the middle of the canal. Because we were in a wide part of the basin I was able to turn the barge around and move over to the other side where we were due to unload. The agent came and collected the paperwork. Shortly after, the empty casks were unloaded, and then we were loaded with full casks of wine.

I took some coffee and a sandwich down to John and warned him that he would have to stay there until we got moving later in the morning. I was just deciding what to do next when a German motor cycle and sidecar came bumping down the road to the jetty. Pete was sitting in it, looking very pleased with himself.

Pete climbed out and handed the German something; he turned the motor cycle around and drove off.

'How much did that cost you, Pete?'

'A lot more than what you're worth, Marçel. I was quite determined I would get rid of you tonight and let the army boys in England sort you out.'

We compared injuries. Pete had a bad cut on the side of his face and a very puffy nose while I had a black eye and swollen lips. I started the engine, reversed the barge and we moved off.

'I really don't understand how you manage to persuade the Germans to do these things for you, Pete.' Pete put his hand in his pocket and showed me several blank gold coins. 'This, my boy. This is a very persuasive language. The morale of the average German at present is pretty low. They have a good idea where Germany is heading and they will go on fighting to the end, but they realise that the war is nearly over and gold is the only thing that will help them survive.'

Pete took over the wheel. 'Last night, Marçel, was a classic example. The Germans at the café were not *Gestapo*. They held back while we beat each other up and then rounded us all up and took us down to the prison. The Germans need the boat people, so when the *patron* from the café produced a few of these coins, we were all sent home to face the wrath of our wives and sweethearts. However if they had found the RAF officer, boy, it might have been a completely different story. Speaking of which, he could come up for a while.'

Flying Officer John McDonald was much relieved to be coming out of the tank and tucked enthusiastically into our cooked breakfast. We had ten miles of the wide and beautiful Erdre River before we entered the first canal and we expected to arrive at our meeting point at about nine pm.

I had mixed feelings about leaving the barge. Seeing the last aeroplane a ball of fire didn't do much for my self-confidence. I put all my things in a bag under my bunk except for my friend, the bayonet, which was now part of me anyway and which I might possibly still need tonight.

———

It was almost dark when we arrived at the rendezvous. We tied up to a derelict jetty and waited. At ten, two well-armed Resistance men appeared. One was to stay and guard the barge until Pete got back. He would warn Pete in case the Germans discovered the barge.

We set off with the other Resistance man, Pete and me each carrying a Sten gun. We walked in single file; I followed a little way behind as rear guard. We walked for an hour without incident along a dirt track until we reached the forest. By now we could hear planes overhead and the rumbling in the distance of the bombs that were falling on St Nazaire.

Arriving at a road that ran at right angles to our track, we were met by another Resistance man. He signalled us to turn right and follow the road. The trees had been cut back on both sides of it, presumably as a fire break for the forest. The road was quite wide at this point.

We were met by yet another man, who told us to wait by the side of the road. A few minutes later we heard the sound of vehicles approaching. We crouched down in the long grass. The convoy of trucks passed by and then we heard the sound of our aircraft overhead.

I don't know how the Resistance had managed this timing, but from somewhere ahead we heard loud explosions coming from the convoy of trucks followed by a lot of gunfire.

The *Lysander* landed on the road just in front of us. I embraced Pete, handed him the Sten gun and then ran with John to the aircraft. As we reached it, a man jumped out—my replacement. We scrambled in, the plane moving off as we closed the door. John fixed my safety belt and we were airborne.

Looking down I could see the trucks on fire. I hoped Pete would get back to the barge safely and then move on, well away from this area.

To the left I could see a large red glow coming from St Nazaire. It must be hell there at the moment; I hoped the U-boat pens were being demolished.

———

This was my first flight in an aircraft and I was not frightened, just excited at the prospect of arriving in England. We were joined by two other aircraft, one on each side. I could see their exhaust flames and it was comforting to know we had an escort. Looking down I could see water. We were crossing the channel.

Dawn was breaking as we approached the south coast of England. I could just make out the faint outline of the coast. The two other aircraft dropped away, we were now on our own. I could feel the pressure on my ears as we started to descend. We made a very bumpy landing on the grass runway just outside Exeter, and taxied across to some buildings. It was now quite light.

The pilot jumped out and helped us climb out from the back seats. 'Enjoy the trip chaps? At least I don't have to clean up any vomit this time. Anyway welcome to England.'

Chapter 15

A jeep with an officer and driver pulled up alongside the aircraft. The army captain shook hands all around, the pilot and John walked off to the control tower and I scrambled into the back of the jeep. The captain sat in front with the driver and we passed out through the airfield checkpoint and drove for about an hour.

The countryside was quite different to Brittany. We were somewhere on the moors when we finally reached a large army camp. We drove through a maze of Nissan huts and eventually pulled up outside one.

An army sergeant was waiting for us and the three of us went into the hut. There was a small room just inside the door, the NCO's quarters; a line of beds as yet not occupied filled the rest of the hut. A door at the bottom end of the hut led to the washrooms.

'I am Captain Norton and will be responsible for your training and all your needs while you are here. Sergeant Bennet will very soon make a man out of you—that's if you survive his training course. You will be joined by fourteen other men in the next few days. You will be undergoing an officers' training course, which I assure you is tough. After this, you will continue on a special training course that has been specifically designed for you. This will run for several months, at the end of which you might possibly receive a commission.'

I took an immediate liking to Captain Norton. He was cheerful and friendly but, as I was soon to find out, very tough and ruthless. I was to see a lot of him in the next few months.

'I'm told your code name is Piglet; it has been decided that while you are training in England you will assume the name of Simon Phillips. Welcome to Britain, Simon. I understand you have already seen far more action than a lot of us. I must say I was expecting someone a little older. Sergeant Bennet will take you for your medical and will get you fixed up with kit. After that, I suggest you get some food and sleep. Be ready to be escorted to your interrogation at six pm. Any questions? If you have any problems come directly to me.'

The jeep moved off with Captain Norton, and I was left with the sergeant. 'Right, young man, your kit is ready on your bunk, the toilets and washroom are through that door at the end of the hut. Get yourself cleaned up and when you get back, put on this battle dress and the boots and I will take you across for your medical and after that to the canteen for some food. We can always change your boots if they don't fit.'

I nearly froze to death under the cold shower but that was nothing to the cold I was to experience in the next few months.

———

I was surprised to find how well the uniform fitted and the heavy boots were just right for me.

'Stand up straight, boy, and follow me.' Sergeant Bennet marched me to the medical centre where I gave my age as seventeen. I received a full medical examination and was passed as extremely fit. I had certainly changed in the last few months—I had grown to five foot eight, weighed eleven stone, shaved every day, and had a strong sex drive.

We crossed over to the canteen where I lined up in the queue. That first breakfast of bacon and eggs was the best I have ever tasted. I was then marched back to my hut and spent the rest of the day catching up on sleep.

At five-thirty pm, I was taken over to the camp headquarters and at six, entered the room where I was to be interrogated.

I was reminded of the interrogation back in St Helier.

I sat on a chair opposite three officers who sat behind tables; Captain Norton was one of them. Once again I had a strong light focused on me—I was not impressed.

The senior officer, who looked old and rather pompous, addressed me. 'Private Phillips. We are here to establish who you are, your background, and the all events leading up to your arrival in England. We will then decide if you are a suitable person to receive the benefit of our special training. We expect absolute respect and obedience from you while you are here. Any breach of our rules, because of your background, and you will be sent to a prison for the rest of the war.'

We had started on a bad note and I could feel the anger rising inside of me. This was not what I had expected and I had not come to England to be addressed in that way. I stood up straight.

'Sir, I have come here from France to improve my ability to harass and kill as many Germans as possible. I expect to return to France as soon as I have received your expert training. Yes, I will respect and obey you all while I am here, but sirs, I am here of my own free will and I expect equal respect from you. I will certainly not allow myself to be threatened. I have done and will be doing far more for the Allied cause than a lot of you people. In the last few months I have seen good people killed, and in return I have killed several Germans. That you should address me in such terms when you need people like me working for you in France is absurd.'

I sat down exhausted. I had even surprised myself.

I detected a smile on the faces of the other two men but the senior officer was suppressing his anger. 'I am sure we will overcome any differences. You will be treated fairly. You are quite right; you are a volunteer and we do owe you the respect you deserve. However this establishment is run on very strict lines and we expect you to follow them.'

There followed a string of questions regarding my background, my family and the events leading up to my meeting with Pierre. I had to give details of each of my killings and the suicide of *Oberleutenant* Grossman. Luckily, through Pete's report, they had already been informed of most of these events, otherwise I think it might have been hard for them to believe my story.

Three hours later, I was dismissed; Captain Norton followed me out. 'Come with me, Phillips.' I followed him into his office and an attendant brought in some hot coffee.

'You did well tonight. Some of our senior officers, especially those that have come out of retirement, have not adjusted too well to the methods we now adopt in the Services. Tonight you have gained the respect you deserve.' He leaned back in his chair. 'I have met both Pete and Pierre. You have been associated with two good men. They must have realised your worth.'

I sipped my coffee. 'I got on well with both of them, sir, I consider Pete a good friend and the last I saw of Pierre he was hanging from a tree.'

Captain Norton was silent for a while. 'I trained his wife. Gerda is a very courageous woman. Poor woman, I hope she survives the war.'

Somehow, I found my way back to my Nissan hut. The sergeant was reading in his room.

The next morning was chaotic as the fourteen other recruits moved in. They were all several years older than me and had already done their initial training.

I was once again thrown into a completely different world; the next six months were spent drilling, marching, handling weapons and hand-to-hand fighting. I learned to drive heavy trucks, handle explosives and was shown how to kill at close quarters; this I already knew. At night and at weekends when all the other men were relaxing, I was given tuition in French, German, Portuguese and to my astonishment, a little information about wine making.

This was the toughest time of my life; I was transformed from a gangling youth to a tough soldier. The hard physical training kept my mind alert so that, despite the tiredness, I was able to absorb the language lessons that I received in the evenings. I trained myself to sleep from five-thirty pm to six-thirty. After a meal I would study until eleven, I then slept on until six am.

On Christmas Eve I was told to report to Captain Norton.

'I am going to my farm in Hampshire for two days; my wife, children and I would like you to join us.' I was delighted. I had not been outside the camp, except on exercises, since arriving in England. The thought of spending Christmas with a family was an unexpected pleasure. 'Grab your toothbrush. We leave in one hour.'

We set off in a jeep. I was the captain's official driver and this was my first opportunity to see a bit of England. We drove through Exeter and Taunton to a lovely old village near Glastonbury and stopped outside the village inn. This was my first time in an old pub with low ceilings, panelled walls and stone floor. It was lunchtime and the bar was filled mostly with locals and just a few RAF men. The captain was greeted by several of the locals. The place was filled with chatter and laughter, it was Christmas and they had started celebrating.

'Mine host' greeted the captain, 'When are you going to cross the Channel, Bill? If this goes on much longer Britain will start to sink with the weight of all these Americans.' He placed two overflowing pints of beer in front of us.

I suddenly realised I didn't have any English money. No one had thought of giving me any and as I had no need for money in the camp, it had not entered my mind.

'Sir, I don't have any money to buy you a beer. I only have a few Reich marks which I'm sure would not go down too well in this pub.'

'Good God, man, so you haven't. It never crossed my mind. As you are not officially in the army it has been completely overlooked. I will definitely fix that up when we return. In the meantime take this as a loan.' He handed me five pounds, which seemed like a fortune to me.

'Let's go, Private Phillips; my wife Sophie will be waiting for us and I'm dying to see her and the kids. It's been three weeks since I last saw them.

We were met at the cottage door by Sophie, a very attractive brunette. She was quite small and had a lovely figure. She reminded me of an older version of Simone. Sophie threw herself at the captain. When he finally put her down, she turned to me and gave me a light kiss on the cheek. 'And who have we here, Bill? I see you've brought me a lovely young man for Christmas.'

'Let's drop the formalities while we are at home. Sophie this is Simon. Simon, this is Sophie and I'm Bill, until we get back to the camp, Simon. My kids are Buddha and Chips—officially Jennifer and Peter. Chips was the first word Jennifer uttered and it's pretty obvious why we call Peter the Buddha.'

The front door opened directly into a charming living room, Chips was sitting in a playpen surrounded by her toys. She gave me a beautiful 'come on' smile. Buddha smiled at me from his pram; I was reminded of the laughing Buddha.

We spent the afternoon playing with the children and decorating a Christmas tree with lights. After high tea, I went up to the small box room where I was to sleep. Sophie did everything possible to make me feel at home; I had almost forgotten what family life was like!

Later when the children had been put to bed we sat around a cosy log fire and discussed the state of the war. Bill had left his father to run the farm when he joined the army, and was itching to get back as soon as the war ended. I started to feel uneasy talking about peace; I had my own internal war to fight and had enjoyed killing. How would I ever be able to control the power I had, to be able kill a man without feeling any remorse? I had now committed myself to maybe several years of eliminating escaping Nazis. Where was this leading? Could I ever stop killing—would I ever be a normal person again?

My thoughts were interrupted by a loud banging on the front door. Bill opened the door and gasped, 'Good God. What the hell are you doing here?'

He stepped aside to let the visitor in. 'Tracked you down, old boy. How are you? Actually I've come to pick up the Piglet; we have a job to do tomorrow.'

Pete came across to the fireplace and gave Sophie a big hug. 'Pete, how lovely to see you after all this time—I hope you are going to spend Christmas with us.'

'Sorry, Sophie old dear, I'm here to take your guest away.' He turned to me, giving me a quick embrace. 'Marçel, old boy, I need you for a few days. I have a suitcase with some suitable civilian clothes for you; we have to report to the RAF at Dunkeswell by six pm tomorrow.'

Sophie took Pete's arm. 'Pete dear, you must stay the night. We'll have an early Christmas lunch and you can easily make Dunkeswell by five.'

Peter was delighted with the idea. Bill went and fetched a girl from next door to come and baby-sit and the four of us set off to the pub.

After an hilarious evening, we returned to the cottage, all a lot worse for wear. Pete and I squeezed into the box room, collapsed onto the bunks and promptly fell asleep.

We woke up to the delicious smell of cooking. Sophie was preparing lunch. By the time we got ourselves together and I had dressed in a shirt and tie, supplied by Pete, it was time for lunch. After real Christmas fare of turkey, Christmas pudding and all the trimmings, Bill produced a bottle of Port wine, which we finished between us.

We made our reluctant farewells and set off in Pete's red sports car to Dunkeswell. It was raining all the way and dark when we arrived at the Air Base. We went into the office that was under the control tower where several other well-dressed civilians were waiting. Outside I could just make out the outline of a *Lancaster* bomber, only it was not camouflaged but appeared to be peacetime silver.

I was unable to contain my curiosity any longer, 'Where are we going, Pete?'

Pete tried to look casual and stifled a yawn. 'Porto in Portugal, old boy!'

I tried not to be impressed and waited for Pete to continue. He remained silent. A flight sergeant came in and advised us to go to the toilet, as there were no such luxuries on our aircraft, and that we would soon be departing.

He was certainly right. The inside of the fuselage was unlined and you could see the cables that ran down the sides of it, which controlled the tail end. There was a row of seats running down each side. We each had a seat belt and a blanket—this was to prove necessary when the aircraft climbed up into the cold air.

When we took off, the noise was deafening and we just sat there as the hours slowly went by. Sleep was impossible.

———

Eventually we heard the engines slow down and my ears started to pop as we descended, and eventually, after several heavy bumps, landed. So much for the glamour of flying! The sun was well up and we were in for a fine but cool day.

We spent some time with immigration but as we only had a small amount of hand luggage, we quickly passed through customs.

We were met by a smartly dressed man who spoke quite good English and introduced himself as Alfonso Baidassaris. He ushered us into his equally smart Renault saloon and we set off heading south.

'Gentlemen, I think I have found the perfect property for you. The main buildings consist of an old renovated castle, which is right on the side of a deep river. This river runs into the large inland waterway from which you may gain access to the ocean.' He paused to negotiate several sharp bends in the road and continued.

'The property includes a very large acreage of vines. Before the war the people who ran this estate dispatched regular supplies of their excellent wine to Northern France and Germany.'

Pete leaned forward. 'So why is it all up for sale now, Alfonso?'

'The war, my friends. The wine used to be delivered by road, a long slow process. When the war started it became impossible to continue and after three years the winery had to close down and the owners went bankrupt.'

We were now travelling along a straight road; the country around us was quite low lying with a number of streams and wetlands.

'Alfonso, what happened to all the staff at the winery? Are they still about?' I could see Pete was becoming quite enthusiastic.

'Most of the workers moved on but the original "wine master" is still there; he and his wife are the caretakers of the property.' Alfonso gave us a lot more details of the property and the surrounding area. After a while, we found we were driving alongside a large estuary where several rivers converged before eventually reaching the ocean. We turned left off the main road and crossed a small bridge and then turned right, down a narrow road until we came to an imposing entrance—we had arrived at the property.

The track continued through acres of vines, they all looked neglected and sometimes were hidden by the tall weeds. In the distance we could see an area of trees, and rising above the trees, the old castle.

We drove through an archway into the courtyard. On three sides were buildings where the wine was made and stored, and on the fourth side an imposing building, which was the owner's residence. The wine master and his wife were waiting at the large studded front door to greet us when we got out of the car.

Alfonso introduced us to José and Maria, his wife. They were both in their fifties, José was able to speak a little English and they seemed very happy to see us. I had a feeling we would get on well with this couple.

José gave us a tour of the house while Maria went off to prepare lunch. It was an impressive entrance hall with a superb wide wooden stairway, leading up to the bedrooms. Upstairs, a passageway ran the length of the back of the building. It had several skylights, as the back wall was part of the old castle wall. There were six bedrooms and three bathrooms. They were all fine rooms but the whole house was run down and needed to be completely redecorated.

On the ground floor along one side of the hallway, double doors led into a large lounge and then an archway through to the library. A door then led on to the study or office. The office had access to the courtyard. On the other side of the hallway there was a large dining room and beyond that, the kitchen and staff rooms.

Maria had prepared a superb lunch for us. She produced an enormous baked fish with a surprising assortment of fresh vegetables. José fetched some bottles, which he carefully opened. It was a very pleasant light white wine, which was his pride and joy.

After lunch we inspected the outbuildings where the wine was made and eventually bottled and then we went down to the cellars where the rows and rows of casks were stored.

'We still have a lot of good wine in store. This will be ready to sell when the war ends, but there is also a considerable amount that is now only fit to dump.' José gave a sigh, thinking of all the hard work gone to waste. 'It will take two seasons to get the vines back into production, but as we still have a lot of wine to sell, we can quickly get back into business. I know that because of the long rest time, some of the more recent plantings will produce much improved wine.'

We piled into an old truck and José took us on a tour of the winery. It extended for miles around but we could see there was a tremendous amount of work needed to clean up the vines before they became productive again.

It was dark when at last we got back to the castle. José produced a bottle of his sherry. I could see it was going to be a long night.

The four of us retired to the office. 'What do you think, Marçel? Do you think this would suit our purposes?'

I nodded my head enthusiastically. 'Yes, providing we are able to take a boat out to the ocean.'

Pete turned to José. 'José, would you and your wife be prepared to work for us, you as wine master and your wife as housekeeper?'

José was smiling. 'We have always hoped that one day we would be able to bring this great winery back into production.'

Pete continued, 'We intend to run the winery as a successful business. We are also working for a Government agency that is helping to rid Europe of certain undesirable people. Our job is to bring them here and to then take them out to a ship that will transport them on to a country in South America. This country is prepared to accept them.'

Pete paused and gave José a piercing look. 'This would mean you and Maria would be working in absolute secrecy with regard to this matter.'

José remained silent for a minute. 'My wife and I would not want to be involved in anything illegal. We would be happy to run the winery and the house for you. What you do after that is entirely your own business. We would not be involved in anything other than running the winery, and as your servants, would be absolutely discreet and loyal to you.'

Pete looked satisfied and leaned forward eagerly. 'We would want you to start bringing the vines back into production now. The house would need to be completely redecorated to accommodate us and our guests.'

José was delighted. 'Sir, you will have no regrets, Maria and I will be delighted to serve you and we will be so very happy to bring this winery back to its old glory. We will need to engage some of the old workers and of course it will need a fair bit of money to restore everything.'

'José, go and talk to Maria now and make sure she is happy with our arrangements and is prepared to be our housekeeper.' José shook both our hands and almost ran out of the room to tell Maria the news.

We spent the next few hours discussing the details. Pete made Alfonso an offer well below the asking price. After a somewhat heated argument,

Alfonso accepted the offer on behalf of his clients, the bank. After arranging to pick us up early afternoon the next day, he set off to the bank to inform them of the sale of the property.

Later, José appeared with a bottle of Madeira and we discussed in detail the improvements that we wished to make to the house and the work that had to be done to the winery. Eventually Maria came and collected us. She had prepared a delicious meal of roast duck.

'José, do you think you could organise a boat trip for us in the morning?' Pete asked. 'We would quite like to see how far it is to the ocean entrance from here.'

José walked over to the phone. 'My brother has a motor boat. I will ask him to pick us up from our jetty in the morning.' He put the phone down. 'He will be with us at nine am and will take you to the entrance and back. He has a fine fishing boat.' It had been a long day with no sleep the night before so we decided to make use of the cold and uninviting bedrooms.

———

A door in the castle wall led from the courtyard to the jetty. We stood on the jetty and watched the motor boat approaching. The river here was about fifteen yards wide and looked quite deep. The boat came alongside, we jumped aboard, José introduced us to his brother and we set off down the river.

About two miles down, the river ran into the estuary. I was surprised how well the channels were marked. The estuary was wide with several small islands. It looked an ideal place for a boating holiday. We followed the channel for an hour and arrived at the entrance; this was a tidal area and I could imagine it would be very difficult to exit in stormy conditions.

As we went out through the entrance, I saw a small village on one side and dunes on the other, there was quite a swell and the tide was running fast. Once out in the ocean, it was a clear run to Porto to the north or Lisbon to the south. We headed back to the estuary, riding the swell as we passed back through the entrance.

'This is perfect; we have deep water all the way from the castle to the ocean. We could bring a large ship through here without any problem.' Pete was delighted. I could see our plans were taking shape.

After lunch, Alfonso arrived with the paperwork for us to sign. The bank had accepted Pete's offer and the castle would soon be ours.

'Alfonso will take you back to the airport, Marçel. I will stay on here and to tie things up, and then I will try to organise the transport from here to northern France. I will meet up with you in about three months' time. I expect the invasion of France will take place early next summer. Thanks to all our hard work, the French Resistance is now so strong, I believe they will be taking over a large part of Brittany in the spring.'

I shook hands warmly with José and Maria and gave Pete a hug. 'You can look after my car until I get back, Marçel. Try not to wreck it.' We set off for the airport. It had been a most interesting Christmas.

—

The night flight back to England was just as uncomfortable and boring. We arrived at Dunkeswell at dawn—it was raining heavily. I found the red sports car and drove back to the army camp on the moors. It was still raining; I changed back into my uniform and reported to Captain Norton who had also returned that morning. I thanked him for their hospitality. I think he knew where I had been but said nothing. He told me where I could safely park Pete's car. The holiday was over and discipline resumed.

The next three months were pretty tough but by April, I was able to speak French and German quite well, I could handle any type of weapon and drive every possible type of vehicle. I was one hundred per cent fit and itching to return to France.

Chapter 16

It was towards the end of April when I was ordered to go to Exeter airport. Pete was waiting there for me. After a warm greeting, he laughingly examined his car for any scratches. 'Something very interesting has turned up in France, Marçel. We are going back tonight but first we have to meet my boss, who is a fair distance from here.'

We set off in Pete's red bombshell and arrived at Ashmore Manor at midday. We were immediately ushered into Stephen Harvey's office.

'Good to see you, Pete; so this is our infamous Piglet. Sorry about that; welcome to our club, Marçel, I'm afraid it is going to be short lived, as you and Pete are to be killed off when you return to France tonight.' Stephen indicated to us to sit down. 'Seriously, the time has come for you to disappear. We want the Resistance to believe you are dead so that you can prepare yourselves for your next operation, which is operation "Deserting Rats".'

Pete was grinning. 'How do want us to die, Stephen? I hope it will be quick and painless!'

Stephen leaned back in his chair. 'I have one last job for you in France, Pete. I expect you are wondering why I asked you to take a barge load of gravel and cement to Pontivy.' Stephen smiled at Pete's look of horror.

'No, not that Pete—something very interesting has turned up. We have been informed that three U-boats have been holed up in a creek on the Blavet tidal estuary. We understand the torpedo tubes have been removed and trucks are entering the compound loaded with crates that we believe are stolen art treasures.'

Stephen had us both sitting up—this sounded interesting.

Stephen continued, 'We have known for some time that the "King Rats" would want to take their nest eggs to South America. This looks like an opportunity for us to save some of these precious items from disappearing forever.

'We believe the French Resistance will be taking over the whole of

Brittany in the next few months so we need to delay the escape of these U-boats until that time.' Stephen leaned forward.

'I want you to fly back to Brittany tonight. We will drop you, and a batch of explosives, which the Resistance boys will deliver to your barge. I want them to watch you all the way; you will go down the Blavet canal in time to arrive at the Blavet estuary just before dusk. About a mile down the estuary on the right-hand side you will see some camouflaged netting and behind that a lock gate. Make sure that you have your explosives well placed, bow and stern. When you hit the lock gates, you press the firing button—you will have forty-five seconds to get as far away as possible from the explosion. I want the Resistance to believe you died there.'

Pete was not smiling. 'So this is where we get killed, Stephen. Forty-five seconds to get away? Not easy; I need smoke bombs to go off just ahead of the explosives. We will have to swim up the estuary and land on the same side, as the Resistance boys will be watching from the opposite bank. Good; if we get that far, then I have no worries about getting away and travelling to Paris and then across to northern France. The Germans are far too occupied preparing for the invasion and fighting the Resistance.'

After a little more discussion we shook hands and left and drove back to Exeter airport both deep in thought. I was thinking of Churchill's words. Was this to be the end of the beginning or the beginning of the end? We stopped off in Exeter for fish and chips and arrived at the airfield at seven pm.

———

As usual Pete was able to produce suitable bargemen's clothes from his suitcase, and then to my horror I was told we would be landing by parachute. I had done some training at jumps and landings and we had all made one actual parachute jump from an aircraft, but that was in daylight. We were both fitted with a parachute and instructed to count to five before pulling the cord that opened the chute. Pete slapped me on the shoulder. 'Don't worry, Marçel; we will bail out north of Pontivy. You should see the canal from the air. When you land if you can't find me, look for the canal and then head south until you get to Pontivy. We'll meet up on the barge.'

Our aircraft took off at ten pm. I was feeling sick, worried about a night landing. What if I landed in a tree or in the canal? At last I felt a tap on my shoulder. Pete was shouting in my ear, 'Time for little pigs to fly.'

I stood by the open door frozen with fear—the pilot raised his hand

and Pete gave me a push—I was out in space and I forgot to count, then I started to count but thought this ridiculous so I pulled the cord and felt a heavy jerk on my shoulders, then I breathed a sigh of relief. A little way ahead, I could see Pete's parachute and the canal on my left. My euphoria didn't last long. I saw the trees rising up towards me. I braced myself and fell in a heap between the trees. I quickly released myself and pulled in and folded the parachute. I found a large bush and stuffed it out of sight.

Pete must have been quite some distance from me so firstly I had to find the canal. It had been on my left side as I descended but I had spun around several times since then. I heard the distant rumbling and could see a pink glow in the distance. That would be an air raid at Lorient to the west. I headed south.

I soon came to the canal and followed it until I arrived at Pontivy. I crept cautiously past some buildings until I arrived at the jetty. There was someone on board. I edged around the outside of the cabin until I could see through a porthole. Pete was making coffee.

We sat silently for a while. 'I hope that was a once in a lifetime, Pete. Thanks for the push. For a moment I was just unable to move.'

'Some people do it for pleasure, Marçel. We were both lucky tonight not to break anything. You will find a big change here since last year. The Germans mostly stay in their barracks, unable to cope with the now powerful French Resistance. This means we will be able to travel more freely.'

There was a thump on the deck. The Resistance men had delivered the explosives. They dropped them in the wheelhouse and quietly left. We placed most of them down in the chain locker in the bow of the barge and the rest in the engine room close to the stern of the barge. It was starting to get light and I felt it was time to move.

'Let's get going, Pete. There should be someone at the first lock by the time we get there.'

We started the engine, untied the ropes and moved out. We had thirty-seven miles and twenty-eight locks to the Blavet estuary. It was not possible to make it in one day as it would be dark well before we reached the estuary. We had to find a safe spot for the night and we could not risk being searched with all the explosives we carried on the barge.

By early afternoon we were passing through a forest when we spotted a small creek. We turned the barge and slowly moved through the reeds and water lilies until we found a spot under the overhanging trees. We were completely out of sight from the river.

Pete and I spent the rest of the day fixing detonators to the explosives and running cables back to the wheelhouse. Stephen had supplied us with smoke bombs which we attached to both sides of the barge. By evening we were both ready to catch up on our lack of sleep the night before.

Next morning we checked over our work and were satisfied that the barge would be destroyed forty-five seconds after we pressed the button. There would be no second chance.

'This might be a good place to leave our gear; it's a fair distance from our destination, which is good, because after the explosion we will have to move fast. We need to be unencumbered with our packs.' Pete agreed.

We walked through the forest until we came to an outcrop of rock. From the top of this rock we were able to see that the forest extended for miles in both directions. We could see no sign of habitation. 'Excellent. On the way back we can keep the canal in sight and this outcrop is a perfect landmark. Let's get our gear, Pete, and conceal it at the foot of the hill.'

We packed a change of clothes, some food, the Sten guns and revolvers, a few hand grenades and water bottles in our packs and concealed them in a crevice at the bottom of the outcrop.

After a good lunch and a bottle of red wine, we set off on our last journey with the barge. It had been our home and the base from which we had been able to achieve so much.

The light was fading when we passed through the last of the locks; we had only a short way to go to reach our target on the right bank. We slipped into shorts and tied our shoes to our belts. We were wearing only light shirts and were both shivering, partly from cold but mostly excitement. We were travelling at half speed when I spotted some camouflaged netting. As we got closer we could see the lock gates. Pete and I shook hands. 'We'll meet up at the creek, Marçel. Good luck, old boy, and don't be late!'

With the engine at full speed, Pete turned the barge and headed straight for the lock gates. It was almost dark now and we were travelling at full speed ahead. We were now very close—as we approached the lock gates head-on Pete fired off the smoke bombs; locked the steering wheel and pressed the firing button 'GO! NOW!'

I dived off the stern being careful to keep well clear of the propeller. It seemed ages before I surfaced—all I could see was black smoke and then a deafening crash as the barge hit the lock gates followed by the ear shattering explosion. I saw an enormous red flash through the smoke and then I was hit by the shock waves—I swam as hard as I could to get away from the flames that were lighting up the sky, burning bits of debris were falling in the water around me. Suddenly it became very quiet, the barge had settled on the bottom and the flames extinguished. I could hear a siren screaming and Germans shouting and yelling. I kept swimming as fast as I could back up the river; I wondered if Pete had got away in time.

The smoke and the darkness enabled me to get well away, unseen by the Germans. I kept going for about thirty minutes and then climbed up the bank and rested where it was very quiet. I could not resist going back to see if we had been successful. The tide was low so I crept along the narrow beach until I came to a fence that ran down to the water.

A guard was standing on top of the bank. I waited. As soon as he moved off I slipped down into the water and around the fence. I was in the compound. I moved along a small beach at the bottom of the bank and came to a wall. There was no sign of a guard so I climbed onto the wall and was able to look down on the entrance to the canal. Floodlights were shining down on the lock gates, which had been completely blown inwards. They appeared irreparable. I could just make out part of the bow of the barge stuck in between the two damaged gates; the rest of the barge was under water.

I slipped down off the wall and crept back the way I had come. No sign of the guard. They evidently were not expecting a second visit that night. As soon as I was well clear of the fence, I broke into a fast walk as I had a long way to go to our meeting point. Our attack had been completely successful—the cement would set on top of the gravel. It would take a long time to clear the canal. The U-boat was safely locked in behind our barge.

My training of the last six months was paying off; I was able to keep up a steady pace for most of the night. I kept well clear of all the lock gates but stayed most of the time within sight of the canal. It was dawn when I eventually arrived at the rock face. I was just about to reach into the crevice to retrieve our pack when I felt cold steel pressing into my neck.

'Getting a little careless aren't we? Why have you been so long?' I felt stupid—I had just broken a golden rule and could have easily walked into a trap.

'That was stupid of me, Pete. Definitely won't be repeated. I went back to see the damage. The gates were completely destroyed and the barge perfectly placed to seal off the entrance.'

We were both feeling elated and relieved that we had come out unscathed from the event. 'The Resistance were waiting for us on the other side of the estuary. They will assume we were blown up with the barge. Marçel, you and I are now dead.'

We decided to rest up for the day. We climbed to the top of the rock and took it in turns to catch up on sleep.

Later in the day, we ate some of our food and discussed our future plans. We were now partners in a business, with a large winery in Portugal to run. Our war in Brittany was over and we were now going to conduct a business that in some ways would be far more dangerous than anything that we had done so far.

Our biggest problem for now would be avoiding the French Resistance; the last thing they would want would be to see German war criminals being helped to escape, with their gold, to Portugal.

Because of our sponsors, we would not be able to reveal the fact that these people were to be eventually killed and dumped at sea. Our enterprise would only succeed if we were able to maintain complete secrecy. We had no illusions—if our activities came to light, our sponsors would not hesitate to remove us from the face of the earth to avoid embarrassment.

—

As the light began to fade, we set off on our three-hundred-and-fifty-mile journey to Paris. Our intention was to get away from Brittany. As we were now presumed dead, we had to be careful not to be seen by anyone who might inform the Resistance that we were still alive. Our plan was to go to Paris for a while and then proceed to north-eastern France where we would set up our escape route to Portugal.

Chapter 17

We decided to head southeast, skirting Redon, and then head east past Le Mans and Chartres and on to Paris. We would follow the minor roads avoiding towns and would try to get lifts from passing farmers whenever possible. By doing this, we were able to travel part of the way in daylight.

When passing through built-up areas we separated and took it in turns to enter shops when it became necessary to buy food. Most nights we were able to find a shed or an open barn to shelter in. On several occasions while walking on the road, we had to slip into a ditch or hide behind a hedge as German patrols passed by. We had a few lifts from passing vehicles but there was always a chance of meeting up with a roadblock, so we were cautious when approaching or leaving a town and never stayed too long with any one person.

Finally, we arrived at the outskirts of Paris. We then split up, agreeing to meet at a café on the Boulevard Montparnasse where Pete would be able to make contact with Stephen in England. I acquired an old bicycle that someone had carelessly left outside a shop, and arrived at the café that evening. Pete had done even better. He had stolen an old van, which he had left parked two streets away from the Boulevard where we were meeting.

I went into the back room of the café. Pete was drinking a glass of wine and flirting with a very attractive French girl. 'Marçel, I've been in touch with Stephen. He's delighted to know that we are both dead. I also have a nice surprise for you. Gerda will be at the café Paradis at seven tomorrow night.'

My mind went back to Gerda's parting words—I was looking forward to meeting her again. I wondered if I really would go to bed with her.

'*Mirelle, cherie*, untangle yourself from me and go and get us some food; we have not had a decent meal for the last two weeks.' Pete poured me a glass of red wine. 'This is Stephen's Paris office and where both Gerda and I are able to make contact with him. It's also a very safe house; even the Resistance don't know of its existence so there is little chance of the Germans ever finding it. However we have to be constantly on our guard, so always be extra careful when coming and going from here.'

Mirelle's father appeared with two large steaming bowls of 'soup d'onion' and a basket of bread. 'Marçel, meet our good friend, Jean. He will be looking after you here for quite some time. I'm going off to organise the truck which we will be using to deliver our wine to northern Europe.'

Pete leaned back in his chair. 'The Allied invasion will take place at any time now which means there will be absolute chaos in Paris from then on. So be ready to move out as soon as I get back, and perhaps by then, our first clients will be ready to leave. Keep an eye on Gerda as I think she might have gone too far making contacts with the Germans.'

After our meal and second bottle of wine, Pete showed me to my room at the top of the building. It was an attic with a low ceiling and had a fantastic view of Paris. Pete went back downstairs and I collapsed on my double bed. When I woke up it was almost noon.

Down in the café they were serving lunch so I tucked into steamed trout and boiled potatoes. Pete had left so I took a walk along the Boulevard to the railway station, the Gare Maine Montparnasse. There was very little traffic on the roads but I noticed crowds of German soldiers waiting at the station. They were leaving Paris and heading for the coast.

———

At seven I found the café Paradis; it was in a side street just off the Rue d'Assas. Gerda was sitting at an outside table and I was shocked to see the change in her. She looked pale and drawn and had lost weight. Gerda had only been in Paris for six months but in that time she appeared to have aged at least ten years. When she saw me, she jumped up and ran towards me. We embraced. She hadn't lost her infectious laughter. 'Marçel dear, I am so pleased to see you.' The feeling was mutual. I held her in my arms and we kissed. 'Come, Marçel, I will show you my apartment. We have so much to talk about. I am so happy to see you again.'

I held her hand tightly. 'You are looking great, Gerda. Paris must agree with you. It's good to be with you again.' That last bit I really meant.

Gerda's apartment was only a few streets away. It was a smart building and must have been built just a short time before the war. We climbed a wide staircase to the second floor and Gerda let me into her delightful apartment. Her lounge room was large with a high ceiling. French windows led out to a small balcony. Her delicate furniture looked good with the polished floor and Afghanistan rugs. Gerda took off her coat. She had lost weight and now had an even more superb figure.

'You are looking so well, Marçel; in six months you have grown so big and strong and now I have you to protect me and perhaps who knows …'

We both curled up laughing. I could see the colour returning to her cheeks but I was waiting to hear what it was that had made her so stressed. 'What is it, Gerda? What has happened to you in the last six months?'

'Dear boy, let us finish the champagne. What I have to say is not at all pleasant. I need to talk but it is hard to start and I don't want to spoil this moment.' Gerda emptied her glass and moved over to the window.

'In the last few months the most horrific truth of what is happening in the concentration camps has been revealed to me. Thousands of men, women and children are being killed every day. A relatively large number of the *Gestapo*, my people, are torturing and killing innocent people all over Europe in an effort to stamp out resistance and wipe out all the Jews. The German population stand by and do nothing; with all the bombing of our cities and living in constant fear from the *Gestapo*, they have been completely traumatised.

'I have met some of these evil men; they are no longer human. When I talk to them I feel I am talking to men of ice. The coldness coming from them makes me shake not from fear but from absolute horror. They are no longer human beings but are creatures from hell.' Gerda paused. 'I will do everything in my power to help you to eliminate these creatures. They cannot be allowed to walk on this earth.' Her voice broke and there were tears in her eyes, a mixture of compassion and anger. I stayed silent to give her time to collect herself. Gerda shook herself, forced a smile and changed the subject.

'Marçel, very soon when the invasion of France starts, the Germans will withdraw from Paris and the French Resistance will take over. For a time there will be a period when they will punish the collaborators. There are many French people with scores to settle—some collaborators will be killed; both men and women. Already I have seen women beaten and their heads have been shaved. Believe me, the people in the Resistance will show no mercy to the girls that have given themselves to the enemy.'

Gerda filled her glass and took a long sip before continuing. 'I shall personally be in great danger until the Allies arrive. In order to collect a lot of the information that I have sent already back to London, I have had to mingle and even flirt with several German officers. They have also made several visits here to my apartment. This has not gone unnoticed. I believe I am a marked woman.' Gerda came behind me and put her hands on my shoulders. 'Once the liberating forces arrive I will be safe. I will be taken on to Germany where I can continue my work and be safe while working with the Allied Forces.'

I got up and put my arms around Gerda. 'It's obvious you are already in great danger, Gerda. From now on don't go anywhere without me. As soon as things turn really nasty you must come to our café and stay in my room. As you know, it's very safe there but you will have to stay indoors until the Allies arrive to take you away.'

Gerda took my hand. 'Dear Marçel, once again you come to my rescue, my knight in armour. I still have much work to do but it will be good to know you are somewhere about when I have to go out into the streets. But come, Marçel, we still have lots of celebrating to do.'

Gerda led me to her bedroom—it really was a splendid double bed.

———

It was after midday when I made coffee and returned to find Gerda asleep again. She looked lovely lying there. Gerda was six years older than me, but in one night she had taught me how to make love. She was both gentle and passionate. I felt very warm towards her; we would always have a very special friendship, but no one could ever replace that one magical evening spent with Simone. That first love would always remain with me.

Later that afternoon we set out to explore Paris in the spring; we walked for miles holding hands and laughing. Even in those difficult days, Paris in spring was something extra special.

During the next few weeks, whenever Gerda was not working, we spent our time together. Some nights I stayed with her but many evenings she had to meet up with the German officers. I tried not to feel jealous. I knew she hated having to play up to these often revolting men. I could see she was making herself a prime target and would soon be in great danger from the loyal French people.

We were walking through the Jardin Luxembourg one day, when Gerda told me that she had four clients for us, with two more likely to join them. They were all men who had worked in the death camps and wanted to get out of Germany while they could. I told her we expected them to pay five thousand US dollars or the equivalent in Swiss francs up front. She thought this quite reasonable and wanted to know if we would soon be ready to start our operation.

It was several weeks since I had heard from Pete. I expected him to turn up at any time. I wondered if he had found a suitable truck by now.

And then one day I heard gunshots coming from just a few streets away. Several German armoured cars went rushing by. After a while the shooting stopped. The next day we got the news—the Allied forces had landed in Normandy.

I went around to Gerda's apartment. I made her pack a bag and almost had to drag her over to the café. Once there, I managed to get a small room for her next to mine. Later I went back and collected all Gerda's paperwork and as many of her personal treasures as I could find.

Over the next few days we could hear sporadic fire coming from all directions. German vehicles were passing up and down the Boulevard all day. The firing continued at night. The Germans would stamp out one small group only to find they would start up again a few streets away.

Gerda wanted me to collect some of her books and a favourite painting, so I returned to the apartment to find it had been broken into. It had been looted and trashed. There was nothing left. I wondered what would have happened to Gerda if she had been there at the time.

A week later a heavy truck loaded with large wine casks arrived outside the café. Pete was back and ready for action.

———

It was a superb truck. It had been concealed on a farm throughout the Occupation and was in perfect condition. Pete had bought it on the black market through one of his many contacts. He had taken it to a remote repair garage in a small country town where he was able to convert it to suit our needs.

The truck had a canvas cover similar to the covers on the army trucks. Pete had got an old wine cask maker to attach three extra-long casks to the rear of the driver's compartment. Loose casks were always kept stacked in front of these casks. Behind the driver's seat there was a concealed trap door. A man could just squeeze through into one of the wine casks.

Once inside the cask, another trap door led through to the second cask and then on to the third cask. There was room in each cask for two men to stretch out or to sit up. The casks contained a mattress, pillow and blankets, water, a sealed can for toilet purposes, a container for food and a small electric light that ran off the truck's batteries. I was reminded of our hiding place on the barge.

In case of an accident, each cask had a concealed emergency escape panel on the top of the cask. At least that is what we told our clients! There was plenty of ventilation on the underside of the three casks, which was essential when travelling in hot weather, especially in Spain and Portugal.

Extra fuel tanks, spare wheels and a water tank had been fitted to the truck. Stephen's department in London had somehow managed to send over Portuguese number plates, registration and insurance papers, all stamped and legal. Pete and I now had Portuguese passports, which showed that we had recently arrived in France from Portugal via Spain. I was now Marçel Beaumont and Pete, Pierre Lonsdale. 'I'm pleased, Marçel, we have been able to retain our first names; it can become so confusing.'

The three of us sat around a table. Mirelle brought us a large bowl of *Pot-au Feu* and I explained to Pete the dangerous situation that Gerda was in and that her apartment had been raided and destroyed by the Resistance. I also told him that Gerda had possibly six clients ready and waiting to use our services.

'It would seem that it is time for the three of us to move out. We now have the transport and a legitimate business in neutral Portugal. I have taken over the lease of the property, which used to be the northern depot for the pre-war distribution of the Portuguese wines, so we now have a base to work from.' Pete had not wasted any time in the last few months. It looked as if we were now ready to start our real business.

'If we move to our depot, which is near to Colmar and only a few miles from the Rhine River, are you still able to make contact with those clients that are ready to travel, Gerda?'

I could see a distinct change in Gerda; she had come to life again and leaned forward eagerly. 'I am in direct contact with these people and furthermore they are just across the Rhine near the town of Freiburg. At present it would be easy for them to join us.'

Pete slapped the table. 'Well, that's it, chaps! The sooner we get out of Paris the better. Gerda, you can be the official manageress of the depot until the district is liberated. You will be unknown there and no one will bother you. Marçel and I can make our first trip to Portugal where by now everything should be ready for us.'

We finished our meal. Pete asked Mirelle to close the café while we loaded the truck with all Gerda's gear, which we put in one of the casks. Pete and I kept our two bags in the cab of the truck. We stowed the Sten guns, pistols, hand grenades and explosives in another hidden container. This was concealed below the space under the passenger seats, which held all the tools for the truck. I went quietly back into the kitchen, wrapped a meat knife in a cloth (my faithful bayonet was still in England) and fastened it inside my trousers.

When all was ready we waited until no one was in sight. Gerda slipped quickly out of the café and climbed into the cab of the truck. She wriggled through the trap door and into the cask. I put my head through. 'Don't panic, Gerda. As soon as we are well clear of Paris we will let you out.'

———

We had about two hundred miles to travel so we decided to stop for the night before reaching the town of Nancy. The next morning would be an easy run to Neuf Brisach, which was close to our destination.

We were stopped twice on our way out of Paris. Our papers were checked and were found to be in order. At one place we had to make a detour as the road was blocked. We could hear guns firing; the Resistance men were shooting from some of the buildings nearby. The Germans were beginning to find themselves in an impossible situation, which would finally force them to withdraw from Paris.

At last, well clear of the city, we helped Gerda out from her, as she said, quite comfortable bed. Three very cheerful people sat in the cab of the truck singing bawdy songs, and for the moment forgetting all the horrors that they were to face in the months to come.

We stopped at an *auberge* just outside Nancy that also sold fuel. Pete had to pay black market prices for fuel that had been stolen from the Germans. We bought bread and some cheese from the *auberge* and moved on to a quiet parking spot near the main road. Pete decided to sleep in the cab where he was able keep a watch on the truck. Gerda and I cuddled up in one of the casks. I'm sure not many people can boast that they have made love in a wine cask!

Next morning we passed through Nancy without a problem Gerda stayed in the wine cask. At Colmar, we stopped at a factory that made equipment for wine producers and bought some new equipment, including a small conveyer system, which we would take back to Portugal for José.

123

Just outside of Colmar, we were stopped at a roadblock and searched. The officer in charge carefully studied our papers and passports. We explained that we were taking the equipment in the back of the truck to Portugal. 'I wish I could come with you. We will be lucky to survive the next few months.' He gave us back our papers and we continued on.

We stopped at Neuf Brisach where Pete collected some keys and soon after, arrived at our newly-acquired depot. I unlocked the gates and we drove into a yard. There were two large sheds on one side of the yard and a house on the other.

We parked the truck in one shed; the other larger shed was used for storing wine. Gerda scrambled out and joined us. 'You can now resume a normal life, Gerda, your papers will cover you while you are here and you'll have no trouble from the Resistance. You are now the manageress of our French depot.'

An office took up most of the space in the front of the house, Pete had already had the power and the telephone connected and there were desks, filing cabinets and a typewriter. Although the place was in a mess, we soon cleaned it up. The previous occupiers must have left in a hurry.

The house was the same. It had been well furnished but there was a lot of work needed to make it habitable again. The three of us set to and a few days later, we had a comfortable home, an organised office, clean sheds and a tidy yard.

Gerda and Pete went to Colmar and returned with a stack of bits and pieces for the house and a good stock of food and wine. This was to be our second home.

Gerda had spent some time in the office and had made contact with our clients. We expected to meet up with them the following week.

We had decided that, for our own safety, there could not be a preliminary meeting with our clients. They had to be desperate enough to take us on trust. Once committed there would be no turning back for them.

We, in our turn, had to take the chance that their money might be forged. If at any time they became too difficult or attempted to turn back, we would have to kill them. This could be a problem for us as we would then have to dispose of all six of them before arriving at our winery in Portugal.

Three days later, we arranged to pick up our clients at a quiet spot close to the Rhine River at five am. They would be crossing the Rhine in a small motor boat, which in itself was going to be very risky.

We guessed they must be paying a heavy bribe to someone to bring them across. Crossing the Rhine without being detected would be extremely difficult unless they had the help of local authorities.

If they were seen and followed, we would then be at risk. We had to make sure that at the slightest hint of trouble we would be able to slip away undetected.

Chapter 18

It was a cold misty morning when we met our clients at a disused sand pit close to the river. Pete had dropped me off two hours earlier. I had been watching the sand pit from a distance to make sure only six people got off the motor boat, which had just crossed the Rhine.

I walked over towards the group. I had them covered with the Sten gun and was quite prepared to use it if it turned out to be trap. I was joined by Pete and we approached this sorry group of men.

As instructed, they each carried a small suitcase and were all dressed in drab-looking civilian clothes. I made them stand in line while Pete carefully searched each one to make sure they were not carrying weapons. They became angry when Pete searched through all of the suitcases. Every suitcase contained a bag or box filled with gold, diamonds and valuable gems. Pete ignored this and handed back the cases to each of the men. There were no knives or guns.

Pete carefully explained to them that they would be travelling in the truck's hidden compartment by day, and would be allowed out for a short spell at night for exercise and food. The journey would take five days; they would then rest for a while before starting their long sea journey to Salvador. They were to make as little noise as possible. If they heard one hoot from the truck, they were to remain silent; two hoots would be the all clear. Anyone who made trouble on the journey would be jeopardising the safety of the whole group and the group would have to deal with that person themselves, or we would be forced to kill him.

We set off along a track that led out of the sandpit and turned up a side track, which soon became a footpath with high bushes on either side.

The truck was parked in a small clearing out of sight of the main road where we could have made our escape if things had gone badly wrong for us.

Pete gathered the Germans around him. 'You will enter the truck through the small trapdoor behind the driver's seat and you will pay me before you enter.' Pete pulled back the driver's seat and exposed the entrance to the barrels.

'There are three double beds, so select your partner carefully, as you will get to know each other intimately in the next few days. You will pay me as you enter the truck.' We showed them how to enter the casks with their cases. Pete collected their money as they climbed in. Thirty thousand dollars was a good start towards covering our costs.

We drove back to the depot and Pete gave Gerda the money. She was to deposit it into our bank account in Switzerland, which was not far from where we were. We passed six food packs through the trap door to our clients. I gave Gerda a big hug and a kiss—I wished she could have joined us—and we said our farewells and set off.

Pete had already carefully planned our route, which cut across France using minor roads all the way to Bayonne, via Chalon, Limoges, crossing the Garonne River at Marmonde and then on to Bayonne.

We would cross the Spanish frontier at Hendaye, at San Sebastian we would then head south to Vitoria Gasteiz with a straight run across Spain via Salamanca, and then finally cross into Portugal near Guarda and on to Aveiro, which was only just a short distance from our castle.

I was soon to realise how much organisation and work Pete had put into this route over the past months. Not only had he carefully worked out the route, which he had gone over several times, but he had also arranged the night stops, which would also be our fuelling depots.

At the end of each day we arrived at a secluded building. Sometimes it was an old farm house and at other times a deserted factory. Pete had gone to the trouble of leasing these buildings; they were always kept locked securely and were well away from inhabited buildings.

At each stopping place, there was a store of tinned food, blankets, spare mattresses and pillows, and a large stock of fuel. In France Pete had purchased quantities of fuel on the black market, in Spain and Portugal there was less of a problem, but he still made sure there was always a good reserve of fuel at our stopping points.

Pete and I took turns to drive, usually in four-hour shifts. It was dark when we arrived at our first stop, which happened to be an old canning factory on the outskirts of Moulins. We drove into the yard and I locked the gates behind us.

Our clients climbed out of the casks and exercised themselves around the yard. We both kept a revolver in our belts as we did not want anyone straying off, and they had to stay in sight at all times.

I went into the locked storeroom, which Pete had equipped with everything we needed. There was a long table but no chairs. I found a primus stove and opened a few tins of soup. We had ample bread, which we had brought with us. Outside, Pete had made the clients bring out their toilet containers from the casks, which they then emptied and washed out ready for the next day.

We herded them into the storeroom where they helped themselves to the soup. I made some coffee while Pete and I waited for them to finish eating. We were most surprised at how submissive they were. They must have realised that far from being the sadistic bullyboys, they were now dependent on us and that we had complete control over their destiny. They talked very little amongst themselves. They all had so much cruelty to account for in the last few years of their lives, any trust for each other had long gone.

I understood what Gerda had said; they seemed to exude evil. Their expressionless faces no longer appeared to be human, each one with his bag of blood money taken from his dead victims.

When they had all finished feeding themselves we let them walk around the yard for a short time and then herded them back into the casks. Pete fixed the lock on the trapdoor in case anyone decided to stray in the night.

We fed ourselves and cleaned up the storeroom, refuelled the truck and checked the water and oil. This was to be our routine for the next few nights. Pete slept in the cab and I climbed into the back of the truck. I was quite pleased with our first day; we had collected them without any problem and they had not given us any trouble so far.

At dawn we exercised the clients, gave them coffee and bread and were ready to set off on the next leg of the journey. We continued across France to Limoges without any problems. We saw very few Germans on the way; they were fully occupied in northern France by now.

Our next stop was at an old farm north of Bergerac. This was in a very quiet part of the country with no other properties in sight.

Our clients seemed to be suffering from the exhaust fumes; they were very quiet, and not interested in talking amongst themselves or in taking any exercise, so I applied a little pressure on them.

I remembered the circle of slave workers I had seen way back, when with other boys we had witnessed the beating of those starving men. I soon had them running in a circle and I stood in the middle of the circle, urging them on and on until I could see they were ready to drop, but I refrained from using a whip. To my surprise, they obeyed me without a murmur—they too seemed to be traumatised.

The next day was a much shorter run, so we left a bit later in the morning and drove a little slower, for our benefit as well as for our passengers.

A group of German soldiers were waiting at the bridge that crossed the river Garonne. I gave a single toot on the horn to warn our clients to keep quiet. Our papers were examined very carefully and our truck was searched for the first time by the *Feldgendamerie*. Much to our relief, we were told to continue on our way. As soon as we were well clear of the bridge, I gave the all clear with two toots on the horn much to the relief, I'm sure, of our six passengers.

We arrived at our last stop in France, a quite respectable house with a large shed at the back. We were able to park the truck in the shed for the night as well as being able to feed and exercise our clients.

Early the following morning, having warned our clients to be extra quiet that day, we set off for Hendaye where we were to cross into Spain. There were still a few Germans at the checkpoint but I wondered for how long. They would soon have to retreat to northern France or be cut off from Germany.

The Spanish officials seemed quite casual as we showed our papers and passports and quickly passed through the checkpoint. We now had a long run to Salamanca on very poor roads. It was well after midnight when we finally arrived at the farm just a few miles from Salamanca. Our clients were in a poor state when we let them out, but by the time I had finished exercising them, they had completely recovered and were ready for food.

I had stopped the truck and bought some supplies on the way, so I was able to cook a good meal. We opened some bottles of wine to restore everybody's spirits.

We were helping the clients back into the casks when I noticed a figure slipping away between the buildings. I picked up my knife and followed. I quickly ran around the back of the buildings until I was able to get ahead of him. I waited in a doorway. As he came level I grabbed him holding the knife at his neck; he froze. I was about to slit his throat, but I knew he was one of our clients, and we had a much more fitting end for him.

'You were lucky this time, my friend, don't try that again or your colleagues will tear you apart.' I led him back to the truck. Later I could hear thumping and some stifled moans coming from his cask.

The next day we had a much shorter run but we had to negotiate some very bad roads through very rough country. We crossed the border into Portugal, drove through the town of Guarda, and finally came down to the flat lands by the coast arriving at Aveiro. We were almost there.

It was late afternoon when we drove through the archway into the courtyard of our castle and José closed the gates behind us. We had made it.

We were all relieved to leave the truck, five of the guests looked quite cheerful as they descended but the sixth one was a mess. He had been well and truly 'done over' by his travelling companions!

José and Maria were at the front door to welcome us; the inside of the house had been redecorated and looked superb. Maria took our clients upstairs. They all seemed quite happy to share rooms—maybe having been locked up together in the casks for a few days they had become attracted to each other. All the showers were soon in use, thank goodness. After five days in the casks the Germans were in need of a good shower.

Maria and José were delighted that we were back. Pete declined Maria's promise of a celebration dinner that night. 'Maria, we will have a celebration party as soon as our guests have left.' José wanted to take us on a tour of inspection around the winery but first we went out to the jetty to inspect the launch, which had been delivered the day before. Our launch had arrived at night and the crew had immediately boarded a second launch and left. We presumed they would be returning to England or possibly Gibraltar. Our yacht was a converted ex-Royal Navy motor launch. It had been painted white and all signs of any armament had been carefully removed. It was now a pleasure yacht.

In the large wheelhouse, on the chart table, we found the registration papers. The boat had been registered in Porto in our names and was fully insured. There was a letter from Stephen wishing us good luck and also stating that we now owed his department just over half a million pounds.

The wheelhouse was fully equipped including a two-way radio, radar and safety equipment. On the chart table were charts of the Portuguese coastline, and the local waters.

Forward of the wheelhouse, there was a galley and a dining area and ahead of that, four double berth cabins and a bathroom. At the rear end, the stateroom had been converted into a lounge area, with leather-covered seats and a large polished table in the centre. There were no portholes, just a skylight that had a strong metal grill beneath it and which was firmly locked on the outside.

Back in the wheelhouse, I pressed the starters and the two powerful motors roared into life. We noticed a cloud of smoke coming from the exhaust outlets. Excellent.

We went back into the castle, well pleased with the launch. This was ideal for the purpose we had in mind.

We found Maria in the well-equipped kitchen, busy preparing the evening meal. We decided that our clients should eat first, and we would have our meal later when the Germans had gone to bed.

Having made sure all the staff had left for the night and all the exits from the castle were securely locked, we set off with José to inspect the vines.

A good part of the winery had been cleared of weeds and the vines cut back, and already they were showing a healthy new growth. 'We still have a long way to go but by next season we will have all the vines back in production.' José was a happy man.

It was dark when we got back to the castle and Maria was serving the evening meal to the Germans. They just sat there silently stuffing themselves. I wondered what they were thinking, or were they now just brain-dead? Perhaps the horror of what they had been doing had finally caught up with them.

'While you are here, gentlemen, you will have to stay in your rooms during the day. You can exercise out in the yard in the evening, when all the workers have gone home. On no account must you speak to any member of the staff while you are here—this is for your own safety. As soon as we get news as to when your cargo ship is due, our luxury motor-launch will take you out to your ship, and you will be on your way to South America. It could be tomorrow night.' Pete placed two bottles of wine on the table. 'In the meantime, gentlemen, we invite you to sample our excellent wine.'

Chapter 19

The following morning Pete and I refuelled the motor-launch. José had ensured that we kept a good stock of fuel at the castle. He had also bought us several fishing rods and tackle—this would be our reason for taking the launch out at night.

We concealed the Sten guns and revolvers on board just in case things went wrong for us, but the last thing we wanted were bullet holes in the cabin.

I started the motors and we set out on a trial run to familiarise ourselves with the channel leading out to the ocean.

The two of us had no problem handling the boat and an hour later we headed out through the entrance and then gave the engines full throttle. The launch leaped forward. The waves were breaking over the bow and we were forced to slow down to a safe cruising speed.

We turned around and headed back to the castle, well pleased with the performance of the launch. We would take our guests out to their final destination tonight.

We told the Germans to be ready to leave at ten pm as the freighter would be picking them up at one am.

At ten that evening they shuffled aboard clutching their suitcases. I led them down into the rear saloon. When they had settled down, I closed the door and joined Pete. The engines roared into life, we cast off and were on our way.

After a while, Pete went down to the saloon and opened several bottles of champagne. 'Gentlemen, we would like you all to take a last drink with us before you set off on your final journey.'

Pete left the saloon, closing the door behind him, quietly locking and bolting it.

Sometime later, when we were well clear of the entrance, Pete went down to the engine room and opened a valve. The exhaust fumes were diverted to the saloon through small holes in the floorboards under the table. Pete then went onto the deck and closed the two saloon ventilators.

—

Three hours later, we stopped the engines, opened the hatch and ventilators and shone a flashlight down into the saloon—they were all dead—six empty Champagne bottles and six very dead 'deserting rats'.

They had died in the same way that they had killed so many innocent Jewish families.

We spent the next hour removing the bodies. We carried them up on deck and slipped them into the weighted body bags, which Stephen had thoughtfully supplied us with. Without any ceremony, we dropped them one by one over the side of the boat and into the water.

After removing all the gold, diamonds and other gems, we put the suitcases into weighted bags and they joined their owners on the ocean bed.

We headed back to the coast. It was a calm night so we decided to try our hand at fishing—to my amazement we caught several good-sized fish, later to be our breakfast.

It was dawn when we passed through the entrance and headed back to the castle—we had disposed of all our garbage.

That night we had our celebration dinner with José, Maria and Alfonso. As far as they knew, we had safely delivered our guests to a ship heading for South America.

Pete estimated we must have collected in excess of a million pounds in gold. Not bad for our first run.

BOOK TWO

Escape
to
Death

PROLOGUE

The T-Class submarine surfaced two miles off the central coast of Portugal. It was ten pm. Except for a slight glow coming from the direction of the nearest town Aveiro, four miles inland from the ocean, only a few faint lights could be seen on the coastline.

It was a calm night, with the moon giving just enough light to the crew as they lowered the small inflatable dinghy over the side of the submarine and into the relatively calm water.

The two men stood before their commander, their yellow oilskins covering their uniforms. They each carried a small compass, torch, water bottle and an emergency food pack, and were both unarmed.

'You know what you have to do. Try to avoid entering the castle and talking to anyone. Just board the launch, start the engine and then slip away as quietly as possible. We'll be waiting for you until daybreak. After that we will submerge and follow you out to sea. Head due west until you are out of sight of the land and any other ships, and then we will resurface.' The commander lowered his voice. 'One more thing—if for any reason you do not return to us within the next forty-eight hours, we have been ordered to return to Gibraltar and we are to deny any knowledge of your existence.'

The Commander shook hands with the two men. 'This is a fairly straightforward operation. Our politicians don't want to cause a diplomatic row with Portugal, so you are really on your own. I just hope the launch has enough fuel on board. Once you return to us, we will be able to top up your fuel tanks and you can then continue on to Gibraltar.'

Grover and Hardman slid down the side of the submarine and were helped into the inflatable by crew members. They started the outboard and once clear of the submarine, headed for the shore.

'Bill, we'll head in the direction of that slight glow. That's the town of Aveiro. The seaway into the broad-water should be directly in front of that glow. After that we will follow the marks until we get to the castle. It's good to be working together again, mate—I thought our night adventures were over when the war ended.'

Grover and Hardman were two of the few surviving men who rode on the backs of mini-submarines, and who slid off their speeding subs once they were successfully lined up with the target. If they were lucky, they would be picked up by an accompanying inflatable, or else they would have to swim to the shore and become POWs.

'I never thought we would be going ashore to steal one of our own bleeding boats! This should be a piece of cake, John. No enemy firing at us this time; we might even receive a bounty for this job.'

'I know one thing, Bill, if we get caught, we will be in deep, deep shit, with no help from the admiralty.'

It was a calm night as they rode the long ocean swell and were soon approaching the seaway. They cut the outboard motor and allowed the strong tide to carry them in. There was no one to watch as they followed the lit marks into the broad-water.

Once clear of the seaway, with only a short distance to go, the only sound was the splash as their paddles dipped into the now still broad-water.

John stopped paddling for a moment and studied his compass. 'If we head east-south-east for eighteen minutes, we should reach the mouth of the river and the castle.'

Karl Schmidt stood on the stone jetty at the back of the old castle, staring at the motor launch. He was aware that Pete was in the castle with the winery manager and his wife. Still pondering on how to make his next move, in the faint light he noticed an inflatable dinghy approaching. He signalled his companion to move back out of sight.

Schmidt stood behind the bushes that surrounded the castle and watched as the two men climbed out of the inflatable and scrambled aboard the launch. He realised that they were about to steal it. Keeping his gun out of sight, Schmidt silently followed the two men as they stepped into the wheelhouse of the launch. 'So you have come to steal my boat?'

The men turned in surprise to see Schmidt's gun pointing at them. One of them barked, 'You must be the owner of the castle; we have been ordered to board this motor launch and return it to the Royal Navy. We are taking it back to Gibraltar tonight.'

Schmidt realised that he was facing two men from the Royal Navy and immediately saw the possibilities. A plan began to form in his mind …

'Remove your oilskins!'

Schmidt's companion had joined him and now with two guns pointing at them, Grover and Hardman reluctantly removed their oilskins, revealing their uniforms. Schmidt smiled, this was just perfect.

He needed those uniforms ...

'Start the engines and head out into the broad-water.'

Hardman, closely watched by Schmidt's assistant, cast off the ropes while Grover, under the watchful eyes of Schmidt edged the launch out onto the broad-water.

'Turn right and head for that small island. Take the launch through that patch of reeds. Stop the engines and allow the launch to run onto the mud bank.'

Grover and Hardman were both staring ahead as the launch came to a stop in the shallow mud.

Schmidt fired two shots. The two men died instantly.

After disposing of the bodies on the island and carefully washing away all the blood stains, Schmidt quietly returned the launch to its moorings alongside the jetty.

Pete, Maria and José, unaware of the departure and return of the launch, finished their meal and retired with a decanter of their best port wine to the comfort of their lounge.

José stood up. 'I can hear someone at the front door.'

Chapter 1

Marçel was finding it difficult to breathe. He slowly opened his eyes to find himself on his back, pinned down by the steering wheel.

Looking up at the floor of the cab, he realised that the truck he had been driving was upside down and that he was trapped between the crushed roof of the cab and the steering wheel. He turned his head to the right, and in the dim light, found himself staring into the dead face of the man who had caused this disaster.

In his hurry to get started on this leg of the journey, he had failed to lock the concealed panel behind the driver's seat, so Franz had been able to push his way through.

Franz had been acting in a very strange way at the previous night's stopover. He had not eaten any breakfast. He had simply walked backwards and forwards, and then round and round in a tight circle, quietly muttering to himself.

When the time had come to get back into the truck, Marçel had had to use all his strength to push Franz through the hatch and into the false wine casks fastened behind the cab of the truck. This was where the 'clients' were concealed. Franz had finally blown his top and had burst through the hatch, which was directly behind the driver's seat, screaming and completely out of control.

Too late Marçel realised that Franz had been quite determined to kill him; Franz had put his hands around Marçel's throat and was pulling him backwards until his hands came off the steering wheel. He had taken his foot off the accelerator but it was too late; they were descending from a mountain pass and were just about to drive around a sharp bend in the road.

Marçel remembered two distinct bumps and suddenly they were airborne. It seemed a long time before they hit the side of the mountain, and then rolled and thudded all the way down to the bottom of the valley.

He decided to give himself a few minutes to calm down and collect his thoughts before attempting to free himself from the cab. The possibility of fire had passed by now—he was not in an immediate danger of being burned alive.

There were six clients concealed on this truck—all quite insane; Marçel just hoped they were now all dead. He had to get himself out of the cab, and then set fire to the truck in order to destroy all the evidence of the illicit human cargo. He also knew he would have to kill any one of them that might have survived the accident.

The clients were some of the lowest form of human life; rats running from the scene of their atrocities. Each one of them carried a bag of gold in his suitcase, small bars made from the melting-down of rings, teeth and precious trinkets, which were torn from the bodies of the wretched Nazi holocaust victims, while on their way to be burned in the furnaces of the concentration camps. There were many hundreds of thousands murdered in the concentration and work camps of Hitler's Europe.

Early in 1945, when the war in Europe was rapidly coming to an end, the British and American forces from the west, and the Russian Allies from the east, were closing in on a crumbling Germany.

The death-camp butchers were fleeing in terror as the liberating forces arrived at each one of the concentration camps.

At these camps they often found just a few remaining starving victims; people dressed in ragged clothes, exposing emaciated bodies and their fleshless ribcages. With gaunt death-like faces they slowly ambled about the camps—the living dead.

All the evil sadistic butchers had gone into hiding, knowing that they would soon have to face retribution, and pay for their inhumanity to the thousands of innocent people they had butchered.

Then one day, word got around to some of these evil people that an enterprising group was, for a large sum of money, operating an escape route through France and Spain to Portugal, where a ship would then transport them to a fresh start and a new life in South America. What they did not know, was that this travel service had been conceived and funded by the Secret Services of the Western Allies.

In 1940 at the beginning of World War Two, a separate branch of the Secret Service was established just outside of London. Stephen Harvey, a long time public servant, was appointed to run this section. Stephen had spent most of his life working in the diplomatic service. When the Second

World War started, he had been placed in charge of a special department that worked in conjunction with several other clandestine movements in Western Europe.

Because of his dealings with several of the top-ranking service people in Europe, Stephen had been given the rank of Wing Commander; an appointment that embarrassed him and which he rarely used.

Beneath the quiet exterior of this smallish grey-haired person, was an extremely ruthless and dangerous man. Stephen would spare no one that might harm or endanger his King and country. His job was to quietly remove anyone who became an embarrassment to the nation. Stephen was a person without scruples when it came to protecting his department and his staff.

Marçel's flight out of occupied France in 1943 and his twelve-month intensive training in Britain before being parachuted back into France just a few months before the Allied Invasion had all been organised by Stephen.

At the end of the war, Stephen had stayed on, tidying and covering up some of his wartime operations, including the operation—'Deserting Rats'. His commission was to rid the Allies of certain double agents, and to plan the assassination of several of the untouchable and highly dangerous enemies of the Alliance. It was within this secret branch that Operation Deserting Rats was conceived.

Harvey considered that he had devised a humane way of executing these evil people. On the day that they were to be taken by motor launch to the supposed passing ship that would take them to South America, they were wined and dined, then in the evening, they boarded the launch and were taken down to the saloon of the launch.

As soon as they were at sea, several bottles of champagne were opened for the clients, a last farewell toast. This put them in a more relaxed state of mind, and more able to cope with their last dying moments, a luxury they never offered their concentration camp victims. While the clients were busy celebrating their departure from Europe, Pete and Marçel were quietly closing down the skylights and locking the doors to the saloon.

Up on the bridge they simply opened a valve. This valve diverted the exhaust fumes from the engines to the saloon.

Now it was the camp butchers' turn to die, locked in the gas chamber.

The concentration camp murderers died fairly quickly and, fittingly, they died in the same way they had killed many thousands of innocent Jews.

When the launch was well out to sea, the weighted body bags were thrown overboard and the bodies of the war criminals sank quietly to the bottom of the ocean.

None of the clients ever reached South America. This was their escape to death. The very anonymity they craved backfired, and made it so very easy to eliminate them.

The clients willingly paid ten thousand dollars for these services and they also bequeathed their suitcases containing the stolen gold.

From early 1945 to summer in 1947, many of the butchers had been executed—very few remained alive. Stephen realised there now were insufficient numbers to make these death runs worth their while; this was to be Marçel's last run.

Marçel could see a narrow strip of light at the far end of the cab. If he could free himself from the steering wheel, he might be able to wriggle down and slip out of this very narrow gap.

He eased himself up a little to free the steering wheel from his ribcage. The pain was excruciating, but he was able to move his body clear. Once the pain subsided, he felt sure that none of his ribs were broken. He was then able to wriggle towards the strip of light and to his relief, slide out of the remains of the side window to greet a bright sunny morning.

Apart from a few aches and pains in his chest, Marçel realised that he had been very lucky to survive this crash. The truck had rolled down to the bottom of a narrow valley and was now lying upside down on a strip of fine, river-washed gravel. The loose gravel must have lessened the impact and probably saved his life.

Marçel looked up at the steep side of the mountain but was unable to see the road. He breathed a sigh of relief, as although there was very little traffic on this part of the road, the last thing he wanted was to be spotted before he could destroy the truck, and all traces of the clients.

He started to pick his way through the wreckage. The truck had been purpose-built for people smuggling. Officially, they were transporting wines from their winery in Portugal to their depot in northern France. From there, their wines were distributed throughout France, Germany and Switzerland.

The back of the truck consisted of hoops covered with canvas. At the front end of the truck, there were three large wine casks securely fastened to the floor and all cleverly interconnected with the concealed entry panel in the cab of the truck, behind the driver's seat. The inside of the wine casks contained mattresses, a supply of food and water and even a portable toilet that had to be emptied at every night stop. The rest of the truck was always kept fully loaded with real casks of wine bound for northern France. The truck then had a full load of empty wine casks, and their clients, for the return journey from France to Portugal.

Each night they would stop at their specially prepared depots, which were either isolated farms or deserted warehouses. They had established depots at ten-hour intervals that ran from northern France, all the way to the winery and castle in Portugal.

Marçel crawled under the rear end of the truck; it was a tangle of broken staves from the crushed wine casks. He moved around the wreckage trying to avoid the pools of blood and came across five dead bodies. There was one missing—the woman.

There was a strong smell of fuel slowly leaking from the truck's fuel tank. He managed to find five of the six small suitcases, which he pushed out from the wreckage. He crawled out and looked around for the woman.

Staring at the point where the truck must have left the road, it was obvious to Marçel that if the woman had fallen out of the truck on the way down, she would certainly have finished up here on the gravel. There were no ledges on the steep slope. There were only two ways for her to have gone—up, or down, the river.

He finally spotted her some way downriver; she was sitting on a boulder on the edge of the rushing mountain water, clutching her suitcase. It would be quite impossible for her to cross the white water at this part of the valley.

Marçel decided to dispose of the truck and bodies first, and go after the woman afterwards. He carefully removed the bags containing the gold bars and transferred them, minus the deceased owners' few possessions, into the fifth case. He rammed all the other suitcases back under the truck.

Reaching inside the remains of the cab, he retrieved his leather jacket that contained his revolver, passport and cash that he always carried for the journey from France to Portugal. He decided to leave all the other paperwork and permits inside the truck. He found the spare can of fuel and poured it over the dead bodies. Satisfied that the mountain road was, for the moment, free of traffic in both directions, he threw a lit rag into the middle of the upturned truck.

Marçel stood back and watched as the flames engulfed the truck; there was a slight roar as the wooden casks exploded into flames. He hoped that any cars and trucks passing on the road above would not notice the flames and smoke.

There was no mistaking the smell of burning flesh. The intense heat soon reduced the five men's bodies to ashes, just like so many of their innocent victims, whose bodies had finished up in the furnaces of the German death camps.

Marçel watched the woman who was staring up at the burning truck. At that moment, she seemed to realise that he would be coming after her. She turned and started to scramble over the rocks heading downstream. He could see that a little farther downstream the cliff dropped straight down into the river—there was no escape for her that way.

He slowly walked around the burning truck, throwing anything he could find into the flames. He even threw a small container of water into the fire, after he'd quenched his thirst. There were to be no traces left for a future investigation; the bodies were reduced to ashes, with only the metal frame of the truck remaining.

He dragged the heavy suitcase under some bushes on the side of the cliff face and then started back after the woman. She had reached the point where the rock face dropped straight down into the water, realising that she could go no further.

Making his way over the slippery boulders, Marçel remembered the last woman he had killed. It had been unfortunate for her that she had been in the wrong place at the time, but she had been a collaborator and was about to reveal his presence to the approaching German soldiers.

This woman he was about to kill was quite a different matter—she had worked in a concentration camp and must have been involved with the experimentation and death of many men, women and children. *She deserved to die* … The woman had now become a liability and a danger to the enterprise; Marçel was left with no alternative, but to kill her. He pulled the revolver from his pocket and clicked back the safety-catch.

The woman, who had given her name as Helga Novoske, had disappeared behind an enormous boulder. He decided to climb to the top of the boulder and drop down, taking her by surprise.

His heart was racing as he reached the top of the high boulder. He stared down at the woman's terrified face. Raising his revolver, his finger on the trigger, Marçel moved towards the edge …

He had not allowed for the smooth slippery surface of the boulder, and stepping forward, lost his footing and started to slide down the side of it. At the same moment, Helga threw a rock, which hit him full in the face.

He fell on to the gravel at the bottom of the boulder, his revolver landing at Helga's feet. For the second time that day, Marçel was knocked unconscious.

Chapter 2

Once again, Marçel woke up to the pain of a heavy weight being pressed down on his chest. He thought for a moment he was still in the upturned truck. He slowly opened his eyes to find Helga Novoske was sitting on his chest and leaning forward. Her face almost touched his; she was smiling evilly as she slowly spat in his face.

His arms were pinned down under her legs, his hands securely bound with the belt from his trousers and resting on his lower stomach. Helga leaned back and picked up the revolver, her face contorted with rage.

'You were going to kill me, Marçel, but now it is my turn to kill you! I watched you stash all the gold in that case in the bushes. This was all filthy German stolen gold and now it will be all—*my* gold.' Helga paused for a moment.

She realised that on her own she would have little hope of getting through Spain and Portugal and then finding a ship to take her to South America, or anywhere else. *Perhaps if I spare his life*, she thought, *I could force him to help me. He is probably my only hope of escaping to South America.*

Yes, Helga thought, *I will make him complete his contract. He will take me to Portugal and then he will get me safely on board a ship. At last, I will finally be free of the hell I have been living in these last four years.*

Marçel noticed a slight change in her demeanour.

'I will spare your life, Marçel, if you promise to fulfil your contract and get me safely onto a ship to South America.'

He was sure then that she really was quite mad; she should have killed him and then escaped with all the gold. Marçel decided to play along with her for the time being.

'Anything you say, Helga, but I expect you to give *me* some of that filthy gold.'

Helga spat in his face again. 'You are no better than that scum I was forced to rub shoulders with in the concentration camp! Get me to the ship and I will share the gold with you. You missed your chance to kill me,

Marçel. I am forced to take the risk that you will not kill me on the way to your base in Portugal. Just remember—I have the gun.'

Not being in a position to argue with the woman, Marçel decided, for the time being, to go along with her as they were now safely in Spain, with only one more frontier to cross. Marçel decided to make for their last base in Spain before attempting to cross the border into Portugal. There was just a chance that Gerda, following them in the Renault, would find that they had not yet reached the Valladolid base. Hopefully, she would realise that something was wrong and would come looking for them. They must get up to the road and watch out for her. It would certainly be far easier to dispose of Helga once they arrived back safely at the winery in Portugal.

'Okay, Helga, I acknowledge that circumstances have changed, I will honour our contract.'

He had to gain her confidence and get her to relax. In her present state, Helga was a danger to them both.

'We must get up on to the road and start walking towards Valladolid, in case Gerda, my partner, is already searching for us. We must try to look like two normal people out for an afternoon stroll.'

He continued quietly, 'From now on, Helga, you will be safe providing you do exactly as I say. I will get you to our base in Portugal and then onto a ship to South America. If we can get up to the road, there is a good chance we'll be picked up by Gerda; she should have been following us in her car. Otherwise, we have one more base, which is not too far from here, where we can meet up with her. If that fails, I will have to organise some other form of transport to Portugal.'

Marçel closed his eyes; Helga had released her grip on him. He relaxed and focused on their journey to the winery. He could dispose of her in the usual way—a trip in the boat would make it quick and painless for her.

Drops of rain fell on his face; he opened his eyes. It was not raining.

Helga's face was still close to his, tears were streaming down her face and dripping onto his. Her whole body was shaking; something inside of her had snapped.

Staring up at her, Marçel suddenly noticed a complete change in her appearance. Gone was the face contorted with anger and hate; here was the face of a young woman, a face contorted with anguish and despair. It was no longer ugly but now softened by the tears that ran down her cheeks.

It occurred to him that he might have been the first person for quite some time to have spoken quietly and reassuringly to this girl.

'You think I am just—just like all the other animals you are helping to escape from the punishment that they so rightly deserve!' she sobbed.

'Helping them to escape out of Germany to a new life in America just makes you one of them. You take some of their tainted gold and then you allow them to go free to continue their disgusting evil life in another country!'

Helga leaned back. Tears still ran down her face, as her voice rose. 'Yes, I expect I *am* just as bad as the rest of them. When we arrived at the concentration camp with the children, I had a choice—to stay with the children, or go with all the other women to the gas chambers. The children needed me and I was afraid of dying.'

Marçel said nothing and waited for her to continue.

Helga had calmed down a little. 'In 1943 I was both nurse and teacher at our orphanage in Warsaw. The day the Germans arrived to take away the children, whom they believed to be of Jewish parents, we were told they were being taken to a special celebration party organised by the local *Oberst*. I immediately offered to go with them and keep an eye on them. Little did I know it was to be a one-way journey to a death camp.'

Helga was sobbing again, 'The party turned out to be a train journey in a cattle truck to the concentration camp. My terrified children clung to me. I tried so hard to comfort them; this helped to hide my own terror. I was only seventeen years old at that time.'

Marçel was staring up at the lined face of a woman who looked more like a forty year old. Her hair once black was now streaked with grey; she had scars on her forehead, cheeks and neck. Marçel realised that four years ago she must have been a very attractive young girl. Those years had changed her forever. Marçel was beginning to see Helga in a completely different light.

He closed his eyes again; the cuts to his face where she had hit him with the stone were stinging. Helga composed herself.

'I was taken with the children to a clinic where supposedly sick children were being cared for. The children were taken straight into a ward. But the guards took me into a side room where I was stripped, beaten and repeatedly raped.' Helga shuddered. 'I just wanted to die that night. The next morning I was ordered to wear a nurse's uniform and I was taken to the doctor in charge of the children's block.'

By now Helga had calmed down and continued quietly. 'I was told by the doctor that I was a very fortunate woman and provided I took charge of the children and did not cause them any trouble, my life would be spared.

'I was informed of medical research being carried out on the children for the betterment of the human race. My job was to prepare the children for the operations they were to undergo, and then afterwards to care for what was left of the poor mutilated little souls. I was to live with the children in the ward and have no contact with anyone outside the children's block.

'So began two years of hell where I must have died a thousand times. I stayed there with the children and helped the murdering bastards, only because I felt I needed to help and comfort these poor innocent dying children.'

Helga shuddered. 'Some nights, the German guards would come and take me to their quarters, where I would be repeatedly raped before being returned to my frightened children. The children knew that one day I might not return.'

It was then that Marçel realised that Helga was not one of their usual cold-blooded murderers.

'So what brought you to us, Helga? And where have you been hiding since the end of the war?'

Helga stopped crying, and almost smiled. 'The Americans arrived. The doctors and guards had left days before. Dead and dying children surrounded me. I was immediately arrested and taken to a house where I was again beaten and raped, this time by the American soldiers of the liberating army. I spent the next two years in jail awaiting trial. That is when I learned to speak English. Then one day I had a visitor. A woman dressed in civilian clothes interviewed me. She sat opposite me in the interview room, and after staring at me for a long time, she asked me if I would like to live in South America. I said anything was better than living in that prison.

'She explained to me that they were in some doubt as to whether I was in the same class as the other concentration camp murderers, who were shortly to be tried for their war crimes. For that reason, I was given the opportunity to join a small group of people, who were buying their way to freedom.

'The woman told me that these remaining people were small fry, and like myself, had given the Allies valuable information that enabled them to find and punish some of the top war criminals. If I agreed to take this opportunity to leave Germany, I would be taken to the point of departure, given a small amount of gold to pay my fare, a false passport, and a suitcase with a few basic necessities.'

Helga wiped her face with her sleeve and continued, 'I had no hesitation in accepting this offer. The woman produced a camera and took my photo; she said this was for a passport. She told me that she had no connection with the people who were going to smuggle me to South America. The arrangements were being made through a certain underground organisation.'

Marçel felt a little sorry for Helga; she had no idea that Gerda had sentenced her to death. *Or perhaps Gerda was really trying to help this woman and this is why she had broken the rules and revealed herself to one of the clients.*

Gerda was the third member of the group who normally operated from the warehouse and office near Colmar in Northern France. She had joined the Department in 1943 while her husband, Pierre, had been in the French Resistance movement, later to be hanged by the *Gestapo*. Gerda had turned out to be one of Stephen's very best agents.

Gerda had spent some of her time in Western Germany and was responsible for finding, organising and delivering the clients to the rendezvous on the French side of the Rhine, but she never actually came face to face with any of the clients.

Marçel thought it strange that Gerda had taken the trouble to interview Helga. *This would have been the first time that Gerda had exposed herself to a client; she must have had a good reason for revealing her identity. Maybe she was trying to save this woman but why would she send her through the network? Their job was to eliminate these people, not to help them. Maybe it was time to end the whole operation.*

Marçel now realised why a few days earlier Pete, his other partner, told him he had been summoned to London. Perhaps Stephen was preparing to close them down.

Pete had told Marçel that he would have to make the escape run without him on this occasion. By now, it had almost become a routine job; the clients were submissive and were only too pleased to be on their way to a new life in America. Marçel just hoped Pete would be there to help him with the boat run; this needed two people to cope with the final disposal of the clients.

'So, Helga, do you have the passport? How long ago was it when this woman came to see you in prison?'

Helga slowly lifted herself from his chest. He was able to breath freely again. She stood over him and pointed the gun at his head.

'Don't you move, Marçel. I have not yet decided what to do with you.'

At that moment, he had no intention of doing anything.

Helga put her hand inside her bra and revealed her passport. She smiled eagerly at him, 'Yes, I now have a passport. So at last I am a real person.'

Marçel noticed quite a change in Helga—she was almost looking like a normal human being; she seemed to have recovered from the shock of the terrible accident and his failed attempt to kill her, and now she even had a slight smile on her face. Her outburst must have purged her in some way; it was probably the first time in four years that she had been able to unburden herself to someone.

'Four days ago the woman came back to the prison. That same night she brought me these navy blue slacks, a blue shirt, the heavy jacket and the walking shoes. The prison guards stood aside as she led me out to her car. We drove for about four hours; on two occasions she pulled into a side lane to see if we were being followed.

When we finally arrived at a lonely spot close to the bank of the Rhine River, she told me to get out of the car; the woman passed me a small suitcase, the passport and a note. She—Gerda—said I was to give this note to you; it was most urgent that you should wait for her at the last Spanish stopover for at least one day. If she did not arrive within twenty-four hours, you were to ring the telephone number on the note before proceeding to your base in Portugal. I was not to mention this to any of the other people travelling with me. I never got an opportunity to speak to you alone.'

'Where is the note she gave you, Helga?' Marçel was puzzled that Gerda had given a telephone number to Helga. Something was very wrong.

'The woman drove away. A man appeared out of the darkness, and led me down a track to where the boat and the rest of the party were waiting. We crossed the river and soon after were met by you.' Helga was smiling. 'So my friend, I memorised the telephone number and swallowed the piece of paper. Maybe now I will have a little insurance; I will tell you the number when we get to Portugal.'

'Was this a French telephone number, Helga?'

She looked thoughtful for a moment. 'How would I know, Marçel? I was taken from Poland to Germany and have never been to France.' Helga was still aiming the gun at his head.

'I think I will be safe when this Gerda woman arrives.'

'Helga, untie my hands now and let me get up. And you can give me the gun.'

Helga untied his hands and Marçel returned the belt to his sagging trousers.

'I will keep the gun, Marçel, and you will carry the gold!'

As they walked back past the truck, Marçel retrieved the heavy suitcase containing the gold bars from behind the bush. Helga passed him her suitcase and they continued walking upstream. After about a mile, they found the remains of a pathway, which appeared to lead up to the road. They started to climb the path, which was overgrown with weeds and appeared not to have been used for many years; two thirds of the way up they found out why.

There had been a landslide and for about five yards there was a gap where the path had subsided and left only about six inches of pathway. Marçel decided to risk it.

He slipped his belt through the handles of the suitcases and leaned against the side of the bank. He clutched grass and any plant he could find and edged slowly along the very narrow remains of the path, not daring to look down at the sheer two-hundred foot drop.

'It's okay, Helga. Throw the gun over to me and then come over slowly. Hug the bank and grab anything you can hold onto, keep close to the bank. Don't look down!'

Instead, Helga slipped the gun into the inside pocket of her jacket and started to cross the gap. She had almost reached him when she stopped to look down. Helga froze for a full minute, unable to move.

Marçel forced a laugh, 'Come on, Helga—or are you going to let go and save me the job of killing you?'

That did the trick; her anger returned, and she moved so fast he thought she would slip to her death. Leaping onto the path where he was standing, she promptly stepped up to him and slapped his face.

'I am a survivor, Marçel. You are the one who will die first! And thank you for reminding me that you might still be thinking of killing me when we get to Portugal.'

They finally reached the road without further incident but it had been an exhausting climb. It was midday and quite warm. They lay on the grass bank to rest until they had both recovered from the steep climb. There was very little traffic on this road, just the occasional truck or car heading south, or north to the Franco-Spanish border.

They started to walk down the winding road. Every time a car or truck approached, Marçel took Helga's hand, giving the impression that they were just a young couple out for a casual afternoon walk. He noticed her sharp reaction to being touched. No one bothered to stop to see if they were in need of a lift to the next village.

Eventually the road straightened, and started to gradually descend until they finally reached the fertile valley with its green meadows stretching away into the distance. Here and there they could see the occasional farmhouse and a scattering of cattle grazing in the nearby meadows. It all seemed so peaceful compared to what they had left behind in northern France.

They arrived at a village with just a few houses, a church and one solitary shop. It was early afternoon; siesta time and the village looked deserted. To Marçel's surprise the village shop was open; he went in and soon came out with two large bottles of lemonade, a loaf of bread and a hunk of cheese.

They walked on to the end of the street and sat under one of the olive trees that lined the road, on the outskirts of this very quiet little Spanish village.

They had not eaten since early breakfast. After their long walk, the food and cool drinks were more than welcome. After finishing off the bread and cheese, they stretched out on the thick grass. Helga immediately fell asleep; the climb, and long walk to the village, having taken its toll.

Marçel realised this woman had done remarkably well. Considering the terrible ordeal in the concentration camp, where she must have been starving, followed by her long stay in prison, she would have found it difficult to regain her strength. He let her sleep for a while and then quietly, took the opportunity to retrieve the revolver from her jacket pocket.

They must have walked on for about another five miles before they spotted the black Renault driving towards them. A very tense-looking Gerda was at the wheel. The car slowed down as it approached them. It drove slowly past, stopped, and then reversed back to where they were standing.

Gerda leaned out of the window of the Renault—she was not smiling. 'Quickly get in the car; we can talk on the way!' she yelled.

Helga quickly jumped into the back of the car. Marçel handed her the case containing the gold and then jumped into the front seat next to Gerda.

She immediately put her foot down on the accelerator, and with the wheels of the Renault spinning on the gravel surface, the car roared down the road, back the way they had just come.

Marçel breathed a sigh of relief that they were now on their way to Portugal ... he hoped.

Chapter 3

Marçel told Gerda how Franz, who suffered from claustrophobia, had finally flipped and had attacked him on the road coming down from the mountain. He described the crash, the burning truck, the dead bodies, with only Helga and himself surviving the crash.

'I was going to kill Helga; instead, Helga very nearly killed me. When I heard her story I guessed that you were trying to help her, so I decided to bring Helga to the winery, or rather she decided for me! When she told me that it was imperative for me to meet up with you in Spain, I guessed something was wrong. So why was it so urgent that I contact you here? By the way I think we are going in the wrong direction.'

Gerda reached for his hand. 'I had to make absolutely sure you didn't take Helga along with the other clients when you set off in the launch. I'm trying to help her get away and start a new life somewhere overseas.'

'The telephone number? Ah yes, a friend of mine was going to pass this message on to you in case anything prevented me from meeting up with you. This friend knows nothing about our activities and was only to tell you not to take Helga out on the launch. When I found that you had not arrived at the Valladolid base I knew something had gone very wrong.'

Gerda let go of his hand; the car swerved badly to avoid several sheep that had strayed onto the road. 'Sorry about that! I just had to touch you. We must take a different route to Portugal, Marçel. It seems Stephen and his men are looking for the truck and maybe this car. It's obvious they don't yet realise that you nearly all died in the truck accident this morning. Marçel, I think they intend to eliminate us when we reach the winery. It appears the UN has found out about our activities and we have become a serious embarrassment to both the British and the US Governments. I think that Stephen has been ordered to eliminate all traces of Operation Deserting Rats.'

'Take the next turning to the left, Gerda. We will have to take the minor roads to Medina and then cut across to Benavante. We will keep going west towards the coast until we get to Verin, and then head south to the border post, pass through Vila Real, cross the Douro River, and on down to Aveiro. Fortunately I had studied this alternative route in case we were ever faced with this type of situation.'

They reached the turn off—a dirt road in very poor condition—and headed west for Medina. Gerda had to drive carefully because of frequent large potholes and the low clearance of the Renault.

Marçel glanced back. Despite the bouncing of the car on the rough road, Helga was stretched out on the back seat and was sound asleep.

Gerda continued, 'Marçel, when I arrived at the French depot, to my horror, all that was left was the smouldering ruins of the warehouse, our house and the office. Pete was just standing in the yard, staring at the burnt-out remains of our wine business that we had built up over the last three years. The warehouse with all our stocks of wine had been destroyed. Only the shell of the house and office remained.

'There was just nothing left; this has been my home for the last three years and now I have lost everything including all my clothes, jewellery and all the things that I kept in memory of Pierre.'

Apart from the death-run business, Pete, Gerda and Marçel had by now established an extremely profitable market for their Portuguese wines in northern Europe; they were now making good money and the future for the winery looked very promising.

'Pete looked alarmed when he saw me, his face was white and for the first time since we have been working together, I thought I detected a slight look of fear in his eyes. He put his arms around my shoulders. You and I know that is something very out of character for Pete; he's completely fearless normally. I think the man must be ill.'

Gerda continued, 'Pete told me he had been summoned to London, where he had been given orders by Stephen to close down the operation Deserting Rats. Stephen told him that we were about to be exposed by a United Nations department that was now very much aware of our activities. Stephen said that apparently a Nazi organisation, operating in Brazil, was puzzled as to why several of their colleagues, who were bringing out considerable amounts of gold, had not turned up in South America. They decided to send an agent back to Germany to find out what was going on.'

Gerda was silent for a while, recalling her conversation with Pete.

'Apparently this man was able to make contact with one of our clients in Germany, and he decided to follow the group all the way down to our base in Portugal. Stephen showed Pete a copy of the statement made by this German from South America, shortly after he was arrested at the French border with Spain, and when he was later interviewed by a French intelligence agent.'

'I wonder how the Nazi from South America managed to find our starting point on the French side of the River Rhine.' Marçel asked.

After negotiating two sharp bends in the road, Gerda responded.

'I'll try to give you the exact words of the man's statement as Pete related it to me. The Nazi from South America said that when he was told of the meeting place on the Rhine, he realised the group would have to cross the river. He decided to go to a spot on the French side of the Rhine, which was opposite the spot where the party were meeting on the German side of the river; it turned out to be an old sand mine. He concealed his car a little way back from the now-deserted sandpit, then climbed to the top of a sand hill where he could watch the river and the approach road to the sand mine, and waited. It was nearly midnight when he saw the headlights of a vehicle approaching. A large covered truck drove into the sand mine. A few minutes later, he watched a small launch arriving from the German side of the river and six people walked over to the truck. He watched the driver get out of the truck; he appeared to be talking to the six people. Then to his amazement, he watched the six people climb into the cab of the truck followed by the driver.'

Marçel chuckled. 'I bet that got him thinking!'

'It's not funny, Marçel. He returned to his car, just in time to follow the departing truck. The truck eventually turned into the gates of what appeared to be a large warehouse. He drove a little way down the road and again waited.'

Gerda continued; it was her German upbringing that enabled her to be so precise in the way she recounted Pete's words, plus her ability to have total recall of past events.

'Much later, just as it was beginning to get light, the truck came out through the gates. Keeping well behind, he was able to follow it through Colmar, Dijon and all the way down through France, Spain and Portugal. Each night when the truck pulled into one of safe depots, he went off to refuel, get himself food and return to a spot where he could keep watch. He was able to snatch several hours sleep before the truck reappeared at daybreak. Halfway down the coast of Portugal, the journey ended at a large riverside castle, surrounded by a very extensive winery.'

Gerda paused for a few minutes to collect her thoughts, then she continued, 'For two days he waited out of sight close to the castle and eventually watched them all board a motor launch, which they kept moored at a jetty, just the behind the castle walls. They set off from the castle crossing the waterway and headed out to the open sea. The launch returned several hours later, but with only two people on board the launch. The next morning he drove to Porto and talked to the port authorities and was told that no large cargo ships had passed up that part of the coast during the night. While still in Porto, he wrote a full report of his findings and posted it off to his masters in Brazil. He knew his mission had been completed and decided to return to Germany and then back to South America.'

Marçel was shocked. They had been followed all the way from the River Rhine to the castle in Portugal and neither he nor Pete had been aware of it.

'Gerda, I can't believe that someone could shadow us all the way from the Rhine, to the castle and not be seen by us. The man must be a genius; he has certainly outwitted Pete and me.'

'That is more or less the gist of his statement. Pete was told that when the man arrived at the French border, on his way into Spain, an astute immigration official at the French border noticed a likeness to a photo of one of the many people on the United Nations' "Wanted" list. On his return to France, the immigration official again spotted him and the man was put under arrest. When eventually questioned by United Nation officials the whole story was revealed. Shortly after this, the agent became one more unfortunate person to join the many prison deaths, having taken his own life. I suppose something like this was bound to happen, Marçel. I wonder just when this agent sent his report to the Nazi bastards in South America and whether these people in South America have actually started to do something about us?'

They could both see the enormous repercussions if the press were to get hold of this information regarding Operation Deserting Rats. Marçel and Gerda realised that all hell would then break loose. Obviously, the British Secret Service, the Allies and the UN would have to immediately suppress this embarrassing information and wipe out all traces of the Deserting Rats operation.

'Pete was told to close down the winery and get rid of any of the staff that might have been involved in our operation, Marçel. If he had any doubts about anyone involved, Stephen said that they might have to be eliminated. Pete informed Stephen that the last batch of clients had already left Germany, and they were now on their way to Portugal. He was not sure where they were at present. He said he was quite prepared to close down our activities regarding the people smuggling, but saw no reason to close the winery or to kill any of the staff or associates.

'He said there were only five people involved who had any knowledge of the operation—Marçel, Gerda, José the wine master, his wife Maria the housekeeper and himself. They were all completely trustworthy. To close down the winery would in itself raise suspicion, but he did think it might be a good idea for the Royal Navy to come and remove their motor launch, after we completed this last death run. Pete said that as he left the office, the last words he heard were: "Get rid of it all, Pete, or we will have to do it for you."

Marçel and Gerda realised Pete must have been convinced that the Department had sent men over to burn down the French depot, and they would now be heading for Portugal to do the same thing. They may also have had instructions to kill all three of them, as well as wiping out all trace of the operation.

Tears started to run down Gerda's face. 'Pete and I just stood there staring at the burnt-out buildings. After a while, Pete told me to take the car and try my best to catch up with you before you reached the castle. He said I must warn you to park the truck somewhere safe, and check out the situation at the winery before taking the truck into the castle. In his state of mind, I just couldn't tell Pete of the added problem of Helga and just hoped to catch you at the Valladolid base. Pete said he would drive to Paris and then fly down to Porto the same day to warn the manager and his wife. He said he would pay them a large bonus, to enable them to go down to southern Portugal where they could retire in a quiet village. There they would be safe and financially secure for the rest of their lives.'

'What the hell is going on, Gerda? You and Pete are two of Stephen's top operators. They are putting Pete in an impossible situation. I know he would never want to desert his friends but I also know he would not hesitate to kill, if he thought it necessary to protect any damage to his country's reputation.'

Marçel leaned back in his seat, angry and confused. He was trying to make sense out of the situation.

Everything they had achieved in the last three years appeared to be falling apart. Peter Lonsdale, his best friend, was the finest and strongest person he was ever likely to meet. He was also the one person in the Department who could be relied upon to do any of the dirty work. Pete was Stephen's hit man and was known to have rid the Department of several of their most unreliable agents.

Pete had dedicated his life to serving his country. Marçel remembered how Pierre, Gerda's husband, had brought Pete to him when he was hiding on an old damaged barge on the River Rance in Brittany. Marçel had been sixteen at the time and had already killed three Germans. They worked together for several months before Pete had him flown back to England, to take a year's intensive training. Marçel had returned to France a very efficient killing machine.

He thought about the time they had worked together in Brittany, right up to the liberation of France. They had killed together, often taking enormous risks. They had worked with the French Resistance, when the RAF landed secretly at night to pick up shot-down Allied airmen. They had been able to do extensive damage to the German forces in Brittany, by blowing up bridges and passing useful information to London, prior to the invasion of France by the Allied forces. For the last three years, under instructions from London, they had been quietly executing a number of war criminals that would otherwise have been allowed to escape punishment.

'We were lucky you were following us down to Portugal. Thank goodness you found us, Gerda. I'm quite sure we will be safe on this route, but I doubt if we can get to the winery before the clean-up men arrive.'

Gerda skidded around a sharp bend in the road.

'Perhaps now that the clients, except for Helga, are dead we should go straight on to Lisbon and find a ship to take us somewhere overseas, Marçel. It would seem that we are no longer needed by the Department, and in fact they want to be rid of us.'

'That's quite ridiculous and definitely not an option, Gerda. Tell me about Helga, while she's asleep. Why are you helping her?'

'Did Helga give you my note?'

'She swallowed it but told me she had memorised the telephone number. She said it would give her a little insurance.'

'I can understand that. When she realised you were about to kill her, she must have been very frightened, Marçel. We had finally run out of clients and I knew this was to be our last operation. I decided to do something about Helga. I had known about her for quite some time, and how she had been forced to work in a concentration camp. I also knew that she had, under impossible conditions, done her best to help the children under her care who were undergoing unspeakable cruelty. I do believe, Marçel, her courage and dedication helped to save quite a few lives, and she must have given a lot of comfort to some of those poor dying children. It was my last chance to help her escape from what would be a long jail sentence in Germany. I knew if I could get her down to our Portuguese base, I would be able to save her from the final death run in the motor launch. That's why I gave her the telephone number for you to ring. It was a French friend of mine who was to tell you not to take the girl who was travelling with you to Portugal out in your boat. I hoped we could then get her to Lisbon and find a ship that would take her to South Africa or Australia.'

Helga was now awake and listening to the conversation. She leaned forward. 'What is going on? Is something wrong?'

Marçel didn't want to alarm Helga right now. 'It seems we have run into a spot of bother. We are having a change of plan, but don't worry; we will still do our best to get you to a safe country overseas. You will be able to start a completely new life, and perhaps one day you might even raise a family of your own. In the meantime, you'll have to trust us. Just stay calm, Helga, and do exactly what you are told.'

'I'm quite sure Gerda will look after me although I'm not so sure about you, Marçel, but I don't have any choice now, do I?'

Marçel touched Gerda's arm. 'Gerda, it is now imperative we meet up with Pete. We have to find out exactly what the situation is at the castle and then we will have to decide what to do.'

Their base, an old converted castle on the Portuguese coast, south of the old city of Porto, stood in the centre of its superb vineyard.

Pete and Marçel had bought this property, under instructions and with a substantial loan, from the Department in London. They were to operate this winery as an entirely separate business, owned and operated by Pete and Marçel, but with no connections to the covert government department they served.

The whole idea was to establish a cover for Operation Deserting Rats. Gerda had been appointed as the go-between with the Allied intelligence section that was supplying the clients, while Pete and Marçel were to dispose of these so-called clients.

Gerda met the clients at a starting point on the German side of the Rhine River and they were brought by launch across the river, close to the base in northern France. From there, they were transported to the castle in Portugal before finally disposing of them at sea.

In return for this, the castle and winery were to remain the property of Pete and Marçel, after paying back the loan for the purchase of the castle.

The converted motor launch, which was used for the final death runs, was on loan from the Royal Navy and was to be returned when the operation finally ended.

They were allowed to keep the gold and other valuables carried by these evil clients—this was the reward for services rendered and in lieu of any form of payment, which might one day compromise the Department.

When they took over the castle, the first thing they did was to re-employ the previous wine master; he had been made redundant three years earlier when the original owners had gone bankrupt. His wife, an absolute treasure, became the housekeeper for the extensive living area. This was to be a guest house for the clients and a home for Pete and Marçel.

The old castle was in excellent condition. The carved stone archway with the heavy studded doors which were still in use, led through to the paved courtyard. The high castle walls, with the battlements and the four corner towers would have made this a very safe retreat in days gone by.

The living area consisted of a fine old granite building, which stood at the far end of the large courtyard inside the castle walls. Several wide stone steps led up to the arched granite doorway and into the large hall with its paved stone floor and high ceiling.

Doors led off into the several large, if a little austere, living rooms on the left side of the hall, the dining room and beyond the kitchens. On the right, there was a spacious lounge, with a small door leading on into the estate office.

A fine carved wooden staircase led to the five bedrooms and four bathrooms. A passageway, behind the bedrooms, ran the full length of the house with a small staircase at one end, which led down to the kitchen.

Outside in the courtyard there were rooms in the castle walls, which were used as wine storage areas for the winery. A small door in the wall of the castle led out to a large stone jetty and the river.

The tree-lined river flowed alongside the castle and into the large broad-water, which stretched for miles in all directions. Several other small rivers flowed into these extensive marshlands that bordered the broad-water; a few small islands were dotted between the castle and the seaway that finally led out to the Atlantic Ocean.

Pete and Marçel had brought most of the old vines back into production and had planted hundreds of new vines in the last three years, giving them one of the most productive and successful vineries in this part of Portugal.

When they reached Medina, Marçel took over the driving from Gerda and two hours later, they arrived at Benavente. Marçel left the two women at the local hotel and went to find a garage that was still open. He filled up the car with fuel and bought an extra five-gallon can of petrol, so they could drive through the night.

Back at the hotel, Marçel noticed that Gerda and Helga seemed to be getting on extremely well together. They were both about the same age; they must have spent quite some time 'tidying up' and were now looking gorgeous.

Gerda was a fine-looking German blond—tall and elegant with a lovely slender figure. Her well-shaped face, smallish slightly turned-up nose and kind blue eyes always delighted Marçel. Gerda was aware of her good looks and her slim figure. She had dreamed of becoming a top model, but then she had met Pierre and that had changed her life forever.

In the last years of the war, devastated by Pierre's murder and after receiving intensive training from Stephen, Gerda had returned to Paris and had used all her looks and charms to seduce and gain valuable information from senior German officers; this information was then passed back to Stephen in London.

In complete contrast, Helga had black slightly-greying hair, dark brown eyes and the dark skin of a gypsy girl, which she had inherited from her father. Her very slim figure with her wild gypsy look and irrepressible sense of humour made her a very attractive young woman. Gerda had helped Helga cover up the scars on her face with make-up. Marçel wondered how he could have killed a person like her just a few hours ago; he certainly would find it difficult to kill her now.

After an excellent meal and two bottles of the best local wine, they were quite prepared to face the long night drive. For a short while they were able to forget the problems that they would have to face the following day.

Gerda drove for the first three hours and Marçel sat back and kept her company. She was an excellent driver and seemed to enjoy driving on the hazardous roads.

They had been lovers and they still occasionally slept together.

The last few days before Paris was liberated, hunted down by both the *Gestapo* and the French Resistance, who considered her a collaborator, Gerda had shared Marçel's small attic hideaway; those had been tense but extremely passionate days.

When Gerda married the French lawyer, Pierre Dubois, just a few months before the start of the Second World War, they had lived in a lovely old house in a small Brittany village in northern France. When France was occupied in 1940, her husband Pierre became involved with the French Resistance and Gerda, who hated the Nazi regime, had helped him to establish communications with London.

In 1943, Gerda's brother *Oberleutenant* Grossman, stationed in the occupied Channel Islands, was on the run. *Gestapo* agents were about to interrogate him in view of his brother-in-law's connections with people they suspected of being in the French Resistance movement. *Oberleutenant* Grossman knew that as his loyalty was in doubt, he would be given the choice of shooting himself or facing execution. Grossman knew that to desert meant certain death; the French Resistance was out to kill any stray German officer they could find—*Oberleutenant* Grossman had nowhere to go.

In the Channel Islands, at the age of sixteen, having just come off the beach after a fishing trip, Marçel, whose name then was Robert Riley, was arrested and brutally raped by two drunken German guards. The rape, followed later by the beating he received in the Jersey prison, had changed him from a quiet schoolboy into a cold-blooded killer.

The two guards were executed without trial, but to save face, the *Wermacht* accused Robert of spying on the German gun emplacements that overlooked the beach; the arresting officer was *Oberleutenant* Grossman.

Robert, handcuffed to a guard, was taken from prison. They boarded a motor torpedo boat, which took them from Jersey to St Malo in France, and then a train from St Malo to Paris, where he was to be interrogated.

Because of the frequent strafing of the railway system in France by the

RAF at that time, they had to take a night train to Renne, and then they were to change trains for the journey on to Paris.

Robert and his father had made this train journey to Renne several times before the war. He knew that the railway line ran alongside the canal for several miles. There were also two bridges that criss-crossed the canal at that point.

Robert's mind went back to the rape and the beatings he had endured.

Although it had happened only two days ago, he was still traumatised by the experience ...

It occurred to him that perhaps he could turn the terrible degradation he had suffered to his advantage. A plan formed in his mind; a trip to the toilet. He would then entice the guard to release him from the handcuffs, somehow escape and jump from the train into the canal.

Robert decided that now was the time to make his escape.

Well before reaching the part of the railway track that bordered the Rance canal, Robert spent time flirting with the guard and allowed him to touch his private parts. Robert then persuaded the guard to take him to the toilet. The guard, believing that he was dealing with an over-sexed teenager, knelt down on the floor with his back to the toilet seat, fully expecting to have oral sex with Robert.

The German guard foolishly left his belt with his bayonet attached, on the toilet seat. The train crossed the first bridge. Carefully pulling the bayonet from its sheath, with all his strength Robert brought the bayonet down through the guard's neck, almost severing his head.

Robert had killed his first German.

Robert came out of the toilet; the slow-moving train was travelling alongside the canal and crossed the second bridge; time to jump. With no one in sight, he opened the door, jumped from the train and rolled down the bank into the canal.

Much later, having walked the rest of the night as far away from the railway line as he could, he passed through a village. A little way further on, he came to an isolated house. Robert decided to break in and steal some food.

It was while he was waiting for the morning to make his move, that he realised after all that had happened, he could never go back to face his family in Jersey. The rape, and then the murder of the German guard, now his hatred and desire to kill Germans had changed him forever. He was starting a new life in France and he realised that the first thing he had to do was to adopt a French name. He decided that from then on, he would be Marçel Beaumont.

Marçel watched the owners drive away in their car, and then thinking the house empty, he entered the house through the back door.

Oberleutenant Grossman was waiting for him.

By sheer chance, Marçel had chosen to break into Pierre and Gerda's house—Grossman had arrived a few hours before to warn his sister and her husband on their impending arrest, trying to persuade them to flee France and head for Spain.

Grossman talked to Marçel for some time, telling him about his situation and how, quite rightly, his French brother-in-law had refused to help him.

'A strange turn of events that you should come to my sister's house, Piglet. It was only two days ago that I arrested you in Jersey. I called you the Piglet—I expected the Piglet to be taken to Paris, tortured and then slaughtered. Instead, I find the Piglet is a killer on the run from the Gestapo, just like me.'

Sometime later, to Marçel's surprise, the Oberleutenant told him to go.

'Unfortunately it was my duty to arrest you for spying after I had ordered the execution of two of my men for raping you. For your own safety, you should try to join up with the French Resistance. You might then be able to return to England and your own people. You should never have been arrested. Go—Rauss!'

As Marçel was leaving the house he heard a shot. Curious, he went back.

Grossman had killed himself.

The next day Pierre, who by then had decided to stay on in France and work with the Resistance, found Marçel asleep in a bomb-damaged barge that he had found abandoned in a backwater of the river Rance; that was the start of Marçel's involvement with the Resistance Movement. The name Piglet was to be remembered by both the Gestapo and several members of the Resistance.

It was one year later when Marçel took Gerda to join up with Pierre and his Resistance group near Brest.

They found Pierre and several other Resistance men hanging from a tree. A disgruntled member of the Resistance had betrayed them; Pierre and his men had walked straight into a German trap.

Marçel spent the next night hiding in an empty water tank with Gerda, trying to comfort her.

—

'I was sweet seventeen the first time we made love, Gerda, and you were so experienced. I will always be grateful to you for teaching me how to give pleasure and satisfaction, making gentle and caring love. Since then we have always been good friends and from time to time when we have slept together, our lovemaking has always been tender and beautiful.'

'You used to wonder if I was making love to Pierre and not to you in those final passionate moments, but you were wrong, Marçel!'

Gerda kept up a steady speed on this road and they were now almost at Verin, and close to the Spanish border with Portugal. Gerda pulled into the side of the road. Because of their frequent trips to and from the winery, they both carried Portuguese passports; they also carried British passports but decided not to use them on this occasion.

Helga, unused to drinking wine, was sleeping soundly on the back seat. Gerda leaned over and gently removed Helga's newly acquired British passport, which Helga had concealed inside her blouse. The passport, though forged, was now her most prized possession.

Marçel took over the driving and drove quietly through Verin and on to the border post. It was almost midnight when they arrived at the border. A sleepy guard lifted the barrier and they drove straight through the Spanish side to the waiting Portuguese soldiers. One of the guards leaned in the window on Gerda's side and looked at the sleeping woman on the back seat. Marçel handed him the three passports and he disappeared into his office. He returned a few minutes later smiling—he had found the bank notes Marçel had put inside his passport. The guard handed back the three stamped passports and they were on their way.

They were heading south down a very rough and twisting road that ran through the centre of Portugal. Gerda gave Marçel another short break, driving along the twisting road to Vila Real. Marçel slept briefly and then took over; he was feeling refreshed and ready to cope with whatever lay ahead.

Shortly after crossing the Douro River, they turned off onto a minor road which eventually led to the castle turnoff.

It was just becoming light when they left the road to pass through the old stone archway; the entrance to the winery. Marçel switched off the lights and drove silently through the acres of vines until they came to the tractor sheds, which stood a little way back from the castle.

Marçel drove into one of the sheds.

'Gerda, I want you to stay here with Helga. Give me twenty minutes; if I am not back by then get the hell out of here and drive south to Lisbon.'

'You'll be back—you won't be able to keep away from two young attractive women.' Gerda squeezed his hand.

He removed his revolver from the glove compartment and walked towards the main entrance of the castle. The heavy studded doors were open. He slipped into the courtyard. It was deadly quiet. Marçel waited a minute and crossed the courtyard to the front of the house. The lights were on and the front door wide open. He climbed the steps, went through the front door into the hall. He turned right, opened the lounge door and walked in.

Marçel could smell the carnage before he saw it. There were two bodies lying on the floor. His dear old friend the wine master and his kind lovable wife were stretched out in front of the fireplace lying in pools of blood—they had fallen still clutching each other—they must have died in each other's arms facing their executioner.

He moved over to the third person sprawled across the back of an armchair. He was still clutching his revolver, his body was riddled with machine-gun bullets—Marçel slowly lifted his head. It was Pete.

He stood back frozen to the spot. For the third time in his life, Marçel was overcome with a cold black rage. He had not felt such anger since he had been raped. He heard a sound behind him, followed by a scream. Marçel swung around.

Gerda had walked into the room followed by Helga. For a moment they both stood there staring, shocked at what they saw.

'Stop! Don't come near and don't touch anything. Go straight back to the car and wait for me there. We are not only in danger from these assassins but now we will have the police to contend with.'

They backed out of the room having taken in the full horror of the scene and started back to the car.

'I'll join you in a few minutes—we must get away before the winery staff arrive; no one must know that we have been here.'

As soon as they had gone, Marçel slipped into the office, which was next to the lounge and unlocked the safe with his personal key. He found a briefcase by the desk and then removed several papers from the safe, which he stuffed into the briefcase. All the remaining paperwork was only relevant to the day-to-day running of the castle and winery. Marçel left all the Portuguese money that was in the safe, but took the 18,000 US dollars kept there for emergencies. Only Pete and Marçel knew about this cash reserve; he relocked the safe.

Marçel went back through the lounge. He took one last look at Pete and his other two dear old friends. There was nothing he could do for them; they had been dead for several hours. Looking at Pete's bullet-ridden body,

Marçel swore he would avenge his death. No matter how long it took he would track down Pete's killers. He closed the lounge door carefully, and walked across the courtyard to the small door that led out to the jetty.

The door was unlocked and the jetty was deserted. The bastards had taken the motor launch. There were several empty fuel drums on the jetty. Whoever had taken the launch must have filled up the launch's fuel tanks with the intention of travelling a long way—possibly Gibraltar.

Was it possible that the Department had arranged for the Royal Navy to assassinate Pete and the caretakers when they came to collect the launch? The launch would now be on its way, with the Royal Navy assassinators returning it to the base in Gibraltar.

That he could not believe. It must have been the South American mob—but why take the launch?

Marçel returned to the courtyard, taking care to leave everything undisturbed and hurried back to the car. He realised that the workers would soon arrive; they would find the bodies and immediately call the police. If he and the girls were seen leaving the winery by anyone, they would certainly become the prime suspects, the last thing he needed.

The girls were sitting in the back of the car; this time it was Helga's turn to comfort Gerda. Marçel knew Gerda would cry for a long time. He started the car and drove quickly back to the winery entrance and out onto the main road. They had been lucky. They had got clear of the winery before any of the staff had arrived for work.

No one spoke as they drove to Aveiro. The three of them, still in shock, were finding it hard to believe what they had just seen. Marçel had made very few friends since he had left Jersey in 1943, and now he and Gerda had just lost their three best friends.

Marçel decided that the best thing they could do now was to drive down to Lisbon, and hopefully smuggle the girls onto a ship out of Portugal to somewhere safe overseas. They had gold, so it should not be too difficult to find a ship's officer who would be pleased to take on the two stowaways.

But first Marçel needed to talk to their bank manager, Alfonso De Freitas, to find out if Pete had already spoken to him regarding their intention to close down the winery, and to sell the castle and their wine business. He headed for Aveiro to wait for the bank to open.

He would explain to Alfonso that he had just arrived from France and was calling in on him on his way to the castle.

Chapter 4

It was early morning when they drove into the delightful town of Aveiro. Its canals, bridges and coloured fishing boats presented a view such as seen in Holland. Gerda and Helga decided to explore the town, waiting for the shops to open. Marçel thought it would be safe at this time of the morning as neither of them were known in Aveiro.

The girls wanted to buy some more suitable clothes so that they would be less conspicuous amongst the locals; Marçel gave Gerda a handful of notes. 'Try to find a local camping shop and buy a small tent and all the necessary camping gear as we are now on the run. It will no longer be safe for us to stay in hotels.'

As he sat outside the bank, Marçel went over all the events that had taken place since the accident with the truck.

He and Helga had survived an appalling accident. Then he'd discovered she was someone they were going to help, instead of one of their usual clients. They had luckily met up with Gerda, and travelled safely to the castle, only to find the murdered bodies of their three best friends. Now they were on the run from either their own people, or the thugs from a Nazi organisation in South America.

Marçel started to shake with anger but it soon passed, leaving him feeling cold and emotionless—'The Piglet' was in his most dangerous frame of mind.

Marçel's thoughts went back to the winery and the three dead bodies lying in the lounge. It was well after dawn when they had left the winery, so the workers should now have arrived to start their day's work. Perhaps Pete had already closed down the winery? He would have dismissed all the staff, and last night he was possibly in the process of paying off the manager and his wife.

He thought about the position of the bodies. Pete must have been taken completely by surprise, which meant the killers were allowed into the room.

So Pete must have known who his murderers were, but had no idea they were all about to be killed.

The launch had been taken—Pete would never have expected naval officers to be assassins; neither would he. At his recent meeting in London, Pete had suggested that the Royal Navy should come and collect the motor launch, so he would not have been surprised to see the arrival of Royal Navy personnel.

He had to get back to the castle. There might be some evidence there which could help him discover who the killers really were. He must also contact José's brother Marco, and warn him that his life might be in danger.

Marco Perestrello, a local fisherman, had helped Marçel on several occasions in the past. He had shown him how to navigate the tricky local waterways and had also taken them to some of the best fishing spots in the area. José had made up a story for Marco, telling him that they were involved in helping a few refugees to get away to Brazil, and that the refugees paid them in gold. Marco was quite unaware of their real activities; José had later given Marco a small amount of gold, swearing him to secrecy.

Marçel would have to warn Marco to stay away from the winery for a while; hopefully London was not aware of his existence and would not come after him. The rest of the winery staff would naturally assume that the groups of visitors to the castle were all part of a wine tasting tour.

The bank was opening. Marçel crossed the road, walked up the steps and entered the impressive old bank with its high ceilings, carved timbers and highly-polished counters and asked to see the manager.

Two minutes later a side door opened. 'Good to see you again, Marçel.' Alfonso De Freitas shook his hand vigorously. 'It's been a long time, my friend, come on in.'

Alfonso had negotiated the purchases of the winery for Pete and Marçel; now four years later he had been promoted and was the manager of their bank in Aveiro.

Alfonso looked diminutive behind his enormous carved desk. He was grinning like a satisfied cat. Life had been good to him and Marçel and Pete had always been two of his best customers. 'I've been expecting you, Marçel, after Pete came to see me the other day. The papers are all here and ready for you to sign.'

Marçel concealed his surprise and nodded.

'I take it that you agree to the sale of the castle and the winery?' Marçel nodded again and let Alfonso continue.

'You boys have been very fortunate. As you know I was approached a few months ago by one of the largest wine producers in the district. For some time now their company has been looking for another winery in order to expand their business; they have always been keen to acquire your winery, but until now you've not been interested in selling your rapidly expanding business.

'They were delighted when I was able to tell them that you had decided to part with your winery. I can tell you that you have got yourselves an extremely good price for the business. All the hard work and the money that you invested have now borne fruit. Excuse the pun!'

Marçel glanced down at the contract and stifled a gasp, finding it hard to believe that their winery could be worth so much in the short time since they had bought it.

'Just sign next to Pete's signature and that will complete the deal. The money has already been transferred to your joint account in Geneva. I understand it is later to be transferred to your trust account in Switzerland.'

Alfonso produced more papers for Marçel to sign. 'This, sadly, closes all your accounts with our bank, Marçel, the remaining balance will now be transferred to your Swiss account.'

'I must thank you, Alfonso, for all you have done for us since we came to see you in 1944. Do you have a large envelope? I wonder if you could post these documents for me. It's most urgent they catch the first post.'

Alfonso passed him a thick registered envelope, which Marçel addressed to their Geneva bank. He slipped in the documents that he had taken from the castle safe. Alfonso handed him all the relevant documents regarding the sale of the castle, which he also put into the envelope. He then carefully sealed it before handing it back.

The documents contained a copy of a will that Pete and Marçel had drawn up some time ago; the original was already in their Geneva bank. Pete had no living relatives and Marçel had cut himself off from all his family in Jersey.

Pete and Marçel had decided to put all their assets into a trust account in Switzerland. In the event of one of them dying, the trust would pass to whichever one survived. In the event that they both passed on, the interest from the trust would be donated to several named world-aid agencies. They had also opened a separate Swiss account; this contained a large sum of money for Gerda, which would make her financially independent in the event that they ever ran into serious problems in the future.

Alfonso offered Marçel a glass of sherry, which he declined, thanking him again for all his help.

'Alfonso, when are the new owners taking over?'

'In three weeks' time, Marçel. You are free to stay in the castle till then; this will give you plenty of time to move your personal possessions out. They are taking over the estate exactly as it is, so all the winery equipment and the house furnishings are to stay. This will enable the new manager and his family to move straight in.'

'All the staff, except for José and Maria, whom Pete said would be retiring, will be re-employed when the new owners take over. I expect they will enjoy having a good holiday in the meantime. Good luck, Marçel. We shall miss you. You and Pete have been good customers and you have also been very generous to the local community.'

'Alfonso, I'm sorry this has all happened so quickly. I had an urgent call from Pete to come down and sign the documents, so I have not yet been to the castle to discuss the wind-up of the business with him.' They shook hands; Marçel was sorry to say goodbye, and to have to lie to such a good old friend.

Marçel wondered what Alfonso would think when the police discovered the three dead bodies at the castle; the letter would be well on its way to Switzerland by then.

It was a warm sunny day outside. Gerda was waiting by the car, with a concerned look on her face. She was alone.

'Where the hell is Helga? We can't hang around here.' Gerda looked confused, and pointed in the direction of the park.

'How did you manage to lose her?'

She threw her parcels in the back of the car. 'Helga seemed to be in a daze. We were walking in the park somewhere near the hospital. I went to the park toilet briefly, and when I came out, she had disappeared.'

'She can't be too far away; she must have wandered into a shop close by. Hospital, did you say? Hmm, I think I might know where to find her; jump in the car.'

They drove to the hospital just a few streets away, parked the car, and ran up the steps into the hospital reception area, following the sign to the children's ward.

Marçel found Helga sitting on a bed, next to a rather puzzled-looking boy who was about seven or eight years old. She had her arms around him, and was crying. Helga had seen the hospital and her mind was cast back to the concentration camp; she became confused and for a few terrifying minutes—she was back there.

At that moment, a nurse joined them at the entrance to the ward. Marçel told both ladies to wait outside for a minute, moved to the bed and sat next to Helga.

'What a lovely little boy, Helga. What is his name?' Helga told him his name was Phillip; he had fallen over and hurt his head but was feeling better now.

Helga whispered to Marçel, tears running down her face, 'So what will happen to this child now? Will he be given more operations until he eventually dies?'

Marçel put his arms around both of them and spoke quietly to Helga, 'There are no more operations now, Helga. That part of your life is all over. Phillip will be going home very soon to his parents.'

In the meantime, Gerda explained to the nurse that Helga had lost her children in the war and introduced herself and Marçel as Helga's friends, who were helping her to get over her loss. The nurse came across and took Helga's hands in hers.

'Phillip is better now, dear. His mother and father are coming to fetch him this morning. Phillip comes from a very happy and loving home.' Helga kissed Phillip's forehead, after which Marçel put his arm around Helga and led her out of the hospital.

The nurse followed them to the top of the steps. She smiled, 'I can tell that woman has suffered; she is lucky to have such good friends. Take good care of her.'

Walking back to the car with his arm still around Helga, Marçel realised that he was feeling a deep sympathy towards her, and even a little warmth. Strange to think that only a few hours before, he had been quite prepared to kill her. Maybe it was *he* and not Helga, who needed some help.

Marçel decided they must find a safe place somewhere in the area to camp for the night. They went to the camping store to pick up the tent and other essentials, and then found a shop where they were able to stock up on food and wine. Marçel raised an eyebrow when he saw they had bought the last two sleeping bags in the shop, one single and one double.

'Who has the single, Gerda? I promise I won't snore.'

'You can snore as much as you like, Marçel, because you won't even be in the tent, smarty!'

During the past three years, Marçel had been able to spend a lot of time exploring the local waterways. He had discovered the many creeks and small islands that surrounded the inland waterway. The waters abounded in fish, and supported the local fishing industry. He knew that one day this would become a very popular holiday area, and the castle was bound to profit from this.

Marçel remembered a perfectly secluded spot that he and Pete had discovered and where he felt sure no one ever visited. They could make their camp there, knowing that they were safely hidden from the outside world. Only the occasional fisherman passed that way. To get to this spot they had to take the road that passed the winery entrance and encircled the entire waterway.

'Marçel, we must get rid of the car. Our enemies, whoever they are, will be looking for it,' Gerda prompted.

'You're right. First we must set up camp and then we'll go to Porto.'

Five miles past the winery they turned off onto a rough dirt road that circled the extensive inland waterway and eventually arrived at the spit of land that divided the broad-water from the ocean. On one side were the Atlantic Ocean breakers and on the other, tranquil waters.

Several miles down this dirt road, Marçel turned off onto a disused and overgrown track. The high bushes parted as he drove down the sandy track, winding through the trees and bushes, until eventually it opened out onto a grassy strip of land that surrounded a small lagoon. A sandy beach ran down to the crystal-clear water of the lagoon. An old disused fisherman's hut close to the water's edge would be their new home for the time being.

On the far side, trees and bushes grew right down to the water's edge. Overhanging branches and a bend in the channel concealed a small entrance to the lagoon from the main inland waterway.

The two girls were delighted.

To Marçel's surprise and completely without any sign of embarrassment, they stripped off and ran into the clear water. Marçel was entranced—this was something new to him, two naked girls being not exactly what he was used to.

'Come on, Marçel, what are you waiting for?' Gerda was waving for him to join them. Marçel didn't need further persuading; he stripped off and ran into the water, keeping a discreet distance between the girls and himself.

Watching the two women playing in the water, he realised they were still girls at heart and despite the traumatic events they were experiencing, were able to break free for a short while and behave like normal young women. He decided that from now on he would treat them as such.

There was an old fireplace in the hut. Later they had a good fire going using some of the driftwood scattered around the lagoon, on which Helga cooked them bacon and eggs. They sat around the rickety old table, drinking a bottle of wine and eventually discussing their sleeping arrangements.

'I will sleep in the hut as it's pretty draughty and probably not waterproof. You girls can sleep in the tent.'

'No way, Marçel, don't be such a spoilsport! Anyway it will be much safer if you sleep in the tent with us,' Gerda insisted.

'You can keep us warm, Marçel, and you never know your luck!' Helga was laughing, both girls insisting that they all sleep in the tent. Marçel, though surprised, was certainly not going to argue with that.

Marçel's thoughts again turned to Helga. He was coming to realise how this girl had managed to survive the last three years. Helga had guts and an irrepressible sense of humour.

Porto, the second largest town in Portugal, was only twenty-five miles up the coast. Marçel said he'd go to a garage where he knew he would pick up a good second-hand car. 'My friend Fernandez is a surprisingly honest car dealer, and anyway the Renault needs updating. To be on the safe side, I won't trade in the Renault, but we'll bring it back here and conceal it in the bushes. A second car might come in handy.'

Helga agreed. 'I'll be quite happy to stay at the camp and enjoy the warm sunshine while you and Gerda go into Porto.'

'Okay, Helga, come and help me find a place to hide the gold until we decide what we are going to do next.' Marçel was still not sure how Helga felt about the gold, and in the interests of being open with her, he thought it best if she knew exactly where it was hidden.

They found a suitable spot and concealed the case under some large rocks.

Helga took his hand. 'This is not my gold, Marçel. Who needs gold when you have friends like you and Gerda?' She put her arms around him and gently kissed him.

Marçel had to use all his strength of mind to walk her back to the car. He could not believe the change in this girl in just two days. The wild bird had been released from her cage. The freedom and the kindness and understanding she had received had, for the moment, transformed her back into the happy young girl from Warsaw, though he knew it would take a long time for Helga to get over the terrible events of the past.

This was certainly not the time to get emotionally involved with her.

'We won't be too long. Just keep your eyes open. If you see or hear anyone, keep out of sight until we get back. I'm pretty sure no one ever comes this way.'

Gerda and Marçel drove to Porto, deciding to park the Renault in a side street well out of sight of the garage. They walked back to meet Marçel's friend, Fernandez, the garage owner. Fernandez always kept a good selection of cars.

Marçel chose a post-war Peugeot, a large dark blue saloon with plenty of luggage space. Fernandez was delighted when he paid him in US dollars and he gave Marçel a generous discount on the deal.

They drove the almost-new car back to the parked Renault.

'Gerda, you take the Peugeot. Go and buy some more provisions on your way back, especially wine and a bottle of the local port. I'm heading for the castle.'

'That's not a good idea, Marçel. If you have to go back, why not wait until it gets dark?'

'Don't worry, I'll park well away from the castle and the car will be out of sight. I can slip into the castle by the jetty door and I'll check to see if the police have arrived.' He knew Gerda was right but he had to find out who the murderers were.

'I will probably be late back, but if I am not with you by morning, pack up and drive down to Lisbon.'

Marçel leaned out of the Renault's window and squeezed Gerda's hand. 'Use some of the gold to find a ship to take you and Helga to South Africa or some other safe country.'

Gerda bent down and kissed him as he started to move away.

'Do you know your way back to the lagoon?'

'Easy, Marçel, I'll conceal the car amongst the bushes when I get back, but just make sure that you come back. You might even get lucky and share the double sleeping bag with me!' she yelled.

Marçel drove back to the winery, through the archway and then turned sharp right, taking the track that followed the riverbank. He came to a clump of trees on the side of the river and parked the car in amongst some high bushes, well out of sight from the track. He followed the footpath to the stone jetty at the back of the castle. In days gone by, this had probably been the main access to the castle. Marçel wondered if in earlier times many pirates and smugglers had used this castle as a base for their activities. They might even have set sail from here to explore the coasts of Africa and South America, bringing back stolen gold, slaves and treasures from the ancient civilisations of America.

Marco's fishing boat was tied to the jetty; the door into the castle was open. Marçel cautiously walked through. The courtyard was still and hot in the afternoon sun. He crossed the yard, entered the front door and peered into the lounge.

Marco was standing in the lounge, staring at the three bodies. He turned; his face white and puzzled. 'Marçel—who—who could have done this?'

Marçel was unable to answer. He walked across the room, removed a flattened bullet from a crack in the stone wall and picked up a spent shell case from the floor. While undergoing special training in England, prior to his return to occupied France, Marçel had spent part of his time learning to handle all types of small arms that were then in use.

He stepped past the two bodies on the floor to join Marco. 'I found the three bodies like this when I arrived here early this morning, Marco. This is a Russian bullet and was fired from a Russian hand gun.'

Marçel stood over Pete's crumpled body, still unable to believe that a man of his experience could have been taken by surprise by these assassins. 'I realised that the police would have to be called and the situation could become very messy.'

He continued, 'As the sole remaining partner in the business, I would become the prime suspect. I had two women with me and they had to be kept out of this affair. I decided the best thing to do was to take the two women away and just wait for the winery staff to alert the police when they arrived for work.'

He moved over to where the gunmen would have been when they shot Pete. 'When the assassins entered the room they would have been standing behind these armchairs, and Pete would not have been able to see the Russian hand guns that the men were carrying.'

'Did the women see this—this *carnage*, Marçel?'

'I'm afraid so, but they will remain silent on this matter. I decided not to touch anything. I took the two girls to Aveiro.'

'They must have been shocked at seeing this.'

'When I realised that the staff had been dismissed and the winery closed down, I came back to decide what to do next.'

Marco and Marçel embraced and for a full minute they stood with their arms around each other, silently sharing their grief.

'But what brought you here, Marco?'

'The motor launch; I was out fishing early this morning at the far end of the broad-water when I spotted the launch. It appeared to be abandoned and partly hidden amongst the tall reeds, so I went alongside and boarded the boat. There was no one on board.'

'You were extremely lucky that there was no one aboard.'

'There were bloodstains in the saloon and in the wheelhouse. Remains of food were on the saloon table, and I spotted a pile of clothes on the floor that might have been uniforms. I decided to come straight here to see what had happened.'

Both men were still in shock at losing their closest friends. They just stood there silently for a moment, lost for words.

Marçel noticed then just how much Marco had aged. His wrinkled old face reflected his anguish and tears welled in his eyes.

Marco's grief turned to anger. 'Who could have done such a thing, Marçel?'

A picture was forming in Marçel's mind. The killers had used Russian guns; he knew then that these were not their own men from London. There must be a Russian connection somewhere.

If it were the Nazi organisation in South America seeking revenge, they would also know about the gold and would be seeking to retrieve it. It was possible that they had connections with an East German gang who would be only too happy to supply them with weapons for a share of the gold.

Marçel concluded that at some point Pete must have spotted the Russian guns and realised that the men who had come into the house, dressed as Royal Navy officers, were in fact assassins.

They must have killed him when he drew out his gun and wounded one of them—that would account for the blood on board the launch. But where had they got the Royal Navy uniforms?

Afterwards, the men must have questioned the old couple before killing them in cold blood. Now they would be out somewhere hoping to intercept the truck. No doubt they would be looking for him and Gerda. He realised that they intended to kill them all and take the gold.

Marçel didn't want to tell Marco about the Nazi connection. The less he knew, the better, as he was sure that at some stage he would be interviewed by the police.

'Marco, I feel sure that this was a professional gang from northern Europe. I think they came down here looking for the gold, which they believed we were keeping in the castle. I can tell you now, any gold we might have collected from the refugees, is now safely deposited in a Swiss bank.'

'So why aren't we calling the police?'

'If the police come here and find the bodies, we could all end up in deep trouble. We might even be accused of killing José, Maria and Pete.'

Marçel wandered towards the front door and stood staring at Pete's body lying across the chair. He wondered what Pete would do if he were in his position. Then he realised what he had to do.

He joined Marco who was sitting on the top step just outside the front door, his head bowed. Marco turned to Marçel as he sat down beside him on the steps.

'Marçel, I would like to have given José and Maria a decent funeral and have buried them in the local cemetery, but I realise we can't do that. We have to conceal their bodies somewhere, as you said. If the police find them, we will all be in big trouble—this country is in the hands of President Salazar, and his fascist secret police have no mercy on the Portuguese people.'

Marçel put his hand on Marco's shoulder. 'I think I have a plan that will make it look like an accident; no one will ever know what really happened. But first we must bring back the motor launch.'

It was late afternoon by the time they set off in Marco's fishing boat. Half an hour later, Marçel spotted the launch tucked in amongst the reeds. They drew silently alongside it. Clutching his revolver, Marçel climbed aboard and slipped inside the wheelhouse. He carefully looked into all the cabins. All was quiet; there was no sign of life. Stepping down into the main saloon, he noticed a pile of clothes lying on the floor and recognised the blood-stained uniforms of a petty officer and a sub-lieutenant.

He returned to the wheelhouse and pressed the starter buttons. The engines immediately came to life.

They tied a rope from Marco's boat to the stern of the launch, and with both engines at full throttle Marçel was able to reverse the launch out from the mud and the tall reeds. He untied the tow-rope and followed Marco's fishing boat back to the castle jetty.

Marçel decided the assassins must have gone off to look for the truck, which they knew would be arriving from France. He felt sure they would want to intercept it before it arrived, rather than just follow it into the castle.

When they got back, they carried the bodies down to the launch and carefully placed each one into a weighted body bag; Marçel thought it ironic they should end up in the same bags that they had been using to dispose of all the evil German war criminals. Marçel decided that he and Marco were going to give them a decent burial at sea and he hoped that maybe they would forgive them under the circumstances.

They spent the next hour in the house cleaning up the mess and gathering any of the bullets and shell cases that were lying around. Marco carefully scrubbed the blood from the stone floor while Marçel rubbed dirt into several bullet holes in the stone wall, close to where he had found Pete's body draped across the armchair. Hopefully, they had removed all traces of the slaughter that had taken place the previous night.

On the way out, Marçel picked up Maria's anorak. It was starting to become dark, but the channels were well marked with lit buoys and by now he had become used to taking the launch out at night.

It was a calm evening as the launch motored across the broad-water and out through the seaway. Marçel had all the cabin and navigation lights switched on—he particularly wanted to be noticed heading out to sea. Anyone seeing the launch would conclude that the people from the castle were out on one of their night fishing expeditions.

They were soon clear of the land and heading out into the Atlantic Ocean. Marco followed behind in his fishing boat, being careful to keep a good distance between the two boats.

They headed west until they were a good five miles from the shore. With the engines cut, the launch just drifted on the Atlantic swell. Marçel poured fuel from the spare cans kept in the engine room, all over the floors of the saloon, engine room and bridge. He lifted the bilge hatch cover and opened the valves of the two propane-gas cylinders that were in the galley and dropped them down into the bilges. As the gas was heavier than air, it soon spread the length of the hull, as he had hoped.

Marco came alongside, Marçel took his ropes and made fast. As soon as he jumped on board the launch, they carried the three body bags to the opposite side of the launch and gently dropped them overboard. Marco said a prayer, as they watched each of the bodies disappear out of sight.

'Get back to your boat, Marco, start the engine and be ready to move off the moment I jump onto it too; then move away from the launch as fast as you can.'

Marco started his engine and Marçel untied the ropes. He went back into the saloon and lit one of the cushions that he had soaked in fuel. The flames spread rapidly; he leaped back onto the deck and jumped down into Marco's boat, at the same time pushing it away from the launch.

As they sped away into the night, they could see the flames spreading throughout the boat—they were about a hundred yards away when there was a blinding flash and a roar as the gas in the bilges exploded. The launch seemed to lift out of the water before completely disintegrating as it fell back and disappeared into the boiling sea. Bits of debris fell into the water around them; they were lucky not to have been hit by any of the falling pieces of burning wood.

Marçel had watched the same thing happen to a French barge in 1944. On that occasion, the young girl he was so much in love with had been on board. The barge had been carrying German torpedoes to the U-boat pens in Lorient and had received a direct hit from an RAF bomb.

After a while the flames died down; it was strangely quiet as darkness returned. Marco had stopped his engine. Marçel, already feeling sick at the loss of his friends, now witnessed the destruction of this fine motor launch.

'Perhaps we should have left the bodies on the launch; they would have gone down in their burning ship like the Vikings of old. Marco, take your boat back to where the launch disappeared.'

They cruised slowly around the area. They picked up a hatch cover, some life jackets and several pieces of wood. As they passed through a patch of oil, Marçel threw Maria's anorak into it, hoping to provide a clue that José and Maria were both on the launch when it sank.

'Let's go back now.'

When they were about two miles from the seaway, Marçel dropped the hatch cover, the lifejackets and pieces of timber over the side. They would be found the next day. Someone would see the fire in the distance and a search would be made of the area. It would be concluded that the launch had blown up, either by a gas explosion on board, or perhaps destroyed by one of the old wartime mines that were occasionally found drifting down the coast.

They would assume that all on board had perished.

When they reached the seaway, Marco stopped the engine and allowed the strong tide to take them into the calm broad-water. Once clear of the seaway, he re-started the motor and headed across to the castle. They were two very sad people with nothing left to say to each other.

Marçel had a slight feeling of unease as they approached the castle. 'Go quietly up the river past the castle and drop me off on the bank near that clump of trees.'

Marco took his boat a little way past the castle jetty and then turned into the riverbank. He put his arms around Marçel's shoulders and embraced him. They stood there for a while, both silently mourning the loss of their dear friends.

'If you need me at all, Marçel, you know where to find me.'

Marçel jumped onto the bank and Marco's boat slipped quietly away into the darkness.

The car was still where he had left it concealed amongst the trees. He decided to go back to the castle. The door into the castle was still open. He moved silently up to it and peered into the courtyard; a black Mercedes was parked by the front door.

All the lights in the house and courtyard were on and a man, clutching a sub-machine gun was standing close to the front door. He could hear shouting and the occasional bang. It seemed they were searching the house.

There was nothing Marçel could do, so he decided to return to the camp. He walked back to where he had left the car and drove quietly away. Several miles down the road, he turned up a side lane and waited a few minutes to make quite sure that he was not being followed.

Marçel reasoned that there must have been at least three men in the house. His guess was that the Nazi thugs had been out on the road all day, hoping to find the truck before it reached the castle, but by evening they realised that they had somehow missed it, and the escaping Germans.

The Nazis would then have returned to the castle to find the bodies had been removed and the scene of the slaughter completely cleaned up. They must have surmised that the truck had returned, and that somehow they had found the launch, disposed of the truck, their fellow countrymen and the three bodies, and were now hiding on the launch somewhere on the broad-water.

They would be wondering if the police had been involved. Marçel decided that if he were in their position, he would head for Porto for the night and carry out a search of the broad-water for them in the morning. He felt sure they would never find their lagoon.

By the time Marçel got back to the camp, it was starting to get light. He had not slept for more than forty-eight hours.

Marçel recalled the two sleeping bags and wondered … he took off his clothes and put his head inside the tent.

The single sleeping bag was empty! He heard a couple of muffled grunts as he slipped into the empty sleeping bag, breathed in the exciting smell of the two young women in the double sleeping bag and wished he was there too. Then he promptly fell asleep.

Chapter 5

Marçel woke up with a start; something was moving inside his sleeping bag. He scrambled out of the bag giving it a good shake. Two small crabs dropped out of the sleeping bag and scurried away. There were sounds of giggling from outside.

He turned over to see two grinning faces peeping through the door of the tent. The girls burst into the tent, grabbed his naked body and with shrieks of laughter dragged him down to the lagoon. They had already been for a swim in the lagoon and were both unashamedly naked.

They spent a long time in the warmish water and then stretched out languidly in the morning sun. Later, the girls dressed and cooked a late but very welcome breakfast.

Marçel told them how he and Marco had disposed of the bodies and how they had given them a decent burial at sea.

Gerda started to cry. 'Pete would have appreciated that, Marçel. I know he was a professional killer, but he was so devoted to his country. He was also a bit of a romantic and would have wanted to be buried at sea. Oh God, we really are going to miss him.'

'Pete had certainly changed my life, Gerda, but now he's dead, like so many others that I have come into contact with in the last four years.' Marçel finished his coffee and stepped towards the door.

'Pete and I have killed a number of people and lost some good friends. We became very cynical about life and death and because of that we trained ourselves not to spend time grieving for our lost friends.'

For the moment Marçel just felt a deep anger; these were evil people. He would punish them and then move on to another chapter in his life, but he would never forget his friend and partner, Pete.

'Having searched the castle to no avail last night, the Nazis will probably be searching the broad-water for the launch. They will also be watching the castle. I should wait until dark but I will have to return to the castle just in case the police turn up.'

Gerda started to clear the table.

'Marçel, when they can't find the launch, they will return to the castle in case we have returned there. They must believe we have hidden the gold in or near the castle. They are obviously determined to retrieve it and eliminate us.'

Marçel had his own ideas—to avenge Pete's death was one of them. He decided it was time to go back to the castle and report the missing launch to the police. 'I'm going to inform the police that I came back from France yesterday morning and called at the bank at Aveiro. I then took two girls in my car well to the south of Aveiro where they intended to have a camping holiday somewhere on the coast.'

Marçel joined Gerda on the bench and continued, 'I'll tell them that it was evening when I finally got back to the castle. I realised that Pete, José and Maria had gone fishing in the launch. I knew that they quite often stayed out fishing overnight, but became worried when they had not returned by lunchtime today. This would tie in with my meeting yesterday with Alfonso at the bank and our visit to the hospital in Aveiro.'

Helga was staring out of the grimy window; she picked up a cloth and started cleaning it. 'I don't want to go back to the castle. You two cannot imagine what it is like for me, after all those months locked up in a prison cell. To be warm, to see a clear blue sky, and to feel the soft green grass and bathe in the crystal clear water of the lagoon. For me it is like stepping into heaven. I want to stay here forever.'

Marçel didn't want to alarm the girls; he knew they would be safe as long as they stayed at this secluded camping spot. 'I think we should rest here for the next few days; this is a safe and a very pleasant campsite. The Nazis will eventually decide that we have moved on and will either give up, or widen their search to France and Germany.'

Marçel stood up. 'Anyway a few days' rest here will do you both good. And I fancy being spoiled by two very attractive girls!'

Gerda gave him a wicked smile. 'I just wonder if you are up to it, boy!'

Marçel picked up Gerda, carried her across to the lagoon and dropped her in the clear water, Helga who had been following behind, jumped on his back and the three of them became involved in a frenzied water battle.

Later they lay on the grass at the edge of the lagoon soaking up the warm sunshine. Gerda realised that this outburst, though perhaps unwise, was their way of relieving the tensions of the last few days.

It was midday. Marçel felt it was time for him to return to the castle.

'I'm going back to the castle. It's better you stay here out of sight for a while. When the thugs move on we can decide what to do next. In the meantime I must make my presence known at the castle, especially during the day. I don't think the thugs will come to the castle in the daytime as they will be expecting the police to be around. I'll return here tonight.'

Early that morning Marçel had driven the Renault into some bushes, well out of sight of the track and their camp. He had no need for the Renault at present, but it would be there in case of an emergency.

Marçel took the Peugeot and drove back to the castle. Throwing caution to the winds, he drove through the open doors and into the courtyard. There were no other cars in the castle courtyard. He parked the car in front of the house and walked up the steps to the front door. The door was closed but unlocked.

As he entered the lounge, he noticed an empty wine bottle and a single glass standing on one of the small side tables.

The office door was open. He walked over to the open door and stopped. He was staring at a jacket hanging from the key in the open door of the safe.

Suddenly something cold and hard was pressing into the back of his neck. He froze, slowly lifting his hands above his head, and cursing himself for being so stupid.

'You made this too easy for me, Piglet, despite all that special training we gave you. I'm afraid you fell for one of the oldest tricks of the trade.'

'Stephen?' he whispered, and then he heard a chuckle behind him. The gun was no longer pressing into his neck. 'You can turn around now, my boy. You know you just can't afford to be so bloody careless, especially at a time like this, Marçel.'

Marçel turned to see Wing Commander Stephen Harvey. 'This is a surprise, sir. So having destroyed our French depot and stocks of wine in France, you've forced us to close down the winery and sell the castle, and now you want to eliminate us?'

'I suppose we should be flattered that you have come to personally carry out the executions.' Marçel knew the bloody man was laughing at him and Stephen had no intention of killing them.

'Did you know there are now only three of us left to kill, Stephen?'

Stephan sat down behind the manager's desk. Marçel took a chair. He had to remind himself that Stephen was not his school headmaster, but a powerful and ruthless head of an undercover government department, who would have no compunction in killing his own grandmother if he thought it would protect his 'Department'.

Stephen had directed their operations in northern France during the Second World War. At that time he had looked pretty old, but now, four years later, he looked positively ancient.

'Dear boy, I'm sorry that you misinterpreted our intentions. I suppose I went a bit over the top when Pete came to see me. I wanted you all to quietly disappear from the scene, but certainly not to die in the process. So tell me exactly what happened to Pete.'

'Pete is dead. You must have made him so angry that he lost his cool. I don't think Pete had been well for some time, and he could not have been thinking straight. He was expecting your people to turn up at the castle. The bloody fool had allowed his emotions to take over. For once in his life, Pete had dropped his guard and he died for it. Unfortunately, so did José and Maria.'

Stephen leaned across the desk and took Marçel's hand. Marçel could see that Pete's death had really shocked Stephen.

'Pete and I go back a long way, Marçel. I knew his mother long before Pete was born. Pete could have been my son. I watched his unhappy childhood, and later when his father died and Pete was a teenager, I sometimes accompanied them when they toured France and Germany. Pete joined my Department shortly after it was set up in 1941. He was fluent in both French and German. His mother had just been killed in a London air raid and he was still in shock when he came to me. At the end of twelve months' intensive training, I sent him over to occupied France. Like you, he was so filled with hate for the enemy that he became an expert assassinator.

'Pete disposed of several Gestapo undercover men, as well as some of our own traitors. He had just finished one such mission when Pierre brought you two together. Pete has always been my best agent and was a very good friend to us both. I am deeply saddened at his loss, Marçel. However we must move on—that's the name of this game. So now you and I have to finish cleaning up this mess.'

Stephen leaned back in his chair. 'I now have a lot of other important work for you, especially now that we have lost Pete. I would like you to take his place. Of course I will have to clear this with the minister when I get back to London.'

Marçel could not believe his ears. 'The king is dead, so God save the new king! Stephen you are a cold-blooded bastard.'

Stephen remained silent for a while. Marçel could see the pain he was feeling.

'You know as well as I, Marçel, that's the only way we can survive in this business. Now fill me in on what happened to the truck and the six clients.'

Marçel told Stephen about the accident and about Helga, the only survivor, the burning of the truck and all the evidence of their activity, and then the discovery that Gerda was helping Helga to escape overseas. He described their climb up on to the road and how they had luckily met up with Gerda.

'Gerda told me how she had arrived at the base in France to find it burned to the ground. Pete told her you had sent your people in to destroy the depot, and that we were now all in danger from the Department.'

'That was rubbish, Marçel. I admit we came over too strongly when we talked to Pete in London—he got the whole thing wrong. I had a feeling at the time that he was fighting some sort of problem. I shouldn't have been so heavy-handed. The danger was not from us, but from the Nazi organisation that was after you.'

'They must have gone into our French depot and set fire to it shortly after I left for Portugal with the last batch of clients. Well, Pete told Gerda to try to catch up with me before I reached Portugal. He told Gerda to warn me not to take the truck into the winery without first checking to make sure that only he, Pete, was at the castle. He told Gerda he was going to Paris and from there would fly down to Porto to warn José and Maria. He said he was going to close down the winery and wait for us to arrive with the truck. I realise now, he must have intended to take the clients straight out to sea that night.'

'So when you arrived at the castle yesterday morning, you found Pete, José and Maria all dead?'

'Yes, it was one hell of a shock to find the three of them dead.' Marçel continued, 'After Pete's warning, Gerda thought it would be safer for us to take a different route to the winery. We drove all night and arrived at first light, ten hours ahead of our expected arrival time.'

'And the ladies?'

'I parked the car in one of the tractor sheds and walked the rest of the way to the castle. I had asked the girls to wait in the car. Unfortunately they followed me into the house and saw the carnage. My immediate thoughts were to get away from the scene as quickly as possible; I had to get the girls to a place where they would be safe from the killers and of course the police. I realised the workers would arrive soon, and it would be far better if they found the bodies and called the police.'

'Where are they now, Marçel?'

'The girls are now camping at a very safe location. Do you remember the small lagoon where Pete and I once took you? We went out in the kayaks and crossed over the main waterway to that spit of land, between the broad-water and the ocean.'

Stephen paused for a while before answering.

'Yes, Marçel, that was a very good day and a great camping place. Anyway, shortly after my meeting with Pete, our department received an urgent message from our American friends. They informed us that a gang of thugs from East Germany with strong Nazi connections had managed to enter West Germany and were on their way to break up our operation in Portugal. We immediately tried to warn Pete, but we were unable to make contact with him. I believe that when he found the burnt-out French depot, he became very angry and decided not to make contact with us.'

Stephen breathed deeply before continuing, 'The man I sent across to the depot in France called me to say that the depot had been destroyed, and there was no sign of Pete. I guessed then that Pete must have gone straight down to Portugal.

'I managed to persuade my friends in the RAF to fly me to Porto in one of their long-range Meteor jets. From there I took a taxi. It was mid-afternoon by the time I got to the castle. The place was deserted and the front door unlocked so I walked in and when I looked into the lounge I saw the bodies—I had arrived too late.'

So Stephen had known all along that Pete was dead!

Stephen spoke more quietly now. 'I sat down in one of the chairs, staring at the three bodies. Sometime later I heard a motorboat approaching. I went upstairs and looked out of the window. I watched José's brother come into the house; you remember I met him one day when we all went out fishing together. Soon after that, you arrived. I could hear you talking to José's brother—Marco isn't it? So I decided to remain out of sight. I was unable to hear what you were saying, but I did hear the launch mentioned several times. When you set off in the fishing boat, I went down and concealed myself near the jetty and waited.'

Marçel remembered that this was always Stephen's tactic; he never revealed himself unless absolutely necessary. Marçel was surprised that he was sitting opposite him now.

'I saw you come back later with the motor launch and I watched you load the three bodies onto the launch. I knew then exactly what you were going to do. I must commend you for that, Marçel. After you left, I went back into the house to await your return. You were extremely lucky in your timing; I was about to open a bottle of your best wine when I heard a car drive into the courtyard. I hurried back upstairs and stood well out of sight on the upstairs landing. Three men came into the house. I was able to listen to their raised voices.

'They were angry that they had not been able to intercept the truck and they were extremely worried as to where the three bodies had gone. I gathered that after killing Pete and the old couple, they had taken the motor launch and stayed on it that night.

'It seems they had driven out along the road that people would normally use coming from Spain, hoping to intercept you. After studying a map of the area they realised there were at least two other roads that you could have taken, so they decided to return to the castle. On their way back they must have decided to stop off at the motor launch, only to find that it had gone.' Stephen was chuckling.

'I really am amazed, Marçel, at just how stupid these men are. When they got here, they made no attempt to see if anyone else was in the house. I overheard everything they said. But the *piece de resistance* came when their leader said they would now have to spend the night at their Nazi headquarters in Porto. They must be getting all their support from there. This is a valuable bit of information which we will certainly follow up in the future.'

'So that was about the time I got back from destroying the launch. Marco brought me back in his fishing boat and dropped me off a little way past the castle; I walked back to the jetty, looked through the castle door and saw their car. I decided it was time to get back to the camp. Do you think they know that the truck has been destroyed and their colleagues are all dead?'

'It really was quite a coincidence that your truck should have met with a fatal accident, Marçel, and it was quite fortuitous as it turned out. You would have had one hell of a reception if you had turned up at the castle with the clients.'

His voice hardened. 'I think that with both the bodies and the launch missing, the thugs will think that somehow you have managed to outwit them. But they will still be after you and the gold. We have to get rid of these bastards, my boy. Even if this is the last thing I do before retiring from the service.'

'So, you stayed here last night, Stephen. I thought they would have searched the house.'

'They did, my boy; I had been listening from the upstairs landing. When I heard them heading for the stairs I nipped down the back staircase to the kitchen, and out through the kitchen door into the courtyard. I waited there behind some empty casks until I heard them drive off.

'I went back into the house, drank a bottle of your best wine, found some food in the larder and later went upstairs to bed. Slept like a log! I knew you would be back sometime today, so I thought I would set my little trap and wait for you to turn up.'

Marçel got up and crossed to the telephone. 'I'm going to call the police to tell them that the launch is overdue from a fishing trip. I will tell him I am concerned because the launch would normally have returned early in the morning.'

Having made his call, they both sat silently for a while.

'I spoke to the head of police. He seemed quite offhand about the missing boat. He told me a bright light, which could have been a fire on a boat, had been seen last night some distance from the shore. Some life jackets and also a woman's jacket had been picked up this morning. A boat had been sent out to search the area, but he did not think there was much hope of finding any survivors. He said he would send someone over to get a statement from me in the morning.'

'So what's the situation here, Marçel? What's happened to all the winery staff?'

Marçel stood up and removed Stephen's jacket from the safe door and handed Stephen back his safe-breaking key.

'I'm afraid there was nothing there in the safe for you, Stephen. I removed anything of interest. I went to see our bank manager yesterday and completed the deal that Pete had negotiated with the bank. I signed away the whole of our business and the castle. By sheer coincidence, Pete was able to sell the entire package to one of our competitors. These people had been in contact with us for some time, wanting us to sell them the winery. At that time we were naturally not interested in winding up Deserting Rats or parting with our very lucrative wine business.

'Pete telephoned our bank manager who had been trying for some time to negotiate a deal. Pete told him we were prepared to sell, but it would be subject to an immediate transaction as both Pete and I wished to move to Australia, where we were intending to take over a large cattle station. I cannot imagine either of us rounding up cattle! The buyers were delighted; within hours they were at the castle and Pete made a deal that included all stock, equipment, house furniture and fittings. Luckily Pete did not include our enterprise in northern France. He intended to sell that at a later date.

'We were able to achieve an excellent price for the castle and the winery. The staff has been laid off for three weeks until the new owners take possession. The purchasers have already paid the full amount into our bank and by now it will have been transferred to our trust account in Switzerland. The tragic thing is that Pete will not be around to enjoy the money and now I have no interest in running the business without Pete.'

Stephen got up, went to the cocktail cabinet and returned to the desk with two glasses of port wine. 'This doesn't exactly call for a celebration, Marçel, but I think we both need a drink. We will drink to our three dear departed friends, especially Pete, with whom we have both shared so much. It has been both a great honour and pleasure for us to have worked together with Pete. I know that he would be very happy that the Piglet has now become an extremely wealthy man and I also know that he would want you to take his place and continue his work with our department.'

'I'm not too sure about that last bit, Stephen. Maybe it is time for me to quit and really look for that cattle station in Australia.'

They drank the port and smashed their glasses in the fireplace. 'We will talk about that later; now let's do something about these Nazi bastards, Marçel. It's reasonable to expect that they will return to the castle as soon as it gets dark. They will have no idea that I am here; it's lucky that I took a taxi from the airport yesterday. They will have spent their day looking for the launch and I expect they will have had someone watching the castle all day. You will probably have been seen arriving here this afternoon and they will have noted that no one else has come to the castle and that there are no workers about.'

'So you think that they will assume I am alone and will not be expecting them to come here, Stephen? This is what I think we should do. We will let them drive into the courtyard. We will leave the main doors open and lock the door to the jetty. This will prevent them from sending someone in that way; we have to monitor exactly where they are. When their car enters the courtyard, I will step out of the front door. They will then see me going back into the house and closing the front door behind me. They will know that I am in the house, so they will certainly not expect an attack from the outside.'

Stephen looked rather pained, 'Do you expect me to stand in the yard shooting at these thugs while you sit in the house quietly sipping port?'

'Yes, I do. Come. I will show you something you didn't see the last time you came to stay with us.'

Stephen followed Marçel into the hallway. At the side of the old carved staircase, he reached up to a wooden carving on one of the panels and tilted it to one side. At the same time he gently leaned against one of the lower panels. The panel slowly opened and they both stepped inside what appeared to be a large cupboard.

Marçel switched on the light and closed the panel behind them. He lifted a wooden trapdoor in the floor, which revealed a flight of worn stone steps that led down to a long and well-lit passageway.

'The house is only about three hundred years old. It was rebuilt on the site of the original old inner tower, which was then the castle's living quarters. There were dungeons underneath the old tower where they kept and tortured their unfortunate prisoners. When the tower was demolished and the present house built, they retained the dungeons for storage and I expect that they were used for many other unpleasant things. Much later it became a wine cellar.'

Stephen followed Marçel down the stairs along the passage to a large room lined with mostly empty wine racks, a good-sized table, a few chairs and a stove in one corner.

'Pete and I decided to keep a small quantity of our very best wines down here—all the commercial wines are stored in rooms within the castle walls.'

Marçel reached up to a slot high up in the wall and produced a set of rusty keys. They continued down the passageway. On either side were the old studded doors that led into the dungeons. He unlocked the last door and switched on the very powerful light inside. Stephen followed him into the bright white-painted dungeon.

A large workbench stood in the centre of the room and wooden crates were stacked up against the walls. Marçel opened three of the crates; they contained rifles, hand grenades, several light machine guns, one heavy machine gun and a large quantity of ammunition. He placed two Sten guns and six clips of ammunition on the bench.

'Good God, Marçel, where the hell did you get hold of all these weapons? I hope you realise the risk you run keeping all this weaponry here.'

'We have been running a dangerous business, Stephen. Pete and I collected these weapons towards the end of the war to protect us in case any operations got out of hand, or if you had any unfinished jobs in this part of Europe. We have another cache of weapons in France as well if they are ever needed. To save your department any embarrassment, I shan't tell you where they are.'

'I know exactly where they are, Marçel, Pete and I have had several meetings on your barge in France.'

Marçel checked over the two Sten guns, slipped a clip into one of them and handed it to Stephen with two spare clips. Stephen went over to one of the crates and helped himself to a revolver and a handful of bullets, which he slipped into his jacket pocket.

'Follow me.' There was a door at the far end of the passage. Marçel unlocked it and they passed through. A steel ladder led down to what appeared to be a large drain and a flight of stairs led up to another heavy door.

'The drain that takes away all the surface rainwater from the castle is down there. It comes out underneath the jetty at the back of the castle. The drain exit is well concealed, and so this makes an excellent escape route from the castle.'

They climbed the stairs and Marçel opened the heavy door. They were in the tower right opposite the front of the house. At ground level, a locked door led out to the courtyard. They climbed the stone flight of stairs inside the tower; a short way up the stone steps they came to a narrow slit in the wall, which gave them an excellent view of the courtyard and was also facing the front of the house.

'When they arrive, Stephen, I will run straight upstairs and the moment they get out of their car, I will start shooting from one of the bedroom windows. That will be the signal for you to start firing. From here you should be able to take them by surprise, attack them first and then disable their car.'

'That sounds good, Marçel, but just you make sure they are the right people before you start shooting.' Stephen paused. 'It's getting dark now so I might as well stay up here.'

'I'll go back to the house and lock the door to the dungeons behind me just in case things go very wrong; we don't want them coming into the house that way. You can either come out of the tower through the door that leads into the courtyard, Stephen, here's the key—or in an emergency, follow the drain out to the jetty. But, expect to get very wet if you go that way.'

Marçel returned to the house, careful to lock the door to the dungeons. On the way through he collected a Sten gun and some spare clips of ammunition. Back in the house, he switched on all the downstairs lights and the courtyard floodlights, opened the front door and waited.

About an hour later, a black Mercedes drove through the archway into the courtyard. Marçel stepped outside the front door where he could be clearly seen and then returned inside, locking the door behind him.

He dashed upstairs taking up his position at a darkened bedroom window. The Mercedes pulled up a little way from the front door. Marçel carefully aimed his gun at the front window of the car and waited.

After a minute, the rear door of the car opened. The body of a woman was thrown from the car on to the cobbled floor of the courtyard. The car door closed. Marçel hesitated.

As the car started to move forward, the face of another woman appeared at the now open rear window.

It was Gerda. Marçel held his fire.

The black Mercedes drew up alongside the Peugeot. A short burst of gunfire into the tyres of the Peugeot ensured they would be unable follow them. The car made a tight circle, headed out through the courtyard archway and disappeared up the driveway.

Stephen and Marçel both reached Helga's twisted motionless body at the same time. Neither of them spoke. Stephen bent down and gently turned her onto her side. He straightened her twisted blood-covered head and slipped his jacket under it.

'She's breathing—*just*. They haven't killed her—she's their messenger.'

Stephen slowly ran his hands over her. 'I don't think there is anything broken. We had better get her inside. We need something flat to carry her on.'

'Stay with her, Stephen, I'll fetch a stepladder from the kitchen.' Marçel went across to the kitchen and returned with a stepladder, some towels and cushions. They spread out the towels and cushions on the ladder and gently lifted Helga onto them. To save having to move her twice, they took her straight up the stairs and carefully lifted her onto one of the guest-room beds.

Looking down at Helga, Marçel felt another surge of anger. He stared down at her blood-stained and badly torn dress; her legs were badly scratched and still bleeding a little. Her hair was matted with blood and her face badly grazed.

'What the hell did they do to get the girl in such a state, Marçel?'

'They had Gerda in the car. I'd like to know how they managed to find the girls—I was so sure no one could possibly have found them at the lagoon.

'Why don't you make us all a hot drink, Stephen? I'm going to clean up Helga's wounds. It might be better if I'm alone with her when she regains consciousness. When she comes to, she will certainly have a lot to tell us.'

Stephen went off to the kitchen, while Marçel gently covered Helga with a blanket. He went to the bathroom, filled a jug with hot water, added some disinfectant and gathered up some clean towels. Helga was still unconscious when he returned.

Carefully removing her wet clothes, Marçel couldn't help admiring her lovely though badly grazed body. He hoped she would not wake until he had finished cleaning her damaged skin. Marçel took his time, gently cleaning all the cuts and scratches with a towel soaked in disinfectant.

When completely satisfied that he had done all he could, Marçel went to his bedroom and collected some of his own clean clothes for her.

Helga was lying on her back and breathing quite normally, wearing one of Marçel's shirts, a pair of his pants and a warm dressing gown. Marçel arranged two pillows under her head, covered her with a blanket and then went downstairs to find Stephen.

Being the perfect gentleman, Stephen had remained downstairs until Marçel had finished attending to Helga.

'She's breathing normally now. She is probably suffering from concussion, but I don't see the need for a doctor unless she fails to recover consciousness by the morning.'

'You'd better go and sit with her, Marçel, in case she wakes. I'll bring up coffee and warm milk.'

Marçel went and sat beside Helga. He brushed back the hair from her face and held her hand. He felt her fingers moving inside his hand and gave them a gentle squeeze. Helga opened her eyes briefly. He saw the trace of a smile appear on one corner of her mouth.

Marçel held a glass of water to her lips, which she slowly sipped. Helga opened her eyes again and whispered, 'What a nice surprise. It just had to be you, Marçel.' Helga looked around the room and then down at the shirt she was wearing. 'I hope it was just you, Marçel.'

Stephen came in with a tray of hot coffee. 'Ah, I'm Stephen, Marçel's old boss. Would you like a drink of milk? How's the pain?'

'I feel like I'm back in the concentration camp again after receiving another one of their beatings. But they never offered me a glass of milk.'

Stephen poured out half a glass of milk. He produced an envelope from his pocket and shook some white powder into the glass. He gave it a quick stir and handed it to Helga. Her small grazed hands were shaking as she drank the milk; she groaned then closed her eyes again.

'That will kill her pain. She will sleep soundly for quite some time. Very effective stuff, but highly illegal!'

Helga sat up, suddenly wide-awake. 'Where is Gerda? Oh my God, I am to tell you,' Helga started to shake as the events of the last few hours flooded back. 'They are going to kill her if you don't hand over all the gold. They said to tell you that they would be phoning you to arrange a transfer. They said that if you kept them waiting too long, you will receive just a few small parts of her. They are vicious evil men!'

Marçel helped lower her back onto the pillows. 'Take it easy, Helga. They drove into the yard and then threw you out of the car. I spotted Gerda in the car as they drove off. Where do you think they've taken her?'

'I really don't know, Marçel.'

'Okay, Helga, when you feel up to it, you can tell us exactly what happened.'

Helga had stopped shaking; Stephen slipped another pillow behind her head, and she quietly described their abduction back at the camp.

'It was late afternoon and we were swimming in the lagoon. We decided to swim out through the channel to the broad-water. We were a little way out from the shore when we noticed a speedboat some distance away. We swam back to the lagoon and thought no more about it.

A little later while we were having tea in the hut, we heard a motorboat approaching. We came out of the hut to see the speedboat entering the lagoon. We realised it was the same one that we had seen earlier. The two men in the boat were smiling and waving to us.'

'I did warn you both to keep out of sight, Helga.'

'I'm so sorry, Marçel. We really thought that they were friends of yours, so we ran down to the speedboat to take its rope and pull it up onto the beach and then we found two guns pointing at us. The men were no longer smiling. They made us lie face down on the sand with our arms stretched out above our heads. One of the men bent down and tied our wrists and ankles with some rough cord while the other, who appeared to be giving the orders, stood over me forcing his gun into my lower back; I remember thinking I would prefer to be shot in the head than in the back. We were dragged to the hut. I was expecting the worst—these animals usually started off by raping their women prisoners. Instead, one of the men went into our tent and came out with some of our underwear, which he stuffed into our mouths. He then used our stockings to tie the gags in place.'

'What did they look like, Helga?'

'They were not young men. I would say they were in their mid-thirties. One man was swarthy and fairly short and had thin greying hair. The other, who was definitely in charge, was tall, well built with blond hair. He had a really cruel-looking face; I had seen that look so often in the prison camps in Germany. They were both dressed in dark suits, which I must say looked a little out of place. They talked quietly in German. The blond man was definitely a German but the other man came from Eastern Europe or Russia. I could tell by his accent.'

Helga leaned back against her pillows and closed her eyes for a few minutes. Stephen's white powder was starting to take effect.

'They set about searching the hut, the tent, and the area around the campsite. They even poked around in the toilet. It's funny. They came quite close to where you and I buried the suitcase containing the gold but they walked right past it. In the end, the short one came over to us, grabbed Gerda by the hair, and removed her gag. He forced his pistol into her mouth and whispered something into her ear. I saw her shake her head. If

it had been me I think I would have told them where the gold was. Then
the animal withdrew the gun from Gerda's mouth and bent over to kiss
her. Gerda spat in his face and told him that the Piglet was on his way and
would tear him apart.

'The blond-haired man came over and told his partner to put his gun
away. He placed a foot on Gerda's breasts and twisted it back and forth
until she screamed. He laughed at her and told her how pleased he was to
meet the famous Piglet's woman. He knew all about the Piglet who had
made such a nuisance of himself in northern France just before the Allied
Invasion. Now this same Piglet was killing his people and stealing his gold.'

Marçel smiled ruefully. 'I didn't realise I was that famous with the
Wehrmacht, Stephen, but it is a pity Gerda revealed my name.'

Helga continued, 'He told the short man that it was unlikely that the
English Piglet would have kept the gold there and anyway he knew a much
better way of acquiring the gold.'

'Go on, Helga.'

'He said they would return to the castle after dark. Hans, who was
watching the castle, would know how many people were there. They would
dump a messenger in the courtyard, one much-damaged woman; she would
demonstrate that they really meant business. It would also be much easier
for them just to hold onto one hostage.'

Helga closed her eyes again. Stephen went downstairs to make Helga a
cup of tea. When he returned Helga was sitting up and was able to drink
a little. She continued, 'They drank a bottle of the wine we had in the hut
and then dragged us down to the water's edge. Then they tied lengths of
rope to the cord that bound our wrists. They untied the stockings so we
could breathe freely. Then they took the two ropes out to the boat, and tied
them to each side. They pushed out the speedboat, climbed in and started
the motor. As the boat moved forward we were slowly dragged over the
sand and then into the water. They revved the engine and raced across the
lagoon; we were immediately pulled under the water ... I thought that was
the end.' Helga shook her head.

'The boat must have slowed down when it reached the far side of the
lagoon. We were able to bring our heads above the water to take a few
breaths. They increased their speed again and started to zigzag through
the narrow channel to the broad-water. Most of the time we were able to
keep our heads out of the water, but each time they turned close to one of

the channel banks we were swung sideways, and our bodies were dragged along the side of the bank. That is how I got the damage to my body. When they reached the entrance to the broad-water they revved the engine … once again we were pulled under water.

'I don't remember anything after that … I came to, lying on a wooden jetty. Gerda was lying alongside me and did not appear to be as badly damaged. She turned towards me, forcing a smile. I remembered her saying, 'Oh my, you are a mess, Helga. Sorry I can't lend you my makeup just now.' And then she passed out … As soon as it became dark, they lifted us into their car, Gerda was still unconscious. When I started to say something, they stuck the barrel of a gun into my neck … I remained silent.

'We set off in the car. The tall blond German they called Karl … pushed his gun harder and harder into my neck as he told me exactly what I had to say to you. He kept on hitting me across the head … must have passed out again … next thing I remember is … is waking up here.'

Helga's speech had been getting slower and slower. Marçel took her hand and gave it a gentle squeeze. 'Helga, do you think they will kill Gerda?'

Helga closed her eyes and slowly whispered, 'Marçel darling … they intend to kill all of us … quite sure that they have underestimated … the … the power … of the Piglet …'

The drug had taken effect; Helga was asleep.

Chapter 6

Stephen and Marçel were on their way downstairs when the telephone rang. Marçel hurried into the office and picked up the receiver. A soft voice with a cultured German accent asked to speak to Marçel. He was checking to make sure Marçel was alone in the house.

'This is Marçel and you know very well there is no one else here.' Marçel wanted him to confirm this and waited for his answer. 'You are not alone Marçel, you have the woman with you. That's if she is still alive.' Marçel knew he was still unaware of Stephen's presence in the castle.

'You know your other woman Gerda is with me. She has a fine body and no doubt we will make full use of it before we kill her.' He paused for a moment; Marçel remained silent.

'We will give the woman one chance to live. We know now that you must have murdered the five Germans that you brought with you. We also know that between them they were carrying over one million dollars in gold bars.' The soft voice paused. 'So, young Piglet, do you want to trade?'

Marçel slowly counted to eight. 'I believe your name is Karl. Keep talking, Karl.' Marçel thought his name was irrelevant; very soon he was going to kill this lowlife.

'At dawn tomorrow you will place an open suitcase containing the gold, on the edge of the castle jetty. You will stand back against the castle wall where we can see you. When we come in to the jetty with a speedboat, we will pick up the suitcase and drop off Gerda. If you make any attempt to hamper this exchange, we will kill her. I would also advise you to keep your arms above your head until we are well away from the jetty.'

Marçel had no doubt he would have someone hiding near the castle ready to kill him at this point. He waited a while before replying.

'You leave me no choice, Karl, but I expect to see Gerda climbing onto the jetty unaided. If I find that she has been badly injured or sexually abused, I promise you I will hunt you down and kill you.'

'Brave words from the Piglet. Till the morning, Marçel.'

Marçel put the phone down. Stephen had been listening to the conversation. 'Of course you know they will kill you both. They must think you're stupid, but I don't see what else you can do to save Gerda. The silly girl gave him your code name.'

'There won't be a dawn exchange on the jetty, Stephen, because before dawn we are going to pay them a visit.'

'You have a slight problem with that, Marçel. We don't know where they are.' Stephen was silent for a moment. Marçel knew that they were thinking on the same lines.

Stephen continued, 'Yes I believe we both have the answer to that. The Nazi base at Porto must have supplied them with a speedboat, but they no longer have our launch as a base. As they only have a few hours before the exchange, the obvious place for them to go is to your lagoon camp. I'm sure they will leave one man with the car to watch the castle and he will kill you and Gerda as soon as they've made the pick up.'

They both realised what they had to do.

'I take it you still have those kayaks? We will have to take Helga down to the wine cellar for her safety, in case things go wrong. If they have a man watching outside the castle, we will have to get rid of him before we can launch the kayaks.'

Marçel smiled at Stephen. 'That's the least of our problems; you know that removing men on guard duty has always been my specialty.'

They took some bedding down to the cellar. The main room was quite habitable, it had excellent lighting, and besides having a table and chairs and a stove, at one end there was a large couch. They made up a bed for Helga.

It took a while to carry her down the stairs. Stephen was able to wake her just enough to explain that they were going to rescue Gerda. He told her that she would be safe in the cellar until they returned in a few hours' time. Helga was asleep before he had finished talking; the drug would keep her asleep until they returned.

Marçel collected two hand grenades from the weapons store and they returned upstairs, being careful to close the secret panel behind them.

They went across to one of the storerooms in the castle wall and fished out two kayaks, which they took over to the jetty door. Marçel ran back to the kitchen and selected a sharp nine-inch meat knife and slipped it into his belt.

Stephen was waiting at the jetty door with the two kayaks.

'Stephen, I would like you to take one of the kayaks across to the jetty. Make as much noise as you like, but stand there for a few minutes. Their man will think it's me. He will not reveal himself to you but I should be able to spot him.'

Stephen knew it was now the Piglet's call. Marçel was excited but calm. The killer instinct in him had taken over—Marçel had become the cold clear-headed killer.

The Piglet was ready and eager to kill.

It was a perfect night; a slight breeze would partly cover the sound of footsteps; not a dark night, the clear sky and half-moon gave him just enough light to make out any movement. Marçel closed his eyes for a moment so he could adjust to the darkness. His excellent night vision had been his greatest asset when attacking German guards in occupied France.

Stephen walked slowly across to the edge of the jetty. Marçel noticed that he and Stephen were about the same height and build. When he got to the edge of the jetty he stood there staring at the water. At that moment Marçel saw a movement in the bushes. About thirty feet away a figure rose up from one of the bushes. It stayed staring at the figure at the water's edge and then disappeared back into the bush.

That was enough for Marçel. He slipped the knife out of his belt and silently inched himself over to where the figure had disappeared. He was only six feet away when he came across the crouching figure.

Marçel guessed the man was still debating whether he should do something about the person standing on the jetty. Marçel crept a little closer and then launched himself at the man. As Marçel landed on top of him, he pierced the meat knife through his neck and jerked it sideways.

The Piglet was pleased with his work; it had been two years since he had used a knife to kill someone. His victim would not have suffered; he would have died almost instantly. Elated, Marçel went over to Stephen.

'One down, two to go. We can leave him there till morning. Let's get across to the camp while I'm in the mood.'

'You really are enjoying yourself, Marçel. I'm so glad we are on the same side.'

They went back to the castle, picked up the other kayak and carried it down to the water. Marçel handed Stephen a hand grenade. 'You might need this. I just hope I can find the entrance to the lagoon. We'd better get going—we have to get there before dawn.'

An hour later, after some hard paddling, they reached the entrance to the lagoon. They were just able to see the gap in the trees that grew right down to the water's edge. They paddled a little way past the entrance, pulled the kayaks up onto the sand and concealed them in the bushes.

'You're in charge now, Marçel.'

Marçel realised that Stephen was putting him to the test, and his performance in the coming moments would determine as to whether he would be working for Stephen's department in the future.

'Okay. Our plan is to find Gerda, get her away intact, eliminate the thugs and hopefully, if it's still there, return to the castle in the Renault or maybe their speedboat. I would like you to follow behind me, Stephen. I'm going to take you to a spot right opposite the door to the fisherman's hut. If anyone comes out of the hut, you shoot to kill, but first I'm going to find out who is in the tent.'

Stephen gripped his arm. 'This is your operation, Marçel. It sounds good to me. Let's do it.'

They made their way silently through the bushes, making a wide circle around the lagoon until they came to the hut. Marçel found a place behind some boulders about ten yards from the hut door. Stephen checked his revolver; he never missed his mark.

The big question for Marçel—where was Gerda, in the hut, or in the tent? He slipped away from Stephen and crept to the back of the hut. The tent was halfway between the hut and the lagoon. He edged towards the outline of the tent.

Marçel smiled; he saw the giveaway red glow of a cigarette. These guys would never learn. They always made it so easy for him. He crept silently up behind the man who should have been alert, but wasn't. With his left arm he pulled back the guard's head and with his right hand, swiftly slit his throat. The only sound was the gurgling of the blood in his throat as he slid to the ground and died.

Gerda was lying asleep in the tent; Marçel put his hand over her mouth and prodded her. He felt Gerda jump. She opened her eyes. He signalled her to remain silent. Marçel removed his hand from her mouth and replaced it with his lips.

After carefully wiping the blood off his knife, Marçel cut through the cords around Gerda's wrists and ankles. She was wearing slacks and a jumper. He passed her Helga's anorak and signalled her to follow him.

They faded away into the bushes and headed for the dip in the dunes where he had left the Renault. It appeared to be intact. Marçel gave Gerda the keys, which he had been carrying in his pocket.

'Helga is safely back at the castle and recovering. How badly are you hurt?'

'I'll survive—thanks to my knight in shining armour—after a long hot bath and lots of healing ointment, I'll be fighting fit again.'

'Get into the back of the car and wait for me to return. Oh and take this, just in case. I still have a little unfinished business.' Marçel handed Gerda his revolver. He bent down, gave her another passionate kiss and headed back to Stephen.

It was starting to become light when he joined Stephen.

'There is still no sign of life from the hut, Marçel.'

'Gerda is safe,' he whispered. 'She's waiting in the car.' He removed the hand grenade from his pocket. 'Keep me covered, Stephen. Fire a shot into the window when I get close. I think I will take your hand grenade as well.'

Stephen had a pained look on his face. 'You are a real bastard, Piglet.'

Marçel walked quietly across to the hut.

After Stephen fired a shot into the window, Marçel lobbed a hand grenade through the broken glass and ran back.

The explosion blew out the sides of the hut, and it was immediately engulfed in flames. In the bright flames they could see two men. One man had collapsed on the floor and the other was staggering to the empty doorframe. Both men were on fire. Stephen ran forward and fired several shots at the burning figure; he fell back into the blazing inferno.

'Give me a hand, Stephen.' They ran around to the tent, pulled it down and threw it and all the contents of the tent into the burning hut. Stephen helped him lift the body of Gerda's guard into the speedboat, which they pushed out into the lagoon. Marçel released the catch of the other hand grenade and lobbed it into the boat.

They scrambled back up the beach and flung themselves down in the tall grass. Stephen saw a figure running towards them. 'Lie down!' he screamed. As Gerda threw herself to the ground, the speedboat exploded in a ball of fire and was blown to smithereens. They were showered with water and bits of debris, but amazingly they were unhurt.

Stephen slowly stood up. 'That was a little too close for comfort, Marçel, and not really necessary. After all that effort, we nearly lost Gerda.'

They walked over to her where she was lying face down and sobbing. 'Stop shamming, Gerda, and get up. There is someone here who wants to talk to you.'

Gerda slowly rolled over and looked up at them. 'Stephen …'

She leaped up and flung her arms around Stephen. 'What the Hell are you doing here? And oh, what a wonderful surprise! Oh my God—have you come to save us or to kill us?'

Stephen gently kissed her on the forehead. 'You really don't think I would harm my favourite female agent? As for saving you—well, you certainly don't need me around while you have Marçel to look after you.'

Marçel was getting twitchy, 'Stephen, do you think you could tow the second kayak back to the castle? I will bring Gerda back in the Renault after we have cleaned up and removed all traces of our stay here.'

'No problem. But remember, I'm the one that's supposed to be giving the orders around here,' Stephen chuckled. 'Perhaps you are thinking of taking on my job when I retire; somehow I don't think you are ready for a desk job. We are going to need you for something with a little more action first.'

They found a short length of cord in the bottom of Stephen's kayak, and Stephen set off, towing Marçel's kayak. 'Don't forget to bring back the gold, Marçel!' Stephen was still chuckling as he paddled off to the castle.

Gerda and Marçel walked around the campsite throwing anything they could find into the still-burning hut. Then they walked back through the long grass to where Helga and Marçel had hidden the case containing the gold. Surprisingly, it had remained undiscovered. Marçel threw it into the back of the car.

Gerda put her arms around Marçel. 'You really are quite something, Marçel. You have already saved my life on two other occasions in France and now you have done it again.'

Gerda reached up, pulled his head down and gave him a long and very passionate kiss. All the horrors of the last few hours seemed to drive them on; they tore at each other's clothes as they slowly sank down onto the thick grass. Throwing their arms around each other, they kissed, first gently, then more urgently.

Their lovemaking was passionate and violent. Gerda groaned as Marçel thrust himself into her, their bodies furiously working together. Gerda dug her fingernails into his back, Marçel ran his fingers through her long blond hair and pulled back her head. He covered her lips with his hungry mouth and then, at that very moment, he thought of the two men that he had just stabbed to death, and suddenly they both exploded into a long and wonderful climax. As they lay there, their arms around each other, Gerda clinging to him quietly sobbing, his heart ached for her as at that very final moment of making love, Gerda had whispered, 'Oh, Pierre.'

Her only true love, the husband that she had lost forever.

Marçel was shocked to realise that it was not the first time that night that he had reached the heights. His lovemaking had been powerful, lustful and ecstatic. All the pent-up tensions of the last few days had been released in those few passionate out-of-control moments.

It was then he also realised that his twisted mind had mixed up his sexual feelings with the two killings. He had enjoyed the killings as much as the sex …

What was wrong with him? Was he a psychopath? At that moment Marçel thought that he could never be a normal person again. With such a twisted mind, could he ever hope to marry Gerda or any other woman? But then maybe he was just not the marrying type. He convinced himself that he only killed people who were a menace to society, people who really deserved to die. So … what the hell.

The early morning sun warmed their relaxed naked bodies. 'Time to get going. Stephen will be getting worried.' They put on their crumpled clothes. Marçel held Gerda in his arms as they gently kissed, both still trembling from their passionate lovemaking. The passion had passed and was replaced with the warmth and afterglow. They both knew they would always have this strong physical desire for each other, and that their friendship would last forever. But neither of them, in the present circumstances, could envisage a future life together.

'We must be really mad, Marçel; after all the shootings, the fire that burned their bodies and all the evidence of our stay here—you and I lying here making passionate love after all that has happened.'

Marçel put his arm around Gerda's shoulder.

'Do you think this is the end of it all now, Marçel?'

'Hard to say. It depends whether there are others, and if the Nazi cell in Porto will continue to seek revenge. As for the lovemaking, I think that passion was the result of what had happened to us earlier last night.'

They had no problem reversing the Renault out of the bushes up the steep slope of the sand hill and out onto the track. They were soon out on the road and heading back to the castle.

'I know one thing. We have to get out of Portugal as quickly as possible and we have to get Helga on board a ship to a safe country overseas. Have you any idea what you would like to do, Gerda?'

'I think I would like to go overseas with Helga. I have had so many bad memories of my life in Europe over the last few years. I would like to go somewhere and start a fresh life. Helga and I get on extremely well and we seem to have a lot of things in common. Neither of us has any living close relatives left and I think Helga will need help to rebuild her life. She has boundless energy and I have the money. Australia would probably be a good place to make a fresh start.'

Marçel noted that he had not been included in Gerda's future plans and at that moment, to his surprise, he felt relieved.

As they approached the winery, a black Mercedes pulled out from the entrance and came racing down the road towards them. The driver was staring straight ahead as he tore past. He had blond hair and his face was clouded in anger. 'I don't think he even noticed us in his rush to get away from the castle, Gerda.'

Chapter 7

When Gerda and Marçel entered the front door of the castle, they were greeted with a strong smell of freshly made coffee and fried bacon. Stephen and Helga, who seemed to have made a remarkable recovery, had prepared breakfast for them. Their appetite was dampened though by the knowledge that Karl was still alive.

'Helga was still asleep when I got back, but apart from all those nasty cuts and bruises, the long sleep has done its job. Helga is almost back to her normal self. By the way, are you quite sure you killed that man by the jetty last night, Marçel? There was no sign of a body when I looked a few minutes ago. I wondered if he had slipped away.'

'He was very dead when I left him. We've just seen a Mercedes driving away from the winery. Karl the blond one, who seems to be the leader of the group, was driving. Obviously he was not one of the men we killed at the camp. He must have been hoping to join his man on the jetty. Finding him dead and no sign of the other men, he would have decided to take away the body and go and find out what happened at the lagoon camp.'

Stephen gave an exasperated sigh. 'This means we are still in danger.'

'By now this Karl fellow will have realised there are at least four of us in the castle.'

Marçel made a quick phone call to his garage friend in Aveiro asking him to deliver and fit another new set of tyres for the Peugeot.

He rejoined the others at the table. Four tired and hungry people, thanks to Stephen's efforts in the kitchen, tucked into a hearty breakfast, finishing with toast, Maria's superb citrus marmalade and washed down with lots of hot strong coffee.

The two girls had been talking quietly for some time about their future. They had agreed that together they could start a new life in a new country. Gerda had her arm around Helga's shoulder. 'Helga and I have decided we would like to go to Australia as soon as possible.'

'Okay, but let's get back to the present, girls. We still have to get rid of that fellow Karl.'

Marçel finished his coffee. 'The Chief of Police is coming over this morning to interview me about the missing launch and the probable drowning of Pete and the old couple. He believes that I am alone here at the castle, so we had better get the place tidied up as quickly as possible.'

'The moment we hear the car arriving, you three had better go down to the cellar and stay there until he goes.'

Stephen pushed aside his empty plate and leaned forward. He was now very much in command. He had made his assessment of their situation and had decided on the next move. He paused to study each of his cohorts sitting around the table. Marçel had the utmost faith in Stephen and knew he would come up with a suitable solution to their problems.

'We must all leave Portugal as soon as possible. My first priority is to cover up all traces of Operation Deserting Rats.' Stephen leaned forward and held both the girls' hands.

'In view of your involvement in Deserting Rats and the events of the last few days, I think it would be unwise for you two to try to board a ship sailing from Portugal. It's also possible the police will be on the lookout for you and could be asking you both some very difficult questions. But your main danger now is from Karl Schmidt and his thugs. I've done a little digging and in view of his contacts and the attitude of the present regime in Portugal, I think it could be dangerous for you to try to get you out of this country in the normal way at present.'

Stephen finished his coffee. 'I don't have that problem as no one knows I've been to the castle. Marçel is well known at the border crossings so he certainly won't have any difficulties.' He turned to Marçel.

'Marçel, you need to get the girls to a safer place. You have a converted barge in France. We must try to get the girls there. After that we'll have plenty of time to organise a passage for them to Australia.'

Marçel agreed; on his barge they would be very comfortable and could stay out of sight indefinitely. Some time ago, Marçel and Pete had bought the barge and converted it into a second home and it was moored in a small but beautiful and secluded estuary connected to the Canal de Nantes à Brest, close to the town of Brevet in France.

'Stephen, the problem is we still have to get them from here to France.'

'I'll come to that in a minute. Now first, you must get things sorted out with the police. The girls and I will move down to the cellar, which we will make fairly comfortable as the girls might have to stay down there for a couple of days. I have a man, an Australian by the way, that I will try to contact. He lives on a large sailing boat, moored at a small fishing village near Vigo, about one hundred and twenty miles up the coast, and just across the border in Spain.' Stephen continued, 'Mick is a leftover from the Spanish civil war. When the fighting ended, he decided to stay on in Spain. He did a lot of good work for our department during the Second World War sailing his fishing boat up and down the coast, from the Bay of Biscay down to the coast of Portugal. Mick was able to pass us lots of very valuable information, on the whereabouts of some of the German U-boat packs that operated in the Atlantic.

'We have got to get rid of the arms cache in the cellar. If I can get Mick over here with his boat, he could pick up the girls, the gold, the arms, and anything else you wanted to remove. He could get the girls out of Portugal and safely deliver them to your base in France. As I said, it will be much easier to organise the girls' passage to Australia from there.'

'That's a great idea if it can be arranged, Stephen. I will get Marco and his fishing boat to meet up with this Mick chap; he will guide Mick's boat through the seaway and across the broad-water to our jetty. He could be in and out of here within an hour or so, if all goes well. This could solve all our problems. It would give me a couple of days to wind things up here and I could then drive back to the barge in France. That will still give me plenty of time to prepare the barge and bring it down to the coast.'

Stephen got up from the table, 'Right, let's get the place tidied up. Take everything you think you might need to keep you comfortable in the cellar for a couple of days, including water and food, girls. Marçel, as soon as I have made contact with Mick, get on to your policeman and get him here as quickly as possible. I want to leave as soon as I know everything is under control. I will go straight to Spain to brief Mick. Where do you want him to take the girls when he gets to France by the way?'

'St Nazaire, at the upper part of the Bay of Biscay. We carry a powerful transmitter on the barge so if Mick has a good radio I could make contact with him and do the transfer of the girls at sea, with no questions asked!'

'I'm sure he has all the necessary equipment. How long will it take to get from here to St Nazaire?'

'It's getting on for seven hundred miles; I would guess sailing and weather permitting—at least four or five days.'

'It all sounds feasible, providing Mick is prepared to do the trip and his boat is ready and seaworthy.' He paused. 'I think the man with the tyres for the Peugeot has just arrived.'

Marçel left him and went out to check that the tyres were being replaced. A few minutes later Stephen came out. 'All fixed, Marçel. I hope to be with Mick late tonight. He said, for a price, his boat would soon be ready to go and he would be delighted to rescue two *sheilas* in distress.'

As soon as Marçel's friend from the garage had finished fixing the new tyres, Marçel paid him, and then carefully parked the Peugeot out of sight; two cars in the courtyard might raise questions. He phoned police headquarters—Chief of Police Cardoso was on his way.

He called out to the others, 'Time for the little rats to go underground, *Toute suite, mais énfants!*'

Gerda gave him a punch below the belt. 'Only one rat around here, Marçel—the king rat and he stays upstairs, *Mate.*'

A few minutes later Police Chief Cardoso arrived. Marçel took him straight into the office and poured out two large glasses of port wine before they sat down. They raised their glasses and enjoyed one of the winery's best products.

'I am very sorry about Pete, José and Maria. As you know we became very good friends over the last three years. José and Maria were good people. It is tragic that they should have died like that. I know some very strange things have been happening here at the castle, but I cannot believe that Pete would be involved in anything dishonest.'

Cardoso got up and walked to the window; then turned to face Marçel. He spoke slowly, carefully choosing his words, 'When he came to see me the other day, Pete told me the castle and winery had been sold. He also told me he expected one or two problems to arise here in the next few days.'

He lowered his voice, 'What I'm about to say, Marçel, is in the strictest confidence. I know I can trust you.'

Marçel nodded, wondering what was coming. 'Of course, you know we are old friends, and nothing you say will go outside of these walls.'

'Pete asked me to ignore anything unusual that might be happening at the castle, until the new owners took over. I agreed, as I have always trusted Pete. He also told me about the Nazi cell that operates from Porto. I told him I already knew about this group, but as you know, people in high authority in this country are connected to the Nazi party so at present my hands are tied. Life for men in my position can be very precarious at times.

'Pete has always been very generous to me, especially with regard to my pension. He added a large amount of cash to my pension fund at our recent meeting.'

Cardoso came and sat down, and continued in his normal voice, 'So I promised to turn a blind eye to any ... *goings on* ... at the castle until the new owners take over. I will sadly present the matter of the three deaths at sea, as a tragic accident caused by the explosion of gas bottles on the launch. I will make sure not to involve you in all the necessary procedures that will follow this tragic accident.'

'Thank you for that, Chief Cardoso, Pete was a good man and you know how much I will miss him. We have indeed had a few problems here recently, including a brush with the local Nazis. But now everything is in order. I shall spend the next few days winding up before returning to France.'

Marçel concealed a sigh of relief. Thank you, Pete, for your generosity to the Police Chief. He refilled the glasses and they drank a toast to Pete.

'We will miss you two boys; you have done a lot for the district since you came here. I will be retiring shortly and would be delighted to see you if you ever come back to visit us in the future.'

After a brief chat, Marçel carried a case of their very best port wine out to his car.

'A word of warning, Marçel, there are some very dangerous men in this Nazi group. They have very long arms, which stretch from here to Spain and France. But I'm afraid at present I am unable to help you in this matter.'

They shook hands and Chief Cardoso drove out of the castle. Marçel realised he was a very worried man.

There were sounds of laughter when Marçel opened the cellar door; Stephen was launching himself into another of his smutty jokes. There was obviously a party in progress. There were already two empty wine bottles on the table. Helga shrieked with laughter when Stephen reached his punch line. 'Stephen, you really are a dirty old man but I love it.' Marçel realised that Helga, having made such a quick recovery, was far tougher than many of the men he knew.

It was hard to believe that in four short days this woman could have changed so much. She had been battered almost to death, and now with her arms around Stephen's shoulders, she was behaving like a normal, healthy and happy young woman.

Stephen noticed the look on Marçel's face and waved him over to the table. 'Don't worry, Marçel, your girls need a little light relief. I shall be leaving you in a few minutes. A little corruption of your delightful protégés will not go amiss. Come Marçel, have a glass of wine, lighten up, let's drink to us all safely meeting up on your "royal barge" in a few days' time in La Belle France.'

Stephen's little speech was interrupted by a loud crash.

'Merde!' Gerda's French broke the silence. 'Someone slammed the secret panel door.' They heard a gunshot as Gerda rushed up the stairs to slip the bolt on the inside of the trap door.

'Shit, I have been bloody careless!' Marçel cursed. 'I must have left the secret panel open. But I wonder why they have come back in daylight? They must have seen Chief Cardoso leaving.' He turned towards the passageway. 'They don't know about the entrance from the tower. Gerda, come with me. Stephen, you have a gun. Stay here with Helga.'

Marçel had automatically taken over, the situation requiring some quick action. They stopped off at the dungeon where the guns were stored and loaded two Sten guns; he knew Gerda was an expert with this weapon.

They ran to the end of the passageway and out through the tower door, which Marçel carefully locked behind them. They crept up the stairs and looked out onto the courtyard. The Renault was the only car parked in front of the house.

Two men dressed in dark suits came running out of the front door, crossed the yard and ran out of the door to the jetty. One of them was Karl Schmidt.

Marçel and Gerda quickly ran up the next flight of stairs and looked down to see Marco's fishing boat tied to the jetty. They watched as the two men ran down the track to their parked Mercedes and drove away.

As they hurried across the courtyard, Gerda turned to Marçel.

'You know who that shot was for, Marçel—the bastards!' They entered the front door. There was no mistaking the smell of cordite.

Marco was lying in a pool of blood. Marçel bent down, his face close to Marco's. He was still breathing and trying to say something, Marçel bent closer to catch his words. 'Sorry, Marçel, he—followed me in. Managed to close door—cellar.' And then Marco died.

Gerda opened the secret panel and then beat the trapdoor with her fists in anger and frustration. 'You can come out now. They've gone.' Helga and Stephen stepped out into the hall, and stood silently staring at Marco's body.

Stephen broke the shocked and angry silence. 'Right. I've got to go. Sort this out, Marçel. I don't know how you are going to explain this one to your policeman friend. Just another drowning at sea? I don't think so.'

Stephen gave the two girls a quick embrace. 'Enjoy your trip to France; cheer up, things can only get worse! Mick should have his boat ready by the time I get to Vigo tonight. I will tell him to phone you before he leaves, hopefully late tonight. You will have to take Marco's boat yourself, and meet him tomorrow night. And don't forget to arrange an identifying signal with him when he telephones. Good luck, my boy, see you in France. I'll take the Renault, as I'm sure they won't be looking for it at present.'

Marçel walked with him to the car. 'The bastards must have watched Marco arrive at the jetty and then followed him into the castle. Marco saw the open panel and managed to close it before Karl and his mate entered the hallway. He gave his life for us; he was a brave man. I will take Marco's body out to sea tomorrow night. Perhaps the police will assume that, in his grief for his family he took his own life.'

'That's probably all you can do, Marçel. When you get to the barge in France, call me. I will be in London. I will come over and join you. After we get the girls off to Australia, you and I will have to get rid of the remaining Nazis.'

'We were both careless this time, Marçel,' he called as he drove off.

It was early afternoon. Vigo was about one hundred and thirty miles of very hard driving along the coast road. Stephen crossed into Spain at Valencia, and arrived at the Vigo waterfront at six-thirty pm.

Meanwhile, back at the castle Gerda and Helga had cleaned up the mess in the hall and had wrapped Marco's body in a blanket. Between them they carried Marco across the yard to the tower. Marçel decided he would take the body out in the boat when he set off the following night.

Marçel decided to hide Marco's boat just in case the thugs came back and tried to disable it. He towed one of the kayaks behind the fishing boat, and crossed the river to a small well-concealed creek. The only access to this part of the river was by water. He left the boat hidden amongst tall reeds and returned to the castle in the kayak.

Back in the castle, he bolted and locked the two heavy doors at the courtyard entrance, as well as the door to the jetty. Anyone trying to enter the castle now would have to scale the walls.

They spent the rest of that day and the next day winding up all the paperwork in the office. Marçel left most of this job to Gerda as she was fully acquainted with the winery accounts.

Helga helped Marçel pack his clothes and his few personal possessions into two large suitcases, which he locked in the boot of the Peugeot. The new occupiers of the castle would find everything they needed and everything in order when they moved in. Marçel was certainly not happy to leave behind so many items that Pete, Gerda and he had collected over the last few years. He realised he would have to start a fresh life back on the barge in France; but this time he would be on his own …

That first evening they were able to relax and enjoy a good meal using up some of the supplies that Maria had kept stocked in the pantry. After consuming several bottles of their very best wine, the girls eventually decided to go to bed.

'Do you realise, Marçel, this is the first night that Helga and I have been able to sleep in a large comfortable bed?'

Gerda put her arms around him and with an impish look on her face, kissed him lightly on his nose while pressing her body against him. Marçel felt a little weak at the knees as Gerda gazed seductively into his eyes. 'So why don't you join us, Marçel?'

Marçel returned to the office to wait for Mick's call. It was just on midnight when the phone rang. He grabbed the phone.

'Mick here.' There was no mistaking the strong Australian accent. 'G'day mate, I hear you want to have a party tomorrow night. I'll meet you two miles to the west of the Aveiro seaway at midnight tomorrow. I will flash VE, which is dot dot dot dash dot—okay, mate?'

'That sounds great, Mick. I will reply with two dashes and a dot. Keep your navigation lights on till I get close to you, then you can turn them off.'

'Good on ya, mate; the weather forecast is good—see ya later.' And he was gone.

Marçel went upstairs and quietly opened the girls' bedroom door. Gerda and Helga were locked in each other's arms, lost to the world. He closed the door and went back downstairs.

Marçel spent the rest of the night sitting at a window overlooking the courtyard. He had thought that they were quite safe behind the stone walls of the castle but now he realised he couldn't underestimate the determination of the Nazis.

Thinking about Gerda and Helga, who were planning to start a new life overseas, made him reflect on his own situation. Four years had passed since he had been brutally raped by the two soldiers. That experience had completely changed his character. The shame, the humiliation and the pain. That monstrous event had created his tremendous hatred of the enemy, which had enabled him to plan to kill his first German.

From that time onwards, helped by the special training that he received soon afterwards when he was flown back to England, he went on to become an extremely accomplished killer. But the worst thing about it was that each time he killed a person, he realised that he was enjoying the act of killing.

Because of all this, he had cut himself off from his family, his parents, brothers and sisters and all connections with his early life in the Channel Islands. All the events that he had been involved in during the last years would now prevent him from ever returning to his past life back in Jersey. He had left the island as a boy, and now as a man he had a completely new identity. The family in Jersey believed that he had died somewhere in France or Germany in 1943. He had no reason to let them think otherwise, so he would not return.

Now he had so much blood on his hands. And he knew that as he was working with Stephen's department, the killing was more than likely to continue for some time to come. Marçel had decided that it would never be possible for him to have a close and lasting relationship with a woman, and although he had been able to live a secret and dangerous life in Europe, he knew that in the end, he would have to move overseas somewhere and start a new life.

Marçel decided that it was not the time to consider options. *Money would never be a problem for him. He was now a very wealthy man ...*

'Wake up, my little snoring Piglet!' Marçel woke up with a start. Gerda was standing over him with large cup of coffee; she looked down at him smiling. 'Naughty boy! I saw you put your head around the door last night. We were waiting for you, but when you didn't appear ... we had to make other arrangements!'

'Who corrupted who, Gerda?'

She bent down and kissed his forehead. 'You, of course, darling, you made us both so frustrated! What else could we do?'

'I'm afraid I might have had a bit of a problem satisfying the two of you; I've had so little sleep lately. I must say I like the idea of making love *à trois*. Maybe another time.'

Gerda ruffled his hair. 'Just be grateful you're alive this morning, darling. The mood that Helga and I were in last night—you might never have survived.'

Gerda was able to sense when Marçel was in one of his darker moods, and she usually managed to blow those moods sky-high, leaving him feeling on top of the world.

Chapter 8

Gerda leaned back against the bulkhead, her legs stretched out on the cockpit seat. She was sitting alongside the main hatch that led down to the saloon.

Enjoying the motion of the boat, she could feel the sun warming her body; it had been a rather cool night at sea. Through her half-open eyes she watched Mick. He was holding the steering wheel, and occasionally giving it a slight turn as the ketch cut its way through the long swell that rolled in from the Atlantic.

Gerda admired his slim, powerful and bronzed body. He was wearing a stained white shirt, shorts, and had a worn peaked cap pulled low, covering his long, once-ginger hair. Gerda liked his strong lined face that was almost hidden behind a greying straggly beard. She put his age at between thirty and thirty-four.

It was well after two am when they finally headed out through the seaway. As soon as they were well clear of the land, and heading out to sea, Mick turned the ketch into the wind, allowing the sails to flap while he went below with the girls. He helped them to make up their bunks, so that they wouldn't fall out if they ran into bad weather.

With only a few hours before dawn, the girls 'turned in,' and were soon asleep. Mick returned to the wheel and got the ketch back on course. It was after nine when the two girls appeared on deck completely refreshed, and excited at the prospect of a few days cruising on this yacht in such superb conditions.

Mick, who was starting to feel tired after twenty-four hours at the helm, was having other ideas.

Gerda watched the bubbling wake of the ketch as it faded away into the distance. She loved the dark blue colour of the ocean against the clear blue cloudless sky above. In the distance she could see the coast of Portugal, with the dark line of the mountains in the background.

'We should be in Spanish waters at about four this afternoon. We are about five miles off the coast at present. Nice steady north-westerly breeze and we are making a good six to seven knots.'

'Good on you, matey!' Helga's mop of black hair popped out through the hatchway holding a tin mug of tea in each hand. She spilled a lot of it as she battled to keep her balance. 'Come and slice your main braces with a cuppa, Mates.'

Mick took one of the mugs. 'Talk to your skipper like that and we'll have you strung up. You'll be getting six lashes of the cat-o-nine tails, me lady!'

Helga passed Gerda the other mug and muttered, 'He's gorgeous. He could tie me up anytime and …'

'Can you steer a boat?'

Gerda moved over and took the wheel from Mick. 'I used to go sailing with my late husband but in much smaller craft. I can steer by compass.' Mick stood behind her and noticed how relaxed she was.

'You'll be right. Just keep heading due north and when you see the sails start to flutter, just pay off a little then bring her back on course. You girls better know right now, you are not on a holiday cruise; you are both going to work your passage to St Nazaire. And believe you me, I'm a really hard taskmaster.'

He then completely spoilt the effect by putting his arm around Helga and giving her a hug. 'You come below with me, Helga; I'm going to show you how to read a chart. By the time we get you to St Nazaire, I'm sure you will both be able to sail this boat single-handed.'

Down in the cramped chart room, Helga was very conscious of Mick's closeness to her as they bent over the chart. She had a feeling that this man was somehow going to become a strong influence in her life. Helga had to try hard to concentrate on what Mick was saying as he drew lines on the chart showing her their route to the top of Spain and then across the Bay of Biscay to St Nazaire.

'So we head north past the top end of Spain and then, in theory, we head northeast to St Nazaire. Unfortunately it's not as simple as that—in the Bay of Biscay we will meet with some heavy seas and possibly some very stormy weather. It could become quite unpleasant, but luckily this is a good time of the year to cross the bay.'

They moved into the spacious saloon, which had a bunk seat on one side and a folding table, then an open area giving access via a narrow passageway to the forward cabins. 'Tell me about your ship, Mick. I would be happy to be your cook and bottle washer for this trip.'

'This is a fifty-eight foot long ketch with four main working sails, a jib, a foresail, a mainsail and on the stern—the back end—a mizzen-mast and sail. And it'll need a cook, cleaner, deckhand, watch keeper and bottle washer for this trip. As you know, you two girls have your cabin up forward. I have my small cabin next and with the toilet and shower opposite. Then we have the main cabin and lastly the chart room opposite the galley, kitchen to you. Under the cockpit there is a small diesel engine, which is there for emergencies only and is also used to charge up the batteries. I think we'd better go and see where Gerda is taking us.'

Up on deck, Gerda had been reflecting on the previous night's events.

By late afternoon they had completed the entire winery accounts, loaded Marçel's car with all his worldly goods, and stacked up the cases of arms ready to load onto Mick's boat.

Marçel had had a long telephone conversation with his bank manager in Aveiro. He had arranged for a caretaker to come to the castle the next day and stay until the new owners took over. That evening they had enjoyed a slap-up meal and tidied up ready to leave.

Later Marçel had wandered around the back of the castle, carrying a Sten gun over his shoulder; to make sure no one was there. When he was satisfied, he took one of the kayaks and crossed the river to collect Marco's boat. The girls had helped him carry Marco's body down to his fishing boat, and then Marçel set off to meet up with Mick.

Much later they had watched as Mick and Marçel brought the ketch skilfully alongside the jetty. They had been up in the tower and had rushed down to take the ropes, oblivious to the fact that the Nazi thugs might now be waiting for them outside the castle.

They had carried the boxes of arms and two cases of wine to the jetty door, and were now able to quickly load them onto the boat. The girls gave Marçel a hug and a kiss, threw their cases onto the deck of the ketch, and climbed aboard.

Marçel passed the extra-heavy case of gold bars over to Helga and told her to stow it carefully down below. Marçel then untied the ropes, gave the bow a hefty shove and the ketch moved away from the jetty before slowly disappearing into the darkness.

Half an hour later, when they were clear of the seaway, Mick had switched off the engine and hoisted the sails. They were on their way.

Gerda was brought back from her reverie as an extra-large wave bore down on the boat; she automatically swung the wheel until the bow faced into the oncoming wave. This brought the boat up into the wind. There was a crash as the boat broached and the boom swung across, just missing Gerda's head. Once over the crest of the wave, Gerda swung the wheel again and the boat came back on course. There was another crash as the boom swung back.

'Well done, Gerda, that was your first big one; you handled it well. Next time take in the main sheet; that's the rope that brings in the main sail and the boom, when you turn into the wind. Girls, watch your heads as the boom swings across, we don't want you knocked overboard.' Mick came up on deck followed by a slightly pale-faced Helga. Mick put his arm around a rather shaken Gerda. 'You handled that very well for a sheila. We'll get the odd big one occasionally girls, especially when we get into the Bay of Biscay. So keep your eyes open and you'll be right, maties.'

'Sorry, Mick, I must admit my mind was far away. That was a good lesson. I think you should show us how to handle all the ropes, just in case.'

'That, me beauty, is exactly what I am about to do, but firstly we must teach Helga to steer the ship.'

Mick stood behind Helga to hold her wrists as he gently helped her to get the feel of the steering wheel. He made her swing the boat, first to port and then to starboard, and then back on course. Mick showed her the points of the compass, and how to bring the ketch onto the different compass bearings. Eventually Helga, shaking with excitement, was completely familiar with the compass and the feel of the steering wheel. She felt a little disappointed when he removed his hands from her wrists and could no longer feel his warm breath on her neck.

'Right, Gerda, you come with me.' Mick showed Gerda, who was already familiar with small sailing boats, every one of the sails and each time he called to Helga to turn the boat into the wind. He made Gerda lower and hoist each sail until she became familiar with the ropes and the sheets that controlled the position of that sail. When they got to the mainsail, he had to help Gerda to hoist it up.

Mick then made Gerda take the wheel and went through the same process with Helga. When he was satisfied that Helga was quite familiar with all the ropes, he leaned against the safety rail and made the girls go through the whole process again.

'Right me beauties, if you have to hoist the mainsail, whoever is at the wheel turns the ketch into the wind and goes and helps the other person. That's when I expect you to move like blue-arsed flies.'

Mick finally took the wheel and looked down at his two exhausted but smiling sheilas. 'You're still smiling. I've a good mind to make you do it all over again. By the time we get to France you'll be able to do that in half the time. Well done, maties.'

'Now, the watches. We should reach St Nazaire in about four or five days. We are doing well at present, but I doubt we can maintain this speed. We will work four-hour watches. Helga will start at four this afternoon till eight this evening. Gerda at eight till twelve and I will take the watch from midnight till four and so on. In practice you will get around two hours' sleep at a time, because the rest of your time off you will be needed to help run the ship. It's just past midday now, so I'll take over till four pm.'

'So when do we eat?' Helga piped up in a small voice.

'Right now I reckon, Helga. Can she cook, Gerda?'

'I don't know, Mick; I certainly can't.' Gerda was an excellent cook, but she felt unable to face cooking in the small galley while the boat was punching its way through the rough seas. 'So it's you or her. Just hurry and make up your minds—I'm starving!'

'Guess we will give Helga a trial right now. Helga, we will relieve you when you prepare food during your watch. I'm afraid the stores in the galley are a bit limited. There's plenty of tinned meat, potatoes and vegetables and bread for today. After that you will have to make bread, that's if you can. As you know I had to leave my base in a bit of a hurry.'

Helga disappeared down to the galley and was surprised to find how well it was stocked. There was plenty of canned food and a good selection of herbs and sauces. Minutes later Helga returned on deck with a large plateful of delicious sandwiches and a bottle of Chardonnay.

'This is just a snack. I'll cook up some food, which should be ready when I go on watch at four pm.'

Helga then spent an hour in the galley cooking an enormous hotpot using up the last of the vegetables, some potatoes and a large tin of beef. She hoped this would last them for a few meals.

'That was really good, Helga, I'm not even going to try to compete. I reckon she's got the job. I'm going below to sleep it off.' And with that, Gerda disappeared.

'When you have finished stuffing yourself, Helga, you can take over; it's your watch now.' Mick was looking astern. A small aeroplane was heading towards them. 'What the hell is he doing out here? He's miles out from the shore and much too small to be flying across the Atlantic.'

They watched as the light aircraft flew over the ketch, before abruptly turning and heading back to the land.

Mick looked thoughtful. 'Somehow I don't think your troubles are over yet.'

Chapter 9

It was a calm night as Marçel set off to meet up with Mick's sailing boat. Once he was well out to sea, he reluctantly dropped Marco's weighted body over the side and watched it sink into the deep dark water. Marco had deserved a much better burial than that.

At midnight he spotted the VE signal and flashed—dash, dash dot in reply. He spotted the navigation lights some way ahead so opened the valve in the bottom of the hull and allowed water to start filling the boat. By the time Mick's ketch came alongside, the water level in the fishing boat had almost covered the motor.

Once alongside, Mick joined him. They both stood on the gunwale of the fishing boat, allowing the seawater to flow over the side and completely fill it. As it started to sink, they both jumped back onto Mick's boat and watched the fishing boat disappear to the bottom of the sea.

When they were just a short distance from the seaway, Mick dropped the sails and started his auxiliary motor. On the way in through the seaway, Marçel pointed out all the lit marks, making sure that Mick would remember them on his way out.

The girls were waiting to take the ropes as they came alongside the jetty. There was no time for introductions. Marçel left the girls to load all the gear onto the ketch while he wandered off towards the track with one of the Sten guns, ready to meet any attack that might come from that direction.

Later, having agreed on which radio frequency they would use when Mick was approaching the French coast, Marçel handed the case of gold to Helga.

Marçel was relieved to watch the ketch disappear into the night with Gerda and Helga on board. He had a nasty suspicion that when they were loading the ketch, that they were being watched and had fully expected an attack from the Nazis.

He was halfway to the castle door when he heard a faint click. He swung around and flung himself to the ground, all the while firing his gun in a wide arc.

He could just make out a vague form moving towards the track. He decided not to follow, as whoever it was would probably be expecting him to do so, and he would then be a sitting duck.

Marçel got up and slowly moved backwards to the castle door, carefully locking the door behind him. The Nazis must have just arrived, just in time to see the departing ketch.

But now they knew that he was alone in the castle.

Marçel realised it was prudent for him to get away as soon as possible. A small charge of explosives would easily blow open one of the doors to the castle and he would stand little chance if several of them were to break in. Anyway, he was now keen to get back to the barge in France.

There seemed to be limitless numbers of these Nazis, even though he had already killed three of them. Their man Schmidt seemed to be a powerful and determined leader and he was still very much alive. Marçel thought it strange that these brutal assassins should be so determined to recover the gold. This must be just part of a much bigger plan. He had to find out who this man was, who could go to such extremes to achieve his goal.

Marçel needed to snatch a couple of hours' sleep, as he had to face a long drive ahead, but dared not take the risk at this time. Two hours later and after several cups of hot strong coffee to keep him awake, Marçel went into the office and found a large envelope, which he addressed to Alfonso at the bank.

As he left the house, he turned off all the lights and locked all the doors behind him. Marçel placed his revolver in the glove compartment of the Peugeot and the Sten gun on the floor beside him; he would have to dispose of the gun before he reached the Spanish border.

It was just starting to become light when he quietly drove up to the main doors. He switched off the engine and opened the doors. All was quiet. He drove out and quickly slipped back to lock the heavy doors—still no sign of anyone.

Marçel drove without lights until he reached the main entrance to the winery and was on the road to Aveiro. He noticed a car following a short way behind him. Pulling up outside the bank at Aveiro, he slipped all the castle keys into the envelope and walked over to the night safe.

Alfonso would be able to hand them over to the new caretakers when the bank opened in the morning. Marçel was too concerned about his present situation to indulge any regrets he might have about leaving the castle for the last time. Marçel jumped into the Peugeot, did a U-turn and drove up alongside the black Mercedes …

They both lowered their windows at the same time.

For a moment they just stared at each other.

Marçel found himself looking into the eyes of Karl, the young blue-eyed blond German—the pride of the Third Reich, one of Hitler's purebred Aryan supermen. The eyes were of hardened steel and the lined face of this man exposed the hidden cruelty beneath his skin.

'So. I am face to face at last with the famous Piglet. I'm disappointed!'

'I'm afraid I've not had the displeasure of your name.'

'*Bitte, ich bin* Karl Schmidt and I have come all the way from Brazil expressly to kill you.'

'Good. Stick around, Sunshine, because I'm on my way to visit my old sick grandma for a few days. But I'll be back. You never know, I might have something extra special for you when I return—but it certainly won't be gold. That's now somewhere on the high seas. Somehow, I don't think you will be going back to your mates in Brazil.'

Marçel drove off and left Schmidt pondering. As long as he knew that Marçel had something he wanted, he would stay close enough for Marçel to catch him off guard and kill him, and this he fully intended to do. This man had murdered his friends.

Marçel felt excited; this was a challenge. He was up against a man who would test him to the very limit. What Karl lacked in shrewdness, he certainly made up for with sheer determination. Convinced that Schmidt would either try to follow him into Spain or would have members of his organisation who would track his movements and report back to him, Marçel realised that he would have to be extremely cautious in approaching the barge. Only Stephen, Pete and he knew of its existence.

It was just after six am. Marçel had a long hard drive in front of him and he fully intended to get to France that night.

The road through Viseu and Guarda twisted and turned all the way to the Spanish border. Except for his revolver, which he had concealed under the dashboard, Marçel dismantled the guns and threw the parts into roadside ditches as he drove through the mountainous roads. After crossing the Spanish border, he headed for Salamanca and then northeast through Valladolid, Burgos and Vitoria Gasteiz to San Sebastian.

It was almost seven in the evening when Marçel crossed the border into France. He was aware of tensions at the border crossing; there had been a series of bomb explosions in the Basque area and both sides of the border were on the lookout for the newly emerging Basque terrorists. He was quite *unaware* though of the official who stamped his passport and who then went off to make two phone calls: one to Porto and later, to a man at St Jean de Luz in France. Karl hadn't wasted any time in calling his contacts.

Marçel drove on through St Jean de Luz and soon after arrived at the seaside town of Biarritz on the Gulf of Vizcaya. He had driven over five hundred miles to Biarritz in France on poor quality roads and had met with little traffic on these roads. He was feeling pretty tired when he finally drove onto the esplanade at Biarritz. He went straight to the Hotel Royale—an old family run hotel on the waterfront, where he had stayed several times in the past.

Madame Le Blonde greeted him warmly (Marçel seemed to collect portly Madames, who usually wanted to mother and smother him), 'So good to see you again, *Cheri*—but you are so late. If you need to eat, the only place open now is the old casino. Tonight they have dancing, *Mon Cheri*. You might find a nice girl to keep you warm tonight!'

That was the last thing Marçel needed after the events of the last few days. He opened the bedroom window and looked across the street. The waves were breaking against the sea wall and occasionally spray drifted across to where his car was parked on the opposite side of the road close to some palm trees. He noticed another car pulling out from behind his, but thought nothing of it.

The casino was only two blocks away. Marçel decided that he needed the exercise, so he strolled down to the very tired-looking building—Biarritz, once a very popular holiday resort, was still looking pretty drab after the war years.

Marçel entered the once-brilliant dance hall. A five-piece band was playing to about six dancing couples, the music had a distinctly Spanish flavour to it and his spirits rose as he propped himself up at the bar. Two quick Pernods and he would have been quite ready to tread a measure if Gerda had been with him. Two more, followed by a plate of ham sandwiches and he was ready for bed. Finishing up with a large brandy, he slowly made his way back to the Hotel Royale. As he turned the last corner bringing him to the waterfront, he noticed that someone was attempting to break into the Peugeot.

As the man started to open the car door, there was a blinding flash that lit up the road as the car was blown apart. The man's body was flung across the road where it lay burning in the gutter.

People rushed out of their houses and the hotel. Two men beat out the flames on the dead man. Moments later, the police and an ambulance arrived. When questioned by the police, one of the men mentioned the bystander who calmly walked back into the hotel.

Marçel slipped quietly up to his room. *Schmidt certainly didn't waste time.* Marçel remembered the immigration official at the French border post who had spent quite some time examining his passport. Believing he had now dealt with Marçel, Schmidt would switch his interest to the two girls and the ketch.

Determined to intercept the gold and the girls, Schmidt would have guessed that they would be heading either to France or England. Schmidt could easily set out in a boat from a port higher up the coast of Spain and just wait for the ketch to come to him.

Marçel decided he would to try to make radio contact to warn Mick the moment he arrived at the barge. He could only hope that the three of them would be able to beat off any attack with the weaponry they had on board. Under cover of darkness they might be able to slip away.

Marçel realised that he would just have to wait patiently until they were well into the Bay of Biscay before he could make radio contact.

The noise outside the hotel had died down. He turned off the bedside light and was soon asleep.

Marçel woke up to a crash, his bedroom door was flung open and three armed *gendarmes* stormed into the room. This was followed by a quite unnecessary strip search as he was almost naked in bed.

He was allowed to slip on a shirt and trousers, no belt; then unceremoniously frog-marched down to their waiting van. Two hefty *gendarmes* picked him up and threw him into the van before jumping in after him. One of them deliberately crushed his bare foot under his heavy boot. At the *commissariat de police*, Marçel was dragged out of the van and taken into the station. '*Anglais*,' the duty sergeant muttered with contempt. '*Parlez vous Français, cochon?*'

'*Non monsieur.*' Marçel could speak fluent French but he was not going to make it too easy for them. He thought it funny that he had been called *cochon* (pig); they could not have known that they were addressing the Piglet. 'I am just an innocent traveller passing through your town. Someone put a bomb in my car and then someone else tried to steal my car. I would like a cup of coffee, please.'

The sergeant exploded.

Marçel guessed the mention of coffee really upset him. He launched into a long tirade, abusing Britain, America, the Basque terrorists and finally Marçel. 'Take the terrorist *pig* down to the cells.'

He was taken down to the basement and thrown into a small cell to cool off. Marçel knew that 'cooling off' might take several days and wondered if he would be free in time to meet the ketch when it arrived off St Nazaire. Stephen had no idea how to handle the barge and he was definitely quite incapable of taking it out to sea.

'*Merde*, bloody *merde, quel dommage!*'

Marçel had underestimated Schmidt. He had been quite sure that he had not been followed from Portugal, so the only way Schmidt could have found him was a tip-off from the French or Spanish border posts. He must have a contact at the posts, possibly someone from the Basque terrorist movement and must have instructed his contact to have him followed and killed.

There was nothing he could do at present. The investigating officer would come to him when he was ready. It was just lucky for him that some unfortunate car thief had chosen to steal his car. It was not so lucky for the car thief. It was a pity about the almost-new uninsured car.

Marçel realised he would have to get himself another car, but that was the least of his problems. Marçel had also lost all his clothes and his few precious possessions. He and Gerda were now both in the same situation.

Marçel decided to catch up on his lack of sleep over the past few days. It was late afternoon when he was finally woken up. A tray with a bowl of broth, a large hunk of bread and a mug of water were brought into the cell. '*L'Inspecteur arrive demain matin.*' He would have to spend the night and hopefully extricate himself out of this situation in the morning.

He spent most of the night pacing up and down in the tiny cell. Marçel regretted having slept most of the previous day. He had to get out of this place in the morning; and hoped the police would have checked out his passport by now and would realise that he was a legitimate businessman travelling from his winery in Portugal to his depot in France.

He would have to be careful that they didn't delve too deeply into his activities. Pete and Marçel had recorded the ownership of the barge under a different name, just in case any prying official ever searched it and discovered their secret armoury. Marçel knew he had to get to the barge as quickly as possible. No doubt his killers would be waiting for him to leave the *Commissariat*. He couldn't risk buying a car in Biarritz. It would be safer to take a taxi to Bayonne and purchase a car there.

The day dragged on and on. By lunchtime Marçel was getting really angry, which was, he knew, what they wanted to achieve. *A prisoner would be more likely to slip up when he lost his cool!* *L'Inspecteur* finally arrived at three pm. Marçel was taken to an interview room, *L'Inspecteur* dismissing the guard.

'We see from your passport that you travel frequently between France and Portugal. You have a wine business in France and a winery in Portugal,' he smiled broadly. 'That would not make you too popular with French wine producers. We have identified the body. He was a well-known car thief in the district and finally got his comeuppance. It seems obvious someone was out to get you. You had no reason to blow up your own car.' *L'Inspecteur* gave a big smile. 'Maybe a French wine producer!' Marçel had become quite used to that joke.

'However, *Monsieur*, it seems you have friends in high places and the news of your accident must have travelled fast. I have received instructions from Paris to deliver you to our *Commissariat de Police* at Bordeaux today. For your own safety we will take you there in a police van.' *L'Inspecteur* left the room and returned a few minutes later bearing a tray with coffee, a large plate of biscuits and Marçel's wallet. A *gendarme* brought in the clothes Marçel had left at the Hotel Royale.

'The remains of your car have been towed away and I will dispose of the wreck for you. Your hotel bill has not yet been paid.' Marçel handed him some notes to cover the hotel bill.

'So, when you have finished your coffee, *mon ami*, we will be ready to leave.'

Marçel was not quite sure how to take this move to Bordeaux. Was he being released or just transferred to another department?

As they drove out of the compound, he noticed two other police vans leaving the depot. They all set off in different directions, a good ploy if Schmidt's man was waiting to follow them. They drove around some of the back streets and then through Bayonne before heading out onto the road to Bordeaux.

After he had endured a bumpy ride in the back of the police van, they arrived at the Bordeaux *commissariat* at seven in the evening. Marçel was taken to an interview room. A distinguished old man was sitting there, grinning like a fat cat.

'Thought you might need a little help, Marçel. You're getting sloppy in your old age. It's a good job I kept my eye on you.' Stephen stood up ready to leave.

'Our department is nearly always kept informed when a bomb explodes somewhere in Western Europe. I contacted my counterpart in Paris and confirmed that it was your car and that you were unharmed. I decided you needed a little help so the Paris chaps arranged for me to collect you from Bordeaux. So now it's time for us to get moving.'

Another police van was waiting for them at the back of the *commissariat*. It was dark when they arrived at Stephen's hotel at Blaye, on the north bank of the Gironde, and too late to admire the superb scenery of the district.

'We will have time for a good meal, Marçel, and then I think we should move on. I'm sure for the time being we have lost your unpleasant friends, but just in case we might encounter a crooked policeman on the way, I think we should really press on and try to get to the barge tonight.'

'It should take us about five or six hours to get to Nantes, Stephen.'

'In my car, Marçel—four and a half hours.'

Oysters followed by poached trout and washed down with one of the best white wines from Saumur, and they were ready for their night drive to the estuary which ran off the Canal de Nantes à Brest close to the small town of Blain.

An open MG sports car, although fast, was not the ideal car for a long night drive. By the time they crossed the Loire River at Nantes they were both suffering from the cold night air.

Before they got to the canal and the town of Blain, they turned off into a lane that led them to a small estuary in the Foret de la Groulais. This estuary, which Pete had found, branched off the main canal and made a perfect hideaway. Partly concealed by the overhanging trees, the estuary ran for a short distance through a heavily-wooded valley.

The only access to the water was by a narrow track that ran through the forest. The early morning sun shining through the trees soon helped to warm them up as they drove through the forest to finally reach the water's edge.

The barge was sitting a little way off the estuary bank, moored to some heavy posts that had been driven into the mud. Tall trees shaded the barge from the sun, and concealed it from the few people that might come down to this isolated little creek.

Marçel removed his shoes and trousers and waded out. He was up to his waist before he was able to scramble aboard. He opened the hatch cover, which was in the bow of the barge, and descended into the storage area where they kept the deflated rubber dinghy. He dragged it up onto the deck and inflated it with a foot pump.

Marçel paddled back to the estuary bank and brought Stephen and his gear back onto the barge. He found the key to the wheelhouse, which was always kept concealed in the wooden cage on the roof of the wheelhouse, hidden amongst the life jackets and flares and unlocked the sliding doors.

Pete and Marçel had bought the barge from a *batelier* (barge owner) shortly after the war; the old man had decided to retire to his brother's farm after a lifetime of working the canals of Brittany. They had taken it to St Nazaire for a complete refit.

The barge was only sixty-five feet long, but it was seafaring with a fairly sharp bow, unusual for this type of barge. They had installed a powerful new diesel engine, which could give them a good fourteen knots if required, and they had equipped the engine room with new pumps and a large generator. The slightly raised and enclosed wheelhouse, with specially reinforced glass windows enabled all-round vision. The large steering wheel had a raised adjustable seat for the helmsman and all the engine controls were within easy reach. There was a two-way radio on one side of the large chart table.

Pete had managed to get hold of some radar equipment, which was just beginning to be developed for smaller craft. There was storage for charts, safety equipment and flags under the chart table. A hatchway at the rear of the bridge revealed the iron steps leading down to the engine room and a larger hatch alongside the steering wheel led down into the main saloon. The varnished timber and teak decking gave the wheelhouse a touch of luxury.

Down below, the spacious saloon took up the whole width of the hull.

A padded seat ran the full length of one side with the long table and chairs, which were all bolted to the deck. On the other side of the saloon, several easy chairs and a small table made a pleasant relaxing area. A passageway then ran down the centre of the hull with the fully equipped galley on one side and opposite, a door to the wireless-room.

Stephen's department had installed all the latest radio equipment. The transmitter was for Pete's use; this enabled him to keep in touch with London and the Department's agents almost anywhere in the world.

Two large cupboards filled with books and radio spares, had hidden panels at the back. In these concealed compartments, the cache of arms was kept. Although well hidden and out of sight, it would probably be found in a thorough search of the barge.

Further down the passageway on the portside there was a large cabin with a double bed, toilet and washbasin and then a cabin with two single bunks. On the starboard side of the passage there was a bathroom with shower, washbasin and toilet, and then two small cabins with double deck bunks. At the end of the passageway two steps led up to a heavy steel bulkhead. The watertight door led into the storage area in the bow of the barge. If at any time the bow of the barge were to be damaged, then the steel bulkhead would prevent flooding to the rest of the barge.

On deck the bow section above the storage area was slightly raised. On the long deck area between the bow and the wheelhouse, a section of the deck had been raised two feet and a row of skylights gave ample daylight to all the below-deck areas. From the short mast behind the wheelhouse, an aerial for the radio and transmitter ran all the way to a post on the bow section. A safety rail surrounded the stern deck behind the wheelhouse. This was a clear area except for the engine room vent and a small upturned dinghy; ideal for entertaining or just lying out in the warm summer sun.

Pete and Marçel had been unable to agree on a suitable name for their second home. In the end, after many arguments, they decided just to call it the 'Barge'.

The batteries needed charging. Marçel went down into the engine room and started the generator. He found Stephen in the radio room, sitting in front of the radio transmitter and trying to make contact with Mick.

'I'm not having much luck, my boy. I have the right frequency but they are not answering.'

'We'll try again later. In fact, let's try every hour until we make contact.'

Stephen withdrew to the galley; he turned on the gas, boiled some water and made coffee and carried it and a plate of biscuits into the saloon.

'I know you were quite unaware of what Pete had been up to when he disappeared for several days at a time. Pete had been doing odd jobs for the Department and naturally for security reasons, he was given strict orders not to confide in you.'

Stephen poured the freshly made coffee into two large mugs. 'In the last two years, I have often come down here to discuss some of our operations with Pete, hence the MG parked at Dinard airport. I must say I enjoy the occasional drive down to this lovely part of France. So now you know why I am so familiar with the layout of the barge.'

Stephen helped himself to a biscuit and continued. 'After my meeting with Mick, I got a flight from Vigo to London. As soon as I got back to London, I made an appointment with our cabinet minister to meet the following day. At the meeting amongst other things I told the minister that I thought you would be an ideal person to take over Pete's job. The minister, who had always taken an interest in Pete and was genuinely upset at his death, agreed that you would be the right person, providing I kept a close watch on you until the Department was quite satisfied with your progress. I went back to my office and caught up with the backlog of work.'

Marçel refilled the coffee mugs.

'When I arrived at my office the following morning, I was told that there had been a car bomb explosion at Biarritz. I knew you would be passing that way at about that time so I contacted Paris. I spent the whole day trying to organise your release from prison.'

'How on earth did you manage to get down to Bordeaux in such a short time, Stephen?'

'I left London late afternoon, flew down to the Dinard airport in Brittany. I keep my MG parked in the airport car park. I drove a few miles into Rennes and the next day, the two hundred miles to Blaye, where for security reasons I arranged for a police car to take me to the Bordeaux *commissariat*.'

'You certainly don't waste any time—for an oldie, sir!'

'Let's have a little more respect if I am to be your new boss, young Piglet.'

Stephen was no longer smiling. He spoke slowly. 'You have been well trained by us; we know you far better than you know yourself. Now, just think very carefully before you reply. Do you really want to work for the

Department? We gave Pete some very dirty and difficult jobs. I know you are quite capable of doing all the unpleasant tasks, in fact I wonder if sometimes you are not a little *too* enthusiastic when it comes to killing people.'

As Stephen was looking into Marçel's eyes, his face had suddenly hardened. Marçel knew that this man would not spare anyone who endangered his country or his organisation. 'Remember too, Marçel, we cannot afford to have people wandering about who know too much about the Department.'

'Wow, that last remark had a sting in the tail! In other words—I am already committed to this task or else!'

They were both silent for a few moments. Marçel had just lost his best friend Pete, the castle and the wine business and now had far more money than he would ever need in his lifetime. He was a complete loner but he needed a purpose in life with a little danger and lots of excitement.

'That guarded threat is wasted on me,' Marçel stated calmly. 'I'm quite capable of looking after myself. However I believe this job would give me the challenges I need and the opportunity to maybe right some of the wrongs that surround us in today's world. It would also give me the chance to rid the world of some of the lowest type of greedy scum that are gorging off society.'

'That's settled then. You will receive Pete's salary and your base from now on will be here on this barge. You know you have now committed yourself for life; till death do us part and all that!'

They both laughed at that but Marçel knew Stephen was quite serious about the last bit ...

'I'm also aware that life can be pretty cheap in the Department. I have no need for a salary, but I will accept it as there are lots of people that we can give a helping hand to on the way.'

They shook hands. Marçel knew this man would never let him down. He also felt that Stephen replaced the father that he had lost, when he had been forced to leave the Channel Islands.

'Stephen, I think we should get some stores in today and prepare the barge so that we are ready to leave here early in the morning. We should be able to moor the barge somewhere close to St Nazaire by midday tomorrow.'

'As soon as we make radio contact with the ketch and get their position, we can slip quickly out to sea, meet up with Mick and bring back the girls. That way we won't have any problems with the immigration people.'

'I need to do some shopping to replace my clothes and of course I will have to get myself a new car, which I guess I can now charge to the Department. It's only thirty minutes to Nantes.'

Stephen chuckled. 'No problem, old boy; you're not wasting any time. But try to make this one last a little longer. You still have your old Renault in Spain in case you forgot.'

Stephen dropped Marçel off at Nantes and returned to the barge, hoping to make radio contact with Mick.

Marçel bought himself a new Renault saloon and then went shopping while the garage prepared the car for him. He returned from Nantes mid-afternoon in the new Renault, laden with fresh food supplies. Marçel had replaced his wardrobe and had collected three cases of some very expensive wine that he knew Stephen particularly liked.

'I'm a little concerned that we can't make contact with the ketch, Marçel. I've just tried again. Nothing!'

'Mick should have made contact by now. They must be well into the Bay of Biscay. We'll keep calling on the hour from daybreak tomorrow morning.'

After spending the next few hours sampling the wines, they decided to turn in. Stephen insisted that Marçel, as the new captain of the barge, should take the stateroom, while he took one of the smaller cabins.

Marçel's thoughts turned to Gerda and Helga and he decided that command of a double bed had lots of possibilities ...

Chapter 10

Marçel woke at daybreak to the sound of chattering birds. It was a perfect summer's morning and he could think of nothing better than spending the summer cruising up and down the French canals.

Standing on the deck of the barge, Marçel breathed in the fresh morning air. The sky was clear with a slight breeze that occasionally rippled the calm backwater and bent the tops of the trees. Marçel decided to hose down the decks.

He heard the pressure pump start up in the engine room as he opened the main water valve on deck. The hosepipe snaked along the deck as the pressure built up, soaking him with icy cold water. Marçel found a stiff brush in the bow storage area and spent the next hour scrubbing away at the bird droppings that had built up on the deck and on the roof of the wheelhouse.

He cleaned the windows and wiped down all the varnished wood inside and outside of the wheelhouse. He carefully polished the compass and all the controls. Then he checked that the fuel tanks were full before running the engine for a few minutes. The barge was ready to go.

It was well after six when he dashed down to the wireless room; Stephen was sitting at the desk trying to make contact with Mick.

'I've just heard a weather forecast. It seems it's pretty rough out in the bay with strong winds from the North East which means the ketch will be heading right into it. I have not yet made contact with Mick; he may be having problems with his aerial in the rough seas. I think it might be worth calling him every hour and hope that he will come through to us by six pm.'

'Yes, I wonder how the girls are coping with the rough weather. We must take the barge down to Nantes and be ready to go out to meet them. Let's have breakfast and then we can get going.'

They both sat back feeling more than satisfied, having tucked into scrambled eggs on toast, bread and jam and several large cups of coffee.

'Now that you have become one of us, Marçel, I am able to give you a little background regarding the work that Pete had been doing in the past year.' Stephen leaned across the table.

'We believe since the end of the war with Germany, there has been a steady re-emergence of the Nazi Party in several parts of Europe. We were aware of cells in France, West Germany, Italy and Spain and of course we now know that a powerful cell is operating from Porto in Portugal.'

Marçel's mind was racing. 'Pete must have uncovered the Porto group and so that's why they came after him. Then having discovered our escape to death runs, they decided to wipe us all out. Firstly they destroyed our depot in France and then they killed Pete. The whole thing is becoming clear now. Gerda, the gold and I were next on their list. Having disposed of so many of their fellow countrymen, no doubt they were not too happy with me. I guess, apart from Pete and the old couple, we have all been extremely lucky in the last few days.'

'*Lucky?* I think they became very *unlucky* when they came up against the Piglet.'

Stephen got up and started to clear the table. 'For some time now I have had my suspicions that someone was attempting to bring all these scattered Nazi groups together with a view to eventually making a great Nazi comeback in Europe. I have reason to believe that the masterminds of this plan are based in Brazil; surprising—as most of the German Nazis are now living in Argentina.'

'So why not go to Brazil and wipe them out?' Marçel liked the idea of an expedition to South America.

'Life is not as simple as that; we just can't barge into another country and start a war! We have received some information in London that points to one man, an aspiring Adolf Hitler. We think that this man has come over to Europe; it's quite possible that this Karl Schmidt could be that person. In any event, it certainly seems that somebody pretty smart is directing things. Pity for him he had such incompetent apes working for him.'

'I met him outside the bank in Aveiro, an unpleasant-looking blue-eyed German blond, the same blond Schmidt that we have been dealing with at the castle.' Marçel recounted the words they'd exchanged from their cars outside the bank.

'That would be right, little was known of this man; he was a minor figure in Hitler's entourage. Karl Schmidt took up the position early in the war. He had been a member of the Hitler youth organisation and it was believed that he occasionally spent time alone with Hitler. It was rumoured that he had come from the same part of Austria as Hitler and that maybe, somewhere along the line there was a blood-tie.'

Marçel was intrigued, 'Do you think he might have been an illegitimate son of Hitler's?'

'I very much doubt that, I don't think Hitler was capable of procreation. Schmidt was not in the bunker in Berlin when the Russians found the bodies of Adolf and Eva, so he must have disappeared with several of the other men who were close to the Führer at that time. Eventually Schmidt turned up in Brazil, a very wealthy man and one of the leaders of the Nazi organisation in South America and I now believe him to be a threat to the peace in Europe. It really is possible that they are planning some sort of come-back.'

They both fell silent for a moment; Marçel could imagine the threat to peace that this man, with the backing of a fairly large number of supporters, could be to their future.

'So, Piglet, this is to be your first assignment. As soon as we have Gerda and Helga safely away, you will have to find and kill this man Schmidt. We will never completely wipe out the small Nazi cells in Europe, but without a strong leader they are nothing, and I am convinced that without a leader we will always be able to keep them under control.'

Marçel left Stephen to wash up the dishes. He climbed the steps to the wheelhouse, sorting out a map of the canal area to Nantes and also the chart that would take them out to the ocean to meet up with the ketch.

Marçel thought about his assignment to hunt down and kill Schmidt—he was a menace to society and he had killed his best friend Pete, as well as his three good friends at the castle. He'd even blown up his car and destroyed his few possessions; Marçel would hunt him down and execute him. Marçel thought of the expression, 'For Pete's sake,' and smiled to himself. No problem.

Down in the engine room, Marçel restarted the diesel and allowed it to quietly tick over. Out of the porthole he could see a healthy puff of smoke, which quickly dispersed. Marçel went back on deck and untied the bow and stern ropes and returned to the wheelhouse. With the engine in reverse, he pulled away from the mooring posts until the barge was well clear of them. A touch ahead and they were heading down the estuary through the overhanging branches of the tree-lined banks of the canal.

The barge motored out into the main canal and then headed southeast through the superb unspoilt French countryside. They passed through numerous locks, which kept them busy as they helped the *éclusiers* open and close the lock gates, until they arrived at the Erde River junction.

Once they were in the wide section of the beautiful Erde River, Marçel was able to take the speed up to twelve knots and by late afternoon he brought the speed back to five knots, as they passed through the tunnel at Nantes and then out on to the busy Loire River.

Navigating down the Loire River was quite difficult; Marçel had to take extra care not to let the fast running tide sweep them onto the many mud banks. He was soon able to turn left into the Canal de la Martinière, which ran parallel to the river and was then able to relax until they were almost at Paimboeuf, a small town on the river, which was just a short way from the port of St Nazaire. The barge was now within easy access of the ocean.

It was close to seven pm when they finally came alongside the jetty. Stephen, who had been trying to make contact with the ketch all day, came up on deck and helped tie up the barge. By this time it was blowing quite hard. They both realised Mick and the girls would be having a hard time out in the bay.

'The weather forecast stated that the wind will ease tonight but will swing to the east and freshen in the morning, which unfortunately is not much help to Mick.'

Marçel went ashore to stretch his legs. He found a shop still open and returned to the boat with fresh bread and a large piece of *Pate de Champagne* which they washed down with a bottle of red Bordeaux.

Stephen and Marçel took it in turns that evening to man the radio.

At midnight Stephen woke Marçel. 'I've been calling the ketch and have just heard a faint female voice.'

They listened for a few minutes and after a while they were just able to make out a few almost unintelligible words.

'That's them, Stephen. Tell them to keep trying. We need to know where they are.' They came back almost at once. It was Gerda calling.

She came in very faintly. They were able to catch some of her words, which made sense. '*Mast—damage—Belle Ile—Shelter Pointe de Pouldon—fishing boat shadowing—battery nearly flat.*' It went quiet for a moment and then quite clearly '*NEED HELP*' was heard and then it went dead.

Marçel grabbed the mike from Stephen. 'Got your message—stay where you are—I'll be with you tomorrow midday—acknowledge—chin up.'

A faint 'Received' came back and that was all, but it was enough.

'We will leave at dawn; I can't risk a night run. We will have to batten down all the hatches and put anything that moves to somewhere where it can't. We are in for a very rough trip, Stephen; this will certainly test the barge in a rough sea. I just hope we don't capsize our flat-bottomed boat.'

'I'm not very happy about the fishing boat that's shadowing them, Marçel. I think we might just sort out some of your weapons. Never underestimate the enemy.'

They opened up the concealed armoury and took out two rifles, two revolvers and several hand grenades. 'This should be enough to deter our Nazi pirates, Marçel.'

'I think we should take that heavy machine gun up to the wheelhouse, Stephen, and put it under the chart table for now; there is a mounting for it under there.'

'Pete and I welded a heavy tube to the deck just in front of the wheelhouse. The gun mounting drops into the tube. That gives us a three-hundred and sixty degree clear vision for firing the gun.'

Marçel went up to the wheelhouse and studied the chart, carefully noting all the marks and buoys on the way out to the ocean. He then plotted a course to Belle Ile and found Pointe de Pouldon marked on the chart. It was on the south side of the island. The ketch would get some shelter there for the night.

—

Karl Schmidt was smiling. He switched off his radio and slapped the helmsman on the back. 'We head for Belle Isle and the Pointe de Pouldon. Full speed ahead.'

Chapter 11

At eight pm Gerda took over the helm from Mick. Shortly after, Helga and Mick went below to catch a few hours' sleep.

It was a fine night with a good steady breeze. Gerda was feeling elated. She was enjoying the feeling of control as the ketch glided along at a steady seven knots, the bow lifting as it topped the swell and then surging forward as it descended into the next trough.

Gerda wished she could have shared this moment with Pierre; they had spent so little time together before he had been so brutally murdered by the *Gestapo*. Gerda shuddered as she recalled the night when they had found Pierre and the other Resistance boys hanging from that tree.

Her mind switched back to Marçel and those passionate moments they had spent making love just after he had rescued her at the campsite. Once again dear Marçel had come to her rescue; afterwards she had put her arms around him and pulled him to the ground kissing him ever so passionately.

They had kissed tenderly on occasion, and this usually led on to them making gentle and sensuous love. But this time, all the tensions of the last few hours had been unleashed. She worried that she had not been careful enough and that perhaps this carelessness on her part might have resulted in her becoming pregnant.

Her feelings for Marçel were very mixed. She felt love for him, but it was the strong love that one felt for a very dear friend. Although she loved him, there were times when he frightened her. She knew he had just knifed a man and that he still had blood on his hands when he had made love to her. Was this the cause of their frenzied lovemaking?

Gerda was happy listening to the swish of the sea as it rushed past the hull of the ketch. She wondered how she would feel if she were to carry Marçel's child. It was something that occasionally passed through her mind when she thought of the wonderful times they had spent together. Gerda sighed. If only she could have had a child from Pierre.

Although she loved Marçel, she could never marry him. He was several years younger than her, but that didn't matter. Deep down she knew she would not be able to live with a professional killer, no matter how justified he felt in ridding the world of the worst enemies of society.

Gerda thought of Marçel as a mostly kind and gentle person and also a very just person, but when his anger took over, he was cold and calculating and a man to be feared. But then she still loved this man and still wanted his child. Gerda knew that although she might never marry Marçel, their lovemaking had bonded them forever.

'Why are you looking so happy, girl? Enjoy the calm, because I'm afraid there's a storm forecast for tomorrow.'

Gerda was surprised at how quickly her four-hour watch had passed, her thoughts coupled with the motion of the ketch as it sliced through the waves had left her feeling happy and elated.

'I'm sure we have nothing to worry about with a big hulk of a man like you to look after us.' Gerda balled her fist and gave Mick a light punch below the belt as he took over the steering wheel.

'There's coffee ready for you in the galley. Sleep well, and don't wake that lovely sheila partner of yours!'

Down in their small cabin, Gerda slipped quietly into the lower bunk. The moment her head touched the pillow she fell asleep, despite Helga's gentle snoring and the hissing sound as the hull of the ship cut through the water.

Helga woke up to the sound of flapping sails and a banging on the cabin door. 'Hands on deck, you lazy lubbers!' Mick had turned the ketch into the wind and had come down to wake the girls. Helga, exhausted from the sail-hoisting exercise the day before, had overslept by an hour. 'I need you both on deck to help take in the sails.'

Up on deck it was still dark and the wind had become quite strong. During Mick's watch the wind had swung to the north and he had been forced onto the other tack, altering his course to northwest to stay well clear of Cape Finisterre.

Mick told the girls to put on the oilskins that were hanging in the chart room; they came up into the cockpit looking like two barefooted penguins. 'Helga, take the wheel and keep the bow up into the wind while we change the sails. Gerda, come with me, that's if you can see out from the top end of that oilskin.'

Up in the bow, Mick passed the storm jib up to Gerda through the forward hatch; he then climbed out and edged himself out along the bowsprit as Gerda lowered the sail. Mick unclipped the jib sail and passed it back to Gerda, who then passed him the storm jib. Twice the bowsprit dipped Mick into the sea before he was able to work his way back onto the deck of the ketch. Gerda hoisted the storm jib and then they changed the staysail, stowing the larger sails in the forward locker.

Helga was struggling to bring the ketch back on course; the strong wind was putting it well over until the port deck became awash. 'We will have to reef the mainsail, Gerda; when I give the word, work that lever at the foot of the mast until I tell you to stop.'

Helga turned the boat back into the wind. Mick unhitched the mainsail halyard and slowly lowered the sail. 'Wind it in, Gerda.' She noticed that using the lever, she was able to slowly turn the boom and wind in the mainsail.

Mick decided not to take any chances—the wind was getting stronger by the minute. He took the mainsail right down so that only a small triangle of sail remained.

'Stop turning now. Back on course, Helga.' Mick tightened up the halyard and then showed Gerda how to put sail ties on the shortened mainsail. 'Just once more, Helga.' As the ketch again turned into the wind, he lowered the mizzen-sail and Gerda secured it with more sail ties.

'Don't look so pleased with yourself, Helga; *we* did all the work. Now just you watch out for those big waves.'

Soaked through, Mick and Gerda went below to the saloon and fished out a selection of old shirts, sweaters and jeans. Although they were all much too large for the girls, they were much more suitable for the wet and cold conditions. 'We don't stand on ceremony when a storm is blowing. Just strip off your wet things and put on any dry clothes you can find.'

Mick went into the galley and soon reappeared with mugs of hot tinned soup, the last of the bread and a jug of coffee. Somehow they managed to get their feast up to the cockpit without spilling too much on the way.

'Make the most of this; we won't be getting much hot food to eat in the next few days.' Mick took Helga's place at the wheel, eating and drinking with one hand and steering with the other, despite the erratic movements of the boat.

'Why don't you get below and grab some rest, Mick? We are quite capable of handling the boat without you.' Helga was keen to get back to the helm.

'Good idea, I'm tying a whistle close to the steering wheel, which we can use when anyone is late for their watch. So give me a whistle in two hours' time; we will be due to change course by then. Don't forget or we will finish up in America.'

At eight am, Gerda took over from Helga, who went below to change into some of the dry clothes.

Mick was asleep on the saloon bench seat. Helga found some of Mick's old jeans and a sweater, both miles too large for her, and stripped off. Glancing over at Mick, she noticed he had one eye open. Helga stretched her arms up to the cabin top, wriggled her bottom before slipping into a pair of Mick's old jeans. On her way to the cockpit she bent over him, and lightly kissed his forehead. 'Pervert!'

Despite the small amount of sail, the ketch was maintaining its speed and Gerda, struggling to keep it on course, was relieved when Mick came up on deck and took the helm.

'There is a fishing boat some way behind us; he must be doing the same speed as us because he's been there for some time.' Gerda moved and stood close to Mick. 'It's a bit strange. I thought he could have easily overtaken us by now.'

Mick studied the boat in the distance. 'Okay, Gerda, we are due to change course now. Let's see what happens.' Mick swung the steering wheel. 'I'm going to get on the other tack and head northeast again as we are now well clear of the Cape. Once clear of Spain we should continue to head northeast all the way to St Nazaire, but unfortunately according to the weather forecast on the radio, the wind is expected to come from that direction.'

The wind had eased slightly, but the seas had become wild. They were leaving the coast of Spain behind and heading into the Bay of Biscay. With the wind from the northeast, they would be forced to tack most of the way to St Nazaire.

Gerda slipped down to her cabin to snatch some sleep. Helga had one hour left before starting her watch, so she decided to try to cook a hot meal. She discovered that by wedging herself between the cooker and one of the cupboards, she was able to peel some potatoes and with an oven glove, hold the pan with one hand until the potatoes were cooked. Helga then drained them and added them to the hotpot. Dinner was now ready.

Back on deck, Helga found Mick struggling to keep the bow close to the wind. She stood with him at the wheel. Gerda reappeared on deck looking the worse for wear.

'How are you girls feeling? You seem to be coping very well with this rough weather.'

Gerda pretended to vomit. 'Never been a problem, Mick. We girls have guts of steel!'

'After three years in a concentration camp, my guts have all been vomited up. That's not to say I am now gutless, so watch your step, big man!' Helga ducked as Mick swung a fender in her direction.

'Take a look astern, girls; that will take the smile off your faces.'

The fishing boat was dead astern of the ketch and appeared to be getting steadily closer.

'It looks as if your friends want to know where you are going.'

Gerda remained silent for a few moments, deciding whether it was time for her to take command of the situation. Gerda had been with the Department for several years now, and was quite used to handling difficult and dangerous situations.

'Mick, our friends have realised that we are carrying some gold and they also want us dead. However I don't think they will try to attack us until they know exactly where we are heading. My guess is that they really want Marçel, and they believe we are on our way to meet him. We will have to somehow lose this fishing boat before we get to St Nazaire.'

'And here was me thinking all our worries were over—bastards!' Helga spat over the side.

'We will try to lose them after dark, girls. No navigation lights from now on. In the meantime, Helga, you can bring us some of that delicious smelling food before you start your watch.'

The hotpot had by now cooled off. As they ate, the occasional spray came over the side of the boat and finished up on their plates.

'I think we should unpack some of the guns that we brought with us, Mick. I don't think we will need them just yet, but if they decide to come too close, we should be able to keep them at bay. With a sea like this I'm sure no one will be able to handle their shooters anyway.'

As if to confirm that, an extra-large wave broke over the deck giving everyone a soaking. Mick slipped down the hatchway and reappeared a few minutes later with three lifejackets and safety lines.

'Time to wear these, me hearties. They won't be bullet-proof, but they'll save you from drowning if you happen to be swept overboard.'

Mick fixed a line to the girls' waists and then clipped the lines onto the side rail.

'You're treating us like dogs. Do you really want us to bark as well? Or are we expected to just beg?'

'I don't know why I bother, Helga, I suppose I don't want the trouble of having to go back to look for you when you are swept overboard.'

Mick took over the wheel. 'Now, when you move around the boat, just unclip and then re-clip those safety lines. In this weather, always keep an eye out for your mates, and if someone goes overboard with or without their safety line, throw that lifebelt by the steering wheel overboard and turn the boat into the wind.'

Gerda headed for the hatchway. 'That sounds good sense, Mick. I'm going below to sort out some firearms before catching up on my sleep.'

Mick slipped his arm around Helga's waist. 'You're doing well for a young sheila. I'm going below to get some rest too. We are going to need all our strength in the next few days.'

It was Helga's watch from four until eight pm. Her arms were aching and despite the oilskins, she was soaked and extremely tired. She was relieved when finally a well-rested Gerda took the wheel. The fishing boat was about one mile behind the ketch; it had continued to maintain the same distance between the two vessels.

At eleven pm, Mick came up on deck. After three hours at the wheel in rough conditions, Gerda needed to stretch her aching arms. The wind had dropped a little and the ketch was travelling along at a good seven knots. They could clearly see the lights of the fishing boat following behind.

'I think it's time we gave those characters a bit of a shock. I'll take over. You go below and make some coffee. Go and get some rest, and be back on deck with Helga at two am. Bring up the heavy machine gun and a few hand grenades when you come up.'

'What are you going to do?'

'They feel so confident that they have kept their navigation lights on, but now without our navigation lights on, they will have to stay close enough to follow our wake. My bet is their helmsman will not have his eyes glued to us at two am, so we'll pay them a visit. We are going to close in on him so fast that he will not have time to realise what we are doing. I intend to run alongside of him and lob a couple of grenades into his wheelhouse. If we are lucky we might damage his radio and perhaps his steering gear.'

'Sounds a bit risky but I like it. I'll man the machine gun. It's time we *sheilas* had a little bit of the action!'

'You are going to get more than you bargained for, my beauty. Now get below and brew up some coffee.'

At two am, Helga appeared on deck with a box containing the hand grenades.

'Bring it over here carefully and put it near the steering wheel. Don't drop the bloody things.'

Gerda appeared at the top of the hatchway, struggling with the heavy machine gun.

'Can you girls take the machine gun to the stern and set it up on the starboard side of the transom? And try not to fall overboard.'

Mick took a long careful look at the fishing boat following a short distance behind. 'We'll need a crate from the galley to elevate the machine gun if Gerda wants to aim it at the fishing boat's wheelhouse. And a line too; you'll have to lash the crate to the mizzen-mast and then tie the gun to the crate.'

As soon as Gerda and the machine gun were firmly secured, Mick started to slowly take in the main sheet. The ketch was on the starboard tack heading northeast with the wind coming from the north. Mick yelled out, 'I'm going to ease off and head eastward for a minute and then we will "come about" onto the port tack. I will bring the ketch right around until we are running before the wind. This should then bring the ketch straight down onto the fishing boat. Get up forward, Helga, and be ready to trim the headsails. Once we start heading for the fishing boat, you'll have to come back here as I'll need you to take the wheel.'

Mick turned to Gerda. 'Your gun is secure so come and take the mainsail sheet. As soon as we are running free towards the fishing boat get back to your machine gun, and wait until we are right alongside. When you see the opportunity, just rake the wheelhouse with bullets; we will be coming together very fast, but you might just get lucky and damage their steering and destroy their radio.'

Helga had run up to the bow, ready to take in the jib and foresail sheets. She was almost lost from sight as the heavy spray kept breaking over her. Mick swung the wheel and the ketch turned eastwards but after a minute he turned the ketch back into the wind. There was a loud crash of falling pans and crockery from below deck as the boom swung across. At the same moment the ketch was hit by an extra-large wave.

Helga was almost washed overboard as the sea swept over the deck. The bow rose out of the water as the ketch slowly turned on to the port tack. Helga was lying on the deck clinging to the starboard rail.

To Mick's relief she scrambled up and gave Mick a rude sign. 'Pay out the sheets, Helga, it's no time to be lying down now, girl!' he yelled.

Helga made another rude sign and yelled back, 'Aye aye, *shit*master!' and propped herself against the mainmast.

Mick knew he had to gauge the exact point at which to turn the ketch in order to bring it down onto the fisherman's starboard side. His years of sailing the ketch and his Aussie audacity, enabled him to attempt this tricky exercise.

'Let the sheets run out, Helga.'

Mick eased the ketch around until it was running before the wind. Helga slackened the headsail sheets enabling the ketch to take full advantage of the following wind and joined Mick at the wheel. Mick turned the ketch until it was heading southwest, which was a little way ahead of the fishing boat's bow.

'Take over now, Helga, and keep on that heading until I tell you to head due south!' He put his arm around Helga's shoulder and held onto her tightly for a few moments. 'You are becoming a great sailor, young Helga. You had me worried for a moment.'

Helga felt a shiver of excitement. She would sail around the world with this man if he would take her. Helga forgot all her aches and pains and how tired she had felt. But her smile froze as she glanced up and saw they were on a course heading straight for the fishing boat.

'Mick, I can't hold this course! My God we are going to collide!'

'Just hold it there, sweetie. I'll tell you when to turn.'

'Mick—Mick you are quite mad!'

Gerda piped up, 'He's an Aussie, Helga. They are all crazy. He thinks he's a bloody kangaroo and we are going to jump over the fishing boat.'

Helga clutched the steering wheel and resisted the urge to close her eyes.

'Stand by and hold tight.' Mick picked up two hand grenades; he looked as if he was about to play a game of cricket. 'Now!'

Helga swung the wheel and the ketch turned in an arc heading down towards the hull of the still unsuspecting fishing boat. There was a crash and a loud scraping sound as the ketch slid down the side of the fishing boat. Mick threw his grenades. One hit and smashed the glass window of the wheelhouse; the other went straight over the other side of the boat into the sea.

Gerda kept her finger on the firing button, watching her bullets slam into the side of the wheelhouse and then seconds later they were clear of the fishing boat.

Someone was firing back from the stern of the fishing boat. The bullets were hitting the mizzen-mast, causing splinters to fly in all directions. One splinter hit Gerda on the side of her head knocking her out and another lodged in her shoulder.

Mick's hand grenade exploded, destroying the fishing boat's wheelhouse; by then they were well clear of her.

'Head west, Helga, I'll take in the sheets. I think Gerda's been hit.'

Gerda was lying very still beside the machine gun. Mick could see blood in her hair and blood coming from a tear in her jacket. He bent down—she was still breathing. He picked her up and carried her over to the hatchway.

'Is she all right? Oh my God, let's get her below!'

Helga turned the ketch into the wind and helped Mick lower Gerda down into the main cabin. Then they carefully lifted Gerda onto the table and supported her with pillows to prevent her sliding off the table. Helga picked up a torch and started to examine Gerda's head and shoulder.

'Get your medicine chest; I am going to have to perform some minor surgery. I don't think she is too bad. Her head has been grazed, but I think it is only surface damage. She should come around soon, but while she is unconscious, I'm going to remove this nasty wooden splinter from her shoulder.'

Helga was impressed with Mick's well-equipped medicine chest and removed a scalpel, tweezers and needles and bandages.

'You better get back on deck and get some wind into the sails. I can't remove this splinter while the boat is rolling so much. I will call you if she regains consciousness or if I need any help.'

As soon as Mick was able to get the ketch back on course, the rolling motion eased. Helga got to work on Gerda's shoulder. First she took off Gerda's jacket and shirt. Then she cleaned up the area with disinfectant, and by gently probing around the edge of the wound, she was able to remove the large wooden splinter from her shoulder. After a while, Helga managed to stop the bleeding, and she carefully bandaged Gerda's shoulder.

She bathed and cleaned the graze on Gerda's head, gently rubbing a small amount of ointment onto the graze. Then she carefully dried Gerda's hair. Gerda was still unconscious but breathing quite normally.

Helga put her head out through the hatchway. 'She's still unconscious but I need you to help me carry her to her bunk. I'm afraid she might roll off the table.'

Mick brought the ketch up into the wind again and between them they carried Gerda to her bunk. 'You've done a great job, Helga. We are lucky to have a trained nurse on board.'

'I think I should stay with her until she recovers. I don't think it will be too long.'

'You do that, girlie, but first we'll have a glass of wine to celebrate our naval victory!'

Mick poured out two large mugs of port wine, which they quickly knocked back. It eased all the built-up tensions of the last hour. Helga put her arms around Mick and for a moment they clung to each other. Mick bent down and gently kissed her on the lips.

Before bringing the ketch back on track, Mick loosened some of the sail ties and hoisted the mainsail higher up the mast. There was still too much wind to give the ketch full sail. Dawn was breaking and it looked like a fine day ahead.

Mick was able to gradually edge the boat to the north. He would hold this course all day and hopefully if the wind veered a little, he would be able to get on the other tack tomorrow and head to the east.

Mick realised Gerda had been very lucky. The bullet had just grazed her head, but the wound in her shoulder would put her out of action for some time. Apart from that, the run-down on the fishing boat had been a great success.

He wondered how much he and Gerda had damaged the fishing boat. If it was disabled they would have to radio for another boat to come out to rescue them, that is providing their radio was kept below deck and had not been destroyed in the explosion.

If they decided to continue following the ketch with another boat, they would first have to find the ketch, in which case they were still in danger of being attacked before they met up with Marçel. Mick thought this highly unlikely as by the morning the ketch would be well ahead and out of sight.

Mick was intrigued with Helga. He had never kissed a girl like her before. Since leaving Australia, he had fought in the Spanish civil war. After the war he had not had any desire to return to Australia. With the money he had saved, some of it looted during the Spanish war, he had bought the old ketch and had spent two years repairing it.

During the Second World War at the request of British naval intelligence, he had sailed up and down the coast of Spain and Portugal, reporting on the enemy shipping movements.

After the war he had just used his boat for pleasure and for taking out the odd fishing party, which he had found quite profitable. It was quite a surprise when Stephen had contacted him and he had to admit to himself that he was now quite enjoying this unusual commission.

Girls had not played a part in Mick's life apart from the occasional woman that he sometimes met in one of the sleazy bars in Spain. Now Helga had put new thoughts into his mind, thoughts that both disturbed and excited him. She made him laugh more than he had done for a long time. And he was fascinated with the way she had taken to sailing and was quite at home on his boat.

He felt certain strong vibes when she came near to him; he wanted to put his arms around her lovely slim figure and hug her, and now that wonderful kiss.

'What have you got to laugh at, big boy?' Helga appeared with a mug of steaming coffee.

'You, you little tiger! I never thought I would put up with so much crap from a young sheila. You've invaded my quiet bachelor's life. And I think I like it!'

'It's time someone pricked your bum, mate! Which reminds me, Gerda has recovered. She is still a little bit shocked, and I told her that we had won the sea battle. She was in considerable pain, so I gave her a shot of morphine from the med-chest and now she's fast asleep. That's the best thing for her.'

'Looks like you and I will have to run this ship from now on. We will take one watch on and one watch off. It's going to be tough. How are you feeling now, girlie?'

'Surprised. It's the first time you have actually shown concern for me and for my feelings. You really must want something, you old sea dog!'

'Yes babe, but not just now. I need to listen to the radio as I might pick up something about that fishing boat mob. It would be nice to know if they still intend to follow us.'

'Go for it. I'm fine for a few hours. Have a look at Gerda afterwards and then grab some sleep. I'll whistle you up if I need you.'

Although she was tired, Helga really enjoyed steering the boat. The wind had now swung around to the northwest and although the sails were still partly reefed down, the ketch was making good speed through the long swells.

It was mid-afternoon when Mick appeared on deck. 'I gave Gerda a mug of tea. She looks much better and has gone back to sleep. We'll share watches tonight. We must have damaged the fishing boat as it's heading back to Vigo and another boat is coming out to meet it. It's possible they might continue to follow us in the other boat. And to add to our problems, I'm afraid there's a gale warning for the bay tomorrow.'

'I'm going to rest for a couple of hours, Mick, and after that we should have something hot to eat. Then I'll take over until midnight.'

Three hours later, Helga reappeared on deck with two steaming plates of the now rather tired hotpot, although this time it was not being doused with spray.

'Only a few plates broken last night. Gerda's had some food, and seems much better. She has gone back to sleep again. She should be back on deck in the morning.'

'I reckon you'd make a good wife to someone, girlie.' Mick was surprised with himself; it was not the sort of remark that he would ever have made. This girl was disturbing him and intruding on his contented bachelor existence.

'I used to dream about that when I was in the concentration camp, Mick. All I know about family life is what I have read in books. I've never had any family. I was abandoned as a baby. My mum had a short but passionate affaire with an Hungarian gypsy and I was brought up in an institution. As soon as I was old enough, I was sent off to train as a nurse. That's when I started to study English, which I really enjoyed and then later, I returned to my children's home as their official nurse. At that time I was able to read lots of books about the family life I never had.' Helga sighed deeply.

'It's a strange thing, Mick, those shocking four years I spent in the concentration camp and then the time in prison now just seem like a bad dream. At the time I was being raped and beaten by those beasts, I swore that if I survived, I would never have anything to do with men. And now, since meeting you, I have been able to push that nightmare to the back of my mind. I feel that one day I could become a normal woman again.'

'I can't imagine the horrors that you must have endured at that time, Helga. I can only wonder at your strength of character.'

'Memory of those horrors, the inhuman treatment and the murder of all the children will never go away but I'm determined to try to live as normal a life as possible, Mick.'

'You've certainly missed out a lot in life, girlie. I suppose in comparison, I was lucky to have had a fairly good childhood. I was reared on a small farm north of Brisbane. Both my parents were fairly old when I was born. They were very poor and not very good farmers. I had to work on the farm as soon as I was able to be of any use. We had a few cattle and some sheep. By the time I was fourteen I was running the farm on my own as Mum and Dad were both too old and sick by then.'

'Were you a happy child and did your mum and dad really love you?'

'They certainly loved me. My mother would spend hours in the evenings giving me a good education. She had been a teacher when she was young and had married Dad late in life. Mum also taught me to cook and become self-sufficient; they both knew that I would one day be left on my own to fend for myself. My dad had been a ship's officer most of his life. He made me work very hard on the farm, but he was always kind and protective. Through him I learned a lot about farming, and he told me so much about the outside world. I knew that one day I would have to go out and see for myself.'

'How did you finish up in Spain?'

'They both died when I was seventeen, within ten months of each other. My mother died first and I'm sure my father died of a broken heart—he just couldn't bear to go on living without her.'

'How sad, and yet so beautiful; they must have been so happy together. I wish I could meet someone like your dad that would love me till I died.'

'I didn't want to stay on at the farm alone, so I rented it out and decided to see the world. I met some other young Australian guys on the boat to England. They were on their way to Spain to fight for the communists, so I decided to join them. I'm afraid they all died in Spain.'

'It was a nasty war, Mick. You must have been fighting the fascists? Will you ever go back to Australia?'

'Yes. It's time I found myself a sheila and went back to my farm. I believe there is good money to be made on the farms at present and now I have sufficient capital to invest in some machinery and buy some good stock.' Mick put his arm around Helga's shoulder. 'I've got to find the right one first; it's a hard life out there for a woman.'

'Go and get some sleep now. It's past eight. I'll keep going till midnight.'

Mick realised just how tired he was. As he disappeared down the hatchway Helga yelled, 'I could milk your cows, Mick!'

At midnight Mick came back on deck. The wind had freshened in the last two hours and Helga was struggling to keep the ketch on course. Mick looked up at the sails.

'I'm going to reduce sail now while we have the chance.' Mick took in the jib sail and then put up the small storm staysail. He took in and tied down the mizzen-sail. 'Bring her into wind, matie, and come and help me take in the mainsail.' Between them they reefed the mainsail, again leaving just a triangle of sail. Then they secured the sail ties firmly in place.

'Go below now to check up on Gerda. You should get some sleep. I'll call you at daybreak. We're going to need all our strength when the storm hits us tomorrow.'

The wind steadily increased during the night; at times Mick had to use all his strength to keep on course. The night seemed endless. Glancing back at the top of a wave, Mick thought he saw for a moment the navigation lights of another vessel. He decided not to mention it to the girls as they were going to have enough to worry about.

Dawn was just breaking when Helga woke up. The ketch seemed to be moving in all directions at the same time. She could feel the surge forward as the ketch dropped down into the troughs of the waves and then the climb up to the crest of the next wave.

Gerda was awake. She slid out of her bunk and was struggling with her oilskins.

'Can you help me, Helga? I really have to get up on deck, I need to get some air and I feel sure I could help with the steering.'

'If you are quite sure you feel strong enough, it will probably be much better for you up on deck.' She helped her put on her oilskins and life jacket before putting on her own. Together they managed to work their way up to the cockpit.

A wicked sea was running with waves towering way above the ketch as it ploughed its way through the heavy seas.

'What kept you, girls? How are you, Gerda?' Mick was remarkably in high spirits. 'Are you strong enough to stay on deck? No cooked breakfast today I'm afraid. It's too dangerous to light the stove; it's ship's biscuits and cold water today, girlies. Both of you take the wheel and see how you go, Gerda. Clip on your safety lines.'

Mick made his way down to the galley and returned with a can of water and a pocket full of dry unappetising biscuits.

'Try not to spit in it, Mick!' Helga yelled as Mick took a long drink out of the can.

Mick, a little surprised, passed the can over. 'You wait till we get ashore, woman; then you really will taste my spit!'

Gerda cut in, shouting to make herself heard over the sound of the wind. 'You are a disgusting, dirty old Aussie. Talking to an innocent young girl like that. And yes, I'm fine and thanks to you both.'

'Don't worry, Gerda, it won't be the first time I've had to bite a man's tongue off!'

Two hours later, the noise had become much louder as the wind screamed through the rigging, as they were now sailing on the starboard tack. Even with the small amount of sail the starboard gunwale was dipping into the sea as the wind pushed the ketch over on its side.

Mick had taken over the steering wheel and was using all his strength to sail the boat.

Helga turned to look at the boat's wake. 'Oh, God! Look behind you, Mick!'

A giant wave, blotting out the sky was bearing down on them. The top of the wave with boiling white foam, started to curl as it towered over them. 'Bloody hell!' Mick yelled. 'Close the hatch cover—get up here with me—wrap your bloody safety lines around the steering column and for God's sake hang on for dear life, I think we're going to capsize!'

The enormous wave broke over the ketch, turning the hull onto its side. The boom swung across and there was a loud crash as the mainmast port stays were ripped out of the deck and the mast snapped and crashed over the side. The ketch disappeared under the wave. Only the broken mast and tangle of sail prevented the ketch from capsizing. The giant wave passed over the ketch and in the following trough the hull gradually emerged out of the sea. It was lying on its side held down by the smashed mast and a tangle of sails and rigging. Three very frightened sailors were still there, clinging to the steering wheel.

The ketch was now wallowing in the trough as wave after wave broke over the hull and poured across the deck. The wreckage of the mast was holding the starboard gunwale under water. Mick realised that unless the mast was quickly cleared away, the heavy seas breaking on the deck would smash open the hatch covers. The ketch would quickly become flooded and sink.

He grabbed the emergency hatchet from the side of the steering wheel. 'Attach your safety lines to the port rail and come and help me clear all the lines attached to the mast or we are going to sink!'

The two shocked, white-faced girls suddenly came to life and leaped into action. Gerda had forgotten her bandaged shoulder. They unhitched the remaining ropes attached to the deck and allowed them to slip over the side.

The waves were continually breaking over them as Mick furiously hacked away at the remaining stays. The hull gradually righted itself and Mick finally cut through the last of the stays and allowed the wreckage of the mast and sails to float away.

'Get back to the steering wheel and try to turn us into the wind!' Mick went below and reappeared with a coil of rope, and the canvas cone-shaped sea anchor. The ketch was still lying across wind with the seas breaking over the deck, but the hull was now in an upright position. Mick scrambled across the cleared deck to the bow and slowly paid out the rope with the sea anchor attached. It took a while for the ketch to drift downwind and the sea anchor to take effect. But gradually the bow came up into the wind. They were safe for the time being, no longer in danger of capsizing.

Mick rejoined the two girls. 'Some wave. I guess we are going to finish the journey going backwards.' Helga's frightened laugh broke the tension, and even Gerda, now in agony, had to smile.

'That's as close as you could ever come to drowning. I think losing the mast at that moment saved us from capsizing and going backwards is going to save our lives until the wind and sea ease off.'

Gerda felt her legs giving away; she slumped down onto the deck. The others grabbed hold of her and managed to get her down to her cabin. 'She's in a bad way, Mick, I'm going to try to dry her out and give her another small dose of morphine.'

Helga found one remaining dry blanket. She stripped Gerda and rolled her in the blanket and again wedged pillows to prevent her from falling out of the bunk. Within minutes Gerda drifted off into a heavy sleep.

Back in the saloon everything was soaking wet. Despite the absolute chaos throughout the boat, Mick had been able to find a tin of tomato soup. Anything, even cold soup, was welcome after their soaking.

Without the mast and sail, the ketch was now rolling badly. Helga, for the first time began to feel sick. She was wet through and cold but there were no more dry clothes to put on. She forced herself to swallow the cold tomato soup, and found that surprisingly it warmed her a little.

'We are safe as long as we have the sea anchor. Luckily we still have the mizzen-mast, so as soon as the wind drops a little, we'll hoist the mizzen. Then we should be able to make a little headway.'

'How are we going to make contact with Marçel, now that we have lost the aerial?'

'I'll have to fix up a temporary aerial to the mizzen-mast. We should soon be near enough to make contact with Marçel. If we send out a 'Mayday' call for assistance, we might encounter too many awkward questions to answer from our rescuers.'

It was midday when the wind swung to the northwest and gradually eased to a strong breeze. Mick hauled in the sea anchor and then hoisted up the mizzen-sail.

Helga brought the ketch around to the northeast and the boat got under way. With only the mizzen-sail, they were only able to move along at three to four knots.

Mick unscrewed a cap in the deck that covered the hand pump and began the laborious job of pumping out the bilges. After about an hour, the pump started to suck air; now the bilges were empty and the hull apparently was not leaking.

With the still heavy sea running, they slowly headed for the land. Mick and Helga shared the long night watches. She had managed to hang out enough clothes to dry, so that they were eventually able to discard their wet clothes. They were soon able to light the stove and heat up tins of soup and drink lots of hot coffee, which helped them stay awake through the long cool night.

Shortly after dawn, Gerda appeared on deck dressed in dry clothes. 'Helga, go and put your head down in my dry bunk for a while. I'm sure I can steer with one arm.' Mick and Helga had been able to take short rests in the saloon, but had not had the luxury of a good sleep.

Helga returned on deck two hours later feeling really good. She insisted that Mick went and had a spell in the dry bunk. 'Go for it while it's still warm, Mick.'

In the meantime, Gerda and Helga had draped the blankets of the other two bunks on the deck ensuring that they would all have a dry bunk the next night. Shortly after midday, Mick appeared with another round of hot soup.

'I think I can see land ahead. It's on our port bow, it looks like an island.'

'Spot on, Helga. That's Belle Isle. We can shelter there for the night and set off for St Nazaire in the morning.'

Mick put his arm around Helga and gave her a gentle hug. 'Would you really like to come and milk my cows in Australia? I think I would like that very much. But it really is a very tough life farming in Australia and it can be very lonely at times for a woman.'

He bent down and kissed Helga lightly on the cheek.

'Lonely? Does that mean I can have you all to myself?

Well, I suppose I will have to share you with all those cows and horses and things!'

'In the last few days, Helga, you have not only proved to be as good as any man that has ever come crewing with me, but you are still able to be one hundred per cent a woman. You are a lovely girl who has completely captivated me. Believe it or not, you are the first woman that has made me feel that I would like to return to Australia and go back to farming again.'

It was almost dark when the ketch finally dropped anchor in a small but fairly sheltered bay just inside Pointe de Pouldon.

Mick took some bearings and made sure the anchor was set and not dragging. He also checked that they were anchored a safe distance from the shore, with sufficient depth of water not to ground at low tide.

Mick managed to run an aerial from the top of the mizzen-mast to the bow of the ketch. Unfortunately the battery for the radio was almost flat. The water in the bilges, after the wave hit the ketch, had flooded the engine, making it impossible to recharge the battery.

Despite the almost-flat battery, Gerda kept trying to make contact with Marçel on the radio.

Helga went down to the galley and heated up a large tin of baked beans and opened a tin of ham and managed to get the saloon into some sort of order so that they could sit around the table and enjoy their hot meal.

Although completely exhausted, they all agreed that it was, however simple, the best meal of their lives, as they washed it down with mugs of hot coffee laced with brandy.

Just before midnight, Gerda decided to try just once more to make contact with Marçel. A few minutes later she called out, 'I think I've got them! Come and listen.' Stephen's voice came over loud and clear asking for their position. Gerda read her prepared message, which Stephen twice asked her to repeat. After three attempts, Marçel's message, '*Got your message—stay where you are—I'll be with you tomorrow morning—acknowledge—chin up.*' came through.

Gerda yelled back, 'Received!' They scrambled back into the saloon and finished off the bottle of brandy.

By now the brandy had taken effect and they dragged themselves to their now dry bunks. Sleep was of the essence.

Except for the sound of the wind in the mizzen-mast, the sea breaking on the shore and the occasional creaking of the boat's hull as it rolled in the now-gentle swell, silence reigned over the ketch …

—

Shortly before dawn there was a loud thud followed by a crash in the galley as the trawler hit the side of the ketch. They heard the thud of boots on the deck and then the hatch cover was flung open. Three men scrambled down into the saloon and burst into the cabins.

Mick was halfway out of his bunk when one of Schmidt's men burst in and struck him across the head with a heavy club. The girls, who were still half asleep, were dragged from their bunks by the hair. Fortunately they were dressed in their slacks and sweaters. They were forced to lie on the floor of the saloon.

A tall man with blond hair stood by as Mick, still unconscious, was brought out from his cabin by the other two men. Using strong fishing cord, the two men tied their hands tightly behind their backs. They then tied their ankles and legs, making it almost impossible for them to move.

'So, we are all together once again; how nice. Tell me, Helga, who is this man that I'm about to throw overboard?' He gave Mick a sharp kick in the ribs, but he was still unconscious.

'If you are just going to throw him overboard you won't need to know his name!' Helga spat at him.

Schmidt grabbed her by the throat and forced her head back against the bulkhead. 'You escaped the gas chambers, Jewish *hag*; but this time you are going to drown. Slowly.' He let go of her throat and then punched her hard in the face; he grinned as Helga's nose started to bleed.

Gerda screamed at him, 'Leave her alone, you Nazi bastard! His name is Mick and he's an Australian! If you met on even terms he'd just grind you into the dust!'

'So you fancy him, you *whore*; well now you can watch him die.' Schmidt was laughing. He stopped, then spoke slowly and menacingly: 'No, I have a much better idea, you can watch each other die.'

'Where is the gold, *Jew*?' Schmidt lifted Helga onto the table. He untied her legs and started to remove her slacks. Then he beckoned over the two other men. 'She's all yours, boys.'

'The gold is on the spare bunk in the forward cabin. Just take it and leave the girls alone.' Mick had recovered and was straining uselessly at his cords.

Schmidt gave him several hard kicks in the ribs before making his way to the forward cabin. He came back into the saloon with the case containing the gold bars. He re-tied Helga's legs and ordered his men to follow him up on deck.

He was about to climb back on to the trawler when he suddenly went back. He grabbed the three lifejackets and threw them into the sea before jumping on to the trawler deck. 'A gift for you, Marçel,' he muttered.

A few minutes later the trawler engine started up. One of the men on the trawler passed a tow-rope over to the man still on the ketch who attached it to the winch in the bow; he then unfastened the anchor chain and allowed it to run right out, saving himself the trouble of hauling in the anchor.

The trawler pulled away, took up the slack in the tow-rope and started to tow the ketch away from the shore. Schmidt left one of his men to steer the ketch and to keep an eye on Mick and the two girls.

Chapter 12

Shortly before dawn, Stephen and Marçel cast off from the Paimboeuf jetty. Thirty minutes later as the sun rose, they motored past the port of St Nazaire. The storm had passed and the wind had eased off, to be replaced by a fresh breeze from the northwest.

All the navigation marks were now clearly visible and several fishing boats were returning from a night at sea. Thirty minutes later they were clear of the land and heading west past the Grand Charpentier buoy.

They altered course and headed west-northwest to Belle Isle, some thirty-six miles away. They would reach the ketch soon after ten am. The barge had no problem with the rough sea and despite its flat bottom, was coping extremely well with the heavy swell.

Marçel switched on the radar and Stephen went down to the radio cabin to see if he could make contact with the ketch.

Later, Stephen came up onto the bridge with two mugs of coffee. 'I can't get any reply from the ketch; their battery must still be flat. I'm a bit surprised that now they are in sheltered water they have not tried to recharge their battery.'

'The sooner we get to them the better. We should see the outline of Belle Isle soon. Take over for a bit, Stephen, I'm going to mount the machine-gun and test it out.'

Marçel slipped the gun mounting into the steel tube and clipped on the heavy machine-gun. He was able to swivel it in almost any direction. He fired a few shots into the sea, scaring off the seagulls.

Marçel returned to the wheelhouse, and took over from Stephen. 'That's a good position for the gun, Stephen. The only problem is that there is no protection for the gunner from any return fire. Sometime I will make up some sort of metal shield.'

'Let's hope you never get to use it, Marçel. However I have a feeling you are going to need that gun today. I think I can just see the outline of Belle Isle in the distance.'

Marçel altered course slightly to the west. Glancing at the radar screen, which was now showing up Belle Isle, he noticed a fairly large boat to the southwest; it was heading away from the island. He looked at it again a few minutes later to find it was still moving away from the island and appeared to be heading in a south-westerly direction.

'Pointe due Skeul is on the southern tip of the island and the next headland is Pointe de Pouldon. We should be there in forty-five minutes.'

Chapter 13

Helga edged herself off the table and rolled onto the floor of the saloon alongside Mick. He leaned over towards her and kissed her gently on the lips.

'I suppose it's as good a time as any for a necking session.' Gerda giggled despite the throbbing pain in her shoulder.

'Helga came close to something much worse than that with those bastards. Now's as good a time as any to show her how I feel about her.'

'It's a good time for you to be a gentleman, Mick. Now roll over, and reach down to help me pull up my pants, instead of just gaping at me.'

'I'm afraid this is all my fault, girls. I should have realised that they were still following us. We should have kept a watch last night. I just hope Marçel will get to Belle Isle before they tow us too far away from the island.'

Gerda wriggled across the floor until she was able to sit up and lean against the galley bulkhead. 'They seem very confident. They took the gold away and didn't bother to remove the guns from our cabin. If one of us could get free, we could easily re-take our boat.'

'These men are real professionals, there is no way I can free myself from this cord. Maybe if we both roll over, Helga, I might be able to gnaw through the cord on your wrists.'

'I would quite fancy that, Mick, but you're going to need very sharp teeth. Anyway they might release us when they decide to abandon the ketch.'

Gerda gave Mick a knowing look. 'I wouldn't rely on that, Helga.'

'Let's just give it a try.'

They both rolled over and Mick was just able to reach Helga's wrists. He started to suck one of the strands, soaking it with his saliva before trying to use his teeth to grind away at the cord.

A few minutes later the man at the helm came down into the saloon. He saw what was happening and dragged Helga through the door to the forward passage way and returned back on deck.

Two hours later, now well clear of the land and with no other ships in sight, Schmidt stopped the trawler's engine. He allowed it to drift back until he was able to edge the fishing boat alongside the ketch; the seas had died down sufficiently for him to hold the trawler alongside it.

He came down into the saloon and ordered his men to lift the boards that covered the ketch's bilges. One man stepped down into the bilge and passed up three heavy rusty pieces of iron ballast. Gerda was dragged well away from Mick. One of the men carefully tied a piece of ballast to their ankles. Schmidt picked up Helga's legs and dragged her back into the saloon, giving her several kicks in the ribs on the way. Then his men tied her ankles to the remaining piece of ballast.

Schmidt ordered his men to return to the trawler. He went into the two toilets and opened the inlet valves to allow seawater to flow into the boat. He cut the cooling hoses on the engine and opened a valve at the side of the engine; water spurted in to flood the engine.

'I had a good idea once you left the coast of Spain you would be heading for one of the French ports in the Bay. The storm gave me the opportunity to catch up with you. Then you fools broke radio silence and told me where you were. No one can provoke Karl Schmidt and expect to live!' Schmidt knelt down beside Mick and murmured, 'A good captain always goes down with his ship. And it's so much more romantic when he takes his lovers with him. Have fun, *kinder!*'

Schmidt was laughing as he stepped up onto the deck and climbed back onto the trawler. The two men untied the tow-rope and also jumped up onto the deck.

'Let her go, men. Helmsman, full speed and head southwest. We are going back to Spain.'

Back on the ketch, the water was starting to rise through the floorboards. Gerda was doubled up with pain and shivering uncontrollably. Helga tried vainly to smile, despite the pain in her ribs. 'We'll most likely die from the cold before we drown. It might be a better way to go. Looks like we're all going down under after all, Mick.'

For once Helga's sense of humour was not appreciated. Mick and Gerda remained silent …

The floor now had water sloshing across from one side to the other as the ketch rolled in the trough of the waves.

Mick dragged himself over to the table. 'We mustn't give up yet as there is still a good chance that Marçel and Stephen will find us. We have got to stay alive, and that means we have to somehow try to stand up.'

'And how can we possibly do that? I can't even move,' Gerda groaned.

'Can you drag your iron weight across the floor, Gerda? Try and move it towards the table.'

'I can't move it at all.'

Helga slid her body around until she had Gerda between herself and the saloon table. 'Wait until the boat rolls away from you and then lean against the bulkhead and push. That's good. Now slide your body around and try to sit up with your back to the table. I will do the same.'

Mick and Helga managed to drag their iron weights across the floor and swing their bodies around until the three of them were lined up with their knees bent and their shoulders pressed against the table-top.

'Right, maties!' Helga had taken over. 'When the boat rolls towards us, lean back with your shoulders against the edge of the table. Then lift your buttocks off the floor and straighten your knees, wriggle your shoulders and push up until your back is on the table.'

After several attempts they were all lying with their backs on the table.

'Bloody hell, Helga this is an impossible position! Our backs are breaking!' Mick was straining forward, trying to relieve the pain in his back.

'Stop whining, Mick. Now when the boat rolls the other way, push with your hands on the table and lean forward till just your buttocks are resting on the edge of the table.'

'That's terrific, Helga. Sorry we can't clap.' By now Gerda was in serious pain and beginning to lose her strength. She had made one superhuman effort and got herself positioned between Mick and Helga. The three of them were now sitting on the edge of the table.

The water had crept over the floorboards and was several inches deep in the saloon. As the hull gradually filled with water, the rolling motion of the boat slowed down and the hull just wallowed in the sea. The water level seemed to be rising more rapidly. With the hull now riding low in the water, the waves were breaking over the deck, and occasionally water poured down through the hatchway.

Another hour passed and the water reached the top of the table. Gerda was fighting to stay conscious. Helga and Mick were trying hard to support her and prevent her from collapsing into the water.

'Do you think we are going to die, Mick?' Helga asked; her eyes large and questioning.

'Never say die until you are dead, if you see what I mean.'

'I think I have fallen in love with you, Mick,' Helga whispered. 'You are the first man I have ever wanted, and now it's too late.'

Mick gave an inward shiver. The ketch was likely to roll over and sink at any time. Even if Marçel arrived now there might not be time to free them before the ketch capsized. 'It's the same with me. I've been around a lot, and now for the first time I have really fallen in love with a sheila,' Mick murmured. 'I've been watching you for the last few days and have not had the courage to say anything. I *can* say it now. I love you too, Helga.'

They both remained silent for a few minutes, thinking of what they had just said. The water sloshed around them. Because their movements were so restricted, the cold water was beginning to take its effect on the three of them. They would soon be overtaken by the cold and unable to support themselves on the table.

'Can anyone sing? How about For those in peril on the sea?'

'How about just saying our prayers, Helga,' murmured Gerda through her chattering teeth.

They all remained silent. No one wanted to admit the fear they felt. Gerda started humming to herself, no longer aware of her surroundings; the tune was unrecognisable.

Helga stiffened. 'Shut up, Gerda! Listen—can you hear anything?'

Mick exclaimed through blue lips, 'Bugger me, Riley; I think it's a boat!'

The sound of the motor got gradually louder; suddenly it stopped.

'All together now, girls, HELP—HELP—HELP!'

Chapter 14

The barge ploughed its way through the rough waters of the Sauvage and entered the bay, sheltered by the Pointe de Pouldon. There was no sign of the ketch. They cruised up and down and then rounded the Pointe to see if it had drifted with the tide, but there was still no sign. They went back to the sheltered bay to see if the ketch might have drifted onto the rocks.

'Looks like some lifejackets floating ahead, Marçel. Get a little closer.' Marçel brought the barge alongside the floating life jackets. It occurred to him that this might be some sort of message.

Schmidt's bravado in tossing the lifejackets overboard was to be his undoing. Marçel felt sure that this was a message. Were they still on board the ketch or perhaps they had been overpowered and were now on the fishing boat?

'That ship we saw heading southwest I wonder? Perhaps Schmidt caught up with them and scuttled the ketch. He may be taking Mick and the girls back to Portugal as we speak.'

'That's a bit optimistic, Marçel. More likely, he has killed them all and is returning to Portugal with the gold.'

Ignoring him, Marçel turned the barge and headed out to sea and opened the throttle to give the barge its full speed. He was thankful that they had installed such a powerful diesel engine and also that the barge had a pointed bow enabling it to cut through the water and travel at a greater speed. Spray was breaking over the bow as they sped through the water and headed southwest after the fast disappearing fishing boat. It was still just visible in the distance.

Two hours later though, the trawler was still well ahead of them, the gap slowly narrowing; it would take another two hours at least to catch up with this boat, and even then it might not be the same fishing boat that had been shadowing the ketch.

'I can see another object ahead. It's just appeared between us and the other boat. It comes and goes, so it must be very low in the water.'

'Well, it's not a U-boat! It might just be some discarded fishing gear floating on the surface.'

They would have gone past it, as it was well over on their port side, but some instinct made Marçel turn the barge.

'Bloody Hell, Stephen, it's a sinking yacht! It must be Mick's ketch. I'm going to take a closer look.'

He brought the barge around to within twenty feet of the sinking hull and switched off the engine. The yacht was a complete wreck; it had lost its mast and all the gear. The main hatch was open and as the sea broke over the deck, they could see water pouring into the cabin.

'It looks as if they have either killed the three of them or else taken them on board their boat.'

And then they heard a faint sound coming from the wreck.

'There is someone on board; the cabin must be almost flooded. They're trapped inside the hull. If we get too close it will probably roll over and sink. I'm going to swim over and see what I can do.'

Marçel stripped off his jeans. 'Throw the inflatable dinghy overboard and be ready to come over to pick me up and whoever else that might still be on board.'

He dived in, hardly noticing the cold water and swam across to the boat. He decided to climb up onto the stern end of the boat in case his extra weight upset the critical balance of the hull. He scrambled over to the hatchway and looked down.

Helga shrieked, 'Marçel—thank God—you took your time—what kept you? I was just about to come looking for you!'

'Better late than never, Helga, and I can see what kept *you*.' Marçel dropped down into the water, found two sharp knives in the galley and swam over to Mick.

'Our legs are tied to weights. Cut us free before the ketch capsizes. It's good to see you, mate.'

'Hi, Mick. This is not a nice way to treat lady passengers.' He quickly cut the cord on Mick's wrists and gave him a second knife so he could free his legs.

It was obvious to Marçel that Gerda was in very bad shape. He dived under the water and cut through the cords, freeing the two girls from the iron weights that would very soon have taken them, and the ketch, to the bottom of the sea.

Helga was able to ease herself onto the table and kick life back into her legs. Meanwhile Mick and Marçel cut through the cords on the girls' wrists.

Gerda had passed out and was about to slip under the water. Mick and Marçel carefully lifted her lifeless body up onto the deck of the ketch, which by now was almost awash.

'Keep in the centre of the boat. We don't want it to roll over just yet. If the mast of the ketch had still been in place, Marçel, we would most certainly have capsized and sunk by now. I don't think we could have lasted very much longer. Thanks, mate.'

Marçel yelled to Stephen to bring over two blankets with the inflatable dinghy.

Mick seemed to have made a quick recovery. 'Marçel, I think it's still possible to save the ketch. Do you have a portable pump?'

'My God aren't you satisfied just to be alive? One extra-large wave and your boat could have rolled over and sunk. Yes, we have a petrol driven pump, but are you able to stop the water flooding into your boat?'

Stephen came alongside with the inflatable.

'Bring it around to the stern, Stephen, and hold it there; we are going to lower Gerda from the transom into the centre of the dinghy.' They gently lowered her down and Helga, who had by now almost fully recovered, jumped into the inflatable and helped Gerda onto the centre seat. She wrapped the blankets around them both.

'I'll stay on board and try to close off all the open valves, Marçel. When you come back to pick me up could you bring over your portable pump?'

'It's certainly worth a try. Our pump is very powerful, and if you can stop the water coming into the hull, we might be able to save your boat.'

Marçel dropped onto the front seat of the dinghy, took over the paddles and rowed back to the barge. It took quite an effort to lift Gerda up onto the deck of the barge, and finally get her down into one of the cabins. Helga got to work; striping off all Gerda's wet clothes and wrapping her up in a fresh dry blanket.

In the meantime, Stephen had brewed hot tea laced with brandy for the two girls. The warmth soon brought Gerda, although still in considerable pain, slowly back to life.

Marçel fished out the petrol-powered pump, which was kept in the storeroom up in the bow of the barge. He jumped into the inflatable while Stephen lowered the pump with the suction hose and a can of petrol into the dinghy, taking special care not to puncture the floor of the inflatable.

Helga, keen to rejoin Mick, appeared on deck wearing some of Marçel's dry clothes. With a blanket around her shoulders and holding a flask of hot coffee, she jumped down into the inflatable. 'Don't laugh, Marçel; I know there is room for two in these trousers. Just think how nice it will feel next time you wear them.' So, Helga was back to normal.

'You will need me to help lift the pump onto the ketch, Marçel, and I will have to ...' Helga smiled archly, '... warm Mick up.'

Back on the ketch, after several attempts, Mick had managed to dive under the water in the toilets and alongside the engine, and had successfully closed off all the open valves. With some difficulty, they lifted the pump onto the ketch's transom. They dropped the suction hose down into the bilges and started the pump.

The powerful pump was soon able to beat the amount of water still occasionally flowing down through the open hatch. After a while it was possible to see the level in the cabin starting to drop, but it was going to take hours to pump all that water out of the hull.

Helga wrapped a blanket around Mick and made him finish the flask of coffee. Marçel was getting impatient; he wanted to go after the fishing boat. Every minute counted. They had to reach the trawler before dark.

'Mick, I think you should leave the pump running and come back with us to the barge. We must get after that trawler. We can come back to the ketch on our way back to St Nazaire.'

'No way, I'm staying here. Once I've reduced the water level sufficiently, I will hoist the mizzen-sail and start heading back to St Nazaire. When you catch up with me you can give me a tow back to port.'

'Okay, then just drop Helga and me back to the barge and then you can keep the inflatable with you in case things go wrong.'

'I'll stay with Mick. I'm sure he could do with some help.' Helga piped up.

'It's much too dangerous for you, Helga. Anyway you are needed on the barge to look after Gerda. Stephen and I want to hear the full story of your journey, and how you came to be almost drowned here in the ketch.'

Marçel noticed the look of disappointment on Helga's face. Then he realised why she wanted to help Mick. 'Don't worry, Helga, it won't take us too long, and Mick I'm sure will still be here when we get back! Since you are still wet, Mick, could you go below and pass up some of the girls' clothes? We can take them back and dry them out; I don't want half-naked girls dancing around on my boat.'

Helga grinned. 'Marçel is such a modest young man, and there we were, planning to do a striptease act for you all.'

Back on the barge they handed Mick a change of clothes, some hot food and a flask of hot coffee to take back with him.

'Mick, we won't catch up with the trawler until late this evening, so I doubt if we will get back to you before morning. I know roughly the direction you will take, so we'll try to keep you on our radar screen. I will have my navigation lights on, so take this powerful lamp and use the same signal that we used when we met up in Portugal.'

Marçel was taken by surprise when Helga jumped down into the inflatable dinghy and she and Mick wrapped their arms around each other. They kissed passionately and then Helga climbed back onto the barge.

As soon as Mick was safely back on the deck of the ketch, Marçel started the engine, turned the barge around and headed off at full speed, determined to catch up with the Nazi trawler.

Helga went below to check on Gerda, who was now curled up in warm blankets and fast asleep. She washed the salt water from their clothes and decorated the wheelhouse with them.

They were now travelling at a good fourteen knots and could just see the trawler in the distance.

'What exactly are you going to do, Marçel?' Stephen had taken the wheel.

'We should catch up early this evening. You said you wanted this Schmidt guy dead, so that's just what I'm going to do. When we catch up with the bastard, I'm going to rake his ship with machine-gun bullets and then when I've killed them all, I'm going to ram and sink his bloody boat. Is that all right with you?'

'That's piracy at sea, but as long as we sink the trawler without leaving any trace, I think that would be a satisfactory conclusion.'

They were lucky that there were no other ships in sight when they caught up on the trawler. Marçel took over the steering wheel. 'Keep your head down, Stephen; I want to draw their fire.'

As soon as they closed in on the trawler, Schmidt and his crew started firing their hand weapons and a sub-machine gun. This was just what

Marçel wanted. First it confirmed that he had followed the right boat, and now he could familiarise himself with their weaponry and their range.

Marçel allowed the barge to pull away from the trawler, but he kept well abreast of it. The trawler was now a sitting duck.

The barge was out of the effective range of their hand weapons, but the trawler was well within the range of the heavy machine-gun.

Gerda appeared on deck with Helga. She was carrying one of the rifles equipped with telescopic sights. She looked like death, but she had such a determined look on her face that Marçel said nothing. They went out onto the stern deck. Gerda made herself comfortable on top of the engine room hatch cover—she was a crack shot, and this woman was out for revenge.

'Maybe the girls should stay below while there are bullets flying around, Marçel.'

'Gerda would probably shoot you first if you tried to stop her now and Helga won't go below while Gerda is on deck. Just take the wheel. Keep this distance away and stay abreast of the trawler until it comes to a stop.

Before Marçel had time to reach the machine-gun mounting, Gerda had started firing at the trawler.

Schmidt and his two mates were crouching on the deck. There was another man in the wheelhouse steering the boat. Two of the men on deck collapsed. Gerda had taken her revenge.

Marçel started firing the machine gun. The wheelhouse glass completely shattered and the helmsman dropped out of sight. The third man, who Marçel recognised as Schmidt, made a dash for shelter behind the wheelhouse. Marçel kept on firing and watched him fall out of sight. He reappeared moments later, staggered, lost his balance, and fell overboard.

Marçel started firing at the waterline at the stern end of the trawler, aiming to damage its rudder.

Without a helmsman, the trawler was now turning in a wide arc. Marçel went back to the wheelhouse. Helga was trying to revive Gerda, who had collapsed after her effort of firing at the trawler.

'We will have to ram the bugger if we want to sink her, Stephen! Can you quickly go below and make sure the bulkhead door between the bow and the main cabin is securely fastened?'

The trawler was slowly turning and would soon be crossing their bow if they kept on this heading.

'All secure below, Marçel. Are you sure the front end of the barge is strong enough to take the impact?'

'We'll soon find out. It will be our steel into their wood. Helga! Hang onto Gerda and hold onto something yourself; we are about to ram the trawler!'

Marçel turned the barge inwards towards the now slow-moving trawler, hoping for a glancing blow, which would penetrate the side of the trawler without damage to the barge.

They hit the boat amidships. At the same time their stern swung around and hit the stern of the trawler almost capsizing it. Marçel stopped the engine as the two vessels drifted apart.

Stephen put his hand on Marçel's shoulder. 'What about the gold on the trawler?'

'I couldn't care less about that tainted gold after what has happened to us. In fact I'm sure no one on this boat would want anything to do with that gold now.'

'You're so right—the best place for that gold is at the bottom of the sea.'

Marçel restarted the engine and turned the barge around to follow the trawler, which had continued on, but with a jagged hole in its timber side. The water must have been rushing in, flooding the engine-room.

They watched in silence as the trawler slowed to a stop. They quietly stood there as it gradually started to sink and then it just rolled over on its side and slowly disappeared out of sight.

No one mentioned the gold bars that went down with the trawler. Marçel knew they all felt the same way.

Stephen and Marçel ran up to the bow to see if they had sustained any damage. There was a large dent in their starboard bow, and what looked like a slight split in the hull, but the damage was all well above the waterline.

'We might take in a little water on board when the bow dips into the waves, but I'm quite sure the pumps will be able to cope with that. This is a tough old barge.'

Stephen went to see if there was any damage below deck. Marçel steered the barge through the area where the trawler had sunk. There was very little left floating on the surface. He fired a few shots with the machine gun to sink any bits of floating debris; they didn't want to leave any trace of the sunken trawler.

Some way astern, Marçel thought he saw what looked like a blond head bobbing in the water, but he chose to ignore it. He gave the engine full throttle and they headed off to join up with Mick …

What Marçel did not see as the light faded, was Helga standing against the stern rail and holding on to a lifebelt. Nor did he notice several fishing trawlers appearing from the southwest. Helga had been leaning over the stern rail of the barge, while they had been circling the last few bits of wreckage, which Marçel was trying to sink. She spotted a bobbing head in the water some way off and realised it was Schmidt.

She knew this was an evil man who represented all the things that she had suffered in the last few years. This was final justice to a man who had done so many evil things in his life, a man who had murdered and tortured hundreds of innocent people. And yet a tiny thought entered her mind. Helga had found a man and Helga had found love. Should she in return for this wonderful gift of love, show a little mercy to a drowning man?

Helga dropped the lifebelt on the deck and returned to the wheelhouse. Justice had been done.

They helped Gerda back into her bunk. She was feeling quite cheerful having found enough inner strength to get herself up on deck. She had taken her revenge for the rough treatment they had all received from the Nazis in the last few hours.

It was obvious that Gerda was still in need of hospital treatment. Stephen decided to take her back to London as soon as they arrived at Nantes.

Helga set to in the galley. Marçel gave Stephen a course to steer and an hour later, Gerda joined them in the wheelhouse where they tucked into a late supper. The girls spent the next hour describing their epic journey from the castle in Portugal, to their arrival at Belle Ile and those final hours trapped in the ketch's saloon. It was the end of quite an eventful day.

'Girls, you really should turn in. You must be completely exhausted by now.' It seemed that Helga was about to collapse with exhaustion.

'Only if you promise to wake me when we get to Mick's boat.' They noticed a slight flush on her face.

Marçel took over from Stephen at midnight. There were several lights in the distance, one where he estimated Mick should be by now, and one or two others from fishing boats ahead and behind them. The sea had calmed right down, with just a long slow swell and a light breeze now from the west.

It was three am when he spotted Mick's signal about a mile ahead.

Marçel nipped down to wake Helga. 'We should be with Mick in about ten minutes, if you want to lend a hand.' She leaped out of bed, still fully dressed. 'Anything you say, *mon Capitaine*.' And followed him back to the wheelhouse.

Mick had hung a lamp from the mizzen-mast; the ketch was now riding high in the water and moving slowly along with the aid of its mizzen-sail.

Marçel brought the barge almost alongside and slightly ahead of the ketch. 'Take the wheel and hold this position, Helga, but don't let the barge fall back onto the ketch.'

Mick was already up in the bow and ready to take the tow-rope. Marçel threw a light line with the tow-rope attached, which Mick caught first time. He pulled in the tow-rope and fastened it to his winch. Mick gave the thumbs up sign and Marçel ran back to the wheelhouse.

Marçel took over the wheel from Helga. 'That worked out well, Helga.' She immediately went and leaned over the stern rail waving and shouting to Mick.

'You will have plenty of time for flirting later. In the meantime come and take the wheel while I dismantle the machine gun and stow it away.'

Helga ran back, flung her arms around Marçel and hugged him. 'Darling, Marçel, thanks to you I have never been so happy in my life!'

Marçel disentangled himself from her and gently placed her hands on the steering wheel. 'You have certainly proved yourself in the last few days and now you have a new life in front of you. You really do deserve to have a very happy future. If you and Mick get together, I know you will give him hell, but it will be a wonderful hell. I also know that you two will have a great life together and I hope lots of children.'

It was just getting light as they passed the first buoy opposite St Brevin. The tide was flooding so Marçel decided to keep going on to Paimboeuf and avoid any awkward questions at St Nazaire from Customs and Immigration. He felt sure they would not be interested in the barge; after all they'd only been away for one night and could not have travelled outside French waters.

The ketch was a different matter. Marçel stopped the engine and allowed it to catch up with the barge, calling out to Mick, 'If the Customs and immigration see you being towed in, they might want to talk to you. You better have a plausible story ready just in case.'

Marçel decided to keep close to the right-hand side of the estuary opposite St Nazaire. Apparently the customs officers were not yet on duty, so they slipped by St Nazaire unnoticed. They passed Paimboeuf and entered the canal de la Martiniere. By late morning they had turned off into a small branch of the canal where they were able to moor the ketch to an old jetty. The jetty was part of a small boatyard near the village of Buzay.

They decided to leave the ketch at the boat yard and return the barge to its secluded canal mooring near Blain. There was no point in Mick staying with his boat as everything below decks was soaking wet and a complete mess. Mick arranged to meet the owner of the boatyard the following day.

Mick dropped any loose gear lying on deck down into the saloon and then he carefully locked all the hatches; Marçel wasn't to find out why until the following day ...

The wind had by now died down and it had become a warm sunny day. They all set off in the barge headed back up the Loire River.

Helga, now fully recovered, served them all a leisurely breakfast on deck. Then she, Gerda and Mick stretched out on the warm afterdeck and were soon happily sleeping, dead to the world.

Stephen had sent a radio message to his office in London requesting the RAF send an aircraft to Nantes to pick up Gerda and him.

They were approaching Nantes when the message came through on the radio that an RAF 'Dove' aircraft would be arriving at Nantes airport late that afternoon to collect them.

Chapter 15

Schmidt broke surface to find the trawler was already some distance away. He noticed it was turning in a wide circle and realised that there was no one on board left alive.

Kicking off his shoes and slipping out of his jacket, Schmidt saw that his shoulder had stopped bleeding. He found he was quite able to tread water and was quite convinced that the people on the barge would soon come and rescue him.

Schmidt watched the trawler complete its circle. The barge then headed straight for the trawler. He watched the barge as it drove into the side of the trawler, then it backed away. To Schmidt's horror the trawler slowly sank out of sight and taking with it all his precious gold.

Schmidt realised then that he was not going to be picked up. He cursed silently; his German pride would not allow him to wave his good arm and cry for help. He was certain they knew he was in the water and were coldly ignoring him. His anger turned to rage as he watched the barge sink all the remaining bits of debris and then it turned away, as it headed back towards France.

As the barge moved off, he realised he would not be able find any debris that would keep him afloat. It was then that he noticed the girl leaning on the stern rail. She bent down and picked up a lifejacket.

He found himself laughing. 'So I am to be saved by the Jewish woman.'

He stared in disbelief as Helga waved the lifejacket at him. Then defiantly, she dropped it on the deck, and walked back to the wheelhouse ...

Furious, he shook his fist and shouted at the departing barge, '*Heil Schmidt*! One day I will make sure that Germany rules the world!' Such was his belief in his own invincibility and his absolute conviction that one day he would rule a Nazi-controlled world!

He waited a few minutes to calm himself before slowly swimming towards the coast of France, which was over forty miles away. He felt quite sure that a passing boat would soon pick him up.

As Schmidt kept slowly swimming, not really knowing in which direction to go as there was no land in sight; his mind went back to the recent events that had landed him in this predicament. He was quite confident that he would be able to extricate himself from this situation. Unfortunately things were going wrong for him at the moment, but he was convinced a passing fishing boat would soon pick him up. He knew he was indestructible and that one day he was to be the ruler of Germany and eventually, the whole world.

He had not yet achieved what he had set out to do since leaving Brazil, he had lost some of the gold, those fools had let it sink to the bottom of the ocean, but he felt sure there must still be much more gold hidden somewhere in that Portuguese castle.

Schmidt decided he no longer needed those pathetic escaping petty war criminals to deliver their gold to him. They were scum, and he would have killed them anyway after they had delivered the gold to him in Brazil.

He was aware that he had an enormous task in front of him. He was also aware that he was destined to become an even greater leader than Adolph Hitler.

Cousin Adolph had deposited a vast amount of gold in South America and now it was all his gold to rebuild the German Empire.

Schmidt was convinced he was about to change the map of the world.

—

In those last few hours of the war in Europe, Schmidt had met his distant cousin Adolph in the Berlin bunker. This was shortly before Adolph and Eva were to die in such ignomiy after having destroyed so much of Europe and causing the death of millions of innocent people.

Cousin Adolph had told him to escape to Brazil before Germany was completely overrun by the advancing Russian army. He had given him a large envelope, which contained the documents necessary to give him access to all the hidden German gold reserves in South America. He was told to wait a few years until Europe had settled down after the war. Then he was to use the vast amount of money to slowly rebuild the Nazi party in all the major countries.

Adolph Hitler was convinced that the Nazis would, by stealth, eventually be able to regain power and take rightful control.

Schmidt remembered how as a small boy he had been sent to a special school from where the very toughest boys, who were by then all in the Hitler Youth movement, were transferred to a secret training camp in the heart of the Black

Forest. *After five years of hell, during which he was completely brainwashed by his Nazi party teachers, Schmidt rejoined the world, convinced that Adolph Hitler, with the aid of the Nazi party, would one day rule the world.*

One year before the start of the Second World War, Schmidt transferred to one of Hitler's crack SS regiments. He was amongst the first of the Germans to enter Poland in 1939.

For the next few years he was involved in a killing spree. It started in Poland then went on to Greece, the Island of Crete, North Africa, Italy, Yugoslavia and finally to Russia. In between these events he had spent months at the headquarters in Berlin where he was given intensive courses on diplomacy, internal and external politics, high finance and all the social graces necessary in a top diplomat.

Eventually he was introduced to his distant cousin, Adolph. The meeting went well. After several private meetings and over a period of a few years, Cousin Adolph, having watched Schmidt's progress and his shared hatred of the Jews, decided that this was the man above all others to succeed him if at any time he were to die, or be assassinated by one of his many enemies.

Very few people in Germany were aware of SS Sturmbannführer Karl Schmidt and his relationship with the Führer. To Hitler's close colleagues and the Nazi Party, the young man was just another SS officer, and a hero in the eyes of the German people …

———

Three hours later, Schmidt spotted the navigation lights of a group of trawlers that were heading in his direction. He waved frantically but three of the fishing boats passed by, unable to see the lone swimmer in the dark. And then about one hour later, when he was beginning to lose some of his self-confidence, a trawler came bearing down on him.

He desperately tried to swim out of the way of the oncoming boat and screamed as the bow wave of the trawler rose above him. He was immediately sucked under water; his clothes were almost ripped off him as he passed down the side of the hull, narrowly missing the whirling propeller of the trawler.

Jean Bouchard, the captain of the trawler, had just come out of the wheelhouse and heard Karl's scream. He immediately stopped his engine.

Some way astern, in the wake of the fishing boat, the body of a man slowly came to the surface.

One of the crew who had been washing down the deck grabbed a hand searchlight, used when they untangled nets at night, and shone it over the water. He spotted the floating body and yelled to the captain to bring the boat around.

As the trawler came alongside the floating body, they used their boat hooks to unceremoniously lift Schmidt out of the water. To everyone's astonishment, he was still alive.

Captain Bouchard, who after only a small catch of fish due to the previous day's storm, had been hitting the bottle. He was not at all clear-headed. He realised that a boat must have just sunk close by and that he had just picked up a survivor from that boat. He circled the area, in case there were any other men in the water. After an hour, not having seen any floating oil or debris, he decided that he must have picked up the only survivor. He decided to continue on his way back to their homeport.

Schmidt looked up at the smiling faces of the two young crew members. He was still alive; he had a splitting headache and his badly grazed body felt as if it had passed through a cement mixer. But he was alive and on board a boat. Carefully sitting up, he found that although badly bruised and grazed, no bones were broken. He noticed his tattered clothes had been draped around the stove in the centre of the large cabin where the crew ate and slept. The younger of the two crewmen ran up the ladder to the wheelhouse to fetch the captain.

'This is your lucky day, *mon ami*. Your time to die had not yet come. What happened to your boat? Were there any others on board?' Captain Bouchard handed Schmidt a pair of trousers and a heavy jersey; it was then that he noticed the look in his eyes. He began to feel afraid of this man they had pulled from the sea.

'Have you informed anyone on the radio to say that you have picked up a survivor?'

Bouchard had decided to talk to this man before reporting his rescue. He was feeling a little nervous now. '*Mais non, monsieur*, I wanted to talk to you first, we are returning from an unsuccessful fishing trip and are low on fuel.'

Schmidt crossed over to the table, picked up a large gutting knife and before Jean realised what was happening, Karl had grabbed Jean by the throat and slipped the knife between his ribs. 'But not your lucky day, my friend.' Schmidt swung around; the other crewman stood frozen to the spot. In a flash he stepped over and quickly dispatched the terrified young crewman.

Schmidt wiped the blood off his hands, and climbed the ladder up to the deck. On deck it was still dark; he joined the other young fisherman in the wheelhouse.

The cheerful smile on the young man's face quickly turned to a look of horror as Schmidt's knife struck him between the shoulder blades. He was quite dead when he was lifted over the side rail and dropped into the sea.

Back in the wheelhouse looking at the chart, it was obvious to Schmidt that the trawler was heading for La Rochelle, which would be their home base. Schmidt studied the open chart that was on the chart table. He knew they would not have a great deal of fuel left on board as they were heading home after several days at sea. He decided to head a little way further to the south, close to the entrance of the Gironde River, from where he could easily get to Bordeaux. There was a Nazi cell at Bordeaux, and he knew he had a contact there.

Leaving the wheel for a minute, Schmidt scoured the deck for a life raft. He found an old inflatable dinghy complete with an outboard motor—perfect for what he wanted.

He needed to get ashore unnoticed.

Schmidt rummaged through the drawers under the chart table until he found a few hundred francs in a watertight tobacco tin.

Shortly before dawn he saw the shore lights. He stopped the engine of the trawler and lowered the inflatable dinghy over the side. Schmidt checked the outboard motor for fuel and gave the motor a quick run. Satisfied, he climbed back on board and went below to open all the safety valves on the trawler. He jumped back into the dinghy and waited for the trawler to sink.

It was just starting to become light when the trawler finally slipped out of sight. Schmidt headed for what appeared to be a deserted part of the coast.

Fifty yards outside of the breakers he used his knife to pierce the sides of the inflatable dinghy and as it sank beneath him he set off towards the breakers, swimming strongly through the heavy surf.

Schmidt lay exhausted on the beach for a few minutes; it had been a long swim through the surf that only a very strong and fit swimmer could have achieved. The beach was completely deserted. It was high tide and only a few paces from the beach to the high sand dunes that stretched away in both directions. From the top of the dunes, in the distance, Schmidt was able to see the road, which led to the small village of Soulac, further up the coast.

Only one or two people were about when Schmidt finally arrived at one of the cafés on the waterfront. The patron stared at this man still dressed in the old shirt and trousers that the trawler captain had given him, but by now dried in the early morning sun. Schmidt drank several cups of hot coffee and ate freshly baked bread, before making a phone call to a telephone number in Bordeaux.

It was now nine am. With only a short distance to the railway station, Schmidt found an open clothes shop where, with the few remaining stolen francs, he was able to change into some respectable trousers, a shirt, jacket and shoes.

A few minutes later, Schmidt was on a train to Bordeaux.

By midday, in a small hotel hidden away in one of the back streets near the river, Karl Schmidt was having a meeting with *Herr* Schiller, the head of the local Nazi cell in Bordeaux.

'You came through a bad storm, *Herr* Schmidt. On the radio this morning it said that at least three fishing boats were lost in the bay, two French trawlers and one from Spain. A de-masted sailing boat was also towed into St Nazaire early this morning.'

Schmidt considered this for a moment. Marçel must have reached the ketch and prevented it from sinking. Having rescued the two girls and the Australian, they had then come straight after him. After sinking his trawler and leaving him to drown, they had towed the ketch back to St Nazaire.

Schmidt's anger returned.

He had lost the gold but Schmidt was even more determined to kill the four of them. It should not be difficult to spot the barge and the ketch from the air and he knew Schiller had an aeroplane.

'I had one or two slight problems but nothing to concern you, *Herr* Schiller. We have given your section several large sums of money in the past, but so far you don't seem to have made much progress here in Bordeaux. However, I understand your group owns a private airstrip where you have concealed one of our wartime aeroplanes. Is it close to Bordeaux?'

'On your orders, *Herr* Schmidt, we established this secret airfield. It is hidden away at a very secluded spot in the centre of very extensive marshland. The airfield is on a small island and is completely fenced with danger signs to warn people off. The only access to it is by boat.'

'And the aeroplane? What sort is it and is it airworthy?'

'Shortly before the collapse of our Fatherland in May 1945 a *Luftwaffe* pilot stole one of the last surviving *Junkers* 87 dive-bombers, the once-famous *Stuka* bomber, and he headed south hoping to reach Spain. But before reaching Spain he ran out of fuel and crash-landed in the middle of this marshland, which is southwest of Bordeaux. Although badly injured, the pilot managed to get to the mainland and was picked up by a fisherman, luckily for him not a member of the French resistance movement. He was taken to a hospital in Bordeaux where he remained for several months after the end of the war.'

'So how did you find him, Schiller?'

'He must have sustained some brain damage; he managed to stay on in Bordeaux living with the many down and outs. We found him lying drunk in the gutter one night. He was a German and we took care of him. Later we persuaded him to join our group. As you know we were very active during the Spanish civil war, but now we are forced to remain a very secret organisation. This man, *Oberleutnant* Huber, a good German, later told us his story and led us to the *Stuka*. He has been restoring the aircraft ever since. That is where most of your money has been spent.'

'So, you have managed to restore the *Stuka* and you now have an airworthy *Junkers* 87 dive-bomber? Next you will tell me that it is armed.'

'As a matter of fact it is. We have restored the two machine guns and we have one bomb, which was recently delivered to us from our friends in Germany. If necessary, we can attach this bomb to the aircraft. For obvious reasons we had to wipe out the aircraft's signs so that we could occasionally test fly the *Stuka* in this area.'

'Tomorrow you will take me to this airfield. If what you say is correct, I will be able to fly this aeroplane. It has been four years since I flew a *Junkers* 87—I shall look forward to it.'

Schmidt, who was still badly bruised and battered, was feeling completely exhausted. After a substantial meal he retired to his room and slept through until the following day.

Early the following morning, driving through this very desolate part of the country, it soon became obvious to Karl why people rarely came along this seemingly endless rough track. They eventually reached the tall reeds that seemed to stretch on for miles ahead. *Herr* Schiller parked the car in amongst the reeds. They continued on foot for another two miles, following the edge of the reeds. They then turned off down a narrow path, which was completely out of sight to anyone passing by.

One hour later they arrived at the water's edge. A tall thin man was waiting alongside a small steel flat-bottomed barge.

'*Reichführer* Schmidt, this is *Oberleutenant* Huber. I'm afraid he doesn't say much as he has become a bit of a recluse since living on the island.'

Schiller would not normally address Schmidt as *Reichführer*. But this was for the benefit of *Oberleutenant* Huber, who still considered himself an officer in the *Luftwaffe*.

The *Oberleutenant* stood to attention, as if on the parade ground. 'I received your radio message, Schiller.'

He turned to face Schmidt; clicked his heels and gave him the Nazi salute.

They climbed aboard the barge. Huber started the slow running diesel engine.

The barge pushed its way through the thick reeds until they reached an almost clear area of water. While steering the barge, the *Oberleutenant* stood to attention and saluted. '*Reichführer* Schmidt, it is an honour to meet you. I wish to serve you as I served *Herr* Hitler. I know one day that with you as our *Führer*, we will restore Nazi Germany to its rightful place as the country that one day will dominate the world. The *Stuka* is all ready for you. It is fully fuelled and armed. I gave it a test flight yesterday. I would consider it a great honour to fly with you today.'

'You *will* come with me, *Oberleutenant*. Today, I wish to destroy an ocean-going barge. On board are people who have harmed our cause and who know too much about our activities—they must be eliminated. Today, Oberleutenant, you will fly to defend our fatherland. This is just the start of a long campaign to restore the Fatherland. You will be given many opportunities to prove yourself in the next few years. We are gathering many friends in Europe and when the time is right, we will emerge as the strongest political party in Europe. We will then return to take over complete control of the Fatherland. After that the whole world will be ours.'

It was only a short stretch of water before they were again pushing their way through reeds. Finally they arrived at a high mud bank. Huber brought the barge alongside a stone jetty with a small crane, which had been used to unload all the necessary equipment for the airfield and, with great difficulty, the 250lb bomb.

The island turned out to be a narrow eight-hundred-yard long strip of rough grass and reeds. At most it was four hundred yards wide. The fencing and warning signs around the island could only be seen after penetrating the thick reeds as these tall reeds completely surrounded the island; no one ever realised that there might be firm dry land amongst all of them.

In February 1945, *Oberleutenant* Huber had been circling over their narrow landing strip in northern France, waiting for the smoke to clear. They had been ordered to attack an American supply column, which was approaching from the west. They had set off in their last three *Junkers 87s*; these were just a few of the remaining outdated aircraft of the once-powerful *Luftwaffe*.

Shortly after take-off just as they were starting to climb, two *Spitfires* attacked them. Huber managed to slip away as the other two *Stukas* were being attacked.

Later, flying back to base, just above treetops, he found his airstrip hidden under a cloud of smoke. The *Spitfires* had completed their mission. As the smoke cleared, Huber realised there was nothing left of the base and the runway was unusable. His friends were all dead, nearly all their aircraft had been destroyed and he realised the war was nearly over.

At that moment, Huber decided that he would save one aircraft and one pilot for a future Germany. He would fly to neutral Spain.

Huber estimated that he had sufficient fuel to get him across the Spanish border. What he had not allowed for was the extra fuel consumption caused by flying at treetop level and the continuous diversions avoiding Allied aircraft.

When *Oberleutenant* Huber finally ran out of fuel, he spotted the narrow spit of land in the middle of a large marshland area and tried to land the *Junkers 87*. He had almost made a safe landing, when unfortunately for him, the undercarriage hit an extra-large rock, and the aircraft nose-dived into a mud-filled gully.

Huber eventually regained consciousness. He found himself upside down, held in the cockpit by his safety harness. He was staring down at the mud six feet below him. Having sustained a broken collarbone and a bang to his head from hitting the side of the canopy, Huber's only way now was to release the safety harness and fall headfirst into the mud. Huber ejected the tiny inflatable dinghy, with which fortunately the *Stuka* was equipped, hoping it would inflate and help to break his fall.

The dinghy inflated but not under the cockpit canopy. He released the catch on his harness and broke an arm landing in the mud, but that broken arm had saved his life. Despite his condition, Huber managed to paddle his tiny life raft across to the mainland and then drag himself through the reeds to the track.

It was several days later when a fisherman found Huber. He was wandering down the track where the fisherman usually parked his van when he went fishing.

The *Oberleutenant* now led them to the far end of the narrow spit of cleared land to a small low hangar. The corrugated roof was covered with a layer of thick turf, making it impossible to be seen from the air.

One side of the hangar had been divided off for living quarters. In the centre of the hangar was the gleaming silver *Junker 87*. Schmidt caught his breath as the memories came flooding back; he had flown this type of aircraft many times and had been privileged to fly as crew in one of these dive-bombers when they had completely destroyed Warsaw in 1939.

Trembling with excitement, he decided he would track down the barge, which had given him so much trouble. Then he would dive-bomb it. He would scare the shit out of Marçel, Mick and the two women with the scream from the dive-bomber, before the bomb exploded and blew them all to hell.

It was after midday when, having eaten the sandwiches that *Herr* Schiller had thoughtfully brought with him, they pushed the aircraft out onto the end of the grass runway. Schmidt put the chocks in place while the *Oberleutenant* brought out the starting batteries on the hand trolley.

'Herr Schiller, you will take away the starter batteries as soon as the engine starts, but don't remove the chocks until I give you the signal.'

The *Oberleutenant* walked around the *Stuka* doing a final check before climbing into the rear seat. Karl examined the 250 lb bomb that had been fastened to the underside of the fuselage early that morning. He was quite satisfied that with the bomb, he would be able to blow the barge out of the water. Then he climbed onto the wing and slipped into the front seat ready for the start up.

After carefully studying the map, Schmidt called Huber on the intercom. 'We will head out to sea, fly up the coast, then turn in towards La Baule before following the coast to St Nazaire. It's one hundred and eighty miles to La Baule, well under an hour. We can cruise up the north side of the Loire as far as Nantes and then return down the south side back to St Nazaire. We will still have enough fuel to comfortably get us back.'

'And the target, *Herr* Führer?'

'The target is an eighty-foot long, converted barge with a machine gun mounting on the deck. But I don't expect they will display that gun now that they are in a French port. We should not have any difficulty spotting this barge; there are not too many boats like this one. If we are lucky, there could be four or more people on board.'

The engine roared into life as Schmidt ran up the engine giving it full throttle and checking the magnetos. 'It sounds excellent Huber. Let's go.'

Schmidt raised his hand and *Herr* Schiller pulled away the chocks. The aeroplane moved forward. Schmidt lined it up on the runway. He held it back on the brakes, lowered the flaps and slowly opened the throttle; the aircraft started to vibrate. As he released the brake, the *Stuka* surged forward and roared down the short runway lifting just a short way from the end.

As the aircraft started to climb and the speed increased, Schmidt raised the flaps and then relaxed. The *Stuka* was the last fighter-bomber to have a fixed undercarriage; this helped to limit its speed and had made it a sitting target for other much faster aircraft. As the war in Europe developed, the *Junkers 87* were no longer used in the major war zones.

Schmidt headed out to sea. It was a fine cloudless day. He climbed up to three thousand feet, then turned and headed north to La Baule.

Forty-five minutes later, he throttled back the engine and allowed the aeroplane to sink down to five hundred feet as they approached La Baule.

'Look out also for a sixty-foot ketch without a main mast, but which still has a mizzen-mast in the stern end. It might be with the smart-looking barge. I think it was towed into St Nazaire by that barge; they could still be together somewhere.'

He circled slowly to the right and then cruised steadily up the Loire River past all the boats at anchor, as well as those tied up at the numerous jetties along the way.

Schmidt was flying along the river at less than three hundred feet above the water, only a short distance out from the riverbank and just a little above stalling speed. 'We will turn around when we get past Nantes and then cruise down along the other side of the river.'

Schmidt was starting to feel a surge of anger. He felt sure the barge must be somewhere here. Well past Nantes, he turned the aircraft and headed down the opposite side of the river.

'*Führer* Schmidt, there is a canal running parallel to the river and at the top end I can see a small canal that runs away to the south. There are some boats moored there.'

Karl swung the aircraft around giving it a little extra power as he turned towards the smaller side canal. 'That's the ketch, Huber; it's moored alongside the boatyard jetty. I can see people standing on the deck but there is still no sign of the barge. We will dive-bomb the ketch instead; it looks as if the people we want are on it anyway. The barge must have gone off somewhere else leaving the ketch here.'

With full throttle the *Stuka* started to climb. Karl kept it in a tight circle until the aircraft was well over four thousand feet high. He levelled out and then looked down at the target. 'Are you ready? The *Stuka* has the siren attached to its belly. We will sound *The Trumpets of Jericho* as we scream all the way down! Those people will probably die of fright before the bomb explodes; block your ears, *Oberleutenant* Huber! Here we go!'

Schmidt pointed the nose down and almost immediately, the *Stuka* started its deafening scream. Schmidt was also screaming with excitement as the *Junkers 87* dived towards its target.

Three thousand.

Two thousand.

Karl saw faces looking up.

One thousand.

The controls suddenly went slack—*the aircraft was not meant to spin!*

Karl Schmidt's scream turned to a scream of fear …

Chapter 16

At Nantes the barge left the Loire River and entered the canal, passing through the tunnel to the centre of the town. Marçel found a vacant spot at a jetty nearby and nipped ashore to find a taxi to take Stephen and Gerda to the airport. Gerda had to be helped up onto the deck and into the waiting taxi. Marçel decided to accompany them to the airport.

A *gendarme* met them at the airport and escorted them to a small office where the immigration officer was waiting. He had already been notified about Stephen and Gerda's departure to England. An RAF Dove aircraft was standing by, ready to take them to Southampton airport. Such was the power and cooperation of the departments both in France and Britain at that time.

Marçel walked out to the aircraft with the two of them. Gerda put her arms around him. 'Look after Helga for me, Marçel. I think she and Mick might be getting together. This would be a wonderful solution for Helga. She's a remarkable girl, Marçel, but she's had one hell of a time and now she deserves to have a good man in her life.'

'What about us, Gerda? Maybe it's time for us to settle down?'

Marçel immediately regretted that remark. He knew that was a silly thing to say at this time and that he deserved her answer, but it still hurt.

'No way, Marçel. I could never live with the Piglet. You will always be an extra special friend and you can come and make love to me next time you come to London. One day you will find another angel, like the one you lost in France during the war. I could never hope to live up to that girl, Marçel, and anyway I believe you might always be hoping you will find her double one day.'

Gerda climbed the steps. When she reached the door of the aircraft she turned and waved. 'Take care of yourself. You're a big boy now. Goodbye.'

He stood rooted to the ground. He could not believe what he had just heard. Marçel knew that she was right, but it was the way she had said it that stung. But he knew of course it was his male pride that was really hurt.

Stephen slapped him on the shoulder. 'Call me in a couple of days when you have sorted things out with Helga and Mick. The Department will pay for the damage to Mick's boat, and will reward him for his services.'

'It would seem that you have finally got rid of that Nazi fanatic, Karl Schmidt, but there is still a lot of work to be done once you have had a good long rest. Good luck, old boy.'

Marçel watched the Dove take off. He walked back to the main building and phoned for a taxi to take him back to the barge. His feelings were mixed—satisfied that he had left Karl Schmidt to drown, and relieved that the girls were now safely back in France.

But then he had lost four close friends as well as the castle and the winery—the business that he and Pete had worked so hard to build up in the last few years.

Marçel felt tired with a slight feeling of anti-climax after all the events of the last few days. He knew Gerda was right; marriage with Gerda was not an option. He was destined to remain a loner.

He and Gerda had shared so much danger together, both during and after the war. And they had often made passionate love after some particularly dangerous operation. Marçel had thought that they were bonded to each other and perhaps at some time in the distant future they might settle down and start a family.

The more he thought about it, the more he realised that he would remain a free spirit. Gerda would want a reliable steady, nine-to-five husband who would work in a 'safe job' and who would always be around for the kids.

That was definitely not for him … Maybe in a few years' time; he might lose his killer instinct and his desire to carry out lethal justice. But for now he could only carry out his career, as an unattached man.

After having been on a shopping expedition just a few streets away, Helga and Mick were sitting on the deck of the barge enjoying the late afternoon sunshine. Marçel could see that they were both deeply engrossed in planning their future. They certainly made a great couple. As he listened to their excited and infectious laughter, Marçel could no longer feel depressed.

He started up the engine, cast off the mooring ropes and headed out of Nantes and onto the Erde River. 'We will head up as far as the first lock near Nerd Sure Order and tie up for the night. In the morning we will go on through all the locks. We should arrive at our moorings by late morning.'

Mick and Helga had joined him in the wheelhouse; Mick had brought up a bottle and poured them all a glass of claret. The bow of the barge was cutting through the glass-like surface of the water at a good ten knots. They were silently enjoying passing through this wide and extra beautiful part of the Erde River.

Marçel was thinking how close to death they'd been just a few hours earlier. Now they were all safely heading back to their secluded moorings on the canal.

'I will be able to take you back to the ketch around midday tomorrow.' Mick had arranged to meet the owner of the boatyard and was afraid that they wouldn't get back to the boatyard in time.

'We now have two cars parked by our moorings. As soon as we have finished tying up the barge, I will drive you back to the ketch. We can all return back to the barge in the evening when you have finished your arrangements with the boatyard.'

Helga put her arm around Marçel's shoulder. 'Marçel, Mick and I have something very special to celebrate with you this evening. Can you believe it; Mick actually got down on his knees and officially asked me to marry him? He is taking me back to Australia to work with him on his farm in Queensland.'

'That's wonderful news, Helga! I realised you two had hit it off and I really am sure you will both be very happy in Australia.'

Marçel shook Mick's hand and kissed Helga on both cheeks. 'Would you like us to organise a passage for you both? I'll tell Stephen to get onto it as soon as possible.'

Mick topped up their near-empty glasses. 'There's no need for that. I'm going to refit the ketch. We intend to sail out to Australia and we will have all the time in the world to get there.'

'Isn't that a fantastic idea, sailing on a slow boat to Australia?' Helga emptied her second glass of wine.

'It's a bit risky, Helga, but you certainly have the right sort of boat for the journey, and you have proved yourself to be a really good sailor in the last few days. So good luck to you both.'

'I'm going below to cook you boys the best meal I possibly can. And it won't be hotpot this time.'

'She's quite something, Marçel. Helga will be a great crewmate and I reckon will make a terrific farmer's wife. We will spend the next few weeks fitting out the ketch, and will then head off to Australia before the winter sets in.'

'You're going to need a fair bit of money to equip the ketch for this long journey, but money won't be a problem. Stephen has agreed to pay for all the repair costs to your boat. You will be able to completely re-equip the ketch for your long voyage to Australia and with no cost spared.'

That evening they tied up just below the first lock gate at the start of the Brest à Nantes canal. Helga cooked them a wonderful roast dinner followed by apple strudel and a selection of the local cheeses, which they washed down with excellent French champagne. It was a meal they would never forget.

The next morning three bleary-eyed mariners were forced to work off the previous night's indulgence by opening and closing numerous lock gates. At midday, fortified with sandwiches and some rather flat champagne, they left the main canal and motored into the narrow canal to the barge's mooring. They quickly tied up the barge to the mooring posts at the very secluded moorings in the quiet creek, just a few miles from the small town of Blain.

Mick was itching to get back to the ketch, so they piled into the Renault and headed back to Nantes. They crossed over the bridge to the south side of the Loire, drove past the airport and then took the road down to Buzay.

A small bridge took them over the narrow canal that branched off from the main canal. They turned left and followed a dirt track until they rejoined the canal. About a mile down the track they could see the ketch tied up to the old wooden jetty. There were several other boats in the water and two large fishing boats that had been hauled up onto the ramps on the side of the canal. Another boat under repair was inside the large shed next to the boatyard workshops.

Marçel drove the Renault up to the old jetty. Mick jumped out and hurried over to the ketch and Helga went and sat in the front seat of the Renault with Marçel.

'You know how the Nazis removed the gold from the ketch and it is now thankfully at the bottom of the sea, well, they didn't take the cases of arms which we had brought from your castle in Portugal. The guns are still on the ketch.'

'My God, Helga, I had forgotten about them. We must get them off the ketch before anyone else sees them.'

They ran over to the ketch. Mick was busy disconnecting the batteries.

'We must get the guns out of here before the boatyard manager comes across. Grab some headsails from the locker and we will wrap them around the cases and carry them out to the car.'

While Marçel was carrying the cases over to the car, he suggested to the others that they conceal two revolvers, a light machine gun and several spare clips of ammunition under Mick's bunk.

He considered this a necessary precaution, as they would need to protect themselves from any pirates that they might meet on their journey to Australia. Mick said he felt sure this would be quite acceptable to the French authorities.

Marçel lifted the last of the cases into the boot of the Renault, Helga dumped a pile of wet clothes and blankets on top of the cases, and Marçel breathed a sigh of relief.

Jean Claude, the owner of the boatyard, came across and joined them on the deck of the ketch. They spent some time inspecting the damage.

Helga was busy emptying the galley cupboards. She lifted a large box with the remaining stores onto the deck and was spreading them out to dry.

It was at that moment that Marçel noticed the aircraft flying low over the canal.

Mick was staring at it. 'It looks just like a *Stuka* bomber; the Germans used them to dive-bomb us in the Spanish civil war.'

A few minutes later, they were standing on the jetty staring at the ketch; Marçel happened to look up and noticed the aeroplane was climbing in a tight circle above them. 'I wonder what he's up to. He looks as if he's going to do some aerobatics.'

Marçel noticed Mick was no longer smiling. He was looking thoughtful, as his mind had drifted back to the days when he was fighting in the Spanish civil war. He was thinking of the times they had been dive-bombed and the terrible sound of the diving *Stuka* bombers.

There was something wrong, Mick thought.

Is that Stuka *circling overhead?*

No, it was just not possible.

They started to walk towards the boatyard office, and then it started. At first they heard a slight wail, and then it grew louder and louder until it became a high-pitched scream. They stood staring at the diving aircraft.

Helga was standing on the deck of the ketch watching. She was transfixed, quite unable to move. She had experienced this once before in

Warsaw; in a matter of days she had watched a whole city being destroyed. Helga became frozen to the spot vaguely aware of her wet legs, but quite unable to control herself. 'Karl Schmidt, you bastard,' she murmured. She started to whimper in absolute fear at the deafening sound of the 'Trumpets of Jericho' as the *Stuka* dived straight towards her.

Mick was the first to realise what was happening. He screamed to Helga, 'Get off the boat!' He ran back and pushed her off the boat; then after throwing himself down into the cabin, he reappeared holding the machine-gun.

He kept firing the gun at the *Stuka* as it came diving straight down towards the ketch.

It took Marçel longer to comprehend what was happening. He started running back to the jetty with the completely confused Jean Claude; they grabbed Helga and flung themselves onto the ground at the back of the jetty.

Mick was still on deck firing the machine gun. Marçel noticed that the *Stuka* had started to spin and was curving away from them. Then there was a loud and yet almost muffled explosion. It was suddenly very quiet. The *Stuka* had dived into the marsh about three hundred yards away. Mick watched a thick black cloud rising from the mud. 'I can't breathe, Marçel.'

He was lying on top of Helga. Jean Claude was sitting up just staring at the black smoke.

'Thanks mate, but there is no need to suffocate her now.' Mick was standing over them grinning. 'I guess it's time I took this young sheila to live in a *safe* country.'

Jean Claude was brushing the dust off his trousers. 'What sort of friends have you got? I won't have your boat parked here if it's going to be used for target practice.'

'Somehow I don't think those friends of ours will be back. I am thinking of the times when I tried to shoot down *Stuka*s in the Spanish civil war without success and now, years later, I must have got him with a stray bullet from this pea shooter. Just a bloody miracle!'

Epilogue

Marçel spent the next eight weeks helping Mick and Helga prepare the ketch for their long voyage to Australia and after two weeks they were able to move in. Marçel remained on the barge and, most days, drove down to the ketch to give them a helping hand. The three of them spent the time scraping and then painting the hull; they were able to put all the trauma of those past few days behind them.

Stephen had decided to leave Marçel in peace for a few weeks, so he was able to enjoy the late summer working on the ketch. By the time it was ready to sail, it had been completely renovated below deck. There was a new galley and a large state cabin complete with double bed for the captain and his new wife. They installed a new mast and a new set of sails and a much more powerful diesel engine, with a separate generator. Stephen donated the very latest in radio and radar equipment. They had fun attaching the radar antenna to the mast-top—Helga had her first experience of going up top!

Early in October, Marçel moved the barge down to the jetty at Buzay and Stephen and Gerda flew down from London. Helga and Mick were to get married the following day and after the wedding would then set off on their honeymoon, sailing away to distant Australia.

Everyone remarked on how well Gerda looked; Marçel thought she had put on some weight. He thought Gerda was a little subdued, putting it down to having to say goodbye to her best friends.

That night Marçel ordered in a banquet from a top restaurant in Nantes; in the afternoon a van arrived with the chef, a waiter and all the ingredients for the wedding feast. Sharp at six pm, Marçel opened the first bottle of champagne to signal the start of a wonderful farewell party for Helga and Mick.

Marçel had decided that they should start the meal with a dozen oysters, a quite unnecessary aphrodisiac for the couple getting married the next day. For the main course there were roast pheasants, with all the trimmings, followed by a very rich hot chocolate gateau for the sweet, and a great selection of French cheeses to finish off the meal. Marçel had carefully chosen some of the best local wines, including one of the last bottles of wine from their winery in Portugal.

Stephen and Mick kept the party going into the early hours with their raucous singing. At two am they all retired to their respective beds, thanks to the watchful eyes of Stephen.

The following morning, the girls dressed all in white, looking absolutely radiant, and the blokes in 'toppers', set off to the cathedral in Nantes, where Mick and Helga were at last happily married. After the ceremony, Marçel stood looking at the two girls, and realised how attached he had become to both of them.

'Don't look so sad. One day you will come and stay on our farm and help us round up the cattle. Dear Marçel, I owe you so much.'

'We certainly had a bad start, Helga. I hope you won't ever want to throw rocks at Mick. I shudder when I think about that. If I had not slipped on that boulder you wouldn't be here today and the world would have lost a beautiful person.'

Two hours later, Mick and Helga were back in their working clothes. They cast off from the jetty and motored down the canal to Paimboeuf.

Stephen, Gerda and Marçel drove down to Paimboeuf and watched as they hoisted the sails on the ketch and waved them goodbye as they sailed down the Loire River to the open sea.

Marçel took Stephen and Gerda back to the airport; they would be back in London that evening.

Stephen cleared his throat and spoke to Marçel, 'Well, we now know that Schmidt fellow is no more. I want you to get yourself a pilot's licence, because your next job is to find out where that *Stuka* came from. By the way, as you know, I have a large house in the country, quite near Newbury and Gerda is coming to live with me. She will be my housekeeper, when she is not working for the Department. You know you will always be welcome to come and stay too.'

Marçel shook hands with Stephen and kissed Gerda lightly on the cheek. He noticed she was crying as they stepped up into the RAF Dove.

Lucky Stephen …

One month later Gerda Dubois and Stephen Harvey were married.

BOOK THREE

Play the Last Card

PART ONE

PART ONE

Chapter 1

T he heavy weight on his back was slowly forcing Marçel to the bottom of the pool. He turned his head to see the gleaming knife, caught by a sunray that shone down to the depths of the pool. Marçel expelled every drop of air from his lungs into the face of his attacker, delaying the thrust of the knife for just a fraction of a second. He touched the bottom of the pool and with his free hand, managed to roll himself over onto one side as the knife came down striking his left arm. With both legs, Marçel kicked his assailant away as they struggled to the surface. As he tried to grab the knife, it struck his assailant in the upper leg before sinking to the bottom of the pool.

Breaking the surface together and clinging to the side of the pool, they fought to recover their breath, the water rapidly turning red with their blood. For a brief second their eyes met; Marçel was shocked to see so much hate coming out of such a beautiful face.

Before he had time to speak, the woman had scrambled out of the pool, run across to the gate and up the steps to the parked cars. Seconds later with its engine revving wildly, her car disappeared down the driveway and out onto the highway.

Marçel heaved himself out of the pool. He felt quite sure that the woman, whoever she was, would not be coming back to finish her botched attempt to kill him.

He dived to the bottom of the pool again to retrieve the knife and then climbed out to examine the cut on his arm. The knife had only grazed the skin and the bleeding had stopped. He walked over to the pool cleaner and dragged the suction pipe over to the blood-stained water. Within minutes the pool cleaner had sucked up all traces of blood. He then carefully wiped the tiles where the woman had left a trail of blood on her way to her car.

Stretching out on one of the several deckchairs scattered around the pool, Marçel allowed the sun to dry his muscular sun-tanned body. He had spent these last two weeks relaxing at Stephen's villa on the outskirts of Dinard in northern Brittany and was quite happy to be thoroughly spoilt by Marie, Stephen's French housekeeper.

It was Marie's day off, and until now Marçel had been enjoying a peaceful day by the pool. It was to be an opportunity for him to catch up on some reading, with an occasional dive into the pool to cool off from the powerful midsummer sun.

He reached across to the icebox and pulled out a bottle of beer; knocking off the cap he emptied the bottle before putting it down on the tiled floor. Leaning back in the deckchair, he wondered why such a beautiful woman would want to come and kill him in the middle of the day, and in Stephen's swimming pool. On reflection he had to admit that doing his freestyle laps provided one of the few occasions that a killer could easily creep up on him undetected.

The woman had reminded Marçel of an advertisement he had seen for a top brand of shampoo. She had long black flowing hair and was wearing a man's shirt, pants and a wide weighted leather belt. She was tall and slim, with a superb dark honey-coloured skin. Marçel guessed she must be in her late twenties or early thirties. There was a distinctly Spanish look about her, reminding him of the women he had recently met in Brazil; that was an experience he was not likely to forget with so many beautiful girls trying to teach him the tango!

The woman had driven away in a light-blue Mercedes hatchback; there were not too many of those in the village. Marçel carefully examined the knife; it was an antique dagger with a lethal blade about nine inches long with a silver handle inlaid with pearl. The initials KS had been engraved into a silver panel on one side of the handle and the Eagle with a small swastika and the initials AH on the other side.

Thinking about the dagger, Marçel allowed his thoughts to drift back to past events. Two names immediately came to mind. Karl Schmidt and Adolph Hitler … and they were both very dead.

He decided to go down to the local hotel; maybe someone in the hotel bar might have seen her, so he borrowed Stephen's moped, and rode down the dirt track that ran from the back of the villa to the village.

The blue hatchback was parked outside the one and only hotel in the village square, the driver sitting at a table on the terrace in front of the hotel.

Marçel slowly walked up to her.

'What kept you, Piglet? I've been waiting half an hour for you.'

'I was cleaning up your mess. Do you usually make a habit of spilling your blood in other people's swimming pools?' Marçel pulled out a chair and sat down opposite her, noticing her change of clothes—no doubt her wound would have been dressed by now. 'You seem to know me. Very few people know that name you used; so who the hell are you, and why come and spoil my swim and mess up my pool?'

The woman leaned back in her chair and with an innocent smile on her face said, 'I must admit that was a bad mistake—I nearly killed a super hunk of a man, and you and I would never have met.' She laughed. 'My name is Lolita. You killed my man, Marçel, and I had come all the way from Brazil to destroy you.'

'And a real mess you made of it. Was your husband's name, Karl? If so, I did you a good turn; but in fact he killed himself. He was trying to dive bomb my friends and me with a clapped-out old *Stuka* bomber.'

Lolita looked surprised and smiled sweetly. 'I'm surprised, Marçel. Karl was a crack pilot and you must have been very lucky that day. I was told later that the *Stuka* had been previously damaged and was really not airworthy. Karl allowed his anger to override his knowledge of *Stuka* dive bombers.'

'From what I was told, I was expecting you to be very young with pimples and pink cheeks.'

Her anger returned. '*You* were the cause of Karl's death and the loss of much of his wealth! When he died, unfortunately all his wealth went to his successor, the new head of the Nazi party in South America.' She emptied her glass.

Marçel handed her the silver dagger. 'This was Karl's; it looks like a present from Adolph Hitler. Karl knew how to use it, but you certainly don't. If I were you, I'd sell it; it could be worth a lot of money.'

'Karl was a very cruel and extremely dangerous man.' She sighed. 'But now at last I'm free of him. Unfortunately, I am left without any of his large fortune. I had become so used to spending it and so now I am denied all the luxuries of the past. So you must see, Piglet, that I have a good reason to avenge Karl's death.'

'Money isn't everything, Lolita.'

'It was to you, you *bastard*!' she snapped.

Marçel leaned forward speaking quietly. 'Karl's money was all blood money, stolen from the Jews he helped to murder; I've been able to hand back a lot of that money, which has since been used to help some of the death camps survivors.'

'Which brings me back to you, Piglet, and all your money ...'

'But why try to kill me, Lolita?'

'I admit I lost it. I had gradually been building up so much hate towards you that in the end, I just knew I had to come and kill you. However, now I have seen you, I have a much better plan in mind.'

'I'm afraid you've lost the element of surprise, dear girl. But tell me, Lolita, what do have you in mind this time?'

'I know all about "Operation Deserting Rats", Marçel. Although I was not personally involved with Karl's work, I know enough to expose you to the International Press.' Lolita paused for a moment. 'But for, let's say ... one million dollars?'

'You're mad.'

'Or maybe ... I could make you marry me.' She smiled.

'I'm a wife beater.'

'I'm a man eater.'

'Would you go to bed with a piglet?'

'I'm not a Jew.'

'Then let's just go to bed.'

'Sure, Piglet—when I get my million dollars.'

'That makes you an expensive woman.' He sighed. 'I'll talk to my boss.'

'I'm a deadly serious woman. You have forty-eight hours to make up your mind.'

Marçel climbed onto his moped and as he started to move off, she yelled, 'I'll call you in two days' time. Your employer better have some good news for me or else we will "Meet the Press"!'

Feeling angry and frustrated, Marçel put the phone down. After thirty minutes of heated discussion with Stephen his boss, Stephen's last words had been, 'Marçel, the woman is dangerous and she has to go. You know what you have to do—remember this is exactly what we pay you for.'

He knew Stephen was right. With her knowledge of the Department's past activities in Portugal, Lolita could create a scandal that amongst other things could cause enormous damage to Britain's trading relations with Europe and would expose all the activities of the Department, which was quite unthinkable.

Stephen had been running the Department since 1940. Marçel had joined the Department in 1945 at the tender age of eighteen. By that time he had become a fully trained agent working in Northern France with the British and French Resistance groups.

In occupied Jersey in 1943, having been checking his fishing lines before curfew ended, Marçel was arrested by two guards who happened to be drunk at the time. He was first beaten and then raped by these two men. While this was going on, their officer appeared on the scene and promptly shot the two guards.

To justify his actions the officer arrested the boy and he was sent under guard to Paris in France to be interrogated and probably executed. On the train to Paris, the boy tricked his guard, killed him and escaped from the train. The events had in less than twenty-four hours turned an innocent sixteen-year-old boy into a savage killer.

Realising he could never go back and face his family, Marçel decided to carry on his own war in France; he changed his name and vowed never to return to Jersey. He found that with the use of a bayonet taken from his first victim, he could surprise and kill German guards at key points like bridges and railway junctions, without compunction. Later, he was secretly flown into England for special training, having been recruited into a special branch of the Secret Service controlled by Stephen.

He spent the rest of the war in France collaborating with the Free French underground movement. What Marçel did not know at the time was that following his escape from the train, his whole family in Jersey had been rounded up and sent to a concentration camp in Germany. None of his family was ever seen again.

Having worked with Stephen for the last eleven years he realised that although Stephen was completely ruthless in running his department, they had become friends. Stephen had always supported him and treated him almost as a son, except when there was a crisis in the Department; then Stephen spared no one.

Lolita phoned Marçel at six am two days later. Marçel, Stephen's hit man, reluctantly agreed to Lolita's demands. They arranged to meet at the Dinard Airport car park at midday.

Marçel had parked his recently-acquired *Auster* aeroplane at the airport, which was only twenty minutes' flying time from Jersey. At their rendezvous in the car park, Marçel offered Lolita three quarters of a million dollars, which she surprisingly accepted. He then persuaded her to fly with him to

Jersey. He explained to her that in the morning, they would go to his bank, open an account in her name, and transfer the money into her new bank account as this would give her the added benefit of Jersey's low taxation system.

He had not decided yet just how he was going to kill her. It had to be done sometime before they went to the bank in the morning.

'Okay, Marçel, I don't mind going to Jersey with you. I phoned London last night. A letter describing all the details of your disgusting work in Portugal is in the hands of my London solicitor. He has instructions to deliver the letter to the London *Times* newspaper if he doesn't hear from me in the next forty-eight hours.'

'Don't you trust me, Lolita?'

'Why should I? I know you are the hit man in your department,' she smiled. 'As this is a night stop in Jersey, I will have to go back to my hotel and collect an overnight bag. But don't you get any ideas, Marçel; this is strictly a business trip.'

'I'll meet you upstairs in the airport restaurant at two-thirty. Don't bring too much luggage; it's only a very small aeroplane.'

At two-thirty, with his flight-plan and pre-flight checks completed, Marçel found Lolita propping up the bar, completely engrossed in a serious political discussion with the barman.

'So you speak fluent French, Lolita? You won't need that in Jersey as most people speak English, though the local language is Jersey French, which is still used by a lot of the farming community.'

'Are you an experienced pilot, Marçel?'

'I should be; I have thirty-five hours in my logbook.'

'Oh, my God—he's fresh out of flying school.'

'I'll let you have a feel of the controls once we are airborne.'

'I don't need to feel your controls, or anything else, Marçel! I've got five hundred flying hours in *my* logbook!'

With clearance from tower control, Marçel taxied the *Auster* out to the end of the runway, ran up the engine, checked the magnetos, and was ready for take-off. Marçel gave the engine full throttle and the *Auster* gathered speed down the runway; as the tail lifted Marçel pulled gently back on the joystick and they were airborne.

At five hundred feet they passed over the crowded beach at Dinard—a superb day for the start of the French holiday season. At one thousand feet, Marçel levelled off the *Auster* and was called by Dinard tower who instructed him to change frequency to Jersey approach. Jersey instructed him to call Jersey tower on reaching Corbière lighthouse. Lolita, having watched Marçel's take-off with interest, was leaning back in her seat and appeared to be asleep. With only thirty miles to go, Marçel settled back, allowing his mind to wander.

Marçel had very mixed thoughts about Jersey. He thought about the events back in occupied Jersey in 1943 and how he had been unaware of his family's fate.

It had been some time after the war when he eventually visited Jersey, only to discover what had actually happened to his family. Returning immediately to France, it was several weeks later, having recovered from the shock, that he decided to maintain his new identity and wipe out his past life on the Island.

In the end, Marçel returned to the Islands and decided to use Jersey as a tax haven. He opened bank accounts and transferred some of his post-war savings from Switzerland to Jersey. It was while visiting the Island that he decided to learn to fly and joined the local flying club, living in a renovated cottage that he'd purchased on the north coast of the Island. Surprisingly no one recognised him—his old school friends had moved on and the events of the last seven years had changed the sixteen year old's appearance from a pink-faced boy into a now hard-looking man.

Lolita interrupted his train of thought. 'What is that lighthouse called, Marçel?'

'That's Corbière lighthouse. In olden days before the lighthouse was built, lots of ships were wrecked on that reef. There are strong tides running around Jersey; occasionally a swimmer gets caught in these rips and is swept away and drowned.'

Marçel called Jersey tower and received clearance to land on runway nine zero, with wind at one-four-zero.

Lolita was now wide awake and wondering what sort of touchdown Marçel would make with what appeared to be a strong crosswind on the runway.

Coming in on finals, the aircraft was hit by a sudden up-draft. Instead of a nice steady three point landing, Marçel overcorrected and the *Auster* sank too fast, landing heavily on the concrete runway.

Lolita was laughing, 'I think our pilot needs a good woman to show him how to touch down!'

'That sounds very interesting, Lolita!'

They parked the plane outside the club and strolled over to the customs office. As there was no one there, they wandered back to the club where Marçel called his bank and made an appointment for ten the next morning. 'I'll hire a car and take you to a very nice hotel on the north coast of the Island. It overlooks Bonne Nuit Bay.'

He would like to have taken Lolita back to his cottage, but knew that this was definitely not the right time to start an *affaire* with a blackmailer that he had been ordered to kill. In fact Marçel was wondering how he could possibly kill such an attractive woman. And when he did, how exactly was he going to do it?

As it turned out the problem was solved for him.

The Bay View Hotel at Bonne Nuit was situated on the side of the hill overlooking the small stone harbour where local fishing boats were moored in neat rows. Along the harbour wall was a row of fisherman's huts where the fishermen kept their gear and where they would sometimes stay overnight, in order to catch the early morning tide.

The bay was surrounded by high cliffs covered with pink flowering heathers and bracken that stretched away in the distance. Across the bay on the very tip of the headland, a small castle that had once helped to defend the Island from French invasions and heavily armed by the German occupying forces during the war, completed the picture.

Marçel was admiring the view when Lolita joined him in the bar looking stunning in a short skirt and low-cut top. After their third gin and tonic, Lolita put her arms on Marçel's shoulders and gazed seductively into his eyes. 'I would like you to show me a little of the Island before it gets dark, Marçel. Then we can come back here and have dinner; it will be my treat as I'm going to be a millionairess tomorrow.'

'Okay, I'll take you to see Mont Orgueil Castle, and on the way we'll stop off at St Catherine's Breakwater. It's a very long jetty with a great view of the local coastline and a haven for the local fishing enthusiasts. We'll certainly get a good meal here; they specialise in fresh lobster at this restaurant, and after that ... who knows?'

'Don't get ideas above your station, big boy; maybe after our visit to the bank tomorrow.'

Marçel drove the car into St Catherine's car park and they decided to walk to the end of the breakwater.

'You were right about the view; it really is something. What's the breakwater for anyway?'

'It was built about one hundred years ago. The admiralty in London decided to establish a naval base here. They completed this part and started to build the second arm, which you can see in the distance; it's just by that Martello tower on the other side of the bay.' Marçel pointed across the ocean to an imposing structure deepening in shadows. 'Apparently they discovered that the bay was silting up, and as their ships were getting bigger all the time and there was less of a threat from a French invasion, they decided to abandon the whole idea.'

It was still quite a warm evening and they were both perspiring by the time they reached the end of the breakwater. Marçel walked over to where several fishermen were leaning on the safety rail, holding onto their fishing rods. Looking down he could see the water rushing past the breakwater and flowing out towards France. The rip was so strong that he could see small overfalls, making it quite impossible for anyone to swim in that tide-race.

Marçel turned to point this out to Lolita, but noticed that she was heading for the stone steps that were just a few yards from the end of the breakwater.

He reached the top of the steps and looked down to see Lolita standing on the bottom step wearing only her pants and bra. 'Lolita—you can't swim here! It's far too dangerous at this state of tide!'

Lolita looked up at him, waved, and then dived into the sea. She surfaced a little way out and waved to him to join her. 'Lolita, come back, you're in a strong rip tide!' She kept swimming. 'Lolita, come back you bloody-stupid bitch!' She waved but kept swimming; he could see that she was already caught in the rip.

Suddenly realising her situation, she turned and started to swim back towards the wall, but it was too late. Lolita was no longer smiling. Seconds later she disappeared behind the wall at the end of the breakwater.

Marçel dashed across to where the fishermen were standing at the end of the breakwater. They were just standing there in silence, quite unable to believe what they had just seen.

There was no sign of Lolita in the boiling rushing rip.

A young man turned to Marçel. 'She come around the corner so fast, sir. And then she was gone. Swallowed up she was, sir. One of them overfalls.'

Several fishermen and Marçel ran up the steps to the small lighthouse that marked the end of the breakwater and scanned the rushing tide in the hope that Lolita had resurfaced, and would be able to swim across and out of the rip.

Marçel just stood for a moment, unable to move, unable to speak. It had all happened so fast. There was nothing that he could have done.

'Best go and call out the lifeboat, sir. She must be a goner by now ... They might be able to pick up her body further out to sea.' An elderly man put his arm around Marçel's shoulder. 'At least it was quick. There was nothing you could possibly do.'

Feeling sick in his stomach, Marçel ran all the way back to the car park. He found the telephone box and called emergency, explaining to the officer on duty what had happened.

The lifeboat was dispatched from St Helier Harbour but it was two hours before it was able to reach the breakwater and begin to search the area; by then it was almost dark. Meanwhile several fishing boats set out from the breakwater slipway, and boats from Gorey Harbour joined in the desperate search.

It was all to no avail. Lolita's body was never recovered.

Soon after Marçel's call, the *Connétable* of the Parish of St. Martin, with several of the parish voluntary police, arrived at the car park. In Jersey, the Island was divided into twelve parishes, each parish having a *Connétable*, equivalent to a mayor and responsible for the law and order of the parish. Marçel and the fishermen, who had by then all returned to the car park, were told to accompany the police back to the parish hall, where they then all made statements describing what they had seen from the time when Lolita and Marçel arrived at the end of the breakwater, to her disappearance in the boiling current. The fishermen were then allowed to leave.

Marçel told the *Connétable* that his name was Marçel Beaumont and that he had a holiday home at St. John in Jersey. He explained to him how he had met Lolita Schmidt, a Brazilian national, while on holiday at Dinard. They had flown over from Dinard that afternoon, and were due to return to Dinard the next day. He then related how he had booked Lolita into the Grand View Hotel at Bonne Nuit and that they had gone to look at St. Catherine's breakwater.

The *Connétable* stared hard at Marçel, 'You watched her being swept away and made no attempt to dive in and save her.' He paused. Marçel remained silent. 'It would have been pointless anyway; we would have had two deaths to deal with.' He turned and spoke to his senior police *Centenier*, after which he shot Marçel a sharp look. 'An inquest will be held in the next few days. You will not be required to attend. I think it will be a clear-cut case of accidental death by drowning. Did the lady have any luggage?'

'Just hand-luggage, sir.'

'*Centenier* De La Maye will accompany you to the hotel; we will need to take possession of her luggage, which I hope contains her passport. I'm sure this whole event is most upsetting for you, though I must say, you seem to be taking it remarkably well.'

Marçel thanked the constabulary for all their help. The *Centenier* took Marçel back to pick up his car from the breakwater and then followed him back to the Bonne Nuit Hotel.

Bill, the hotel manager, was shocked to hear of Lolita's drowning. 'It's not the sort of publicity a hotel needs at any time. But at least it wasn't in our harbour.'

'Bill, do me a favour; keep the *Centenier* talking in the bar for a few minutes? I need to collect the things from her room—I'll bring them down for him.'

'No problem, Marçel, I'll get you her key.'

Marçel left the official busy talking to Bill and headed for the toilets. When out of sight, Marçel went straight up to Lolita's room and tipped her holdall out onto the bed, carefully going through her belongings—pants, bra, a pair of shorts and top and a large bag containing makeup. He found a purse full of French francs, her passport and a diary, which he slipped into his pocket. He put everything back into her holdall, had a quick look around the room and returned to the bar.

'I thought I'd save you a job. These are all her worldly possessions; in Jersey anyway. There is a passport and a purse full of money.'

Centenier De La Maye examined her passport. 'There isn't any entry in for today.'

'There was no one at the customs office when we came through.'

'Just be careful in future; otherwise you could land yourself in trouble. We don't need all you English people moving into Jersey and buying up all our farms.'

'I only have a small cottage; anyway I'm sure most good farmers wouldn't want to sell their farms. Are we finished now?' Marçel was starting to get irritated and wanted to get back to his cottage.

'Well, I suppose this must be upsetting for you losing your girlfriend like that. Oh, I need her address in Dinard so that I can contact the French police and recover the rest of her luggage.

'I don't know it, but try the Hotel Du Nord in Dinard.'

Marçel returned to his cottage, feeling depressed. He poured himself a large whisky; violent death was something he had grown used to, but this was different—at least he had been saved the job of killing the woman. He realised that he had been quite taken by this very unusual lady. Anyway he doubted that when it had come to the point, he would have been able to kill her. At least Stephen would be satisfied, and then he suddenly remembered her letter that was being posted to *The Times* the day after tomorrow.

He picked up Lolita's diary and started to thumb through it. Right on the back page he found the name and telephone number of a solicitor in Knightsbridge.

It was past midnight when he called Stephen. Roused from a deep sleep, Stephen was not at all happy at being woken up.

'What the *hell* do you want at *this* time of night, Marçel?'

'I thought you would like to know. She's dead. She drowned off the end of St Catherine's breakwater.'

'Well done, Marçel, I knew you would find a way to eliminate her.'

'Well as it happens, she did it for me. But the point is that letter will still be delivered to the press by her solicitor.'

'And we don't know who the hell he is, Marçel.'

'Stephen, I've found a solicitor's address in her diary. If this is the one, then I'm sure your department will be able to stop that letter being posted.' Marçel gave Stephen the name and telephone number.

'If he's our man, then the letter will certainly be destroyed. I will get right on to it. Thanks, Marçel.'

Smiling, Marçel knew several people would now be roused from their beds and if that was the right solicitor, the letter would be destroyed before the morning.

Chapter 2

Marçel returned to Dinard the next day; he spent the next few weeks living it up, spending time on the beach in the day and at the Casino at night. An Englishman who could speak fluent French had no difficulty finding girls, especially in August, when all the attractive young Parisians came down to the seaside for their annual holidays. By now, all the German mines had been removed from the beaches and most of the large remaining hotels were once more open for business. The young French people were now catching up on some fun, determined to make up for the lost war years.

After a while, Marçel found he was becoming bored with Dinard's high life and decided to fly down to Nantes in southern Brittany to spend time on his converted barge. He and Pete could not agree on a name at the time so they named it, *The Barge*. It was moored in a very quiet offshoot of the Brest à Nantes canal, close to the small town of Blain.

Marçel flew into Nantes, parked and tied down the *Auster* and then carried his backpack across to the waiting taxis. He took a taxi to the garage in Nantes where his Renault saloon was stored. On his way, Marçel stopped off at the small town of Blain to buy provisions.

On arriving at the mooring site, he parked his car under the trees that surrounded this long-forgotten part of the canal, the overhanging branches concealing the entrance to this secluded offshoot of the main canal, and *The Barge*, moored on one side amongst the trees, was almost hidden from sight.

He took off his shoes and trousers and waded out carrying the provisions on his head. Marçel climbed on board, found the concealed keys and opened the wheelhouse door. Sitting on the raised engine-room hatch cover, he gazed around the canal. It was midday and the only sound was the singing of the birds high up in the trees. Very few people ever came to this delightful tree-lined backwater; that was why they had chosen it.

The Barge, which had a sea-going hull, had been purchased at the end of the war by Stephen's department and had been converted into a very comfortable home for the use of the Department's agents, Peter and Marçel. It was equipped with a powerful new engine, which had proved very useful on several occasions in the past. It had all the latest radio and radar technology enabling *The Barge* to keep in contact with the Department's agents anywhere in the world, while a secret panel in the radio room masked a well-equipped armoury. This had been Marçel's second home since the end of the war. It was from here he often received Stephen's instructions. Sometimes Stephen would drive down from Dinard, where he kept his MG sports car, and drive down to *The Barge* so that he could discreetly direct certain operations in Europe.

Marçel's assignments often involved him in assisting one of the French Secret Service agencies to track down wanted war criminals. The French authorities were aware of *The Barge*, but had decided to turn a blind eye, as long as they were allowed to operate their own secret base in England.

Marçel spent the afternoon washing down the decks, which always collected large quantities of bird poo. After that he cleaned the wheelhouse windows and polished all the brass fittings on *The Barge*. When it was dark, he went below to open a bottle of wine and cook his supper. He decided to call Stephen.

'I thought I should let you know that I'm back at *The Barge*, Stephen, and getting it shipshape again. Is everything okay regarding Lolita?'

'I'm glad you called, Marçel. I was just about to contact you. We had a call from the French police. When they were going through Lolita's case in Dinard, they found some correspondence that indicated Lolita had been staying in Bordeaux with a known Nazi operator called Franz Schiller. Remember, he was the character that supplied Karl Schmidt with the *Stuka* bomber, which nearly wiped you all out three years ago? Do you remember his address?'

'How could I forget? The slimy bastard; at the time he was able to talk himself out of any responsibility and the French police let him go. There was also some talk at the time that Schiller was connected to a paedophile network in that part of France.'

'You'd better pay him a visit; he might know too much about operations in Portugal. Go and talk to him. If you think he knows too much, kill him.'

'Is that all, Stephen?' He smiled. 'I think I'll enjoy this one.'

'Just for now, Marçel, let me know how you get on. You're right; he is connected to a very large paedophile syndicate in that part of France. And please be discreet; we don't want to upset our French friends.'

'As always, Stephen. Good night.'

It was nearly nine when Marçel woke up the following morning. He was feeling excited—today he would catch up with one of the people he really despised. Stephen had given him the green light to get rid of this animal. He would have to be especially careful how he disposed of this disgusting paedophile; he didn't want to spend the rest of his life in a French prison.

Marçel showered, shaved and then cooked himself a large breakfast. After clearing up the galley, he clipped the holster with his dagger to the inside of his jeans and fitted a silencer to his revolver, attaching the leather strap holding the gun under his armpit. Launching the rubber dingy, he rowed himself to the canal bank, tied the dingy to an overhanging branch, jumped into the Renault and set off for Bordeaux.

It was about one hundred and eighty miles to Bordeaux; Marçel guessed he would be there about two pm, which was too early, so he decided to stop off for lunch and get to Bordeaux around four.

Marçel's mind drifted back to the day when Karl had dive-bombed them at the boatyard on the Loire River. It was the end of a chapter and they had closed down the operation in Portugal. For almost three years, they had been offering war criminals a safe passage to Brazil, secretly transporting them to their castle in Portugal, relieving them of their stolen gold, and then finally dumping their dead bodies into the Atlantic Ocean. Marçel considered they were doing the world a favour and were able to return a good portion of the stolen gold to some of the holocaust survivors.

After they had foiled Karl Schmidt's attempt to steal back the gold, Schmidt had used his Nazi party influence to persuade Franz Schiller, the head of the Bordeaux group, to let him to use their hidden *Stuka* bomber so that he could take out his revenge on them.

Marçel remembered visiting the small island in the middle of an extensive marshland with the French police; the restored *Stuka* had been kept at the hidden airfield there. At the time Schiller had sworn that he had only rented the island to a man called Huber and had no idea it was being used as an airfield. The police decided not to pursue Schiller. Marçel reckoned Schiller to be just a minor player in the international Nazi organisation, but if Lolita had confided in him, then he was, like Lolita, a danger that had to be removed.

Schiller had a florist business; the shop was down a side street in the poorer part of the town. Marçel drove slowly by the shop, wondering how

Schiller could possibly make a living selling flowers in this part of Bordeaux. As he passed the shop, he saw Schiller talking to a customer. Marçel circled the back streets and parked just a few yards away.

At five pm, he watched Schiller take the buckets of flowers from the pavement back into the shop. Marçel got out of his car and started to walk towards the florist. He saw the lights go out; Schiller appeared, locking the shop door behind him and set off down the road.

A narrow lane ran down by the side of the shop. Marçel decided to have a look. At the back of the shop was a stone wall with a heavy door leading into the backyard of the building. He was able to look over the wall, being careful of broken glass embedded into the top of the wall. In the yard, there were several old bins, one full of dead flowers. Several fishing rods were also propped against the wall at the back of the shop. He noticed two large doors, which were folded back exposing stone steps leading down to the cellar under the shop.

At that moment, a black Citroen started to reverse down the narrow lane. Marçel quickly moved down to the next house, which appeared to be empty and stood in the shadows of the doorway. The car stopped outside the yard door. Marçel watched Schiller, who was followed by another man, unlock the door. He moved forward and was just in time to see the two men disappear down into the cellar.

The light was starting to fade. Marçel heard voices and carefully looked over the wall; the two men reappeared, the other man carrying a large hessian sack. Schiller opened the yard door and the man carrying the sack opened the back door of the car. Marçel moved a little closer to get a better look. As he lifted the sack onto the back seat of the car, Marçel thought he saw a small foot coming out of the bottom. The driver quickly jumped into the car and started the engine. Schiller attached two fishing rods to the roof of the car, locked the yard door and got into the back seat next to the sack.

Marçel watched the car drive out into the street, heading he guessed, in a westerly direction. He took off his jacket and placed it over part of the broken-glass topped wall. He climbed over the wall without cutting himself; not so his jacket.

The doors to the cellar were closed but not locked. Marçel descended the steps. He noticed a light switch on the wall at the bottom of the steps and turned it on. The cellar was quite roomy and piled up with years of old rubbish from the flower shop. He noticed a large pile of rusted frames, which looked as though they had been collected from the local cemeteries. A door at the end of the cellar led into a room that appeared to be Schiller's workshop. In one corner, he saw what looked like a large birdcage. There was a small mattress with blankets on the floor of the cage, a low table with half a glass of milk and some biscuits. Marçel turned to the workbench, on which was a tray with several used syringes, but nothing else. *The bastards.* He was suddenly overcome with a blinding rage. He realised what they were doing and he knew exactly where he would find them.

Marçel looked around the yard at all the junk and spotted a small kayak and close by—a paddle. Luckily, he had added a roof rack to his car; he pushed the kayak over the wall, climbed over and quickly tied the kayak to the roof rack. Jumping into his car, he drove as fast as he could in the direction the other car had taken. He had a vague idea how to get to the spot in the marshland where they kept their boat, but he couldn't remember how to find his way through the reeds to the island.

Driving his car to its limits, he got to the long straight road that led to the marshes and spotted the lights of a car far ahead in the distance. Marçel turned off his lights and kept his foot down on the accelerator.

Twenty minutes later, Marçel noticed the car in front turn off the road and disappear into the high reeds. He slowed down and drew off the road about five hundred yards from the other car, untied the kayak and quietly carried it and the paddle on his back towards the other car. He had almost reached the black Citroen when he heard the punt's engine start. Running down the track between the high reeds carrying the kayak, he reached the wooden jetty and watched the metal punt disappearing in the distance. He dropped the kayak into the water, lowered himself into it and started paddling after the disappearing punt.

Marçel had not had time to examine the kayak and wondered if it was going to stay afloat and to complicate matters, by the time he was clear of the first lot of reeds, he realised he was sitting in water. The moon was shining through a gap in the clouds giving Marçel barely enough light to see the faint white line of foam left from the wake of the punt, which was way ahead on his left-hand side.

The punt slowed down to pass through another large mass of reeds, enabling Marçel to catch up. Unfortunately the reeds slowed him down considerably; he was unable to use the paddle properly because of the lack of room to swing it. He eventually broke through to see the punt heading for the island. By now the water in the kayak was covering his legs and he guessed he wouldn't make the distance. Marçel stopped paddling, knowing he would be able to swim faster than trying to paddle a waterlogged kayak. He managed to remove his shoes and slid out into the dark water. Still he had about five hundred yards to go, but being a strong swimmer, was soon able to cover the distance.

He finally reached the reeds that concealed the island and waded through the mud until he came to the sharply rising bank. He climbed up the bank, feeling the stones cutting his bare feet. Standing on the long uncut grass of the old runway, Marçel could see a faint light ahead. He ran silently through the grass to the old hangar.

The heavy doors in front of the hangar were locked with a large padlock. Marçel found another door on the side and was able to peer through the dirty window alongside the door. At the far end, he could see two oil lamps on a workbench, which were giving a dim light to the inside of the old hangar. Close to the workbench, he could see an old armchair, lying back in which Marçel thought he saw a young girl who appeared to be sleeping. The two men were standing close by, both holding wine glasses in their hands. Marçel could hear them laughing; there were several bottles of wine on the workbench.

Marçel took out his revolver, wiped it dry and waited.

Unable to hear what they were saying, he watched for a while as they topped up their glasses and continued their conversation. Later they appeared to be arguing. The one that had been driving pushed Schiller away, walked over to the girl in the armchair and started to shake her violently.

Unable to contain himself any longer, Marçel flung open the door and started running towards the two men brandishing his gun. For a moment they just stood there rooted to the ground; then Schiller darted to the workbench and picked up what appeared to be a shotgun.

Marçel was halfway across the hangar floor when he started firing his revolver, aiming at the two men's legs. Schiller turned towards Marçel, screaming and firing his shotgun at the same time. The shot had gone way over Marçel's head and Schiller collapsed on the floor clutching his left kneecap. The other man reached down quickly grabbing the shotgun; he turned to point it at Marçel who had propped and fired two quick shots at the man's head. The man dropped the shotgun and sank slowly to the floor.

Stepping over the dead man, Marçel saw the now wide-awake and terrified girl staring at him. He quickly turned the armchair around, away from the two men; he had one more thing to do. Bending down alongside the moaning Schiller, Marçel pressed the revolver's barrel against Schiller's forehead.

'No! Don't kill me!' he shrieked. Marçel kicked him in the ribs.

'I *will* kill you if you don't truthfully answer one question, you skunk.' He then pressed the gun hard into the back of Schiller's neck.

'You had Lolita staying with you last month. What exactly did she tell you?'

Tears were running down Schiller's frightened face; he was quite unable to speak.

'What was Lolita going to do? Your life depends on a correct answer. Did she tell you about Operation Escape to Death? Nod to me if yes.'

Schiller shook his head.

'Was that a yes or no, Schiller?'

'If I tell you what I know … will you spare my life?' he whined.

Marçel smiled down at Schiller. 'Just tell me.'

'Karl Schmidt never talked to anyone like me—L—Lolita told me about your operation in Portugal and—and I told her she would find you in Jersey.'

Marçel stepped back, fired once and turned away from the two dead men.

The girl was screaming, Marçel picked her up and held her tightly in his arms.

'It's all over, sweetheart … you're quite safe now; you will soon be going home to your family.'

The girl, who must have only been about eight or nine years old, was clutching tightly onto Marçel, sobbing quietly. He held her close until, still under the influence of the drugs, she fell asleep in his arms. Marçel gently lowered the sleeping child down into the old armchair. He wondered what he should do. Obviously, there was no telephone, but he had to talk to Stephen. Maybe there was an old radio transmitter in the hangar but it would have to be battery operated.

Marçel searched the store cupboards that lined the wall behind the workbench. He found a dust-covered transmitter on the top of one of the cupboards. It needed power to operate it. He noticed there was a small generator under the workbench. It started first time and the workbench was immediately flooded from an overhead light. Marçel managed to lift the transmitter onto the bench and connected it up to the aerial that ran from the bench up into the roof of the hangar. He waited for it to warm up and then tuned in to the Department's London frequency.

He was able to hear a faint voice above the loud crackling of the old transmitter.

'This is Marçel Beaumont; I need to talk to Stephen Harvey. Can you connect his telephone to this frequency? It really is urgent.' He knew that if Stephen was at home, they would very quickly have him on the line. Three minutes later to his amazement he was talking to Stephen.

'Do you have a problem, Marçel?'

'Just a small one, Stephen! I'm on a deserted island with two dead men at my feet, and I have been holding an eight-year-old girl in my arms but luckily she is sleeping now as she's been heavily sedated.' Marçel quickly went on to describe the situation and everything that had happened.

'So, Stephen, what do I do now?'

'Just stay where you are, Marçel. I will explain the situation to our French counterparts. They will contact the French police, who will be told that one of our agents, having tracked down a small paedophile group, was forced to take drastic action to save a child. We have your frequency; I will call back in thirty minutes.'

Marçel left the radio connected and walked around the hangar, not sure whether to pick up the sleeping child, or to let her sleep on in the armchair. He decided that as long as he was close to her if she woke up, he could quickly pick her up again and calm her.

Looking down at the two bodies, he felt no remorse at having killed them—they were low scum that should not be allowed to live. The death of Lolita had really upset him, but he had no problem with killing the low vermin that prayed on society, especially children. Marçel was a killer with high principals and that was why he was so valuable to the Department. The war had taught him to kill; now the Department was pleased to have him, especially when elimination was the only option.

The radio crackled; Stephen was back.

'Marçel, the French police are on their way. They are delighted that at last these two men have been nailed. You will not be at all involved in what has happened, as they wish to take all the glory in having killed these paedophiles for themselves. As soon as they arrive with the parents, just fade out of the picture and get the hell out of there.'

'Don't I even get a thank you from the Department?' Marçel laughed.
'What do you think we pay you for? Just find your own way home.'
'Yes, sir. I'll pinch the paedophiles' boat. Go back to bed.'

Marçel dismantled the radio and returned it to the cupboard. He left the generator running, turned on all the lights and walked to the door. After a few minutes, he could see lights flashing in the distance. He was sure they would be using an inflatable boat to cross to the island. Their torch lights appeared as they pushed their way through the reeds.

Marçel ran down to the punt, started the motor and headed away from the approaching lights. From a safe distance, he watched as the French police landed on the island and entered the hangar. He turned the punt and headed for the shore, landing very close to where he had parked his car.

Chapter 3

For the next year, Marçel spent most of his time in London, sifting through endless files and following the movements of known criminals and some of the extreme political activists who were operating in different parts of the world. The boredom was lightened by the occasional stay on *The Barge*, when he had been instructed to track down violent criminals who were hiding in France, or one of the other countries in Western Europe. In between these more dangerous missions, Marçel sometimes found time to enjoy the peace of his cottage in Jersey.

In early September 1957, when Marçel returned to England after helping to track down a group of illegal arms dealers in Italy, to his surprise, Stephen had invited him to come and stay at his country estate in Buckinghamshire. 'Gerda wants you to come and meet young Peter,' he had insisted.

Marçel had not seen Gerda since Peter's lavish christening party held at Stephen's home in 1949. Gerda and Marçel had wandered out into the garden, when Gerda had suddenly turned on Marçel. She told him that she was in love with Stephen, and now that they had Stephen's child to consider, she had decided that it would be better if they never met again. 'I'm sorry, Marçel, but because of the passionate affaire that you and I had when we were in Portugal, I could never feel at ease with you hovering in the background. Nothing is ever coming between the love I have for Stephen and Peter.'

Marçel was speechless. They had wandered back to the party.

Shortly after they returned to the house, Marçel made his excuses, kissed Gerda lightly on the forehead and returned to London. That night, a very drunk Marçel was escorted by two hall porters from the hotel bar to his bedroom. The next day he returned to *The Barge* in France as Stephen had another job waiting for him in Paris.

Marçel had always been a little puzzled as to why she and Stephen had been married so soon after she had gone to stay at Stephen's home. But when in 1949, Gerda had given birth to Peter, he realised that Stephen must have indulged in a little pre-marital sex. They had named him Peter, after their best friend Pete, who had been murdered in Portugal by Karl Schmidt, Lolita's husband.

So now, years later, he was about to meet up again with Gerda and her eight-year-old son. Marçel had mixed feelings about this reunion—he had been badly hurt all those years ago and he wondered why Gerda had had a sudden change of heart.

He flew across the Channel, landing at Stephen's private landing strip, to be greeted by Gerda. 'It's so good to see you again, Marçel, it's been so long. How's the cottage in Jersey? It's interesting that no one in Jersey has recognised you from your past life.'

'I do get some funny looks at times, Gerda, but I keep a low profile when I'm in Jersey. Everyone there assumes I was murdered by the *Gestapo* and my cottage in the country is fairly isolated. The people I meet at the Aero Club are not the same group of people that I grew up with. I've also come to terms with losing my family; after all, I killed a lot of Germans and more than evened *that* score.'

'All the same, you must still have bitter memories.' Gerda put her hand on his arm giving it a gentle squeeze. Marçel stiffened for a split second but then laughed to cover his embarrassment at reacting to her touch.

'Life goes on, Gerda. So, how about your lovely son, Peter? You and Stephen certainly didn't waste any time.' He paused for a moment, feeling that was not the most tactful thing to say, but continued on brashly. 'Looking back, Peter could easily have been mine. Anyway, I could never have made such a good husband and father as Stephen.'

They had just sat down at the table on the balcony when Stephen appeared carrying a tray loaded with sandwiches and a bottle of wine. Following Stephen was his housekeeper, who was leading Peter by the hand.

'Good to see you again, old boy. These last two jobs you've just completed prove you have not yet lost your ability to, 'sort out' our little problems. It's been a very long time since you came down here; anyway welcome back and meet junior, my lovely wife, and my faithful housekeeper, May.'

Still living in the previous generation, May gave a little curtsey. 'Pleased to meet you, sir. Born on the first of May I was, sir.' She released Peter's hand and shook Marçel's, while Peter, feeling a little shy, ran over to Gerda.

Marçel stared in disbelief at the child.

He thought he was looking at himself.

In the days that followed, Marçel felt inexplicably drawn to Peter. He wanted to spend most of his time just playing with the boy. He wondered if this could possibly be his child.

His mind went back to those traumatic days in Portugal. The night they had killed three of Karl's men, rescued Gerda, and destroyed their campsite by the small lagoon. That was the last time that they had made love. It had been powerful and passionate, the reaction to those last few hours, when they had both come so close to death.

He wondered if it were possible. Could that have been the night Gerda became pregnant?

No, he decided; Gerda would have told him. Instead, she had gone to stay with Stephen at his country estate and soon after they got married. Yet he felt sure the child looked like him; why was he drawn so close to him? Peter was born only eight months after Gerda and Steven were married. He wondered if he should bring up the subject. He decided against that; better to wait for Gerda to say something. *Surely she must notice the likeness between us, and the way Peter and I are drawn together.*

The four of them spent the next three weeks exploring the small country towns and villages in the area, making day trips to Salisbury, Bournemouth, the Isle of Wight and Brighton. They hired a boat at Marlow and explored that part of the Thames and finally, they spent a day taking Peter to the London Zoo. Unfortunately, on that occasion, Peter was not feeling at all well and Marçel had to spend most of the day carrying a very unhappy child.

Weeks before and with Gerda's blessing, May had promised to take Peter to a visiting circus near Newbury. The day before Marçel was due to leave and return to his cottage in Jersey, they set off early in May's Morris Minor car.

Later that morning, Gerda asked Marçel if he would take her for a flight in his aircraft. It was a perfect day and Stephen was quite happy to have a quiet day to himself. Gerda and he had also realised that it was time for Marçel to be told that Peter was his son. This would provide the perfect opportunity.

It was the first time that Gerda and Marçel had spent time alone together and for once they were able to almost feel relaxed in each other's company. They flew over the Marlborough Downs to Swindon; then they turned northeast and crossed the Vale of The White Horse to Oxford.

From there they flew south and landed at White Waltham Airport near Maidenhead.

They decided to take a taxi to into Maidenhead where they found a restaurant overlooking the Thames River. They spent a leisurely lunch watching the punts and pleasure boats travelling up and down the river and talked about some of their war and post-war experiences.

Gerda felt a strong urge to put her arms around Marçel as the memories of all those events and especially their passionate lovemaking came flooding back. She realised that this was the right moment to tell him about Peter, but she just couldn't bring herself to break the spell of the moment.

'Do you remember, Gerda, when we parted in Nantes and you were going back to live in Stephen's house? You told me you could never marry me, and although you loved me, you could never live with someone who was a professional killer.'

Gerda looked down and nodded.

'I was hurt at the time but understood because I also knew in my heart, that although I loved you, I could never settle down and be a good husband. But I still do love you, Gerda.'

Gerda laughed, 'I think you just love the memories.'

'I remember at the time you said when I ever came up to London we could make love. And then you went and married Stephen ... I'm really happy for you though.'

'Stephen is old enough to be my father, but he has turned out to be a wonderful husband, I know now he really does love me. And, Marçel, as you know, I shall always be very fond of you.'

'That's good,' Marçel replied a little sharply. 'Well, I think it's time to get going; by the time we get airborne the light will be fading and we don't want to be flying in the dark.'

'Are you safe to fly, Marçel? You've had rather a lot of wine to drink.'

'Don't worry, sweetheart. Even if I can't see the road now, I can certainly see it when we are five hundred feet above it,' he mumbled.

Gerda was not quite so sure.

They were on their way back, flying past Newbury to Stephen's airstrip, which was just southwest of Newbury when Gerda, who had been putting off the moment for the last few hours, decided that it was the right time to tell Marçel that Peter was his child and not Stephen's.

Marçel, although he had been a little puzzled at Peter's likeness and his strong feelings towards the boy, was at first shocked and then he became very angry. 'Why didn't you tell me this before, Gerda? How could you have done this to me?' He turned to Gerda allowing his emotions to take control—Marçel released his safety harness to put an arm around Gerda to hug her, his anger now quickly replaced with the joy of being Peter's father.

For a brief moment Marçel forgot that he was flying an aeroplane—the nose of the aircraft had gradually crept up—it lost speed and stalled. Marçel grabbed the controls, gave the engine full throttle and at the same time pulled back on the joystick. They had lost height but were flying safely just above the tree tops heading for Stephen's airfield. Marçel had eased back the throttle. Suddenly as the trees gave way to pasture they saw the power lines, both having forgotten that they ran by the edge of the forest. Marçel gave the engine full throttle pulling back on the joy stick; the engine coughed twice. The *Auster* started to climb but the landing gear just clipped the power lines. The aircraft spun over onto its back as it crashed to the ground, just half a mile from Stephen's airfield.

Chapter 4

Stephen had been watching the aeroplane approaching; he knew that Gerda would definitely have told Marçel that Peter was actually his son, and that she had become pregnant well before her marriage had been consummated by Stephen. He wondered what sort of mood they would be in when they returned.

He loved them both dearly. During the war years, they had been working for him; he had sent them out on many dangerous missions. Each time he had prayed for their safe return and always thanked God when they did. He had not been that surprised when Gerda had told him that she was going to have Marçel's child. She told him that she couldn't bring herself to marry a man who could kill so easily, even though he had been ordered to do so by the Department.

Stephen had offered her his home in Buckinghamshire where she could live and bring up the child. Gerda accepted but insisted they get married. After careful consideration Stephen agreed, but felt that at some time in the future, Gerda should tell Marçel that it was his child, and that Stephen was not the real father. Stephen had always loved Peter as his son and he realised that he would find it very hard to lose the child if Marçel tried to take Peter away from them.

Stephen stood watching the aeroplane approaching but suddenly froze.

Something was very wrong. The nose of the aircraft had dropped and it was heading straight for the power lines that bordered his land. He watched in horror as the plane hit the power lines, catapulted to the ground and burst into flames.

Rushing indoors, he called the emergency services, then ran out, leaping into his Land Rover and drove flat out across his fields to the still-burning wreckage.

Stephen stood, staring at the remains of the plane. He heard the bells of the approaching fire engine and ambulance. He could only see one body in the burnt-out cabin of the aircraft. His heart began to pound and his legs almost gave way from underneath him.

'Over here, sir.' Wilson the local policeman was already on the scene. 'In this bush, sir—I think he's still alive.'

Those words galvanised Stephen into action and he quickly joined Wilson, followed by the two ambulance men. He watched as the three men gently lifted Marçel out of the undergrowth and onto the stretcher.

'He really is in a mess, sir. He's very lucky to be alive, but has sustained a lot of damage to himself. We'll send him to the Reading Hospital and what's left of the other person.'

Stephen grabbed his arm. 'That other person … was my wife, Wilson!'

'Oh, my God, sir—and she with your dear little boy—what can I say? I'm so very sorry, sir.'

Gerda had died on impact. The *Auster* burst into flames, leaving very little of her left when her body was finally recovered from the ashes.

Marçel, minus his safety harness, had been catapulted from the aircraft and was found several metres from the burning aircraft in the middle of thick undergrowth. This saved his life but tore his skin to pieces and left him with almost every bone in his body broken.

'Wilson, instruct the ambulance men to deliver Marçel to this address in North London. It's a private hospital run especially for top civil servants; he will get the very best attention there. The local undertaker will look after my wife's body.'

'Right, sir. If you don't mind, I'll join you back at your house. I will need your wife's details, the pilot's and also what you saw of the crash.'

With the fire extinguished and the ambulance on its way to London containing Marçel, who was fighting for his life, and Gerda's remains being taken away by the local undertaker, Stephen climbed back into the Land Rover and drove slowly back to the house. Stephen was devastated; in his mid-sixties, he had suddenly lost Gerda, the wife he adored, and perhaps Marçel, whom he had always treated as a son. He realised he was left with little Peter, a child without a mother. He had always cared for Gerda ever since she had joined the Department in 1944 and had been worried about their age difference when they first got married, but he had soon grown to love Gerda as his wife. And now she was gone.

Marçel regained consciousness the following morning. Stephen watched as Marçel's eyes slowly opened. He bent down and wiped away the steady stream of tears that came flooding from his half-opened eyes.

Marçel, straining to speak, finally managed two faint grunts, 'Gur … deh?'

Stephen held his bandaged hand and whispered to him, 'Yes, Marçel, Gerda is dead … it was instantaneous … she wouldn't have felt a thing.'

Marçel had received multiple fractures to his arms and legs and dislocated both shoulders. His torn and punctured skin though extremely damaged, would gradually heal leaving a few more scars to add to his already scar-marked body. Marçel's mental health was probably far worse. Suffering from a feeling of guilt at the death of Gerda, the mental scars would take much longer to heal, some remaining with him forever.

That first night after the accident, Stephen had telephoned Helga and Mick, who were Marçel and Gerda's best friends. They insisted on leaving their farm in Australia to fly back to London to attend Gerda's funeral.

Pulling a few strings, Stephen managed to arrange a flight for them in a *Sunderland* flying boat, flying from Sydney Harbour to the Solent in Southampton.

Helga and Mick arrived just in time for the funeral, which was held in the Nortonbury Village Church, close to where Stephen lived. It was a quiet funeral, Gerda, like most of the Department's agents, had very few living relatives. Only a few locals who had occasionally met Gerda in the village turned up to join Stephen, Helga, Mick and May, who held Peter's hand throughout the service and the burial. Peter was the first to step forward to throw dirt down onto the coffin; he turned, put his arms around May's waist, buried his face in her long black shawl and wept uncontrollably.

After the funeral, they drove over to the nursing home to see Marçel while May returned to the house with Peter. Marçel was now quite conscious but still in a state of shock. Stephen bent over him and whispered, 'I am aware that you know that Peter is your son. You must recover for his sake. He loves you very much and also knows that you are his father.' He squeezed Marçel's shoulder gently.

Despite being in terrible pain, Marçel managed a smile when Helga bent down and kissed him. She whispered, 'Stephen told me that you must now know that Peter is your child. I know she loved you, Marçel, and was so happy when she found she was carrying your child. When you are better, why don't you bring Peter out to Australia? Gerda and Stephen told us how Peter and you had bonded very closely. You know you can stay with us just as long as you like.'

She started crying, Stephen gently led her over to a chair by the door. 'Oh, Stephen, I feel so sad for you. We all loved Gerda so much—we were one big family and now we have lost her forever.'

Marçel winced when Mick touched his shoulder but still managed a smile and a slight nod. 'She's right, mate, I could do with some help on the farm when you're ready to come out to Australia.' He went over to Helga who was still quietly crying.

Stephen held Mick's hand for a few minutes; they both had tears in their eyes. After a while, Stephen leaned over and murmured to Marçel, 'Peter's fine. He knows Gerda is not coming back. May, our housekeeper, is taking good care of him and for now he's actually staying in her cosy little flat in the west wing of the house. That's something that he's always wanted to do—May has always spoilt the little monkey! His grieving will come later and last much longer though.'

Mick and Helga stood in the doorway. 'See ya later, Marçel,' Mick called, and Helga, still crying, just waved to Marçel as they left the room.

Stephen took Marçel's hand again. 'We'll come back tomorrow, Marçel, especially as Helga and Mick will have to return to Australia in the next few days.' Marçel nodded; then closed his eyes.

At dinner that night, Helga, Mick, and Stephen had a serious talk about Marçel and Peter's future.

'Now that Gerda is dead and Marçel knows that Peter is his son, I think, as soon as he is well enough, Marçel, I'm sure, will want to get involved in Peter's life,' Stephen said leaning back in his chair.

Mick helped himself to a second helping of the delicious roasted grouse. 'Surely this is the best place to bring up the child, Stephen. It's obvious that you are devoted to Peter.'

'So is Marçel. I wish we could take him back with us; I would so like to be able to look after him.' Helga sighed. 'Stephen, our boy, Michael, is nine now, it would be just wonderful to bring them up together.'

'Marçel is not in a fit position to make any decisions at present. Peter will stay here; May and I will look after him until Marçel is well enough and then Marçel and I together can decide on Peter's future.'

The next day Helga and Mick set off on their return journey to Australia.

Helga couldn't wait to get back to Michael, even though she knew he would be well looked after by her neighbour Jenny, who already had five children of her own to care for.

Six months later, Marçel in hospital and with still many months to go, was able to send a thank-you card to Helga and Mick for coming all the way from Australia for Gerda's funeral. Although all the cuts and bruises to his skin had by now almost healed, he was having difficulty with some of the bad fractures, which had to be reset. For Marçel, it had become a very long and painful process.

Chapter Five

I t was just over one year before Stephen was finally told that Marçel would soon be well enough to leave the hospital. The doctors suggested that Stephen, if he wished, could take him back to recuperate at his country estate.

'Marçel, I've just spoken to your surgeon. He tells me you are ready to be discharged. You have to take things very slowly for some time to come, and of course by now you must be so physically unfit. It will be many months before you are back to your old self.' Stephen moved over from the window and placed his hand on Marçel's shoulder. He noticed the pain on Marçel's face when he touched him.

'You will come and stay with me in Buckinghamshire, where I can keep an eye on you and where you will be able to completely regain your strength.'

Marçel sighed. 'That's very generous of you, Stephen. But I can't possibly impose myself on you … especially after being responsible for Gerda's death.'

Stephen held Marçel's hand. 'That's just bloody ridiculous, Marçel. What happened was a most unfortunate tragic accident. You have to put all that behind you now and just move on. Besides, I have an active interest in you; remember you still work for the Department.'

Stephen moved to the door. 'I'll pick you up on Friday at eleven am. Be ready, crutches and all! There's a little boy who can't wait for his father to come home.'

At first, Marçel was finding it quite difficult to walk and he had lost so much weight that Stephen had to go up to London to buy him a new set of clothes.

Thanks to the loving care of Stephen and May, Peter had gradually accepted the fact that his mum would never return. But now with Marçel to talk to, he was soon able to also accept the fact that although he had lost his mother, he now had a father that he knew loved him and whom he worshipped.

The school bus picked up Peter every morning and brought him home at four-thirty pm from the village school, but Stephen and Marçel realised that the following year Peter would have to travel to Newbury to a prep school. Therefore they would have to consider sending him to a boarding school.

Marçel spent the next year making steady progress. In between the long sessions he had with his physiotherapist, four months after leaving hospital he began to take short walks, gradually increasing the length of his walks as the days went by. He was soon able to started jogging along the leaf-strewn country lanes. Although there was now an autumn chill in the air, every day Marçel swam in Stephen's unheated pool. By the following summer he realised that he felt far fitter than he had been before the crash.

His mental state was a different matter.

The death of Gerda weighed heavily on Marçel's conscience. His mind kept going back to the moments before the crash; Gerda had died because of his stupidity. He had been flying an aeroplane and had done the unthinkable—he had let go of the controls, but he had also allowed his emotions to take over. Marçel then started to thinking of all the people he had killed in the last fifteen years. He knew that all their deaths had been necessary and were part of the job that he had been trained to do, but this time it was different. He had made a bad mistake and was responsible for the death of someone he loved.

But now things were going to change; Marçel decided that his killing days were over. He would ask Stephen to relieve him from his job with the Department and he would now devote his life to his son Peter, whom he adored.

Money was certainly not a problem for Marçel. He and Pete, his deceased partner in the Department, had stashed away large amounts of money in Switzerland, mostly from the sale of their castle and their successful winery in Portugal and, as the sole survivor, he was now a very wealthy man.

Sitting out on the wide balcony of Stephen's house in early September with a glass of Shiraz in his hand, Marçel watched the sunset. It had been a beautiful late summer's day and he hoped Stephen would soon be back from London in time for a sundowner. Peter, on holiday from his boarding school, had gone camping with his friends and was due back the following day.

Marçel watched Stephen drive through the main gate and park his car at the side of the house.

Four days a week, at seven am, Stephen drove to the station in Newbury and caught the train to London. At Paddington he took a taxi to his office in Whitehall. Although the war years were well behind, Stephen's department was kept very busy, keeping a watchful eye on the small splinter groups of the Nazi party, and some of the most extreme Communist party groups that were operating in several European countries.

A very tired Stephen came up the stone steps and collapsed in the deckchair next to Marçel.

'Been a hard day, Marçel; all these bloody stupid people that keep fighting amongst themselves, instead of helping the people they are supposed to represent.'

Marçel poured Stephen a large gin and tonic. 'I think it's time you took a break, Stephen.'

'Funny you should say that, my boy. Guess who's coming to stay?'

'I've no idea. Not your friend Winston, I hope.'

Stephen stretched back in his chair and smiled. 'Winston is a great talker and very interesting to listen to. No, it's someone we are both very fond of. It's Helga. She telephoned me at my office. Helga has been over to Warsaw to see if she could find anyone from her past life. She wasn't able find anyone that she knew from the past. Helga reckons that by the end of the war the *Gestapo* had killed off all the people she once knew.'

'When is she arriving here, Stephen?'

'Tomorrow lunchtime. We will go and fetch her from Newbury station at two pm.'

Marçel decided to talk to him about his decision.

'Stephen, I'm becoming bored just sitting around here these days. I feel it's time I found something to do.'

'That's good; that's just what I wanted to hear. It's time to eat.'

They had finished their meal and moved into the lounge, Stephen poured out two large glasses of Port.

'I have a feeling that you have something to tell me, Stephen?' They both sat down in the two comfortable recliners.

'An interesting new job has just materialised, Marçel, but it means returning to Portugal.'

'I'm sorry; no more killings, Stephen. Even if it means losing my job, I have really decided to give up that side of my life. In fact I would like you to give me the sack.'

'Nothing like that, old boy. This is a piece of cake; no killings—at least not by you anyway.' Stephen turned his head to one side, smiled and emptied his glass. He leaned forward. 'It's twelve years since you sold the castle and the winery. We, the Department, are convinced that we now have a complete cover-up of 'Operation Deserting Rats', thanks in part, to your efforts in silencing anyone who knew or might have guessed at what we were doing in Portugal.'

'It certainly was an expensive operation, Stephen, but we did manage to silence, not just by killing, but using a lot of the Department's money, and a little blackmail to block up any future leaks.'

'Anyway, Marçel, what you didn't know at the time was that the real buyers of your castle were not your wine producing competitors but, via a very devious route, HM Government. Thanks to a very generous commission to Alfonso, your bank manager, we were able to keep this secret, even from you.'

'My God—I wondered why it was so easy and quick to sell. So what now?'

Stephen recharged the glasses and continued. 'Since you left, the whole place has been neglected. The staff members were all paid off, quite generously I'm told, and the house has been left empty ever since.'

'I don't believe this, Stephen. How could they leave such a fine property with a very successful winery to run down?'

'I went and had a look at the property while you were in hospital. It certainly is very sad to see it today.' Stephen stretched, and then leaned back in his chair.

'What we are proposing now is that you go down to have a look at it and then you can decide whether you would like to buy it back.'

'You mean I go back and clean up the mess! What do you think the locals will say if I just turn up again having just walked away from them all in 1949?'

'You can have it back at forty per cent less than the price we paid you for it. The wine business is still pretty good. Although President Salazar runs an oppressive government, he is now doing great things for the economy.'

'You're quite right about that, Stephen; I believe there is a great future for tourism in Portugal. With its wonderful beaches and sunny climate, it will always be a great holiday spot. As European economies improve, and travel becomes cheaper, Spain and Portugal will both become important holiday centres.' Marçel paused. 'But what's the catch?'

'Ah, well.' Stephen leaned forward. 'We would like you to run a sort of nursing home for us. It will be all above board, at least on the surface,' he chuckled. 'Think of it as a sort of training ground for some of our younger people.'

'It sounds very suspicious to me, Stephen. But then you have always been a devious bastard. I must say I would very much like to own the castle again. However, I have Peter to consider. I'm sure he would love it there, living in a castle with all the waterways to explore. He would have to bring all his friends down during the school holidays.'

'I think this is just what you need, Marçel. Get stuck into all those vines; when our job is finished you can have the castle to yourself.' He paused. 'You could turn the castle into a hotel.'

Marçel stood up. 'And is this nursing home where the patients come to die? It seems just a little like *déjà vu*. I'm certainly not going through that trauma again.'

'It's not at all like that. This will be a safe haven for threatened witnesses involved in serious political scandal and a rest home for two of our very badly brain-damaged agents, who were involved in an exchange programme with two East European agents. It's also an opportunity for us to retrain some of our people, away from the attentive eyes of the press.

Stephen stood up and stretched himself. 'It's getting late, Marçel. I've given you something to think about, and why don't we call it a day—perhaps you could sleep on it.'

'Sleep, Stephen? You must be joking.'

'Good night, Marçel.'

Chapter 6

Stephen and Marçel, with Peter close behind, walked onto the platform just as the train arrived. The doors of the train opened and the passengers from London poured out onto the platform.

Helga came running towards them, her swinging light suitcase helping to clear a way through the crowd. Completely ignoring Stephen and Marçel, she dropped her suitcase and swept Peter up in her arms. Hugging him, she did a complete circle, kissing the slightly confused and embarrassed eleven-year-old boy on both cheeks and rubbed noses with him. Peter, now laughing loudly, put his arms on Helga's shoulders and looking into her eyes, said, 'You really do remind me of my mum.'

'I'm not your real mother, Peter, but I'd like to be your second mum.'

Still holding Peter and with tears in her eyes, she turned to the two men. 'How wonderful to be back again with my three best friends.' Releasing Peter for a moment she hugged and kissed Stephen and Marçel while Peter stood laughing at them. He said to Marçel, 'Daddy, stop kissing my number two mother! You know she's already married.' Helga turned to Peter again. 'That's because your naughty father just loves kissing.'

Stephen rescued Helga's abandoned suitcase, Marçel and Peter each took one of Helga's hands, and the happy group headed back to Stephen's house.

After dinner that night, Peter had gone to bed telling Marçel and Helga that this had been one of the best days in his life, while Helga tried to describe her feelings on returning to the suburb in Warsaw where she had been brought up.

For a short time at the beginning of the war, she had worked as a nurse at the children's home in Warsaw until that fateful day when she had accompanied the children to the concentration camp in eastern Germany.

At the death camp, Helga had been forced between joining all the other women who were heading for the gas chambers, or to stay with the children as a nurse at the hospital where the children were to be used for experiments. Helga remained in this hellish situation, caring for the dying children, until eventually the American forces arrived, when she was arrested as a war criminal by the Allies.

'I found it very hard to leave Michael and Mick in Australia, Stephen, but I really had to find out if I had any friends or relations still alive in Poland. I searched everywhere for two weeks but found no one. All the records had been destroyed and so had most of the buildings in our streets. Do you know what struck me most of all? There were still very few people around and they were mostly men who had survived the work camps, but no children. It would seem a whole generation of children have been wiped out. Of course this area was mostly inhabited by Jewish people, but I was overcome by a strange feeling of silence around me.

'I am amazed, that having lived through those terrifying years, when I found myself trying to care and save so many of those poor doomed children, I was able to survive and become an almost normal person again. Well … almost—the horrors and the nightmares will remain with me for the rest of my life but thanks to Gerda, to you, Marçel, and to you, Stephen, I will lead a normal and happy life and now I am blessed with a beautiful son.

'I came away from Warsaw feeling deeply saddened by what I had seen and felt. It will take many years for all the wounds of the people in Poland to heal.

'So, my friends, I have dedicated my life to the health and happiness of children! I've made a good start with our son, Michael, and this is bringing me on to my reason for being here this evening.'

'You know you don't need a reason for coming to see us. My God, Helga, if I hadn't slipped on that riverside rock when you were running away from me, on our way to Portugal in 1948, I would have killed you. *I'm* the one who deserves to have nightmares.'

'That was a very strange time, Marçel. God was watching over us that day.'

Helga got up and crossed over to Marçel. She sat on the arm of his chair and held Marçel's hand.

'You know how much I love you all, and I grieved for Gerda and especially now, for you, Marçel, and young Peter. Mick and I have built up a successful farm and a very happy home. We would like to share it with you two. We would like you both to come back to Australia and live with us. I'm sure Peter and Michael would get on well together and with my love and devotion to both of them, they will face a great future in this wonderful Australian country.'

Marçel remained silent, taking in Helga's proposal. He was slightly irritated at first; he didn't need any help in bringing up Peter, but then he realised he wasn't anyway—it really was Stephen and May who did all the work.

Stephen broke the silence. 'That's a wonderful and very generous offer, Helga.' He got up and filled their glasses.

'I don't think I could live in Australia, Helga, and anyway I've just committed myself to returning to Portugal. Stephen has some work for me to do there,' he lied. He needed more time to think.

Stephen handed Marçel his drink, 'You're free to go out to Australia, Marçel, if that's what you wish. I think it's a great idea. Peter would have a much better life and education in the warm Australian climate and Helga and Mick could give Peter the love and all those other important things in a boy's life that May and I are too old to give.'

'I don't know, Stephen. I love my son but I realise I'm really not capable of looking after him properly, but I couldn't let Helga adopt him—'

Helga cut in, 'We are not talking of adoption, Marçel. What we are suggesting is that we bring up Peter as one of our family. You will always be Peter's dad. You can come and live with us, or just come and visit us, whenever you want. You know you would always be welcome to come and stay on the farm.'

Marçel stood up and started to pace the floor and then turned to Stephen. 'How would I know if he were happy out there, Stephen? I know that at present he's very happy with you and May.'

'We love having him here, Marçel, but May and I are getting too old to give Peter all the attention that a growing boy needs.'

'Mick and I can do that, Marçel. The two boys can run wild on our farm and grow up eating all the fresh food a farm can provide. That's a wonderful thing for two young boys to be able to do.'

'Sit down, Marçel.' Stephen had, as always, taken command of the situation. 'I think we can solve this problem as to whether Peter would be happy living in Australia. If you like, I will return with Helga and Peter and stay with them for a few months. If Peter settles down and is happy with everything, I will leave him with Mick and Helga. However, you must go out and visit them in six months' time to see for yourself how Peter is settling in with a completely new life.'

'And if he is unhappy, Stephen?' Marçel asked, speaking slowly.

'You bring him back to us in England; I'm pretty sure that won't happen anyway. And by the way, Peter must always retain your name, Peter Beaumont.'

Marçel was won over. He knew he would miss Peter like hell, but realised this was probably the best solution for Peter's future.

'You're quite right, Helga, and I realise that this is a wonderful offer that you have made to Peter and to me, sure—I'll miss Peter and I know Stephen and May certainly will, but I will definitely come and stay with you whenever I can and when he is older I will bring him back to visit Stephen and May.' Marçel paused briefly. 'There's just one condition—apart from an annual contribution for food, clothing etcetera, I will pay for both boys' education including university if they wish and of course any travelling and holiday expenses while they are still at school. As you know I can easily afford this.'

With all the arrangements made in the days that followed, Marçel drove them all down to the marine terminal at Southampton where they were to board a BOAC Airways *Sandringham* flying boat that would take them to Rose Bay, Sydney, Australia. Hopefully they would fly the 35,313 miles in less than six days.

The flying boat was due to take off at eleven forty-five am, so they said their farewells on the jetty by the flying boat. Marçel picked up Peter and gave him a bear hug, promising to come and see him in a few months' time. Peter was too excited to become emotional at parting from Marçel. He shook his father's hand vigorously and stepped down into the aircraft, eager to see the inside of a flying boat.

Stephen took Marçel aside, deliberately preventing him from becoming too upset at their parting. 'I think you should go down to *The Barge*, Marçel. It's two years since anyone has been near it. I'm sure it will be in need of a repaint and engine service.'

'My God, Stephen, hasn't anyone been down there in two years to look at it? It must be in a hell of a state by now!'

Stephen looked down at his feet, pleased that he had made Marçel angry. He knew Marçel well enough to know that his anger and determination to get down to *The Barge* would take his mind off parting from Peter.

'I'm sorry, Marçel; I just didn't have a reason for going down there and I clean forgot about *The Barge*. Look, you don't have to go to Portugal until next spring so go down now and attend to it. You can then spend the rest of the winter in Jersey.'

'When do you expect to come back, Stephen?' Marçel tried to hide his anger.

'I might as well stay until January. Incidentally, I'm due for some leave and I really do feel like a rest. That means no jobs for you this coming winter. By the way, your car is still in my garage in Dinard. You have the keys so you are welcome to go and stay there whenever you wish. Maria would love to look after you again. Good luck.'

After handshakes, hugs and kisses, in October 1960, Helga, Peter, Mick and Stephen climbed aboard the silver flying boat, shortly after, the four Bristol Pegasus engines roared into life and within a few minutes, the *Sandringham* was airborne.

After returning the car to Stephen's house, Marçel called Mary the cleaning lady at his Jersey cottage. He decided to spend a few days in Jersey and would then go on down to *The Barge* in France.

The following morning he packed his bag, took a taxi to the station, a train to London and from Southampton flew over to Jersey.

Chapter 7

Pleased to be back in his Jersey cottage after little over two years, Marçel felt as if he had just left it. Mary his cleaning lady had regularly visited the cottage keeping it fresh and clean for when he eventually returned. So he was not surprised to find the fridge well stocked, and fresh flowers in his sun lounge.

He woke up the next morning to the sound of Mary in full song as she dusted through the house. Mary was more than happy to have this job; she was the younger daughter of one of the local farmers and lived only a few hundred yards from the cottage.

Mary was a happy twenty-one year old. She was a buxom, blonde girl with an open and pleasant face. Mary had been a top student at school but unfortunately, at that time her parents couldn't afford to send her on to a university. So she was pleased to take on the care of Marçel's cottage. This enabled her to continue her studies and save up for a place at university at a later date. The local boys had all found her a little too bright for them, which certainly didn't bother Mary. Mary enjoyed her work and found it an easy house to clean; Marçel was a very tidy person, and with his more than generous cheque coming to her every month, she considered this the perfect job.

Mary called out as she left by the back door, 'Your breakfast is ready, Mr Marçel sir, I have to go to the dentist today, and I'll see you tomorrow.'

With just a few weeks to Christmas, his peaceful but short life in Jersey suddenly came to an end.

Washed, shaved and casually dressed, Marçel came down to the kitchen; the table was set for breakfast, and he poured himself a coffee and tucked into a large plate of muesli. Helping himself to a second cup of coffee, he reached over to the pile of unopened mail that Mary had left for him on the table.

He sorted through the bills, charity requests and bank statements but then came to a brown padded envelope at the bottom of the pile.

Marçel sat staring at it for a few minutes. Something worried him.

He picked up the package and carefully examined it. The stamps were local but the Post Office stamp marks didn't appear to line up correctly.

He turned it over—no return address.

Gingerly manipulating the contents of the package; he could feel a long cylindrical object; a torch battery? The rest of the contents were quite soft and felt like a powdery substance.

Marçel took the package out into the garden and placed it on an upturned flowerpot at the far end of the lawn. He went back to the cottage and returned with his airgun. Lying on the grass at the house end of the lawn, he took careful aim at the package, hoping to pierce it at one end.

He fired at the package; there was a blinding flash and a loud bang.

Marçel walked over to find a burnt patch on his lawn and several yards away the remains of a small, burnt battery.

Marçel decided to go to Dinard the next day to collect his car from Stephen's garage; Maria was delighted when he phoned her in Dinard to see if it was convenient to stay at the house the following night.

The Renault had been standing there for at least two years. He would certainly need a new battery for the car; he would put on a new set of tyres and at the same time have the car serviced before driving down to *The Barge*, to see what sort of condition it was in.

The next morning when Marçel told Mary that he would be away in France for quite a few weeks, he couldn't help noticing the look of disappointment on her face.

'It's a bad time of the year to go travelling in France, Marçel sir.' She turned away trying to conceal her disappointment.

'Cut out the sir, Mary; I'm Marçel to you. Have you seen that burnt patch in the garden?' He put his arm around Mary's shoulder. She shivered a little and then surprised herself by moved slightly closer to him. 'Look, yesterday I found a letter bomb amongst the mail. I exploded it in the garden and no harm was done.'

'Oh, my God! You could have been killed or badly injured.'

'Mary, I want you to keep this to yourself because if the press get to hear about a letter bomb, they will hound you until they get a story, which of course they will and so exaggerate it that it might make it impossible for me to come back to live here again.'

'Good God—sir—Marçel—who could have possibly done that to you?

I handled that package. I had no idea. Shouldn't you inform the police?' At that moment, she wanted to hold him and felt embarrassed at the thought.

'I've just explained that to you. I'm sure it was just a silly one-off case. However when you collect the mail from the mailbox while I'm away, just handle it with care and lock it in that old safe in the garden shed at the bottom of the garden. Here's the key.'

Mary took the key eagerly from Marçel. 'Isn't that a bit dangerous, Marçel?' She felt excited as she realised that Marçel was involving her in some small part of what she suspected could be Secret Service machinations 'Letter bombs only explode when they are opened. So can I rely on you, Mary?

'Yes,' she whispered.

Marçel laughed and bent down kissing her lightly on the forehead. 'So now, Mary,' he chuckled, 'you've really got yourself involved in my secret life! Now drive me down to the harbour please. The ferry for France leaves in forty minutes.'

As Marçel opened the car door to step onto the dockside, Mary leaned over and kissed him on the cheek. 'Come back soon, sir—I mean, Marçel,' she stuttered.

'Mary, why—you are blushing.' He laughed and squeezed her hand as he left the car.

The ferry arrived in St Malo at midday. Marçel caught the Vedette from St Malo, crossed the wide River Rance estuary to Dinard and took a taxi to Stephen's house. Marie the housekeeper, a warm-hearted fifty-year-old widow, whose husband had been killed while fighting with the *résistance* in 1944, greeted him. She tried to persuade him to stay for a few days before going down to Nantes.

'My dear Marie, as much as I would love to be spoilt by you, unfortunately I have business to do in Nantes, but I would love to come and stay here for a few days in the spring.'

Marçel called the local service garage. They came straight over, towed his Renault to the garage, fitted a battery and new tyres, serviced the car and returned it to him late in the afternoon.

Marie was always delighted to have one of Stephen's friends to stay, so she cooked him a superb French meal starting with fresh local shellfish, followed by a grilled steak with a salad that only the French know how to prepare.

Setting off early, Marçel drove south through Brittany to Ploêrmel, then across to Redon where the river Oust, part of the Nantes à Brest canal, meets the river Vilaine. He then followed the minor roads running close to the canal until he arrived at Blain, collected provisions and continued on to *The Barge*.

The tall trees that surrounded this quiet and forgotten waterway had now shed all their autumn leaves; Marçel parked the Renault and walked over to *The Barge*. He was shocked to see the state of neglect; there were patches of rust on the hull and the decks were coated in dead leaves and bird droppings.

He waded out to *The Barge* and climbed aboard. The door into the wheelhouse was open. He stepped in; the wheelhouse was filthy but appeared to be undamaged. He looked at the door leading down to the cabins; it was closed but he could see that it had been forced open and then closed again.

Marçel stood for a while staring at the door. Why close it? He thought he knew why.

The keys were in their usual place hidden on top of the wheelhouse amongst the life rafts. He walked over to the bow of *The Barge* and let himself down through the hatchway into the storage area. From there he unlocked the bulkhead door and stepped down into the cabin area.

The whole of the cabin area had been trashed.

The floor was covered in broken glass, books and bedding. All the kitchenware and the contents of the cupboards had been thrown out into the saloon. In the radio room, the radio equipment had been completely smashed but luckily they had not discovered the secret panel that opened the large cupboard where their guns and ammunition were stored.

Marçel looked into all the sleeping quarters; the same thing there—all the mattresses had been slashed open and everything breakable in the cabins had been smashed.

Marçel went back into the main cabin and walked over to the door that led up to the wheelhouse. He saw two wires running down from the door handle, to a parcel on the bottom step just below the door, and bent down to examine the parcel. He had felt a strong feeling of unease in the wheelhouse when he had been looking at this door. Some instinct had warned him not to open it; he'd learned a long time ago not to ignore those primitive warning instincts.

A homemade effort, but nevertheless quite lethal. He disconnected the two terminals that led from the detonator to the explosive and two that connected the detonator to the door. He unlocked the door and carefully carried the parcel out onto the deck and down onto the canal bank. Unsure what to do with the contents, Marçel carefully undid the packets, emptied the powdered contents into the canal and watched as the fertilisers and paraphernalia drifted away.

Marçel was surprised to see that the hatchway to the engine room was still intact. Not only was it locked but the hatchway cover still had the large padlock fastened to it. He descended the ladder into the engine room. It was all just as he had left it, Marçel's pride and joy. He knew the batteries would be flat, so he topped them up with distilled water and then started the petrol-driven generator to charge them. This would enable him to give the engine a good run the following day.

Back in the saloon, he was pleased to see that none of *The Barge's* electrical wiring had been damaged. He went into the galley; on the draining board, there was a handwritten note.

'To The English Piglet,
If by some fluke you have survived my little surprise, let this be a warning to you. You will not be so lucky next time.
You have messed with a member of the International Crime Federation. We have a very long arm and an everlasting memory; we will hunt you down, like the wild pig that you are.
You are a dead man, Marçel.'

Marçel stood there for a moment staring at the note; he wondered who the hell these people were. Karl Schmidt was dead, and he felt sure that he had eliminated all the other people who had been involved in the Portuguese enterprise. It couldn't have been Lolita. Was it possible that Karl Schmidt's successor in Brazil had followed Lolita to Europe, assuming that she had been eliminated in Jersey?

'I'm allowing my imagination to run away with me.' Marçel carefully folded the note and slipped it into his wallet.

He rummaged through the trash for a while trying to find anything of use in the pile of rubbish that covered the floor of the saloon, but then decided to go back on deck. He went back to the engine room and started the main water pump, after which he went up on deck and began the task of cleaning up, starting with the inside of the wheelhouse. Following this, he hosed the wheelhouse roof and all the decks.

Several hours later, satisfied with his work, he locked up *The Barge*, drove back to Blain and booked into an Auberge for the night.

Early the next morning, with everything covered in a white frost, Marçel returned to *The Barge* and parked his car under the trees amongst some bushes and well out of sight.

He decided that if the engine was in working order, he would take *The Barge* down to his friend, the boat builder on the Loire River. The hull could be repainted there. He would clear out all the rubbish from the cabins and the boat builder could completely refit the inside.

The small transmitter, the radar equipment and all the charts in the wheelhouse had been destroyed but surprisingly the engine controls and the steering gear had been left intact. That was all he needed to take her through the canals and down the Loire River.

Marçel spent the next two hours cleaning the engine room, the engine, generator and the pumps. He carefully checked all the grease points on the engine and main shaft and the batteries were now fully charged.

He pressed the starter, the powerful diesel engine turned over twice before bursting into life; outside, a thick black cloud of smoke came out from the exhaust system. Marçel let out a cheer and ran up the ladder to the wheelhouse and revved the engine a couple of times before checking the water cooling system.

Stretching over to the mooring posts, Marçel unhooked the ropes and then ran back to the wheelhouse and put the engine into reverse slowly allowing *The Barge* to clear the mooring posts. Then, with the engine slow-ahead, she headed out into the main canal and Nantes.

It was a perfect cloudless early winter's day without a breath of wind. *The Barge* cut its way through water that looked like blue-coloured glass. The superb unspoilt French scenery looked to Marçel like the backdrop of a rural stage production, the peaceful surroundings enabling him to relax a little and his mind to wander.

For the first time since that terrible accident with Gerda, Marçel regained a feeling of happiness. The guilt and the sadness at losing her would be there forever, but he had come to realise that life goes on and he must now look ahead to Peter, his son, and their future.

For the next few hours, Marçel was kept busy helping the *éclusiers* to open and close the numerous lock gates. He finally arrived at the delightful Erdre River. There he was able to increase his speed until he got to Nantes. After passing through the tunnel he came out onto the Loire River and followed it down to the start of Canal de Martiniére. Marçel then turned up a small side canal to the boat yard's old jetty.

Jean Claude came out of his office, delighted to meet Marçel again.

'What brings you to us, Marçel? No more *Stuka* bombers this time I hope.'

'Certainly not that again, Jean, but still you never know.'

Jean pointed to the mud flats. 'If we were to dig deep down into that mud, I expect we might still find the remains of the engine, but Carl Schmidt's body must have been burned to ashes in the fireball when he crashed.'

Marçel laughed bitterly. 'The mud with no tombstone makes a suitable burial ground for that evil man. Jean, I need the hull repainted. The interior of *The Barge* has been trashed. We need to clean out all the trash and then refit all the cabins.'

'You are in luck, my friend; I have a few months before my next job. Let's get it up onto the slipway right now.'

Two hours later with all the chocks in place, two of Jean's men started to wash down the hull of *The Barge*; Jean and Marçel were in the main cabin filling up bins with the rubbish. By evening, they had the cabins cleared and washed down. Jean supplied Marçel with a mattress, sleeping bag, a few basics for the kitchen, and after a visit to the local shop, he was able to stay on her until all the work was completed.

It was almost four months later due to a very cold winter which delayed work on *The Barge*—Marçel having spent Christmas with Jean and his family— when she was finally able to slip back into the water and Marçel set off on the return journey to the estuary near Blain.

Marçel moored her to a jetty in the centre of Nantes and went on a shopping spree; replacing all the bedding in the cabins and completely re-equipping the galley with new cutlery, cups, plates, a dinner service and all the necessary pots and pans required for a well-equipped kitchen.

He installed a new two-way radio in the wheelhouse; the radar and wireless equipment in the radio cabin would have to wait until Stephen returned from Australia as the Department would be installing their own radio equipment.

It was raining the next day when *The Barge* came alongside its moorings in the quiet tree-lined estuary. Marçel cut the engine and ran out to fasten the mooring ropes to the pillars. It was then that he noticed the roof of a car in the water. It was his Renault.

He had just finished tying up the ropes to the pillars when a black van pulled up just a few yards from him.

Three men carrying guns stepped out of the van and started to walk towards him. Marçel, realising their intentions, dived back into the main cabin and into the radio room. He opened the arms cupboard and grabbed a Sten gun and several clips of ammunition, slipping one into the gun as he returned to the wheelhouse.

The men were on the canal bank and started firing the moment he appeared. Marçel dropped to the deck and peered over the wheelhouse's twelve-inch high doorstep. He guessed they had no idea that he was armed so raised the gun over the step and fired a whole clip of ammunition at them.

Two of the men had dropped—the third man ran back to the van.

Marçel reloaded and fired a whole clip at the tyres of the van; the third man had disappeared behind it. Bending double, Marçel ran along the deck and released the mooring ropes from *The Barge*; he fired another burst at the van, ran back to the wheelhouse, started the engine and reversed her away from the canal bank.

The third man started to fire again, two bullets shattered the glass in the wheelhouse. Marçel realised that the top of his head was wet with blood; he had been hit by the flying glass.

As *The Barge* turned towards the entrance of the estuary, he noticed that the two men on the ground were not moving. The third man had stopped firing.

Marçel entered the main canal, having decided to return to the boatyard. He stopped at the first lock gate, washed the dried blood from the minor cut on the top of his head, went over to the *éclusier*'s house and made a call to Jean.

'Jean, I'm heading back to you, I've run into a slight problem. I'd like to leave *The Barge* with you for a short while. Have you any place where I can leave it out of sight from prying eyes?'

'No problem, Marçel. What time do you arrive here?'

'About seven o'clock, Jean?'

'I'll look out for you. Try to make it before dark; the Loire River can be very difficult in the dark.'

Marçel, realising that the light would be fading soon after six, jumped back on *The Barge* and pushed ahead as fast as possible in the speed-restricted canal waters. Once he was in the much wider waters of the Erde River, it was full speed ahead until he reached Nantes. He passed through the Nantes tunnel and out onto the Loire River, just after five o'clock.

It was dusk when he reached the boatyard and tied up at Jean's jetty. Marçel explained to Jean that his reason for needing to conceal her for a short time, was because he had upset some colleagues and he was afraid they might revisit *The Barge* and trash it again, while he was away for a few days.

Jean stared at the shattered glass in the wheelhouse.

'That's okay, Marçel. You have woman trouble perhaps?' Jean smirked.

'I always have woman trouble, Jean!'

Early the next morning, Marçel followed Jean's boatyard launch up a very narrow canal to a small lake. The lake was filled with old wartime-damaged barges that had been left there to rot by the departing German forces.

'No one comes this way now, Marçel—all the useful spare parts were taken a long time ago.'

Marçel slipped in between two old barges and tied up to the old timber posts. Satisfied that no one would come to this deserted spot, he carefully locked up, jumped into Jean's launch and they sped back to the boatyard.

'I really do appreciate this, Jean,' Marçel said, handing Jean a substantial roll of francs. 'I really value our friendship and your discretion in our dealings. I'm hoping to get a flight to Dinard today, but I expect to be back in a few days' time.'

'You're a very good customer, *mon ami*. I still think of that wonderful wedding we had here on your barge, with your Australian friend, and his lovely young bride. Now I will take you to our airport; you should be able to get a flight to Dinard today.'

At the airport, Marçel decided to book a flight for the following day—there was something he had to tidy up. He hired a car and drove back to his mooring near Blain. As expected, there was no sign of the van or the assassins. They had done a good job of tidying up the scene except for Marçel's car with the roof just visible under the water. He drove back to a garage in Blain and paid them to retrieve the car and then dispose of it.

It was early April when he returned to the cottage in Jersey. Stephen had decided to stay on in Australia until then. With Mary away visiting relatives in Guernsey, Marçel spent the next few weeks lying low while he considered his options.

Marçel had also spent a lot of time thinking about his situation and his son. Knowing that it was not a safe situation to introduce a child to, he decided to call Stephen for some help.

It was midday in Queensland when Marçel called; Helga was delighted to hear from him and gave him a day-by-day description of Peter's life in Australia. 'He's so happy here, Marçel, and he is getting on very well with our Michael. He wants to talk to you.'

There was a long pause then, 'Daddy, I love Australia and Michael and all the animals. When are you coming to live with us?'

Surprised at Peter's ability to talk like a grown up, Marçel was able to chat to him about all his animals, his new school and Helga, who always made him laugh.

Marçel felt the tears running down his face. He realised just how much he missed his son. It would be a crime to bring him back to England now that he had settled in so well with Helga and Mick.

Eventually Stephen came on the line. 'Good to talk to you, Marçel. I said I would be back in January, but I'm having such a wonderful time here that I'm having a job tearing myself away.' Stephen realised that Marçel was not in the habit of making social calls. 'What's the problem?'

'Stephen, I need to talk to you about something.'

'I gathered that, Marçel. You can talk. The others have run outside. I think all the 'chooks' have escaped from their pen.'

'Someone is trying to kill me, Stephen, and has been out to get me for months now.' Marçel went on to describe the events of the past months and the attempts on his life. Stephen was silent for a few moments.

'That's very strange, Marçel; I'm sure this isn't any of your Nazi friends this time. Which leaves me to think of that last job you did in Bordeaux. I'll call our London people and get back to you tomorrow. I think you might have got yourself into something that is way out of your depth. You are going to need a lot of help to get out of this one. I will call you tomorrow.'

'Say goodbye to the others for me please, Stephen.'

The call had left Marçel feeling depressed and undecided about his future. He realised now how much he cared for Peter and that he must stay involved with his son's upbringing; otherwise, he stood to lose him.

The boy was happy, he now considered Helga as his new mother and he appeared to love Australia and the farm life. Marçel decided he couldn't bring him back to England. He could never make him as happy as he was now.

Marçel wondered if he should go and live either with Helga and Mick, or buy a farm close by. But then he still had to decide what to do about the castle in Portugal.

Marçel's phone woke him up at six the following morning; Stephen hadn't wasted any time, having telephoned the Department in London and several of his contacts in Paris.

'Marçel, I want you to go to my office in London this morning. Charter a plane, if necessary. You will be taken from there to a meeting with a Vincent Shearman at one pm. You are to take your orders from him until I get back to London. We believe you are in serious danger from a very powerful international organisation and you are going to need protection.'

'Is this really necessary, Stephen? I am quite capable of looking after myself you know.'

'For once in your life do what you're told, Marçel, otherwise I'll come over and kill you myself!' Stephen slammed down the phone.

After a few phone calls, Marçel had managed to get a seat in a Jersey Airways *DH Rapide* to Southampton, a train to Waterloo station and a taxi to Whitehall, arriving at Stephen's office at twelve-thirty pm.

Harriet, Stephen's secretary, was very efficient but she was also a very warm-hearted soul—she had fallen in love with Marçel, but unfortunately being old enough to be his mum, she decided it was more prudent to mother him whenever he visited to the office.

'Lovely to see you again, Marçel. We were so worried for you after that terrible accident. Just enough time for a cup of tea; then I'll take you across to Scotland Yard for your meeting.'

Harriet left Marçel at the reception, where a police sergeant checked his driving licence, and took him up to the top level of the building.

The glass doors led into a vast office with more than a dozen people of both sexes working at desks spread around the large room. People were having phone conversations in several different languages, while at the same time others were calling across the room, passing information to those already on the phone. The noise was incredible.

The sergeant led Marçel to a glass-enclosed room, knocked and led the way in.

Vincent Shearman stood up and shook Marçel's hand; the police sergeant quietly withdrew, shutting out the noise from the main office. 'I'm Vincent Shearman; my friends call me Vinney. Please sit down, Marçel. This department was established to liaise with all our European neighbours and as you can see we are an extremely noisy, busy, section of Scotland Yard.'

Vinney continued, 'Stephen is a very good friend of mine. He told me about your three near-death experiences and your recent involvement with certain sleazy characters in Bordeaux.'

'Good to meet you. May I call you Vinney?'

'But of course, but I won't call you Piglet!'

Marçel had taken an instant dislike to this man.

He did not appear to be much older than he was; well built, tall—at least six foot—and looked extremely fit. It was obvious to Marçel that this fair-haired man with steely blue eyes had a sense of humour and appeared to be a man of action.

'I'm sure we will be seeing a lot of each other in the next few weeks, Marçel. I'd like you to tell me all about the attempts on your life and all about the events that took place when you were last in Bordeaux.'

Marçel described to him exactly what had happened in Bordeaux and also the three recent attempts that had been made on his life. When he had finished, Shearman sat quietly tapping his pencil against a small glass statue of Peter Pan.

'Do you have the note that they left you?'

Marçel pulled out his wallet and handed him the folded note.

After examining it, Shearman picked up his internal phone. 'Des, I've got a piece of paper here; could you take it down for analysis please?' He stared at Marçel.

'Did you notice the watermark? That is the same paper that was used by the German SS during the war. This could be our first lead. Marçel, you have got yourself into a dangerous situation and I'm afraid it has taken you well out of your depth. We in Britain, amongst other nations, are trying to investigate a new post-war criminal organisation, which as far as we know, controls crime in nearly every country in the world. They call themselves the International Crime Federation. 'INCRIM', we believe, consists of five men, each controlling a large slice of the world's crime organisations.

We understand that one man controls the Far East, one controls Russia and the Balkans, another controls the Middle East, a fourth person, the Americas and the fifth person, Europe. As far as we know, they meet up once a year to share ideas, settle major disputes and plan their strategies for the year ahead.

'These men control the Mafia, the Chinese Triads and many other minor organisations around the world. They are so powerful today that there are several governments around the world they could easily topple if it suited their plans. We believe that unchecked, they could one day be capable of taking control of the world's oil supplies. They already have control of most of the world's drug supplies.' Vinney leaned back in his chair. 'I know all about your past and how you acquired the name Piglet. Your reputation with the *Wehrmacht* and the *résistance* in France is common knowledge. But this time you have got yourself into a situation where I doubt if we can save you.'

Shearman paused before continuing, 'In fact, Marçel, in trying to wipe you out, it is more than possible that several other innocent people will be killed. So maybe we should just feed you to them!' He smiled.

'I think I'll leave now, Vinney!'

'Relax, Marçel, Stephen still needs you.'

'To hell with that, what are we going to do now?'

'*You* are doing nothing, Marçel. You've stirred up a wasps nest. You are going for a ride in the country. We have a nice country house where we can keep an eye on you.'

'The hell you are!' Marçel stood up and started for the door. His path was barred by two police sergeants and before he realised what had happened, they had slipped on the handcuffs.

'Take him away, Sergeant. Just relax, Marçel, think of it as a nice quiet time in the country; good food, good wine and maybe a little female company if you so desire.'

For once Marçel was speechless.

'I'll come and see you in a few days' time when we have examined that piece of paper and made a few more inquiries. As far as we know these people have not yet established themselves in Australia, so your boy over there should be safe. I will ask Stephen to tell—I think it's Mick—to keep an eye out for strangers. I understand he is more than capable of looking after his family.'

Marçel was escorted to the door by the two policemen. He turned. 'Vinney, I really thought I was amongst friends.'

Vincent Shearman crossed to the door and gripped his shoulder. 'Believe me, Marçel, you are.'

Marçel was escorted through the office, followed by curious glances from the staff. He was taken out briskly through the back entrance of Scotland Yard to a waiting police van and driven for the next four hours to his unexpected new residence.

Chapter 8

'Welcome to Sindrien Castle, sir, in the Southern Pennines, Yorkshire. I am William the butler and I shall be attending to all your needs while you are a guest here.'

William looked the typical old family butler—medium height, stout and a red face; probably through sampling too much of the master's old port wine.

A tall and powerful man stepped out from what Marçel imagined were the kitchens—definitely a policeman. 'This, sir, is Frances the footman, he takes care of all the staff and of course the security in the castle.' William gave Marçel a meaningful glance. 'Now I will take you to your apartment. Unfortunately, sir, we will have to ensure that you remain in your quarters while you are staying with us.'

Marçel was surprised at the luxurious apartment, obviously kept available for any top VIP needing protection. The lounge area with a large floor-to-ceiling window (heavily barred of course), was furnished with a comfortable-looking lounge suite with a low glass table, a good-sized desk with a swivelling chair, a radio and music deck. At the far end of the room, Marçel noticed a grand piano and beyond that a small dining area.

The bedroom had a slightly smaller window with long lace curtains, also heavily barred. A king-sized bed with brightly coloured bed covers, a large dressing table and another small desk were the only things in this room. A door led into the *ensuite* bathroom, almost as big as the bedroom, with bath, shower and bidet. There were two other doors in the bedroom for the wardrobe and toilet.

'I hope you will be happy with your accommodation, sir. Dinner will be served shortly.' William withdrew … carefully locking the heavy door behind him.

Marçel stretched out on the comfortable bed and dozed off. At eight pm, he was wakened by a bell ringing in the small dining room; the food had come up on the service lift. He opened the glass door of the lift and carried the loaded tray over to the table.

Realising that he had not eaten since early morning, he tucked into a delicious steak and kidney pie, followed by a selection of fruits and a cheese board. Staring at the empty Red Bordeaux bottle, he decided that he *had* to return to Bordeaux, where he might pick up a lead that would take him to the people who were trying to kill him.

He noticed a well-stocked bookshelf in the dining room and selected a book on the Loire Valley. That might be a start.

Four hours later Marçel took himself to bed.

Over the next four weeks the routine never varied—excellent food, excellent wine, lots of reading and so boring. He had gone to bed worried that he might not ever get out of his enforced 'rest'. Marçel was beginning to go stir-crazy.

At eight the next morning, Marçel was woken by the bell in the dining room. Slipping on one of the dressing gowns provided, he wandered into the dining room. A covered dish on the tray contained the usual fine fare; bacon, eggs, tomatoes and black pudding, with several pieces of hot toast beckoning from next to a large Thermos flask of coffee.

At nine am, Marçel was just about to head for the shower when there was a loud knock at the door, so he shouted to whoever it was to come in. William entered, followed by a very attractive dark-skinned housemaid. 'Annie has come to do the housework.' He smiled and added in a low voice, 'And anything else that takes your fancy.' William withdrew, locking the door behind him. Annie moved up close to Marçel and gazed into his eyes—he could smell her freshly-washed hair and felt a little embarrassed, standing in his silk dressing gown.

'If you do not mind, sir, I will do the rooms first, then I will be free to do anything else you may require ...'

She then completely ruined the effect by laughing. Marçel had to join in.

Half an hour later Marçel walked out of the shower and came face to face with a completely naked Annie. He briefly thought what an improvement on the crusty old butler who usually did all the cleaning and then, without a second thought, he swept her into his arms and carried her over to the bed.

It was late afternoon. Marçel was half-awake when Annie jumped out of the bed, slipped into her maid's uniform and knocked on the door to be let out of the apartment. 'You really are a naughty boy, Marçel, but oh boy, what a great lover.' She giggled. 'But now unfortunately, I have to go and cook dinner for everyone. See you in the morning.'

Marçel went back into the shower, singing his favourite aria at the top of his voice. 'I think I could grow used to this protection lark!' he shouted.

He suddenly found himself thinking about Mary and wondered why he was feeling a little uncomfortable about his recent lovemaking.

That really is crazy, he thought. Mary is only my housekeeper.

Sharp at eight pm the dining room bell rang; he picked up the tray. Annie had really excelled herself—grilled prawns, baked salmon and an enormous *soufflé* to finish. This time there were two bottles of wine with a note tucked under one of the bottles.

'*Perhaps keep this one for the morning, sir.*'

Retiring to the lounge having overeaten, Marçel sat back in an armchair listening to the *Enigma Variations* by Elga, which he had found amongst the large record collection. As a child he had acquired a taste for classical music, thanks to his father, who had been an organist at the local church. Marçel had been one of his choirboys in his church.

I have to get out of here, he thought. Maybe Annie could help me.

An idea was forming in his mind. Tomorrow he would find a way to get out of this place.

The next day was a repeat of the day before—Marçel had his breakfast, William and Annie came in at nine am. When he came out of the shower, William had gone and Annie was already waiting in his bed. It was an opportunity Marçel did not intend to waste.

Later that morning locked in each other's arms, Marçel was puzzled, wondering why an intelligent, attractive and extremely passionate girl like Annie was working as a housemaid in this prison-like castle.

'What are you doing here, Annie? I'm sure you are capable of far better things than this.'

Annie laughed, 'Kind sir, you sounded just like my father. Well, I'm a prisoner like you, only I'm here because I've been naughty.'

'I wouldn't call this naughty; it's very nice.' Marçel gently stroked the back of her neck. 'If you have committed a crime, why aren't you in prison?'

Annie was quiet for a few minutes, enjoying Marçel's gentle touch.

'Mr Marçel sir, you have captivated me, and as you are not a criminal but just an innocent bystander,' she chuckled, 'I will reveal my murky past.'

'I am an Israeli and I work for the Israeli Intelligence service. Unfortunately, I was caught with my hand in the till while working in the defence department in Whitehall. They didn't shoot me.' She laughed. 'But

I was sentenced to two years' hard labour. I am a well-kept secret within the Department. It's a bit of a cover-up; my infiltration would certainly have been very embarrassing had it been revealed to the press.' Annie sighed. 'So the powers that be decided to send me here. Out of sight and out of mind and as a warning to my government, not to send any more agents into Whitehall!

Annie's smiling face disappeared under the covers; Marçel gave a little yelp and then gasped as Annie did something to him that most men only dream about. It was some time later before he got his voice back.

'That's quite a story, Annie. How long have you got to go before they send you home?' Marçel was getting some strong vibes from this girl. This was something he had not felt with a girl for a long time; however, he still had a slight feeling of guilt. Was this Mary again? he thought.

'I've more than done my time, sir. I am here now at HM's pleasure, which could be a long time, especially if they intend to swap me for one of their people. I just want to go home now.'

Marçel got out of bed and slipped on his trousers. 'I think we could help each other. You help me get out of here, and I'll help you get back to Israel.'

Annie slid out of the bed. 'Do you have some ideas?' she asked, running naked to the shower. 'Because sir, I'm with you all the way—to my homeland.'

The next morning, showered and dressed, Marçel waited for Annie to arrive.

At ten past nine, the door opened and William came in followed by Vinney. Marçel concealed his disappointment. 'What the hell do you want, Vinney? Come to let me out? Or have you found the bastards?'

They shook hands and sat down in the two armchairs. Marçel turned to William, who was hovering by the door. 'William, this calls for a fresh flask of coffee. Go and tell Annie to bring coffee and a few biscuits if possible.'

'I see you have made yourself at home, Marçel. She's quite a girl this Annie, but unfortunately she's given us a few problems. I expect you have managed to extract this out of her,' he said, giving Marçel a sly smile.

'I think you need someone like her to occasionally shake you guys out of your complacency, Vinney. So why have you come all this way to see me?'

Vinney leaned forward. 'We may have a small clue that could lead us on to something useful. You remember the car that Schiller and his accomplice used to take the young girl to their island in the marshes? Well, the guy that owned the car, the one you killed, was Franz Bolhiem, a violent man and a known paedophile.'

At that moment, William reappeared with coffee and biscuits.

'What's happened to my new housemaid, William?' Marçel said, feeling a little disappointed.

Vinney waved to William to leave the room and waited until the door closed behind him. 'I'm taking Annie back to London, Marçel. We need her to identify a body, one of her colleagues, whom we believe got too close to the same people that we think are after you. As I was saying, this character Bolhiem had been under surveillance for some time prior to your meeting him, by the local police in Bordeaux. He had made several long trips to an isolated village to the southeast of Aurillac, which is some way south of the Dordogne. When asked why they had not followed this up, they told us that it was out of their region and that they weren't on very good terms with the police in that region.'

'That's ridiculous, Vinney. We must go over there ourselves and find out what this fellow Bolhiem had been doing there. I speak good French; why don't I go and have a look at this village? This could lead us to this mysterious man at the top who wants me dead.'

'Quite.' Vinney sighed. 'That's exactly why you are staying here until Stephen arrives. Maybe he will consider you to be dispensable.' Vinney stood up. 'I'm going back to London now. Just try to be patient. I'm sure Stephen will soon have a plan worked out.'

Vinney pressed the servants' call button and William appeared. Vinney turned to Marçel on his way out. 'I'll send Annie back to you tomorrow, so just relax, and then you can enjoy her company.'

After Vinney left, Marçel did relax; he found an interesting book and listened to some of his favourite music. After dinner, he went to bed and slept soundly till seven the next morning.

Sharp at nine am, William appeared with Annie and quietly withdrew. Marçel noticed that she was not wearing her maid's uniform but was dressed in navy slacks and a polar necked sweater, her long black hair hanging down her shoulders and back. Marçel caught his breath; he thought she looked stunning. 'I'm glad they didn't send you home, Annie.'

Annie laughing stepped forward and flung her arms around Marçel's neck.

'How would you like a holiday, exploring some of the *Châteaus* in the Dordogne, Marçel? Just you and me with all expenses paid.'

'Looking at you now, Annie, that sounds a fantastic idea but sadly just not possible.' He was puzzled at her suggestion.

'Well, you gorgeous man, I spoke with your boss Stephen yesterday. Believe it or not, I've been seconded to your department, to go with you as your newly-wed wife on a honeymoon holiday in Central France. If our mission is successful, my reward will be my freedom to return to Tel Aviv!'

Marçel was taken by surprise; Stephen as usual hadn't wasted any time.

Marçel liked the idea. He took Annie in his arms. 'I must kiss my new wife,' he chuckled. 'I've already consummated our marriage. Seriously, Stephen must have decided that we are dispensable; this could be a tough mission but also lots of fun!' They both laughed.

'We are to catch the first train to London and undertake two weeks' intensive training and then go straight to Stephen's office for briefing, new passports and I believe, a brand new Triumph sports car!'

Chapter 9

'Yes, Marçel, I *do* think you are dispensable. You buggered up my holiday in Australia!' He thumped his desk and finished up with coffee all over his trousers. 'Seriously, this is a dangerous mission for both of you, but hopefully I will be following not too far behind. I, as an elderly tourist with my man Vinney, will be travelling through France and out for a little you know what, in my sports car.'

He stared at Annie pointedly, while dabbing at his trousers with his handkerchief. 'I'm taking a big chance on you, Annie. I understand you have been a well-trained agent, acting for your homeland, which is now just emerging as a brand new State. You have been a naughty girl infiltrating our intelligence department, but I'm giving you a chance to put that right by helping us on this mission. I also understand you two young people have already formed a close relationship over the last few weeks ... so it will not be too difficult to carry out this husband and wife cover.' Stephen smiled benignly at them.

Marçel realised then that his meeting up with Annie at the castle had been carefully orchestrated by Stephen. The old boy knew he would succumb to a girl like Annie and the past two weeks of training had cemented their relationship. Marçel was not complaining!

'Marçel, as you know the only lead we have on the people who are trying to kill you is the late Bolhiem's car, which had often been seen travelling to a small village called Raulac, somewhere between Aurillac and St Flour we think. As the local police are not interested in following up this lead, I've decided that *we* will. This could be a fruitless exercise but will also be very dangerous for both of you, Marçel.'

Stephen leaned back in his chair exposing his wet, coffee-stained trousers. 'There is something else. After the war, there was a story going around about some missing paintings: The Huberstien Collection of five paintings. They were stolen by a German, SS-Gruppenführer Schitzklien, from a mansion near Warsaw in 1942.

'It was rumoured that they were taken to a *Château* in the Cantal region of France. That, strangely enough, is where Schitzklien disappeared in the last few months of the war. He was supposedly killed by the Resistance Movement in that area, which *kinden*, is where we will be looking. I find this all quite interesting. We could be onto something big, Marçel.'

Stephen moved around the desk and took hold of Marçel and Annie's hands. 'And so my children, by the power vested in me, I declare you both—man and wife.'

'Aren't you going to kiss the bride, Marçel?' Annie put her arms around his shoulders. The kiss took a full minute! 'And now a kiss for my new step-dad.'

Marçel laughed as Stephen backed away diplomatically.

Stephen crossed to his drinks cupboard and produced a bottle of Champagne. 'We might as well do this properly.' Handing them both a full glass, he raised his. 'Here's to a successful operation. And don't worry; I shall be keeping a watchful eye on both of you.

'I want you to go shopping now. There's just time before the shops close, get yourselves some suitable clothes. You are checked in at the Strand Palace Hotel tonight. Here is the key to your sports car, which is in the hotel car park. Oh, and by the way, Marçel, I've arranged for you to go to the hotel hairdresser at seven am; he will re-style your hair. I think you will look good as a blonde and don't shave your upper lip for a while. Annie, make sure yours is also fair, and keep your eyes open in case you find you are being followed. He's your responsibility now, Annie.' He led them to the door.

'Later in the morning you'll drive down to Dover and catch the midday ferry to Calais. We meet up on Sunday in four days' time, in the bar of the Hotel Angleterre in Limoges, at five pm. *Bonne chance.*'

The cab pulled in at the front entrance of the Strand Palace Hotel, where the two newlyweds jumped out of the cab. The hall porter picked up their two new suitcases and followed the couple to the reception desk.

'You have a booking, sir?' a rather pompous-looking receptionist demanded.

Caught slightly off guard, Marçel produced his new passport, 'Oh, err, Mr and Mrs ... err John Tompkins.' He glanced at Annie. 'What are you smiling at? Don't you ever forget your name?'

'You are booked into suite number four and it has been paid for in advance. Just sign in here, sir. Your luggage is already on the way up.'

Marçel remembered to sign J Tompkins. The receptionist handed him the key, giving Marçel a sly knowing smile.

Marçel wasted no time in filling the two glasses from the waiting chilled bottle of Champagne. 'Let's drink a toast to our married status and to our honeymoon in France.'

They both emptied their glasses; it had been a mad rush to finish their shopping in time and now they were able to sit back and relax in the comfort of their luxury hotel suite.

'Are you quite happy with all these arrangements, Annie?' Marçel was being serious for once. 'If not, say so and I will adjust my behaviour accordingly.'

Annie stared thoughtfully at him for a moment. 'Marçel, I don't normally behave as I have done in the last few days. I have to admit, I took a fancy to you the moment I saw you. I think there is some sort of magic between us, but it might only be a temporary thing. I'm very happy to go along with you, and even behave as your wife, for the next week or two. However what happens after that, who knows?'

Marçel got up to refill the glasses and Annie, already standing, flung her arms around him. 'And how about you, hubbie?' she said laughingly.

'Wife, I should just love to be your faithful and loving husband for the next couple of weeks. As you say—after that let's wait and see, but I hope we will be more than just friends.'

The next morning, Marçel woke up to find Annie fully dressed and on her way out. 'I need some exercise, Marçel; I'll see you in the dining room in thirty minutes.' Marçel slid out of bed. It had been an exhausting night, and he needed a shower before heading off to the hairdresser.

Annie took the lift down to reception and headed for the row of telephone boxes. Twenty minutes later, she emerged and stepped out of the hotel entrance to the Strand. Ten minutes later she returned and found herself a table in the dining room—a very different woman.

Annie stifled a laugh as a blonde and embarrassed Marçel joined her a few minutes later. Annie herself looked quite different sporting a blonde wig. After an enormous English breakfast, complete with ribbing, they set off for Dover in the brand new Triumph Sports car; few speed limits and little traffic made driving a real pleasure. With the car safely on board, the ferry set off on the short trip to Calais.

As was to be expected, the boat journey was rough and they were both relieved when they finally arrived in Calais.

France was still recovering from the war years and tourists from Britain were welcomed with open arms. Having passed through customs, they were sitting in the car ready to move off.

'We've got time to spare, Annie; how about going to Paris for a day and then heading on down to Limoges tomorrow afternoon?'

Annie squeezed his hand. 'That sounds great to me. Evidently, your nasty friends didn't catch up with us in London. I'm sure there is less chance of them catching up with us if we go to Paris, and then we can head down from the north, to Limoges. Chocks away, hubbie!'

It was just getting dark when they arrived in Paris. They drove up the Charles De Gaulle Avenue around the Arc De Triomphe and along the Champs Elysées, crossed the river at the Place De La Concord and finally checked in at a smart hotel just off the Boulevard Raspail at Montparnasse.

Later that evening they walked to the *café* where Marçel and Gerda had lived during the last few months of the war. They were greeted by Mirelle. When she saw Marçel, she flung her arms around him, furiously kissing him on both cheeks. '*Ma chérie*, it is so-so goo-oo-d to see you again! And this *belle Madame*—she is your wife, *oui?*' Mirelle finally put him down.

Marçel remembered her lovely slim figure; she had been a teenager when he had last seen her. Now although she had put on a lot of weight, she still looked good and had retained her lovely pink-cheeked face.

'Where is your father, Mirelle?' Marçel noticed sadness in her eyes.

'*Malheureusement, il est mort*. Sadly, he died six months past. It is now my *café*. And now I must cook you a wonderful *petit repas*.' She disappeared into the kitchen and returned with a bottle of wine and three glasses. Several hours and several empty wine bottles later when they were about to leave, Annie went upstairs to the toilet.

Mirelle put her arms around Marçel. 'Is she really your wife, Marçel?'

He looked into her eyes. 'No, Mirelle,' he laughed, 'there's still a chance for us.'

'Be careful, *chérie*; I feel sure I 'ave seen your woman before. I think it was in a newspaper. *Faire attention.*'

Annie came slowly down the stairs clutching the safety rail. They said their goodbyes and zigzagged their way back to the hotel.

Paris in the spring always had a certain romantic magic about it. June, and the city was just entering summer. Paris was one of the few cities in Europe that had not had much bomb-damage in the war, and even still,

Paris retained its magic for lovers of all ages. It was the perfect setting for a young couple to spend a romantic honeymoon.

Hand in hand, Annie and Marçel, mostly on foot, explored the sights of Paris including the Tour Eiffel, Notre Dames and several of the famous buildings. Before they knew it, the day had passed. Marçel decided to take Annie to the Moulin Rouge. By the time they got to bed they were both too exhausted to make love and just went to sleep in each other's arms.

At eight the following morning, feeling the worse for wear but with lots of happy memories of Paris, they set off on the six-hour journey to Limoges.

By nine-thirty, the early morning fog had cleared and they were to enjoy a warm sunny day. They lowered the sports car's hood and with their long scarves trailing in the cool morning air, they were able to enjoy driving through the French countryside on the almost deserted roads.

They stopped at Orléans, famous for its links with Joan of Arc; Annie spent some time looking at the famous statue. Marçel, fancying himself as a tour guide, decided to give Annie a history lesson, giving her his version of the life and death of Joan of Arc.

'She was born in 1412. Joan eventually became head of the French army; she drove the English out of Orléans in 1429 and continued to defeat them in battle, forcing them out of several more towns. Finally captured by the English, she was tried as a heretic before English priests. They found her guilty and Joan of Arc was executed by burning at the stake in 1431.'

'That is a terrible story, Marçel; Joan of Arc must have been one of many who tried to stand up for women's rights. It has taken another five hundred years for it to finally happen.'

'I agree, Annie, religion has a lot to answer for, and even today some religious leaders still don't seem to get the message.'

They moved on to Châteauroux and decided to have a leisurely lunch of local smoked trout and a bottle of Muscadet. At four pm, they arrived at Limoges and checked in at the Hotel Angleterre. An hour later, having showered and changed into more formal clothes, they wandered down to the cosy hotel lounge bar and waited for Stephen to appear.

At five-forty and on their third aperitif, the receptionist came over. '*Madame le telephone. Venez avec mois s'il vous plait.*'

'Annie, Vinney here, we had a problem today. We thought we had a lead but then discovered we were being followed. We gave them the slip but decided not to meet you at Limoges.'

'Do you still want to meet up with us? If so, where and when?'

'Three pm tomorrow, drive past the town square of Aurillac; you will see a sign to Carlat. It's a very rough road; follow it until you get past Carlat. You will be in the mountains. It's a great area, very wild. Three miles past Carlat, you will see a lane on your left. A mile down that lane where there is a gap in the trees, pull off the road; we will be there. Don't go via Brive; take the minor road to Tulle, then down to Aurillac.'

'Is Stephen with you?'

'He says enjoy your evening, it might be your last.'

They did enjoy their evening, having an expensive meal, two bottles of wine and getting rather drunk.

It was late morning by the time they felt well enough to set off for Aurillac, vowing never to touch a drop again.

It was now overcast, but Annie and Marçel were still able to enjoy the drive through some of the best French countryside. They stopped at the attractive town of Aurillac for lunch but settled for a loaf of bread, some of the local cheese and a bottle of mineral water. They arrived at their meeting place at three-twenty.

Vinney appeared out of some bushes and waved them over. They parked their car alongside Stephen's MG, out of sight of the road.

'These villains now know that Vinney and I are making inquiries in the area. They followed us from Bordeaux to Brive. We were in our hotel bar at Brive when we noticed two men, whom we had seen before at Bordeaux, talking to the hotel receptionist. She later told us that they were asking a lot of questions about us. Later, we went for a drive and naturally they followed us. Vinney displayed his driving skills and forced their car into a ditch where it finished upside down.'

Vinney was grinning. 'That's always been my party-piece—the secret is to turn them over without damaging your own car.'

Stephen continued, 'We knew that Bolhiem's car had been seen heading out of Aurillac, so we were able to spend yesterday stopping at all the villages on the way to Espalion. Here we were told that the car had been seen heading out towards the small town of Aumont. I'm amazed just how observant these people in villages and small towns are. I suppose they don't have much else to do and sometimes it earns them a few drinks from the likes of us!'

Annie climbed into the back seat of the Triumph and Vinney slid in alongside her. Stephen jumped into the front seat beside Marçel. 'God that's better, Marçel; gotta watch the old legs now.'

Vinney took over. 'But Bolhiem had never been seen passing through the village of Raulac, though I thought the locals there were a bit cagey. It was in the bar at Espalion, talking to the locals that we found out about the *Château* De Montprécis. It's not too far from here. Apparently the *Château* belongs to the *Comtesse* Ballaine who is a recluse, but no one has been allowed into the castle since the Germans were there in 1945.' Vinney paused, deep in thought for a moment.

'The butler comes down to the village once a week in an ancient Bentley to collect vegetables, meat and groceries for the castle. They reckon in the village that the *Comtesse* must be at least sixty by now and some of the older villagers say that she is a witch who flies out at night to steal children for her supper.'

Annie chipped in, 'That's strange. I wonder if there is some connection with the paedophiles.'

'I'm also wondering if perhaps there is some connection to the missing *SS-Gruppenführer* Schitzklien. We must pay a visit to this *Château*.' Stephen turned to Marçel. 'Or rather you and Annie must, Marçel.'

Annie leaned forward eagerly. 'That sounds great; when can we go?'

'Well first, Annie, we have got to find this *Château*. We must be quite close to it by now,' Stephen said thoughtfully. 'Vinney and I are going back to the Auberge at Espalion for the night. Marçel, see if you and Annie can find accommodation at the Raulac village for tonight—I'm sure you will be able to talk to someone about the *Château*. You can say you are doing some research for a thesis on French *Château*s for your university degree.'

'That sounds good, Stephen. We can use that excuse to call at the *Château* tomorrow.'

'Just be bloody careful in that village. You might be in enemy territory, so stay alert. We will meet back here at nine-thirty tomorrow morning.'

Marçel and Annie drove slowly down the cobbled street; Raulac was a one-street village with cottages on both sides of the road. Halfway down the street they came to a square. On one side was a neglected-looking church with a house on either side, and on the other side a small shop, next door a *café*, which had several tables outside. In the centre of this small square, a stone monument carried the names of the *résistance* fighters who had been killed in the area during the war.

Parking the car outside the *café*, they entered the dimly lit bar. A much overweight patron came over to them and asked them what they wanted.

'*Deux vins blanc s'il vous plais, Monsieur*.' Marçel was not impressed with this barman.

'You English—*n'est pas?*' He slapped the two glasses of wine in front of Marçel, spilling the contents on the bar top. '*Dix francs, Monsieur*. We do not often see strangers here much.'

Annie gave him a warm smile. 'We are looking for a bed for the night. Can you help us?'

A tall dark man stepped up to the bar. 'Of course you can, Francois— and I'm sure you can rustle up a meal for these good people.' He turned to Annie and for an instant their eyes met and they both quickly looked away. Annie coughed politely and appeared to Marçel to be uncomfortable. The strange man appeared not to notice and asked, 'And what's a young couple doing here in central France?'

'We are newly-married, *Monsieur*, and are travelling around France on our honeymoon, but I'm still at university and I'm doing a study of some of the oldest *Chateaus* in France. I hope to do a thesis on this subject when we get back to the university.'

'So, young lady, you are in luck. We have one of the oldest *Châteaus* in the whole of France! I can arrange for you to see this fine old *Château* tomorrow morning if you like.' Marçel noticed him giving the barman a sly grin.

'We would like that very much, *Monsieur*, I'm Annie and this is Marçel. What is your name—'

'He is a German and his name is Kurt and he lives and works at the *Château*.' The barman interrupted Annie. 'Kurt has been here a long time. The *Comtesse* saved him from us, the *résistance*. We were going to kill him with all the other Germans who were living at the *Château* at the end of the war. But the *Comtesse* insisted that he be spared as he had supported France by helping the *Comtesse* to get messages out of the castle to the *résistance*. Also, as he had the makings of a good servant, she said she would keep him as her own special prisoner-servant in the castle.

'And you all fell for that one!' Kurt laughed. 'Later, the *Comtesse* insisted I came into the village every week, and bought presents for all the villagers at Christmas. Gradually as the war memories started to fade into the past, I became accepted by everyone.'

Annie fidgeted, almost nervously. 'Does the *Comtesse* still come to the village, *Monsieur?*'

'Alas, *Madame*, no one has seen the *Comtesse* since 1944. We were told she became very ill and was so disfigured that she vowed never to show her face to anyone outside of the castle again.'

Annie shivered. She gave Marçel's hand a little squeeze, 'I need to go to the loo,' she whispered, 'That man is dangerous, Marçel.'

Marçel ordered another round of drinks for everyone in the bar. A youth came into the bar and spoke quietly to the barman. The barman turned to Marçel. 'This lad says that a group of kids are outside playing with your car. Why don't you go and bring it around to the shed at the back of this building?'

Outside, Marçel found four scruffy kids sitting in the Triumph. 'Allez—Allez!' he shouted, at the same time laughing at the cheeky kids; he then reached into the glove box, pulled out a handful of fruit drops and threw them at the kids. While they were scrambling to pick up the sweets, Marçel jumped into the car and drove around to the back of the building, parked the Triumph in the shed and bolted the door.

Back in the bar, which by now was getting decidedly noisy, there was no sign of Annie. After waiting a few minutes longer, Marçel went up to the attic bedroom. He tried the bathroom and the toilet. Returning to the bar, there was still no sign of Annie.

Not wanting to make a fuss, Marçel went outside to where the car had been parked. The kids were still there, obviously waiting for their parents to come out of the bar. He called to the kids, '*Avez-vous voire une dame, mes enfants?*'

'*Mais oui, Monsieur. Elle départ avec un homme dans le voiture noir.*'

Another small voice piped up, '*Seulement deux minutes, Monsieur. Madame est très, très fâché.*'

Horrified, Marçel realised that Annie must have just stepped out into the yard; the man must have been waiting to grab her and force her into the car. Yes, Annie would have been very angry.

Marçel found some more sweets in his pocket and gave them to the kids; thank goodness he had made some friends.

To his surprise, the bar was empty. His heart began beating a tattoo in his chest—he had been standing outside the *café* and no one had come out that way.

Nearly all the lights had been turned off.

He heard laughter and shouting coming from an open trapdoor at the far end of the bar. A young girl started to scream. Marçel took a step forward. He received a powerful blow to the back of his head and felt his knees slowly bending under him—and then total blackness.

Chapter 10

nnie woke up with a splitting headache; she was staring up at a bright salmon-coloured ceiling and lying dressed only in her pants and bra, on top of the eiderdown on a very large bed. The bed was on a raised dais, at the outer edge of a completely circular room.

Looking around the room, she guessed it was about thirty feet in diameter. It had a domed ceiling but there were no windows and no doors. The lighting came from three chandeliers hanging in a triangular arrangement around the domed ceiling. In the centre of the lights, she noticed what appeared to be a large circular wooden tub suspended from the high ceiling and which seemed to be screening a hole.

Annie slid her feet off the right side of the bed, which pointed inwards; the room was pleasantly warm. The wall was completely bare except for a large curtained-off section off to the right. She stepped over and pulled back the curtain to reveal a shower, washbasin, full-length mirror and a screened-off toilet. On a shelf by the mirror, she found a toothbrush and paste, soaps, hairbrushes and clips and several large towels.

'You've been here before, Annie,' she whispered. 'You might have been born in this room and on this same bed … That beautiful lady I used to dream about could have been my mother; maybe this was her bedroom.'

Annie looked around at the wall and ceiling to see if she was being watched. She was not surprised to notice several small glass discs dotted around the circular room. She also realised that someone else had undressed her, it didn't really bother her; she was proud of her fine figure and hoped that person and the voyeur, if any, took pleasure in her body; as long as they didn't intend to do anything more about it. She shuddered.

Annie noticed a large chest at the foot of the bed; she opened it and found her clothes from the night before, all neatly folded. Her watch was missing, so she had no idea of the time. Then she remembered taking off her watch and leaving it in the car in the hope that someone would find it and give it to Marçel …

Annie took a long hot shower, washed her hair, dressed, sat on the bed, and waited to see what would happen next.

The dais stood in the centre of the room. Annie found that to walk around the perimeter of the room took thirty-four paces. This meant walking three times around the room at a steady pace, took about one minute. She walked around the room one hundred and eighty times and reckoned that one hour had passed; she decided that would be her exercise for the day. Annie lay down on the bed.

What the hell is going to happen now? she wondered. Was this the climax to all the mystery that surrounded her life?

As a baby, she had been dumped in a nunnery and had been brought up and educated by the nuns. It had been a hard childhood; however, she had known nothing else. When she was old enough to realise that she must have had a mother and father, she demanded to know how she had come to the nunnery and who her parents were. Sister Clara, who had always been the nun to care for her, had explained that she had been brought to the nunnery by a man called Kurt, who had told them that both her parents had died in an air raid in 1940 when the columns of refugees fleeing from Northern France had been attacked by German warplanes. Because of the carnage at the time, there had been no way of identifying the child's parents.

Every two years, Kurt had come to see how she was progressing and Sister Clara had told Annie that he had been very generous to the nunnery for taking her in. When she was sixteen, he called at the nunnery, leaving enough money for her to attend an expensive finishing school in Switzerland. Annie spent the next two years learning to be a refined and worldly young lady.

Annie was just eighteen when the blackmailing started.

The day before her finishing school closed down for the summer holidays, Annie was told a car had arrived to pick her up and take her to the Grand Commerce Hotel in the village.

That was when Annie actually had met with Kurt face to face for the first time. She took an instant dislike to him and began to feel more and more frightened as he began to explain the reason he had come to see her.

'When your mother died, almost two years after you were born,' he had explained, 'your father decided that he was unable to face the problems of having to bring you up. He instructed me to take you to the nunnery, and to pay the nuns a generous annual sum to care for and educate you, up until the time you were old enough to go on to a university. When the time arrived, the nuns didn't think you would be up to the standard required for entry into a university. So it was decided to send you to a finishing school, before joining your father in the family business.

'I have always worked for your father; he is a top international criminal and is completely ruthless.' He had paused to see the surprised look on Annie's face. 'He intends to get back with interest all the money he has invested in you since the day you were born.'

Annie recalled the shock she had felt at the time; Kurt just kept laughing at her. That was her introduction into the real world.

Kurt then told her that there was a job waiting for her in a private investigator's office at Tel Aviv in Israel. There she was to receive the necessary training for the work her father had planned for her.

He had put his hand on her thigh and squeezed it so hard that she had let out a cry. 'Your father is a cruel man, Annie.' He took his hand away. 'If you make just one bad mistake and if you talk to anyone about your father's business activities, I know he will have no compunction in killing you; believe me, he is a ruthless man and he has spies who will be watching your every move.'

Annie spent the next eighteen months working in Israel. The business in Tel Aviv was engaged in some very shady business deals; she was taught to fight and was shown no mercy by her teachers. She learned how to handle weapons, to break into a safe and read the relevant parts of secret files. To highlight the seriousness of her situation, she was taken to witness the execution of a man who had disobeyed her father.

During this period, she was given a healthy allowance and was encouraged to take part in the nightlife of Tel Aviv, which was considered to be an important part of the education and preparation for her future work.

Finally, she was told by Kurt to go to London and to get herself a flat in Kensington, where for the next six weeks she was briefed concerning her entry into the career that her father had planned for her a long time before.

She was to enter British Secret Service as a junior filing clerk. False papers and letters of recommendation had been prepared to help her to acquire a job in the War Office. Her father had gone to much trouble to infiltrate this office; the reason given to Annie was that it would enable him to gain access to information regarding the movement of large consignments of gold and any other worthwhile opportunities. At the same time, Annie might be in a position to give him advanced warning of the discovery by the departments of any of his underworld activities.

It had been decided that in case things went wrong and Annie's false documents and deception were uncovered, she would claim that the Israeli Secret Service had placed her in the War Office. This would give cover for her real reasons for her being there and so protect her father's involvement in her presence at the War Office.

Annie had no problem getting the job, but soon after it was revealed that her letters of recommendation were false.

After months in solitary confinement, Annie was transferred to Sindrien Castle where she was expected to look after the 'wellbeing' of the people who were forced to spend their time at the castle.

Annie's feelings had been mixed when she had been interviewed by Stephen. She couldn't help a feeling of loyalty to the father she had never seen, but she realised he was an evil man and his evil activities had to be destroyed. Now she had met Marçel and realised she had a strong feeling towards him, but she was in an impossible situation. Either way, she decided, both she and Marçel were in great danger from her father. She would just wait and run with the tide. Anyway, she wanted to meet this evil man—her father.

She was just dozing off when the chain above her head started to rattle. Looking up, she watched the tub, which turned out to be the bottom of a large cage, slowly descending from the black hole in the ceiling. She was unable to see into the black hole. The lift stopped the moment the cage touched the floor. She opened the cage door tentatively and took out a tray, the cage door closed and it was quickly wound back to the ceiling, effectively blocking the hole.

Annie carried the tray to the bed. The first thing she saw on the tray was her watch. Lifting the plate cover, she found a very tempting roast dinner and another cover revealed fresh strawberries. She quickly finished off the food, before reading a letter tucked under the plate.

The envelope was pink in top-quality paper and smelt of expensive perfume. She took out the equally expensive-looking sheet of paper and read the handwritten note.

Dear Annie,

So nice of you to visit an old lady, although I must admit you did have a little help from me! I do not normally entertain visitors at my Château, but when I was shown your photograph, I knew we had a lot in common and it is possible that you might be able to help me.

I would like you to come and see me this evening in my private chamber. The lift will come and pick you up at seven pm sharp. Don't be afraid; no one's ever fallen out of it as yet, even though it's now over one hundred years old. My servant boy will be there to meet you. I promise you this will be a night to remember.

I hope you are comfortable in your room; I'm sure you will enjoy the undisturbed peace and tranquility as a pleasant change from the bustle of your very busy life. By the way dear, your young friend Marçel will be joining us.'

Yours Truly,

La Comtesse Ballaine

'Oh, my God, this woman sounds crazy! So where the *hell* is Marçel?'

Annie looked again at her watch—six pm; one hour to wait. She decided to freshen up and spent a little time in front of the mirror fastening her hair into a ponytail. Satisfied, she sat on the bed and waited. It was then that Annie realised just how isolated she was and began to get a feeling of claustrophobia. She stood up and started to pace the room. 'I must control myself and try not to think about my situation until I have seen the old lady. I'm locked up in the *Château* with the old *Comtesse* … so where is my father … and where is Marçel? He must be somewhere in the castle; at least he is still alive.'

At seven pm sharp the lift came rattling down. Annie climbed inside the cage, and swaying a little, it quickly returned her to the hole in the ceiling. She stepped out of the cage and into a room that appeared to be identical in shape to the room below; only this room had a central pillar that housed the unusual lift.

The pillar ran all the way up to the centre of another domed ceiling, which was glazed with attractive coloured patterns. This upper room had a fine mosaic-covered floor and on the deep red wall, hung a collection of large and quite beautiful oil paintings. There were heavy studded doors on two sides of the room and two small doors on the other two sides; the studded doors on Annie's left were open so she headed towards them.

She was greeted by a small dark-skinned boy with long black hair, who was naked except for a wide leather belt, which held a long curved dagger. He stared up at her with wide frightened brown eyes, took her hand and led her into the *Comtesse's* boudoir to a chair, standing in the middle of the room's polished floor. The boy stood quietly behind her.

Annie found she was staring at long, heavy, dark-blue curtains. Fascinated, she failed to notice the leather strap that the boy quickly passed around her arms and upper waist. The boy tightened the strap before she realised she was fastened to the chair and unable to move her arms. The boy came and sat cross-legged beside her.

She heard a cackle of laughter coming from the back of the curtains and then a rasping voice. 'Well done, Bruno. So, Annie, you have finally come to visit the *Comtesse*; and of course your father. I'm afraid you are in for a disappointment, my dear. Your real father of course died in 1942.'

There was a pause, which allowed Annie to absorb this information.

'Bruno, come and pull back the curtains—I want to look at my adopted daughter.'

Bruno jumped up and ran to the curtains, slowly opening them as if he were trying to make the moment even more dramatic.

Annie was shocked.

She was staring at a man dressed as a woman.

He was sitting on a throne on a raised dais surrounded with bright blue silken curtains that hung from ceiling to floor.

This enormous revolting-looking man was dressed in a white sequin-studded silken gown. He wore a long blonde wig topped with a large silver tiara, studded with gems and set forward on his head, presumably to keep the ludicrous wig from slipping off.

In other circumstances, Annie might have laughed but the evil cruel expression on his fat, ugly face frightened her. He reminded her of a very large evil-looking frog about to spring forward and devour her.

Grotesquely contorting his face into something resembling a smile, he sighed and continued speaking. 'Sadly, my dear, your mother had an unfortunate accident two years after you were born. She died trying to protect your father—a Nazi deserter, Klaus Becker. They had planned to escape to Spain; of course I had to prevent them from leaving the *Château*. The stupid woman fell in love with one of my younger officers ...'

He laughed at the look of horror on Annie's face and continued. 'I should have killed you at the same time but in a weak moment, I decided to be both your mother and your father. As you never seemed to stop crying at the time, I decided to hand you over to the nuns until you were old enough to be of use to me.' His enormous gut shook with laughter.

'You monster! You killed my mother and father!' Annie screamed.

'Yes,' he hissed. 'You were so lucky that I spared your life, Annie, and that *I* made you into what you are today—an attractive and educated young lady. As your father and mother, I have also been able to keep this *Château* with all its wealth until you were of marrying age.'

'No—'

'So now I shall marry you and all this will be legally mine. Be grateful, Annie, I will have given you twenty years of life. Of course when we are married, you will only be an encumbrance to me and you will also have to die.' He cackled.

'You wicked—evil—*bastard*! You'll never get away with this!' Annie screamed. 'Marçel and the French police are onto you now. Your time is over and I *swear* I will tear you apart when I get out of this bloody chair!'

'Bruno, use your knife and cut off some of that girl's long hair.'

The frightened boy grabbed a handful of Annie's black ponytail.

Annie screamed in pain and fear as he pulled back her head and started to mercilessly hack it off.

Chapter 11

Marçel's awakening was slightly less comfortable.

He found himself gazing at a crumbling red-bricked arched ceiling; his eyes wandered around the old stone walls and stared at the rusty iron bars where light filtered in through the tiny cell window. Marçel listened to the loud steady drip of water falling from the ceiling and down to a small stone trough. Presumably, this was the only source of water for washing and drinking. The overflow from the trough created a filthy wet muddy floor, which Marçel lay fifteen inches above on a wooden frame. He sat up and looked around. The cell was about fourteen feet by nine feet. Apart from the wooden bed frame, the only other thing in the cell was the small stone trough. He noticed a hole in one corner of the floor—the toilet.

Marçel's head was throbbing; he gently felt and noticed that the hair at the back of his head was matted with dried blood. Only wearing a shirt and trousers, he shivered. His pockets were empty and his watch and shoes were gone.

Marçel stood up, stretched, performed a few basic exercises and then splashed his feet up and down in the filthy black mud that covered the floor of the cell as his mind cleared and he began to think positively.

I'm quite uninjured and I'm bloody fit! What the hell have they done with Annie! Bastards. I've been tricked by these animals; and now the Piglet is *extremely* angry. When the Piglet gets angry, he becomes cold, calculating, completely ruthless, and extremely dangerous … Someone is bound to come and check to see if I'm still alive. Whoever it is doesn't know me and will be expecting to find a subdued and maybe a somewhat frightened person in this cell today … So let's give him a little surprise …

Marçel waited until he heard faint footsteps approaching; then lay down on his side in the filthy, dank mud in the darkest part of the cell, facing the door. With his eyes narrowed, he watched as the small viewing trap opened. He could see someone's eye watching him. Marçel remained perfectly still and started counting to himself. He reached three hundred and thirty-five; he reckoned that was about five minutes. The door of the cell opened noisily—Marçel remained still.

Kurt hesitated and then walked cautiously over and stared down at him.

Kurt made a fatal mistake.

He bent over Marçel and as he brought his arm down to feel his pulse, Marçel's right hand grabbed Kurt's wrist and heaved. Caught off balance, Kurt would have fallen across Marçel's body, but anticipating this, Marçel slid to one side, at the same time as his powerful right hand hit Kurt across his neck. He felt it crack.

Marçel scrambled to his feet. Kurt was dead.

He lifted Kurt's limp body on top of the wooden bed, turned him onto his back, searched his pockets, unclipped the key ring from his belt and smiling, crossed Kurt's hands across his chest.

'One less scumbag.'

An open stone spiral staircase led up to the small locked door. Marçel found the right key and let himself into the large circular hallway. He noticed the domed glass ceiling, the collection of fine paintings on the surrounding wall and the large pillar in the centre of the room. Marçel stared at the heavy studded doors at the edge of the room. Like Annie he hesitated as to which door to take. It was quickly settled for him when he heard Annie's screams coming from the door on his left side.

Marçel burst into what appeared to be a lady's boudoir of enormous proportions; it was another circular room with deep blue walls and with light coming in from the high, domed coloured glass ceiling.

The sun was shining down on Annie, who was strapped to a chair in the centre of the room. A naked, frightened-looking boy was standing behind the chair holding a vicious-looking knife to her bleeding neck while his other hand clutched some of Annie's hair.

Marçel heard a high-pitched laugh and turned to see a large and very ugly old woman sitting on an elaborately gilded throne, on a raised dais. He gazed at the hideous woman dressed in white silken robes covered with hundreds of sparkling sequins—the blonde wig and diamond tiara making her look like a top-heavy Christmas tree fairy. Beneath her blonde wig, a large, red and masculine-looking face with a bulbous nose and layers of swollen chins almost concealed the small sunken eyes and the cruel line of her mouth.

Marçel was revolted by this strange-looking woman.

From under the woman's skirts, a podgy wrinkled hand appeared holding a revolver, and it was pointing at Marçel's stomach. Speaking in a quiet but grave voice, the woman stared at Marçel with her red piggy eyes.

'Welcome to *Château* De Montprécis, young Piglet ...' the *Comtesse* hissed. 'But what have you done to my man Kurt? I do hope you haven't hurt him; he was supposed to bring you to me. I wanted you to watch my dear little boy play with the knife I gave him for his birthday.' She cackled. 'In Portugal they enjoy eating dried pigs' ears; so I thought we might start with the Piglet's young lady's ears. The little boy is so hungry he won't bother to wait for them to be dried. I had hoped that the boy in this situation would have been sexually aroused, but obviously, he is far too hungry for that. I haven't fed the wretched child for at least a week. Interesting, don't you think?'

Marçel stared at the *Comtesse*. 'Don't worry about Kurt, *Comtesse*; he decided to take a long nap. I believe that he had a late party in the village last night and the wine has taken its toll.'

Staring at the woman's face, he realised it had been recently shaved. This was not a woman. The face, the voice, the way she held the revolver and the things she said, all pointed to *it* being a man. Then, unlike Annie, the truth slowly dawned on him; those pictures in the hall, perhaps they were the missing Huberstien Collection, if so, this must be the missing General—*SS-Gruppenführer* Schitzklien.

'I was admiring your paintings; are they by Huberstien, *Herr* General?' Marçel watched the grotesque face freeze, and then break into a smile. 'You're a depraved old lunatic. So you must be the missing German General, but where is the real *Comtesse* Ballaine?'

The General gave a shriek of laughter but then had a coughing fit, which caused him to fire the revolver; the bullet passing over Marçel's head.

'You stupid children! You thought you could get close to *SS-Gruppenführer* Schitzklien and destroy his comfortable life? Now you are going to pay with both your lives; so, Marçel, if you have damaged one hair of Kurt's head not only will I kill you but I promise ... it will take a very long time for you to die.' He leaned forward. 'What are you waiting for, boy? Cut off the girl's ears!'

The young boy hesitated; he turned and stared at Marçel. 'Don't do it, boy. We have come to rescue you, to feed you and take you home to your family.'

Bruno took a step back and lowered his knife. 'That's another week without food for you, Bruno!' the creature screamed in rage.

'As you and Annie will not be going anywhere, Piglet, I have to admit that you are quite right. They are the Huberstien paintings, and I am the person who brought them from Poland to France in 1941.' *SS-Gruppenführer* Schitzklien sighed.

'The poor *Comtesse* had an unfortunate accident on her way from the *Château* to the village; it was then that I decided to take her place and become the *Comtesse*. I have always had a fancy for cross-dressing and, as you must notice, I am more female than male. Unfortunately circumstances dictated that I had to become a recluse, and so I was denied the opportunity of marrying a rich and handsome Count. He would certainly have had a nasty shock on our wedding night.' Schitzklien's fat body started to shake with laughter. 'Instead, I shall marry Annie and the *Château* will then be legally mine forever.'

'Over my dead body!' Annie hissed.

'Quite.' Schitzklien cackled.

'So you see, young Piglet, I'm living a happy life here in the *Château*. I have complete control over several interesting enterprises in Europe and the one that gives me much personal pleasure, is organising the adoption of small children; there is an ever-growing international market to supply the needs of the many connoisseurs around the world. So after disposing of you two, I shall remain here for many years to come, sampling some of the goods I have to offer to my clients.' Schitzklien started to cackle again.

'You dirty evil *monster*!' Annie spat at him.

'Annie is an attractive young girl; I'm sure she would have made a good wife but alas, she has become a liability to me. Once we are married, I will play with her here in the *Château* until I get bored; then I will kill her. However, maybe there is another option. I have several contacts in the Middle East who I'm sure would love to take her into their harems; as you know, there are no safe returns for girls in that situation.'

He fired the pistol again, narrowly missing the little boy who was still holding his knife, now completely confused and squatting alongside Annie.

'As for your stupid friends, I have just had a phone call from the village; I understand they have returned to the forest this morning, presumably to meet you. By now they are being severely dealt with.' He looked at the elaborately gilded clock on the wall. 'It's the village's annual wild pig hunt today and your friends are the *pigs*.'

He glanced at the little boy. 'Get some more cord from the dressing table drawer, Bruno, and put your clothes on.' He turned to Marçel. 'I always keep rope in that drawer; we sometimes like to play bondage games. So how would you fancy that, Piglet?' He giggled.

Marçel's revulsion for the creature was quietly turning to anger, but the General was quite unaware of the danger signs. Marçel noticed he was tiring a little and had allowed his hand holding the revolver to rest on his lap.

The General turned slightly to look at Bruno crossing the room; Marçel gave Annie a slight nod of the head and then quickly opened and closed his mouth. Annie stared blankly back at him for a moment and then finally got the message—she let out a piercing scream.

As he turned to look at her, the General let the gun slip into his lap. Marçel leaped across the room bringing his cupped hand down on the General's arm preventing him from recovering the gun. Marçel grabbed it, hitting the General on the back of the head with it; his enormous fat bulk collapsed onto the floor.

Marçel then fired the gun towards Bruno, who was standing transfixed in the centre of the room. Marçel had aimed to miss; his intention was to frighten, but not harm him, but had clipped the poor little fellow's shoulder. He indicated to the boy to bring the rope across to him. As he started to tie him up, the General opened his eyes.

'I'm afraid, "*Comtesse*" … your trusted servant Kurt will never wake from his sleep. The Piglet has made sure of that.' Marçel had never seen such an evil face, which was now black with rage.

After trussing up the General, Marçel struck him on the back of his head with the gun again. 'We won't hear your ugly voice again for some time, you evil bastard!' He looked down on Annie. 'That was a mighty good scream, Annie.'

She looked up at him. 'If you don't hurry up and untie me, you'll hear an even louder one, Marçel.' Tears were running down her face. 'I want to kill that creature! He murdered my mother and father. At least I now know I come from this bloody castle.'

'Looks like it's all yours now, Annie, or should I say—*Comtesse?*'

'I'd like to keep that creature in the dungeons until he dies, Marçel.' She wiped away the tears and smiled. Marçel untied her and Annie slowly stood up and stretched herself. 'God where is the nearest loo?' Then she stared at Bruno sitting cross-legged in the middle of the floor quietly weeping and nursing his left shoulder. 'Shooting at him was quite unnecessary, Marçel, I'm sure the poor boy is already frightened enough.'

Marçel strode to the centre of the room, swept Bruno up into his arms, gave him a rough hug and spoke quietly to him. 'You don't have to worry anymore, young man; you're quite safe now and your troubles are over. I am sorry to have wounded you—it's only a little nick really and should heal quickly. What's your real name?' The boy's mouth opened and closed, but no sound came. Marçel was shocked to find just how light he was.

'My God, this child has been starved,' he murmured angrily to Annie. 'I wonder what else the evil beast has done to the poor kid.' He held him tight for a moment; wanting to make him feel secure. 'I'm Marçel. You are safe now. So tell me your real name, lad.' Again the boy opened and closed his mouth without making a sound. 'Annie, I'm sure he is so badly traumatised that he is unable to speak; we should get him to a hospital as quickly as possible.'

Annie came over and gently stroked his long dark hair. 'Firing at Bruno really was a stupid thing to do, Marçel. You're right, the child is not only traumatised, *and* wounded, but I think he has also been drugged; just look at his eyes, the poor little fellow.'

When Marçel put him down, he ran to Annie, putting his arms around her waist sobbing uncontrollably.

Marçel picked up the small pile of clothes that the lad had dropped on the floor and handed them to Annie. 'I'm sorry, Annie, I just wanted to frighten him, but I wasn't quite sure how he was going to react.' Annie cooed gently to the crying child and soon she had dressed him in the robe, using the ghastly wide silk belt to wrap around his shoulder wound. At least the poor lad had some covering now; although Marçel was repulsed by the thought of the horrors he had experienced, all dressed it would seem as the General's slave boy.

The boy could not have been more than twelve to fourteen years old, with darkish skin stretched taut over his thin frame; Marçel guessed that he had come from Eastern Europe; possibly Romania, or Bulgaria.

Annie put her arms around Bruno, held him tight and whispered something into his ear. The boy stopped crying and stared at her for a moment, opened his mouth to say something but made no sound, just a faint smile. 'Marçel, you are right, he's quite unable to speak; come on; let's find Stephen and then get this poor boy to a hospital right now.'

'I'll have to do a thorough search of this vile place first. There may be other children locked up somewhere else in the castle.' He stepped over to the General, gave him a sharp kick in the ribs. 'The bastard is still out. Wait here until I get back; if *it* wakes up knock *it* out again. It shouldn't take me too long.'

Chapter 12

'Where the hell are they? They should have been here an hour ago.' Vinney got out of the car and stamped his feet on the frosty ground.

'Don't worry, Vinney, the youngsters have probably overslept after a heavy night.' Stephen was watching a group of horsemen approaching in the distance. They had parked the car on the side of a frozen dirt track, which ran close to the edge of the forest and was about half a mile from the main road.

'Looks like the locals are out hunting today; they're heading straight towards us. I can't see any prey, can you, Stephen?'

Stephen jumped out of the car and stared at the rapidly approaching horses. Because of the very cold weather, they had decided to hire a Peugeot saloon, leaving the MG with the hire company.

'That's strange, Vinney, those aren't just dogs, they are *hounds*.' His voice rose, 'And their prey appears to be *us*. *Move!* Quick into the car, Vinney!' With the huntsmen following a little way behind, the dogs now seemed completely out of control and were howling and baring their teeth as they bore down on Stephen and Vinney.

They leaped into the car just seconds before the first animal crashed onto the bonnet of the car followed by two others. The rest of the pack was leaping up on the windows, already smeared with their saliva and muddy paws. The leader of the pack was still standing on the bonnet and appeared to be waiting for orders from his master.

'Start the car, Vinney—let's get the hell out of here!'

Vinney turned to him, his face pale. 'The keys are outside—I—I must have dropped them when I got out of the car.'

'You bloody idiot! Can't you see what they intend to do?' Stephen endeavoured to calm down; they were now surrounded by seven or eight red-coated huntsmen, who were looking almost as menacing as their animals. The apparent master of the hunt dismounted, walked over to a pile of wood and came back to the car with a heavy piece of timber.

'Pass me your revolver, Vinney.' Stephen watched the hunt master as he approached the car with a grim look on his face. The hounds escalated their ferocious barking as pandemonium rained down on the car. He brought the heavy log down on the windscreen, shattering the glass, at the same time signalling the pack leader, who leaped at the broken windscreen. As the dog's head came through the broken glass, snapping savagely, Stephen fired the gun into the dog's mouth. It screamed as it fell back and died. Two others followed, meeting the same fate.

The silence that followed was interrupted by the sound of the huntsman's horn; quickly followed by the wailing sound of the police cars approaching from the main road.

The hunt master mounted his horse, waved his whip and screamed at his remaining hounds as they all disappeared into the forest.

Three police cars came bouncing down the track and pulled up behind the mud-covered Peugeot. Eight fully armed policemen jumped out of the cars, headed by the local police chief.

'*Merd*! You stupid English policemen! How dare you come and interfere in police matters in this part of France. It is so lucky for you that we had a tip-off from someone in the village.'

Stephen and Vinney got out of the car and sheepishly stood in front of the very angry police chief. '*Mon Dieu*! If it isn't *Monsieur* Stephen. Do you remember André?' Stephen's face lit up as he recognised the Inspector.

'I used to organise the landing strips for your aircraft in central Brittany.'

He put his arms around Stephen and they embraced each other. 'I will always remember the night you handed me a box and told me it contained explosives. *Mon Dieu*, when I got home, I found it was a bottle of whiskey!'

'Those were exciting days, André my friend, but happily they are over. I am so pleased that you were able to survive when so many of your people in the *résistance* died fighting the German army in France. But now I see you are a very important person in the Bordeaux police force.'

Stephen took André's arm and walked a little way up the track. 'Do you know why we are here, André? We helped you track down the paedophiles in Bordeaux. We believe there is a connection in this area, and we now think an international gang is operating from the *Château De Montprécis*.'

André stopped and turned to Stephen. 'We are here also, my friend, because we were following the same track as you, and then we discovered you were ahead of us. You could be in serious trouble over this when I make my report.'

Stephen gave André a winning smile. 'Let's make a deal, André. I will give you some information that will make you an even more famous figure in the French police service. In exchange, you can just report breaking up a dispute between some English activists, and some farmers out for a good day's hunt. But I'm sure, before the end of the day, you will find a much stronger reason for arresting those scum.'

'You gave us a very good deal over the paedophiles in Bordeaux, Stephen. So what's the information this time?'

'Okay, André, not only do we suspect that crooks are operating from the castle, but we have a strong hunch that the missing General SS-*Gruppenführer* Schitzklien and the missing Huberstien collection of stolen paintings are in the castle.'

André stood silent for a moment. *'Mon Dieu!'*

'I had two of my people staying in Raulac, the village next to the castle; both have gone missing.'

'So what are we waiting for? Leave your car here; we will attend to it later. *À l'avance, mon ami.'* André sensibly called for an ambulance to meet them at the castle.

Half an hour later they arrived at the castle to find the heavy wooden outer doors securely locked. André ordered one of the policemen to place a small charge at the bottom of the doors. They all stood back and waited— the explosion blew them wide open and they drove through the archway and into the courtyard. As they were walking cross the courtyard, the front door to the main living quarters of the castle flew open and out stepped Marçel, holding a bedraggled child in each hand and followed by Annie who had her arm around an older boy.

'You'll find Schitzklien upstairs, he's well trussed up and ready for the slaughterhouse. So what kept you, Stephen?' He smiled as he presented Stephen with the three frightened children.

At that moment, two ambulances arrived and nurses quickly took charge of the two younger children, carrying them to one of the ambulances. Annie insisted on accompanying them to the hospital. 'I'll join you at the hospital later, Annie!' Marçel yelled as Annie climbed into the second ambulance with Bruno.

'Looks like the honeymoon is over for you and Annie. I expect Annie will stay in Bordeaux for a few days. Perhaps she can help sort out this dreadful mess. In the meantime, Marçel, I think we should get away from this place as quickly as possible. You will have to return that new car to London.' They were standing out the front of the *Château* after the ambulances had driven off.

'How about Annie? Do I bring her back with me, Stephen?'

'You had better call into the hospital and talk to her. As far as we are concerned, she has served her time. We told her that after helping us with this task, she would be free to go back to Israel.'

At that moment, André joined them. 'Quite a day, my friends. Thanks to you, we now have an important war criminal and international gangster under arrest, recovered the Huberstien paintings and those three poor children, and I have just been told that my men have arrested most of the horsemen as they returned to the village. *Merci, mes amis.*'

Stephen shook André's hand. 'You have done a pretty good job yourself, André. That should earn you another promotion. I hope you are able to play down our presence here today.'

'I will take you three back to your hotel, Stephen; your car has already been taken there. Then, my friend, you must go straight back to London. We will forget that you were here today—'

'No need for that, André. My car is still in the village and I can drop them back to their hotel on my way to the hospital.'

André laughed. 'That's if you still have a car, *Monsieur* Marçel. I'll take you there now; the sooner I get rid of you people, the better.'

To Marçel's surprise, the Triumph was still in the shed behind the *café* and was exactly as he had left it.

With handshakes all around and with Vinney squeezed into the small back seat of the Triumph, they set off for the hotel. Stephen and Vinney collected their suitcases and set off in Stephen's MG for Dinard. Taking it in turns with the driving, they expected to make Dinard by the following afternoon. Leaving the MG at Stephen's villa, they would fly back to England that evening.

Marçel later found Annie waiting in the hospital reception area. 'Although very much underweight, the children are all in good shape, but mentally it will take a long time for them to recover from their terrible experience. They are to be sent to the local children's home and surprise, it's run by Sister Clara, the nun that brought me up. With Sister Clara in charge, it has now become a really good children's home.'

Marçel could see she was itching to get back to the children. 'So are you coming back to London with me?' Marçel already knew the answer.

'I—I've asked Sister Clara if I could stay at the nunnery with the children for a few days. The local police are quite happy for me to help them to track down their parents. I think that is unlikely. It's usually the poor little orphans that are taken by those evil men.'

'And so what happens to them now, Annie?' Marçel inquired.

'I am going to use all my influence to get these children to Israel. They have come from one of the Eastern Europe countries. Israel can give them a fresh start and a wonderful new life.'

'So … it's bye-bye, Annie?'

'I'm afraid so, darling. It could never have worked for us; sadly our jobs would make it impossible. We are on different sides of the fence, we both love our lives too much to compromise and, darling Marçel, you *are* a bit old for me.' She laughed.

'So will you move into the *Château* and live the life of a *Comtesse?*'

Annie pulled a face. 'Definitely not yet, darling. I will use some of the money and either sell the *Château* or maybe move into it in a few years' time.' She flung her arms around Marçel and they clung together for a while. A tear ran down Annie's cheek as she broke away. Annie turned and headed back to the children's ward.

Marçel realised it was pointless to follow her. Annie was right; their job was over. Maybe one day in the future their paths might cross again, but for the present they were travelling on different roads. Anyway, although they had gotten on well together, he knew she was not the right woman for him.

———

'With all the rapid changes that are happening in Europe today, Marçel, we have decided that *The Barge* in France is no longer of any use to us. One of our politicians with more money than sense has offered to buy it. He intends to keep it on the Norfolk Broads as a holiday houseboat for his family. As you will soon be going back to live in Aveiro, I'm sure you wouldn't want to worry about *The Barge* anymore.'

Back in London, it was a cold February day and missing Annie, Marçel was not in a very receptive mood. 'Whatever you want, Stephen. Do you want it delivered to the Broads? I suppose you've got a good price for it? I shall miss the old *Barge*, but I guess it's time to move on. Anyway I will need a much smaller and faster boat, when I'm living in Portugal.'

'I'm sure we will make a handsome profit from it, my boy.' Stephen smiled. 'If it's seaworthy, we will send two men down to collect it; they can bring it back through the canals to Northern France. Then it's only a few hours to cross the Channel to England; a nice trip for somebody. That's when it's convenient for you to remove all your gear of course.'

Marçel was feeling irritated that Stephen had gone ahead and sold *The Barge*, without any thought for his feelings on the matter. His mind went back to all the good and bad times he and Peter had experienced over the few years they had worked together, during and after the war. After Peter's death, the modest-looking barge had even been involved in a minor sea battle and had proved itself an excellent sea vessel in difficult conditions in the Bay of Biscay.

'I suppose I might as well go down to the castle now. I'll hire a van, drive down to *The Barge*, remove all my bits and pieces and when your chaps come down to collect her, I will drive on down to Aveiro with all my gear. Peter and I had great plans for the winery, but now he's dead I've lost all enthusiasm for the castle and the winery. I was responsible for Gerda's death; my son, Helga and Mick are all living in Australia, and the castle and winery are now completely run down.' Marçel sighed. 'I'll just have to start all over again from scratch.'

Stephen had been looking out of the window; he swung around angrily. 'Don't you talk like that! By a miracle you survived that dreadful aeroplane accident. You were so badly injured we didn't expect you to live, but now two years later, apart from a few scars you are completely back to normal, and in fact you are fitter now than you were before that accident.'

'I'm sorry, Stephen; I just can't get enthusiastic about the winery.'

Stephen put his arm around Marçel's shoulder and gently led him to the door. 'I miss Gerda too, but I know it was an accident and not your fault. Why don't you give Annie a ring? She's still at the Monastery with the children.' He gave Marçel a gentle shove. 'Now piss off, Marçel, and stop your whining. You have more money than you could possibly spend in your life; you're disgustingly healthy, and you are going to live in a much warmer climate while we poor sods have to live in London.'

Later that morning, Marçel took the train down to Eastleigh Airport, Southampton, and flew back to Jersey in a *DH Heron*.

Mary was waiting for him when he arrived at the cottage. She had run down to the cottage after he had phoned and had turned on the newly installed central heating. She soon had a welcoming log fire burning in the old granite fireplace that took pride of place in the low-beamed-ceiling lounge.

'How long will you be staying this time, Mr Marçel sir?'

'It's Marçel to you, Mary. We are in the sixties now, so cut out the 'sir' nonsense. In today's world, thank God, we are all born equal.' He smiled warmly at her and Mary fought to conceal a blush; she was beginning to realise just how much she missed him when he was away from the cottage.

At first she had thought of him as just a handsome man who had given her a well-paid job that she thoroughly enjoyed doing, but as time wore on she realised that this was quite a remarkable man, who seemed to be shrouded in mystery. He was kind and considerate and yet she felt that this man could, when called upon, be very tough and ruthless. She was quite sure he was not a bad man.

From the postmarks on the mail he often received, she guessed that he must be working in Whitehall, London. She wondered if perhaps he was a British spy; she felt a sudden shiver of excitement run down her spine.

'I'll be here for a few days, Mary. I feel like being spoilt by you, and then I shall be going to France for a few days. I must say I will miss the cosy atmosphere of this cottage. You've made this such a homely place for me to come back to.'

'I think I love this cottage as much as you, Marçel, but it is so much nicer when you are here.'

Mary hurried into the kitchen; this time she really was blushing. She wondered if she had sounded a little too forward and giggled when she allowed her thoughts to wander as far as Marçel's bedroom and bed.

The next morning Marçel woke up late, completely relaxed in the quietness of the Jersey countryside. The silence was broken by the pleasant sound of Mary singing in the kitchen. He realised that although Mary had been working for him for over two years—she had come to him two years after leaving school—he had hardly noticed her as she bustled around the cottage; to him she was just a pleasant country girl doing her job.

Yesterday was the first time that he had been relaxed enough to talk to her. Looking at Mary, he realised that this quiet country girl, whom he had thought quite unworldly, was in fact a very attractive young woman and after talking to her about a wide range of subjects, he had realised he was talking to a very intelligent girl. He realised she'd probably had a far better education than he had, his having ended abruptly at sixteen when he had been arrested by the *Wehrmacht* in 1943. Marçel decided that he would try to get to know her better next time he returned to the cottage.

After a full English breakfast of bacon, eggs and tomatoes, Marçel felt the need to take a brisk walk along the cliff paths that ran up and down the hills on the north coast of the Island. When, two hours later, he returned to the cottage; his hands and face felt as though they had been frozen by the strong cold easterly wind that swept across the islands at that time of year. Mary poured him a half a tumbler of whiskey; she added a spoonful of sugar and topped the glass up with hot water. Marçel soon thawed out as the hot drink took effect. He decided it was time to telephone Annie.

After two attempts, he finally got through to the Mother Superior in charge of the nunnery. 'Mr Beaumont, I'm Sister Clara; yesterday Annie and the children went out for a brief walk and have not been seen since. We are extremely worried as all Annie's things are still in her room except for her purse and her passport.' She paused for breath.

'I have informed the police and they are searching the area, but they have not found any sign of them. I don't know what to do next as Annie doesn't seem to have a home address amongst her possessions.'

'This is really serious, Mother Clara. I will contact the people in London who know all about her and they will have all of her details. If she's not back by the morning, I will come down the following day. Don't worry too much, Annie is a very resourceful girl and I'm sure whatever has happened they will be back by tomorrow morning.'

Marçel called Stephen immediately. 'Annie and the children have gone missing, Stephen. I wondered if they might have been kidnapped by some of the remaining members of that paedophile gang. I really thought we had cleaned up those bastards. What do you think?'

'Get up here tonight if possible. We have found out something about our Annie, and the French, bless them, have let the General go free. It's not good news.' Marçel detected the anger in Stephen's voice.

'Stephen, the French police seem to have things in hand there and are searching the whole area. I told Sister Clara, the nun in charge, that I would go down the day after tomorrow to see if I can help.'

'I think we had better leave the searching to the local police force to deal with this time, Marçel. We were lucky not to get a slap on the wrist after our last encounter with them. You and I have to get after that bloody General!'

'I'll try to book a flight to Southampton this afternoon.'

'If you do, get a train to Newbury and I will pick you up at the station. You can stay at my home tonight. It's time we shared a bottle or two of wine.'

Marçel walked over to the kitchen.

'Mary, can I have another hot whisky please? Do one for yourself and come and join me by the fire.'

A few minutes later Mary appeared with two steaming glasses of whisky. 'Is something wrong, Mr—sorry, I mean—Marçel?'

'Come and sit down, Mary. My few days' rest have come to an end. I will be flying back to England this afternoon.'

'Has something bad happened, Marçel?'

'It could be. We have just lost a young woman and three children in Bordeaux. I am going to help look for them. If we do find them and they are in danger, I will try to bring them back to the cottage. I would like you to stay here and keep it warm for a few days, in case I return with the children.'

'That's no problem, Marçel, I would just love to help you in any way I can.'

Marçel got up and phoned the airport about flights to London. On the way to the telephone he stopped, bent over, and kissed Mary lightly ... on the mouth.

Chapter 13

From experience, Marçel knew that it was better to sit and wait until Stephen was ready to talk, which didn't happen until after Stephen had opened the second bottle of wine.

Stephen had met him at the Newbury station and had driven him to his country estate; May had excelled herself with a delicious roast leg of English lamb followed by a homemade fruit pie covered with Devonshire clotted cream. Now sitting comfortably in the deep luxurious armchairs, they were enjoying a fine Port wine and smoking Stephen's large and very expensive Havana cigars.

'I'll start with Annie—as you know we did a deal with Annie; we released her from our detention centre because we needed her to act as a cover for you. Acting as your new wife, she was able to help us in tracking down the paedophile organisation.'

'Afterwards we were allowing her to return back to Israel, so we thought. At the same time, we decided to inform our counterparts in the Israeli Secret Service of her detention by us for the last eighteen months, a lenient punishment for someone infiltrating a section of the War Office. We took the opportunity to give them a strong warning not to try that game again.'

'We now know why they never contacted us with regard to her whereabouts.' Stephen paused to relight his cigar. 'They told us that they had never heard of her.'

Stephen paused again before continuing. 'We know the Israeli Secret Service is in its early stages of development. Anyway, they informed us that as yet they definitely didn't have women out in the field. That I don't believe. Also they couldn't help making a few caustic remarks regarding the efficiency of our Secret Service.'

'Wow, Stephen that must have been very embarrassing for the Department.'

'I'm afraid so; that girl Annie was so convincing that no one got around to checking her story, but also at that time we didn't want the Israelis to know that we were holding her.' Stephen groaned. 'I now have to find out who was responsible for getting her into the War Office and for what purpose.'

'I can answer that one for you, Stephen.' Marçel cut in brightly. 'I really thought you would have known her background. Having murdered the *Comtesse* and the father of her child, Annie, the General decided to adopt Annie. He put her into a convent to be educated and cared for by the nuns. When she became old enough, he sent her to a finishing school in Switzerland and then from there, she went on to Israel where she was trained, for the sole purpose of using her to further his criminal activities.'

'Oh, my God!' Stephen groaned.

'The General managed to get her into the War Office where she would be in a position to pass him information regarding any large government movements of gold, etcetera, and she would also to be able to warn him in case she discovered Interpol getting too close to his activities.'

For a moment, Stephen just sat speechless.

'This infiltration is even worse than I realised. Heads will certainly fall over this.'

'And that's not all, Stephen. Annie will inherit the *Château* and so will now be the *Comtesse*. The General intended to marry Annie and then murder her, so that he could then claim ownership of the *Château* and all of *Comtesse's* assets.'

Marçel picked up the decanter from the sideboard and topped up their glasses.

'This all came out when the General was threatening to kill us and that's when Annie discovered who her parents were. She would have killed the bastard right then if she hadn't been trussed up at the time.'

'Why are you only just telling me now? You didn't mention all this when we were at the *Château!*' Stephen demanded.

'I thought you knew all about Annie. Anyway I reckoned she had been through enough that day and I thought she needed time to get used to the shock of discovering that her parents had been murdered and she was now the *Comtesse*.'

Stephen sat silent for a while before continuing, 'I could not believe it when André called from Bordeaux, to say that the General, when taken before a Magistrate, was given bail. He apparently offered to pay two million francs, which was accepted by the Magistrate. André is furious and is sure the Magistrate must have received a kickback from the General. And now the General has flown the coop.'

'Oh, my God; then all our work has been for nothing, Stephen.' He paused for a moment. 'Do you think this is why Annie and the children have also gone missing? They are certainly in danger from him and if so, where do we go from here?'

'There are two possibilities. Either Annie has been told the General is on the loose and realising he would be coming after her, she decided to go into hiding with the children, or the General has kidnapped them and will no doubt try to get them out of the country. This I think is more likely.'

'We—that is you, Marçel—have got to track them down and when found, the General must be quietly eliminated.'

Stephen finished his Port and headed for the staircase. 'So in the morning, Marçel, you will have to go back to France and look for them; kill the General and quietly hand Annie and the children back to the French authorities. I don't want my Minister finding out about all these unfortunate and embarrassing events.'

'Yours is the blue room, Marçel. Pleasant dreams. We will decide how to handle all this over breakfast at eight-thirty—sharp. Good night.'

Marçel poured himself another drink and returned to the armchair. His mind wandered over the events of the last few weeks. He had been attracted to Annie, and had fallen in love with her. They had gone to bed and made love, before and during their pretend marriage; he had to admit that during that time he had found Annie most attractive but he was glad that it was only a fabricated marriage. She was really not his type.

But now he had to find them and he would have no hesitation in killing the General It was a duty he must perform and it was one that he knew he would enjoy. He had no problem killing people when they were such a menace to society.

Marçel woke to the delicious smell of fried bacon. He hurried downstairs and joined Stephen in the dining room. May had prepared a full English breakfast; Marçel lifted the silver dish lids and helped himself to a selection of bacon, kidney, black pudding, scrambled egg and tomatoes.

'God, where on earth do you put all that food, Marçel?'

'When May goes to so much trouble I feel I have to try a bit of everything. Anyway, I need to build up my strength to find Annie and the children and to hunt down that monster. Oh, I can hear your phone ringing in the library.'

Stephen hurried off to take the call and returned a few minutes later grinning like a Cheshire cat.

'That was André. You won't be going to France after all. The children have been found unharmed. They were wandering along the beach last night at the small fishing town called Port Vendres, which is on the south western end of the French Mediterranean coast. It looks as if they were abandoned a short distance before the General and Annie reached the French-Spanish border.'

Marçel gave a sigh of relief. 'Thank God for that, the poor little devils. This will make our job much easier. The General must be holding Annie hostage, and we know he won't hesitate to kill her to save his skin.'

'André is a first class policeman, Marçel. When the General was released on bail, André followed him back to the castle. Two hours later he drove his Mercedes out of the castle courtyard and headed for the village. He was driving so fast the police car lost him. He probably turned off the main road then doubled back and headed in the opposite direction.'

'That was a bit of bad luck, Stephen. I wonder where they were heading; the roads are all in pretty poor shape in that area.'

'Anyway,' Stephen continued impatiently. 'André returned to the castle and searched through a pile of half-burnt paperwork. He'd left in such a hurry he had not had time to destroy everything. André discovered that the General had a pile of blank false Moroccan passports. So André returned to the village and put pressure on the barman at the *café*, which French policeman are experts at doing, and found out that the General has a house in Menorca and that he keeps a large motor yacht moored at Barcelona, Spain, which he uses whenever he visits his house in Menorca.'

'It looks as if he intended to use the yacht to take them to Morocco. Maybe you can organise an air search in that part of the Mediterranean?' Marçel asked eagerly.

'No need for that now, Marçel. They are both dead.'

'Good God, Stephen, what happened?'

'André put out an alert to the police in Perpignan, the most southerly French town and also to the tiny state of Andorra, which is on the Spanish border. Later that day, that was yesterday evening—they were spotted driving through Perpignan and heading for the coast road; this meant they would have to travel on a winding mountain road to get to the Spanish border. A police car was waiting for them at Banyuls, a small town at the start of this dangerous mountain road; they had already dumped the children and were driving very fast when they passed the waiting police car.

'André told me that when they realised they were being pursued by the police car, the General used all his extra power to get away from them. The road had a series of sharp bends. Predictably, they met a truck heading towards them on one of these tight bends. The horrified driver of the truck watched as they drove straight over the edge of the road and plunged down onto the rocks below.

'As the truck driver got out of his cab, there was a loud explosion. When he and the two policemen leaned over the low wall, they saw a ball of flame. It devoured the car and its occupants.'

Marçel got up from the table and stood looking out of the window. 'Poor Annie. I expect she traded her life for the release of the kids.' He sighed. 'What a horrible way to go … She's had a short and sad life and now, such a tragic end. I suppose there is still some justice in the world; that was a very appropriate end for an evil monster.'

Stephen sat at the table, a satisfied smile on his face, which irritated Marçel.

'Well done to André. That's solved a few problems for you, Stephen, and I bet the Minister will never know the truth about this whole affair.'

Marçel was feeling depressed. 'I think I will go back to Jersey this morning if you don't mind, Stephen.'

'You don't have to go, Marçel.' He smiled. 'Just think of all the poor little children's lives that might be saved now that the General's dead. Annie was a brave girl; she gave her young life for the children, I'm sure that now she will be joining her parents and will be happy in heaven. Annie was a lovely girl.'

The express train to London was just about to leave; Stephen vigorously shook Marçel's hand.

'Time to move on, Marçel. You must start looking for another woman; it's time you got yourself a wife and settled down, my boy. Besides you will need someone to share that castle in Portugal with you.'

'I'm inclined to agree and I think I might already have someone in mind.'

Chapter 14

Three hours later the taxi dropped Marçel off at his front gate. It was a lovely warm sunny day and he walked around the side of the cottage to the large walled-in garden. Marçel noticed a deckchair in the centre of the lawn. He walked quietly across the lawn and peeped over the back of the chair.

'Oh—oh, my God! Mr Marçel, sir.' Mary struggled to find the newspaper to cover her nakedness; Marçel was just a little too quick for her and put one foot on the paper.

'Mary, do I have to keep telling you? I'm Marçel to you, and don't worry, I'm used to seeing naked girls; but not usually in my garden!' He laughed.

Mary tried to get up with one arm across her breasts, and the other shielding her lower part. She gave up, sinking back into the deckchair giggling.

'Marçel, you're the first man to see my naked body and strangely I don't seem to mind. I think perhaps an innermost desire has prompted me to expose myself to you …' she laughed.

Marçel sat on the thick grass beside her, gazing with an appreciative eye at her slim, well-formed body. 'I consider myself very lucky, and honoured, to see a young lady with such lovely figure. It fits well with the lovely natural person that lives inside it.'

'Pass me the towel that you kicked out of my reach and help me up, Marçel.' She smiled.

Marçel draped the towel around her lower half, bent down and eased her up from the deckchair. At the same time, he slipped his other arm around her bringing her close to him; he kissed her lightly on the lips. Mary leaned back, her expression was serious as she gazed into his eyes. She put her hand behind his neck and pulled him down to her waiting lips. Their passionate kiss seemed to go on forever. Mary, standing on her toes, pressed her body against his, delightfully almost knocking him off balance. They finally separated, leaning back and holding each other's hands, breathing heavily and smiling as they looked into each other's eyes. Their hearts were racing as they realised just how much that kiss had meant to both of them.

'I'll go and make some tea, Marçel.' She giggled. 'Better put some clothes on. I'm afraid I left them up in the spare room.'

Marçel held Mary's hand as they walked back into the cottage, passing through the kitchen and into the lounge. Marçel watched Mary climb the narrow staircase. She was nearly at the top when she turned and looked down at him. 'You can come and watch me dress if you like.' She realised her forwardness but couldn't help herself; that kiss had awakened such strong feelings in her.

Marçel rushed up the stairs two at a time and followed Mary into the spare bedroom laughing as they both flung themselves onto the bed.

Instead of Mary getting dressed, she slowly helped Marçel undress. Silence reigned over the cottage for the rest of the afternoon.

It was almost dark when they finally woke up still wrapped in each other's arms.

'You were a virgin and you gave yourself to me,' he whispered. Mary nodded. He kissed her on the tip of her nose. 'I claim you as mine now. I know that I am going to love you forever.' He gently nibbled her ear and kissed her on her neck. 'And to think you have been here in my cottage, living under my nose all this time and I have only just found you.'

Mary sat up and ran her fingers through Marçel's thick dark hair. 'I have known for a long time that I love you, Marçel. But I never dreamed that you would one day want to make love to me. I feel that after this afternoon, we really are bonded to each other. I know that's silly because you will find someone far more sophisticated than me. I'm just not in your class, Marçel.' Mary slipped on her slacks and a sweater and went down to the kitchen to make tea.

'That class crap went out years ago, Mary!' Marçel shouted as he followed her downstairs to the kitchen. 'You finished your education—I didn't. Your parents are farmers, and Jersey farmers are a very special breed of people. So don't ever talk like that again.'

Marçel put his arms around Mary pulling her close to him, her breasts pressing hard against his bare chest. They gazed into each other's eyes. 'I want to take you out to dinner tonight and I think you should stay over.'

'I'll have to go home to change and tell my parents I'm staying the night in the cottage,' she whispered back. 'As you know, they are very conservative and will worry about me.' She hesitated. 'Would you like to meet them?'

'I'll take you there in the car. I should have met them a long time ago, I know.' Mary laughed. 'You know what you are letting yourself into, Marçel?

To them, that's asking for their daughter's hand.' She allowed their lips to come together and kissed him lightly. 'Don't worry, Marçel, I will let you off the hook. Dad hasn't got a shotgun. I'll tell them you are taking me out to dinner as a reward for my good services.' She laughed.

John and Enid Le Vicomier were just sitting down to high tea when Mary and Marçel burst in on them. They both jumped up in surprise, John spilling tea on the clean tablecloth.

'Mum, Dad, I've finally brought my boss Marçel to meet you. He wants to take me out to dinner as a reward for looking after him at his cottage.'

There was slight pause.

'Actually Mr Le Vicomier, I've come to ask you for your daughter's hand in marriage.'

There was a moment of shocked silence, John's mouth dropped open and Enid's face lit up as she moved over to embrace her daughter.

'Marçel—you haven't asked me yet, you idiot!' She laughed. 'Do you really know what you've just said?'

'Mary, will you marry me?' He took her two hands and gazed into her eyes. 'Please.'

Still slightly shocked at this sudden event, John stepped over and shook Marçel's hand. 'Just how long has this been going on, Marçel?'

'I think we have both known for some time,' he lied, smiling.

'Well I shall be most pleased to have you as a son-in law so now I can finally get rid of the girl!' He laughed.

Enid put her arms around Marçel and kissed him lightly on both cheeks. 'I shan't be losing my daughter; I will now be gaining a lovely son.' She smiled. 'So when do you young things intend to get married?'

'I don't think—'

Marçel interrupted. 'I will talk to the Rector tomorrow and arrange to have the wedding in the parish church as soon as possible.'

'That's what I like to hear; get the ploughing done while the sun shines and then plant the seeds and wait for a good harvest!' John laughed.

'Dad … you really are disgusting. Come on, Marçel; take me out to dinner while I'm still in shock.'

Mary ran quickly upstairs, filled a bag with clothes and her makeup. Downstairs she found Marçel having an animated conversation with her parents; she dragged him away to his car and they quickly returned to the cottage.

That night, over a candlelight dinner, Marçel formally proposed to Mary and she accepted. They sat up late into the night discussing their plans for the future and decided that they would go into St Helier the next morning to buy an engagement ring.

'I know you have quite a history, Marçel, and you have already had lots of women in your life. Please don't ever let me down.'

'You are quite right, Mary. I've had lots of experience with lovely women and some wicked evil men; I used to think I could never settle down with a woman after all the dreadful things I have done in the last few years. But now, I know I have found my woman and I promise you, Mary, I will dedicate the rest of my life to you.'

'I guess because I'm so crazy about you, Marçel, I'm prepared to accept your strange and secretive past life. My love for you is strong and I accept you for who you are *now* and I never want to know about your past life.'

'Thank God for that!'

'Stop laughing and take me home. I'm sleeping at the farm tonight and in the morning I will come to the cottage and continue my housekeeping job until we get married! Then you can support me, darling. I'll be ready to go into St Helier with you at midday.'

Marçel woke up the following morning at five. He quickly dressed and decided to take a walk along the cliff paths that ran almost the whole length of Jersey's north coast. It was a bright sunny morning as he strode along the cliff path; heather and wild ferns ran all the way up from the footpath to the top of the cliffs and on the other side of the footpath, a sharp drop of several hundred feet of granite rock ran all away down to the deep blue sea.

Marçel's thoughts were mixed—he knew he had finally found the woman that he wanted to share the rest of his life with and yet it had all happened so quickly. For the last two years he had watched her and had admired her in many small ways; the way she presented herself, always neatly dressed, cheerful, friendly but not at all pushy. He had noticed how she had cared for the cottage as if it were her own, and had always gone out of her way to make sure that everything was there to make him comfortable when he returned after being away for some time.

She had accepted the wage that he had first offered her and had never asked him for a raise, although she was doing far more than when he had first asked her to take care of the cottage. This told him a lot about her character.

Finding her naked in the garden, and then the calm way in which she had handled it, had not only turned him on, but had made him realise just what a strong and lovely character she had. Mary had offered herself to him and he had taken her, knowing that they had both found the partner of their dreams. They had loved and bonded themselves together in that one afternoon.

For the last few years, Marçel had decided that in view of all his activities in France and Portugal, he would never be able to marry a woman after having so much blood on his hands. Mary must have realised that he had an unsavoury history of an active involvement in undercover dealings that entailed life and death situations. Yet she had said, and he knew that she meant it, that she never wanted to know about his past activities in the war and the aftermath.

Marçel wondered how he was going to cope with getting married in a church. He had not entered a church since before the day he had been raped by the two soldiers of the occupation force in Jersey back in 1943. Since then he had killed, and caused the death of so many people. How would God receive him when he entered the church to get married? Would God forgive him for all these killings? He had not had any religious thoughts in these last few years and realised that now to think this way, he must still have faith in God. The more Marçel thought about it, the more he realised that all these years he had been protected. He had never killed in anger or for personal gain, but he had killed to protect himself and others, and had also killed people who were a menace to society and who really deserved to die. Marçel decided that he must talk to the minister at the church where they were to be married.

He took the footpath that led from the cliff path to the village and the Parish Church. As he was walked through the churchyard, past some of the old tombstones, he noticed that the door to the church was open.

Stepping into to the semi-darkness of the Parish church, Marçel looked up admiring the arched granite ceiling of the old church. A soft light came filtering through from the small stained-glass windows that ran down both sides of the church. At the far end of the church, he noticed the minister kneeling in front of the decorated altar, in the dim wavering light emanating from the four large candles.

Marçel walked down the smooth, worn paving stones to the front pew and sat down. He bent forward and tried to pray. His mind froze. He simply couldn't remember any of the prayers he had been taught as a small boy. This was rejection.

Marçel sat there, feeling the hot tears running down his face.

He was about to get up and leave the church when he felt a hand on his shoulder. He looked up—the elderly minister was standing over him.

'What brings you to my church so early in the morning, young man?'

Marçel pulled a handkerchief from his pocket and wiped away the tears on his face. 'I'm so sorry, sir. My name is Marçel Beaumont; I came here because I have just become engaged to the daughter of a local farmer and I wanted to ask you if you could marry us in your church.'

'What is the young lady's name if I may ask? I must say you don't seem too happy about it.' He smiled.

'Mary Le Vicomier. We would like to get married as soon as possible as we are going to live in Portugal and run a winery there.'

'Ah, yes Mary, a lovely girl. She deserves a good man and Enid and John are very good people, who support this church.' The minister sat down beside Marçel. 'You're the young man that lives in the cottage near their farm. So why are you so upset, Marçel? This is a country Parish where there are few secrets.' He paused for a moment. 'I do know a little about you. You were involved with the poor girl who drowned off St Catherine's breakwater. I also know about your experience in 1943 when everyone here believed you were killed in France by the *Gestapo*. Your parents were taken to Germany at the time and we believe that they both died in Auschwitz.' He took Marçel's hand. 'Don't worry; your tragic past is safe with me. I know you fought with the *résistance* in France. I can imagine the hell you must have experienced in the last few years.'

Marçel was taken aback. 'But how did you find out about me? I have taken great pains to conceal my changed identity and my childhood in Jersey.'

'We have a mutual friend; Stephen and I were at school together and he told me a little about you, I was able to piece together your identity from what I already knew. I have spent some time trying to find out what happened to several other Jersey people sent to Germany in the occupation, who never returned. I always knew that you had escaped and I was sure that you were still alive.

'I have not prayed to God since 1943, Father. I came here with blood on my hands to pray and to ask God for forgiveness for all the bad things I did. When I tried to pray nothing came out. My mind went completely blank. Is this a message from God?'

'No, my son.' He smiled, putting his arm on Marçel's shoulder. 'Our God is all forgiving. Come and pray with me and it will all gradually come back to you.'

Thirty minutes later, they came out of the church together. They shook hands.

'So that's settled, Marçel, a fortnight Saturday at eleven pm. And don't be late.' They both laughed.

'Thank you, sir; I feel I am now ready to start a fresh life.'

Marçel hurried back to the cottage. He returned to the smell of fried bacon; picking up Mary in his arms, he swung her around in a circle, gave her a bear hug, kissing her until they were both completely out of breath. They sat down and devoured two large platefuls of fried bacon and eggs after which they went shopping for the finest diamond ring Marçel could find in St Helier's well-stocked jewellery shops.

Two weeks later Marçel and Mary married in the lovely old parish church. Stephen was Marçel's best man. He had come over to the cottage in Jersey with May his housekeeper; they were to be the only friends of the groom at the wedding. May insisted on taking over Mary's job until after the wedding.

The reception was at Mary's parent's farm in the large low-ceiling storeroom next to the large farm kitchen. The decorated centrepiece was the old granite cider press, common in many of the old farmhouses in Jersey. It was a typical farm wedding, with all Mary's friends and farmer relatives enjoying themselves as only farming people can. The wives had prepared all the food, and Uncle Sam had supplied a cask of his very best cider, plus several bottles of home-brewed Calvados to get the party going.

Mary and Marçel quietly slipped away in the evening and were driven to the airport and their waiting aeroplane. Forty-five minutes later, they were at Stephen's villa in Dinard. In the backyard, they found Stephen's wedding present to them; a shining new red MG sports car.

It was early July when Mary and Marçel set off on their honeymoon; Mary had never been outside of Jersey, so they decided to take advantage of the warm summer weather to tour southern Europe before finally driving down to the castle in Portugal.

They enjoyed a few days in Paris and two weeks in Switzerland, which they found interesting and exciting, with still a little snow on some of the mountain passes. At Brig, they drove through the Simplon Pass into northern Italy and finally arrived at Milan. Here in the much warmer climate, they spent weeks just lapping up the wonderful Italian culture. Years later, when Marçel looked back, he remembered they had been some of the happiest days of their lives. Hand in hand, they had explored all the small towns and remote villages in Italy, some still bearing the scars and damage from the retreating German army.

In Venice, Milan, Rome and Florence they spent time exploring all the old buildings and museums. Every day Mary was like a happy excited child, going from one cultural treasure to another. Every night she became a passionate loving woman. Marçel, who had always been haunted by the memory of the young girl he had met and then tragically lost in France in 1944, realised that in Mary he had found that very same girl.

It was early September when they finally passed through the old stone archway—the entrance to the castle's large estate. Marçel was horrified to see the state of the grape vines—in some parts the weeds had grown so high that it was almost impossible to see them.

When they arrived at the sheds where they used to keep the tractors and all the farm equipment, he realised that there had been a fire and several of the buildings had been destroyed. He decided to continue on and come back later to inspect the damage; Marçel was impatient to show Mary the impressive old castle.

They continued down the tree-lined avenue and arrived at the castle gates only to find, a burnt-out and blackened ruin.

All that was left standing of the old castle and dwelling house were the outer walls and even those had collapsed in several places, leaving large gaps in the once-high walls. The grassland, scrubs and bushes that surrounded the old castle were also badly scorched by the enormous heat generated from the burning castle.

They got out of their car and stood in silence, just staring at all their future hopes, now just a tangled burnt-out pile of rubble.

'I just can't believe what I'm seeing, Mary. That was not just an ordinary fire.' He took Mary's hand. 'A normal fire wouldn't damage a stone castle as badly as this. Someone has deliberately set out to destroy the castle and our future together, rebuilding the winery.'

At that moment a police car sped down the driveway; pulling up alongside them and one of his old friends, Chief of Police Cardoso, got out of the car, came over and shook hands with them both.

'I am so sorry, Marçel. We have all been looking forward to you coming back to reopen the winery and live amongst us all again in Aveiro.' He turned to look at the still smouldering remains of the castle. 'And now you have lost everything.'

'What has happened, Cardoso? Who could have done this to us?'

'You have some very powerful enemies, my friend. This happened two

411

nights ago. People miles away heard the explosions. It was just before midnight, and then the fire lit up the sky. It lasted for a very long time.'

They walked through the gap that had been the archway into the large inner square; the house was just a pile of still-smouldering ash and stones. They noticed that there were several large gaps in the outer walls which could only have been accomplished with a large amount of explosives.

Marçel and Cardoso were talking in Portuguese. Mary after a quick look around wandered off. Sitting by the castle jetty, she watched the large flocks of birds that inhabited the vast marshland area of the Ria.

'Cardoso, have you any idea who might have been involved in the blowing up and the burning of our castle? Only someone with access to a lot of explosives would be capable of doing this sort of damage.'

Cardoso put his arm around Marçel's shoulder. 'My friend, this could be political. Your bank manager friend, Alfonso Biadassaris, was arrested last week, charged with subversion. I know Alfonso has strong political views, but he has always kept them to himself. I think someone high up put pressure on him to persuade you not to return to the castle. When he refused, their only option was to destroy your castle.' Cardoso bent down to look at one of the old castle door hinges.

'Marçel, do you remember the Petisqueira Bar in Aveiro?'

'That's one bar we'll never forget, Cardoso, especially the night you arrested us all for creating a disturbance; instead we persuaded you to join us that night and we all got very drunk.'

'Well, one of my contacts told me that three nights ago, a group of men who were well-known Nazis from that still very active cell in Porto, were a bit drunk and boasting that they were going to get revenge on someone who had recently caused the death of one of their very important Nazi leaders in France.'

'That was me, Cardoso; I helped cause the death of their man in France. This man, amongst other things, was a paedophile and deserved to die.'

'Well, as there is still a strong Nazi influence in our Government, someone high up must have supplied these men with their explosives.'

Marçel turned and for a moment stared into Cardoso's eyes. Cardoso stared back without blinking and then he started to laugh. Marçel knew this man was an honest man and was not in any way involved in this business. 'I know you have always hated the Nazis. So where do we go from here, Cardoso?'

'Go home, Marçel. It would be foolish to try to nail these people. Much as I would like you to come back to live amongst us, you are up against our present political system. We are expecting a dramatic change in the next five years in terms of the way we are governed, but for now, Marçel, go back to your home in Jersey, my friend. Maybe it will be possible for you to return in a few years' time.'

'Is there anything I can do for Alfonso? How about his family?'

'His wife and two kids have gone to stay with cousins in a small mountain village. They will keep Alfonso in prison for a while, but once they know you are not coming back to Portugal, he will probably be released. Just stay away from them; you could only make things worse for the family.'

Marçel kicked a stone into the still-smouldering debris. 'We did kill some of the Porto Nazis before we left. I suppose they are still angry about that as well.'

'No one can be trusted in this country; the 'PIAD' Secret Service are everywhere. A lot of us knew what you were doing when you were living here, but we had to turn a blind eye to all your executions. The Nazi party is very strong around here at present.'

They returned to the parked cars and were joined by Mary.

'I am so sorry, *Senhora*, that we had to meet in these unfortunate circumstances. But now I must now return to the police station.' Cardoso shook their hands and got back into his car.

'What are you two going to do, Marçel?'

Marçel put his arms around Mary holding her close to him. 'It's still early; we are going to head straight back to France, Cardoso. When your people let Alfonso out of prison, we will send him instructions to sell the winery and the pile of black stones that goes with it. *Arté logo*, Cardoso.'

'I've been expecting this, Marçel. You now have a lovely wife and there is a little boy in Australia waiting for his father to come and make a home for the three of you. Helga and Mick will certainly be looking forward to you joining them in the 'lucky-country'. Your idea to buy a suitable farm and grow grapes and the four of you setting up a partnership to run a winery is excellent.'

Stephen leaned back in his office chair, blowing perfect smoke rings from his cigar. A tap at the door and his secretary came in and handed him a sheet of paper; she gave Mary and Marçel a warm smile and then kissed Mary on the cheeks.

'Congratulations. You will have your hands full taming that tiger, Mary, but he really is a sweetie. I just wish he was mine, but unfortunately I'm old enough to be his mum.' She laughed and returned to the outer office.

'I hope we are going to track down the Nazi bastards who destroyed my castle before we go to Australia, Stephen.'

Stephen waved the piece of paper that he was holding. 'This is from my Minister, Marçel. We have been given strict instructions not to pursue this matter. Apparently several top politicians in Portugal and my minister in London are involved in a missing gold scandal and as the British government is heavily committed at present setting up important trade deals with Portugal, they cannot afford to have them compromised by us.' He sighed. 'We certainly don't want our past activities at the castle revealed. You were certainly very lucky that our masters delayed the settlement of the castle—now they will have to bear the loss instead of you!'

Stephen made several more perfect smoke rings. 'I think the sooner you leave for Australia the better. There are still people here who want to destroy you for breaking up their organisation; and don't you forget, you now have your wife Mary to protect.'

Several weeks later, with the Jersey cottage sold and their furniture already on its way to their new life in Australia they were all, including May, sitting back in Stephen's spacious lounge after having consumed one of May's special roasts and drinking one of Stephen's very treasured Port wines.

Marçel leaned forward eagerly in his chair.

'I believe it will work very well. With Mick's farming experience, he will be the grape grower, and with my knowledge of making and marketing wines, we will make a good partnership. But there is just one condition, Stephen. We will expect you to come to stay with us to officially open our first bottle of wine.'

'We'll all be sad to lose you from the service, Marçel, but you have served your country very well in the last few years and you certainly deserve your early retirement.'

The following morning Stephen and May took Mary and Marçel down to the Southampton docks. Their luggage had already been delivered to the ship. After numerous kisses, handshakes and a few tears, the couple was escorted to their first class cabin and shortly after, their ship pulled away from the dock and sailed for Australia.

PART TWO

Chapter 15

It took almost a year for Mary and Marçel, having completed an extended tour of Australia, to find and settle in to a small farm north of Cessnock on the central coast of New South Wales. There were already several well-established vineries in the Hunter Valley. They realised that the soil and conditions were ideal for growing grapes; in fact they found that the soil and climate were very similar to the winery they had left behind in Portugal.

Mick and Helga, having sold their livestock and farm in the hills near Mount Pleasant, north of Brisbane, for an excellent price, and with money in the bank, also moved down to the Cessnock property. Helga and Mary got on extremely well and were happy to have each other's company. The two boys growing up together were inseparable and now all Peter's dreams had come true; his dad and step-mum were living together with Helga and Mick.

The first thing they did was build a barn large enough to hold Mick and Helga's furniture and most of Mick's farm equipment, which he had collected during his last few years of profitable farming.

By 1967, Marçel and Mick had an established winery and were producing their own brands of wine. They had built two fine houses on the land and were rapidly expanding their vine acreage in order to keep pace with the burgeoning wine industry in Australia at the time.

When they were old enough, the two firm friends Peter and Michael, returned to England and were both accepted at Oxford University, where they were not learning a great deal, but having a whale of a time. Michael, having decided on a career in the army, trained at Sandhurst and spent the next few years travelling to various hot spots around the world until finally joining his father in the now extensive wine business. Peter, after having been politely asked to leave the Communist Party in Oxford, spent time exploring Europe. He became fluent in French, German, Italian and Spanish before taking up an appointment in the Foreign Office in London.

Marçel and Mary spent many happy years together in Australia, working hard at the winery but often taking long holidays together in the quiet seasons. Their strong friendship with Mick and Helga proved to be a lasting one and they often travelled together to shows and sporting events in Sydney over the years.

Disaster struck in 1985.

Peter had returned to Australia on one of his rare trips to visit his parents and Michael, Helga and Mick. It was soon apparent that Peter was drinking far too much and was rather moody. He seemed to have a lot on his mind.

Marçel guessed that Peter was under considerable pressure from his department in London, but Peter refused to talk to Marçel about his problems. Marçel thought it best just simply to give him some time to unwind a little, before he broached the subject again.

Then one day, seemingly in a better mood, Peter produced tickets for the Opera in Sydney. Unfortunately, Marçel was chairing a meeting in Cessnock that evening and couldn't go along. He knew Mary was keen to see the Opera so he insisted that Peter and Mary go without him. So, they drove into Sydney that afternoon and decided to return to the winery that night after the Opera.

They were just about to pass through Hornsby, north of Sydney, when Peter slowed down and pulled in at a coffee shop. After having a warm discussion about the opera which they had both really enjoyed, Peter took Mary's hand. 'Mum, I expect you have been wondering why I came back and have been such a misery these last few days.'

'I guessed that there was some sort of problem, Peter. You seem to be drinking a lot more than usual and you seem so sad.' She held both of his hands. 'You don't have to tell me, Peter dear, but if I can help in any way.'

'I am in deep trouble—but I don't want Dad to know; he just wouldn't understand.'

'I'm sure you are very wrong about that. Your father is very understanding and he loves you very much.'

'I have serious girl trouble, Mum. I'm in love with a wonderful girl. Unfortunately, she is on the 'other side' and on two occasions I have talked too much to her. This has eventually got back to my department and is about to dramatically end my career in the diplomatic service.'

Mary noticed the tears in Peter's eyes.

'The trouble is I still love her, but I'm told that if I go over to Russia, my passport will be annulled and I won't be able to return to Britain. I really don't know what to do.'

'Are you quite sure the girl loves you? It seems to me that if she has betrayed your confidence on two occasions; maybe you should just be a little cautious and make sure she really wants you.'

'I know what you are saying; love does make one irrational.'

'Why don't we talk to your dad when we get back; I'm sure he'll still be awake and he will understand and support you in whatever you decide.'

'Thanks, Mum, you are always the sensible one of the family. Let's get back home as quickly as possible.'

At four the next morning, Marçel was sleeping when the telephone rang.

Marçel had stumbled to the phone in a panic, barking his shin on the coffee table as he hurried to reach the source of the sound. It had taken a while for Marçel to grasp what the person on the phone was saying to him and he had to ask them to repeat themselves twice. With trembling knees and heart beating a tattoo in his chest, Marçel heard, as if in a nightmare, that shortly after crossing the Hawkesbury River, the Holden motorcar that Peter and Mary had been travelling in had been hit by a heavy truck. It had strayed across the road and right into the path of the Holden, instantly killing the two people in the world he loved more than life itself.

Marçel remained in a state of shock for the following few days leading up to Mary and Peter's funerals. Fortunately for Marçel, Mick and Helga took over and made all the arrangements for the return of the bodies and the double funeral. Marçel was beside himself; unable to function and feeling as though he would rather be dead as well; lying next to them.

For the next eight weeks, Marçel locked himself away in his house only to come out occasionally to collect more wine from the store. Every day Helga called on him and left food for him on the veranda but Marçel steadfastly refused to talk to anyone, preferring his cold and now-empty world.

Mick and Helga were sitting in the main office having their morning tea one day when Marçel, looking old and haggard, walked into the office.

'I have to thank you, my dear old friends, for all you have done.' He went and sat at his desk where over the last few years he and Mick had planned and built up their successful wine business. 'I'm sorry. It was such a terrible shock that I was quite unable to handle the situation. Thank God you were both here to take charge.'

Unsure of Marçel's reaction, they both mumbled their sympathy to him.

'My friends,' he forced a smile, 'I have decided to retire and move up to Queensland. There are too many memories here. I have to get away … I'm giving you all my shares in the business; as you know I am a wealthy man in my own right, so I would rather you have my shares, and when you retire Michael will be secure and able to continue to expand the winery.'

Helga moved over to Marçel and put her arms around him.

'You don't have to do this, Marçel. Please stay here in your house. I promise I will always look after you.' She started to cry.

Marçel stood up, and bending down, gave Helga a long and warm kiss. 'There are far too many memories here, Helga dear. When I am finally settled you must come and visit me. The time has come to start a new life. You can tell Michael he can move into my house. It will be his house now—that's as soon as you have disposed of my furniture and all my old and happy memories.'

'When do you intend to move on, Marçel?'

'Right now, Mick. My new car has just been delivered and my suitcases are already loaded.'

He embraced them both and then turned for the door. 'Please don't come out—I'll be in touch just as soon as I find a suitable place somewhere on the coast. I'll always love you both.' He slipped out, gently closing the door behind him.

Mick held a sobbing Helga in his arms as they watched the Ford disappear up the gravel driveway.

Chapter 16

Many years had passed by. Marçel had found himself a small house on the Gold Coast waterfront. He joined the local sailing club, bought himself a sailing boat and in between racing his boat, fishing, exploring the waterways and swimming, he joined a sports club determined to keep himself fit, and taught a martial art to students at one of the Gold Coast universities.

In May of 2005, Marçel received a letter from Nelson Biadassaris.

Dear Mr Beaumont,

I am writing to you as suggested by my father Alfonso Biadassaris, whom you knew many years ago in Portugal when he was your bank manager in Aveiro. He is an old man now, but he sincerely believes that you are the only person in the world who could help me and my family in our present predicament. I believe you told my father many years ago that if he ever needed help he was to call on you. I only call on you now, as the situation here at present is desperate for my family.

We are all still living at Aveiro in Portugal. If you feel you are able to travel over to us here in Aveiro, we would be most grateful.

Please forgive me for the intrusion into your life. If you are unable to help us at this time, I will fully understand. If you decide to come to us, you can contact me at the Esquadra de polici, Aveiro.

Yours sincerely,
Nelson Biadassaris.

Ever since Marçel's train journey from Brisbane to the Gold Coast in 2000, when a small incident, involving several badly-behaved boys on the train, had brought back all the memories of his own behaviour when he was sixteen years old, Marçel's mind had kept going back over the events that had taken place all those years ago.

It had all started when, at the age of sixteen, on the Island of Jersey while occupied by the German forces, he had been brutally raped, arrested by the *Wehrmacht* and then sent under escort to Paris for interrogation and certain execution. A series of events then took place that changed his life forever.

And now, years later, Marçel was to finally satisfy his strong urge to return to Portugal, prompted by an urgent call for help from the son of his old friend in Aveiro. He realised to receive a call for help from such normally independent people; something very serious must be happening to the Biadassaris family. So, without a second thought he caught the first available flight to Madrid and then flew on to Porto in Portugal.

The letter from Nelson had prompted him to go and revisit the remains of the castle, and the surrounding countryside in Portugal where, during that period from 1943 to 1961, so many dramatic events had taken place both in Portugal and France.

So now he had finally arrived back in Portugal. At the tender age of seventy-five, sporting a strong but greying beard and bushy eyebrows, he still retained a good head of hair. Marçel was taking the train journey from Porto to Aveiro and was about to visit all the places where life had been so harsh for many people.

As the express train sped down to Aveiro, Marçel couldn't believe that so many changes could have occurred in this country that had once been so poor and repressed in the forties and fifties. He was very pleased to see that little had changed in the old part of Porto, but what he did notice was the change in the Portuguese people. In the past they had been very downtrodden after having lived under a harsh dictatorship for so many years. Now at last they were able to talk openly, without fear of arrest and were obviously so much happier in their newfound democracy.

Since joining the European Union, many of the old trains had been replaced by fast modern trains. New railway stations had been constructed to serve all the recently built industrial estates that now lined the railway system. Some of the tiny villages had now become thriving towns, some with rows of high-rise apartment blocks spreading out in all directions.

Arriving at Aveiro, Marçel found a brand new station still under construction. He took the lift up to street level and stepped out into the brilliant morning sunshine.

The front wall of the station still had large areas of blue and white tiles, each one depicting a part of the life of the town. The tiles had been produced locally and many houses had been adorned with these attractive, carefully-designed patterns.

Marçel decided to walk down the Avenida Lourenco Peixinho, the main street leading down to the town centre. He shouldered his backpack and started the long walk; his hotel was at the far end of the *Avenida*, which had always been the main avenue in Aveiro. Now all the once-empty spaces were filled with modern buildings, mostly apartment blocks and shops.

His hotel was close to a bridge that crossed the central canal. The Hotel Arcada, the fine outstanding building, still looked the same from the outside as he remembered it all those years ago. Before checking into the hotel, Marçel decided to sit on a bench by the side of the canal, to rest his aching hips and knee joints. It had been a long walk, and now he felt his age was beginning to catch up with him, besides which, he was still feeling slightly jet-lagged after his long flight from Australia to Madrid.

For his age, apart from the odd aches and pains, Marçel was extremely fit. This was due to regular exercise, distance swimming at the local swimming pool and regular visits to his judo club. Marçel was quite aware that he was still very capable of defending himself against much younger men.

He closed his eyes and with the warm sun on his back, allowed himself to drift into a light sleep.

He felt a hand on his shoulder. 'Is that really you, Marçel?' He was instantly awake, a legacy from those earlier years.

'Good God, it's my old friend Alfonso Biadassaris. I thought you would have died long ago, especially with a job like yours; always trying to claw back the loans you gave to your customers, the ones that came to you at the bank, cap in hand. But when I received Nelson's letter, I thought I had better come and see what trouble you have got yourself into this time.'

Marçel found that after all these years he was still able to speak fluent Portuguese.

'So you have finally decided to come and visit us, Marçel? Not bringing us more trouble this time, I hope?' He sat down beside Marçel and stretched his tired legs. 'It is good to see you, my friend. I didn't expect to see you again after all these years. I told Nelson that you were the only person that could help us. I was surprised when he told me he had written to you.' Alfonso paused for a moment. 'I am even more surprised that you answered our call for help; and to have come from so far away in such a short time … it's certainly a changed world.'

'Curiosity brought me back, my old friend. As you get older, Alfonso, all the memories come creeping back. Apart from seeing if I am able to help you and Nelson, I wanted to see how time had changed the scenes of my misspent youth. You must be at least eighty-four by now.'

Alfonso laughed. 'Curiosity killed the cat; I'm eighty-seven years old this month. My beloved wife passed on in 1980.'

A small dog ran up to him, sniffed his shoes and ran off to join his well-dressed young mistress. Marçel stared at the woman as she walked away. There was something about her that disturbed him …

Alfonso was talking to him. 'Life was hard under the old regime, Marçel. Now with the dictatorship well behind us, plus our entry into the common market, the future for Portugal is looking good. However there are things happening in certain areas that are still very dangerous for some of us.' He grabbed Marçel's wrist.

'I have a son—his wife and my grandchildren are in great danger. I will arrange for you to meet Nelson. It is better you don't go to the *Esquadra*—there are some in the police service you cannot trust.'

Alfonso stood up, shook Marçel's hand vigorously and started to back away.

'You must excuse me now, Marçel, I have to go to Porto; I am booked into the main hospital there for a few days. I hope you will be staying in Aveiro for a while. Tomorrow night, if you like, I will tell my son Nelson to meet you at the Petisqueira Portuguesa Bar. You and I spent a few good times there in the past.'

'I am too old to get drunk now, my friend, but that will be fine. You behave yourself with all those lovely young nurses. *Adieus até logo*—see you later, Alfonso.'

Late that evening Nelson called Marçel at his hotel. He arranged for them to meet in the Petisqueira Bar at eight the following evening.

Just before eight the next evening, Marçel strolled into the noisy Petisqueira Bar. He noticed how it suddenly became very quiet when he entered and realised that he was being carefully scrutinised. There were four men clustered at the far end of the bar staring at him. He ordered a beer.

'You—*Senhor* Marçel?' the barman snapped at him.

Marçel picked up his beer—he didn't like the barman's tone of voice—and half-emptied his glass before answering.

'Why do you ask?' Marçel stared into the barman's eyes. The barman looked down and started to wipe the bar counter with a dirty cloth. The other four men turned away and started talking amongst themselves.

'*Senhor* Nelson was here. I was to tell you to meet him in the Heartbeat Club at eleven o'clock tonight.'

'You need a clean cloth, barman.' Marçel emptied his glass and walked across the square to the Neptune Restaurant. He sat down at a table near the window and ordered grilled *bacalau* once again, his favourite Portuguese dish that he washed down with a bottle of *Mateuse Rosé*.

Later Marçel wandered down to the canal, admiring all the colourful old fishing boats that were moored three abreast on the side of the canal, before turning up one of the narrow lanes that crisscrossed that part of old Aveiro.

The Heartbeat Club was just a few yards up a narrow lane that ran off a small but busy square. Only a small red sign indicated its presence. Marçel rang the bell alongside the darkened doorway. A face abruptly appeared at the grill and then the door slowly opened. The only light in the small room was coming from several red lights at the back of the bar. Marçel sat down at one of the empty tables scattered around the tiny dance floor. It was eleven-fifteen and there was no sign of Nelson—apart from two powerful-looking men and a girl, standing close together at the bar, and a bored-looking barmaid, the club was empty. The barmaid came out from behind the bar to take his order. Marçel decided to stay with port wine.

The girl, who had been standing with the two men, walked across the dance floor carrying her drink and sat down beside him.

'My name is Cleo; what's yours, *Senhor*?'

'Bill, and don't get any ideas, Cleo. I'm old enough to be your grandfather but I'm just happy to talk to you for a few minutes if you wish.'

Cleo walked back to the bar. Marçel recognised her as the girl with the small dog who had walked by him the day before while he was talking to Alfonso; he also noticed that he was being carefully watched by the two men. Cleo rejoined him carrying two drinks this time. Marçel was careful to 'pay as he went' for his drinks; this was not the sort of place where you allowed yourself to run up a drinks bill. Cleo explained that she was from Brazil and wanted to live in Europe, as these days there was so little work for ambitious girls in Brazil.

She was certainly very attractive, he thought, a tall girl with long black flowing hair and with eyes that turned up at the corners, giving her a slightly oriental look. Cleo's tall slim figure he guessed would even be the envy of some of the top models in Paris. For a brief moment, Marçel wished he was forty years younger.

'You surprise me; I would have thought there was always work for a girl like you.'

She narrowed her eyes at that remark, and then moved closer to him. 'Yes, *Senhor*, but there are not many men like you in Salvador.' She looked into his eyes, a mischievous smile playing on her face. 'And I'm sure the *senhor* has lots of money.'

The two men were still staring at him. Where was Nelson? He was beginning to get the feeling that he might be in danger. Marçel remembered the drill—two or three drinks and then the next one would likely be spiked. 'Excuse me, Cleo; I have to visit the toilets.'

Marçel picked up his third drink and walked across the dance floor. The toilets were next to the entrance. He sensed the two men were watching him and at the last moment he turned towards the exit. A doorman barred his way. He turned to see the two men at the bar heading towards him. Marçel flung the glass of port into the doorman's face. With his left hand he withdrew a small knife from his pocket which he jabbed into the doorman's wrist. 'You'll need to see a doctor pretty quick, son.' The doorman held his wrist as the blood spurted from his severed artery. Marçel quickly slipped out of the door; the two men following close behind. Despite his age, he ran down the narrow lane at full speed, closely followed by the two men. Once into the well-lit square, he noticed that the two men had dropped back, and were returning slowly to the club.

Marçel took a few deep breaths, and then used his handkerchief to carefully wipe the doorman's blood from his hands before heading for the Petisqueira Bar.

There was no sign of the barman when he entered the bar, instead there was a fierce-looking *senhora* who could well have been his mother. But there was no mistaking Nelson; he was the carbon copy of his dad way back in 1950. Stocky, medium height, receding hair and a strong face with a drooping moustache, just like his father's. Nelson turned to see Marçel, a look of surprise and then relief on his face.

'When I told the barman you were to meet me here at eight o'clock, Marçel, he told me that you had just called and you were at the railway station waiting for me. Where have you been?' he inquired.

Marçel, using his full height and strength, put his hand on the back of

Nelson's collar, firmly leading him out of the bar and across the square, towards his hotel.

'We are going to my hotel, Nelson, because you have a little explaining to do! I don't like what's going on, so just come along and you can explain to me why I had to extricate myself from the Heartbeat Club.'

'I am very sorry, Marçel. The barman had us both duped. He sent me to the station and you to the Heartbeat Club. It was stupid of me not to realise that the barman was one of the gang; I'm just not thinking clearly at present, especially for a policeman.'

'Yes, Nelson my friend, that was a *very* bad mistake. You must pull yourself together.'

They sat at the table in Marçel's bedroom. Marçel had poured out two large glasses of whisky. 'Cheers, Nelson. Now talk, my friend.'

Nelson, white faced, his hand shaking and spilling whisky, tried to drink from his glass. 'My wife and two children are in great danger, Marçel. Talking to you will put them in even greater danger. However, I realise that if I don't talk to you they will, I'm sure, be murdered by those bastards.'

'I was sent to the Heartbeat Club, where I would, at the very least, have been beaten to pulp, but more probably murdered by the two resident gorillas. So what's going on? And please stop crying, Nelson.'

'They told my father that I had to choose between you, Marçel, and my wife and children! They said they would decapitate my two children if you didn't go straight back to Australia—' He breathed in sharply. 'Someone must have seen you talking to my father and told them you were here.'

'Ah yes … the girl with the little dog.' Marçel whispered.

'They must have checked out the hotel register and realised you had come back to Aveiro. After all these years your name is still well remembered. They must have guessed you had been asked to come to Aveiro to help our family and spoil all their plans.'

Nelson crossed to the window, opened it and anxiously looked out. The room faced a stone wall and there were no other windows that were close enough to enable anyone to gain access to the room. He moved back to his chair at the table and dried his eyes with his handkerchief.

'This goes back a long way, Marçel. It all started in 1944. This was the time when you were having your own private war with the Nazis in Brittany. At the end of World War Two, you established your organisation here in Aveiro. My father realised that although the amount of gold you were able to steal back from those fleeing war criminals was quite substantial, it was only a small part of a much larger amount of gold that had been stolen from the Jews in the death camps. He told me that what you people didn't know was that the bulk of Adolph Hitler's treasures had already been shipped out across the Atlantic in a fast cargo ship from Porto to Salvador in Brazil, and this, under the very noses of yourselves and the Portuguese Government.'

Marçel sat up, slightly shocked at this revelation. 'Good God … and did your father know about all our activities? He was the assistant manager of our bank at the time and later became our bank manager. We certainly didn't reveal any of our activities to him. So how could he have found out about us?'

'Simple, my friend. Like many others at that time, Father was a part-time agent for PIAD, the Portuguese secret police.'

He continued, 'My father discovered that several corrupt government officials were working with a gang of Portuguese criminals. These officials were paid an extremely high commission by the criminals, for allowing and helping Germany to bring in, and load a ship, with a large amount of Adolph Hitler's stolen treasures. The small but fast freighter sailed from Porto and apparently avoided the Allies' naval blockade in the Atlantic and arrived safely in Salvador—the Nazis got their gold.'

Marçel's mind went back to the occasion on the River Blavet near Lorient in France in 1940. He and Peter had destroyed a lock gate that had trapped a U-boat loaded with Adolph Hitler's stolen gold and treasures. The U-boat was still there after the end of the war. Maybe these were the same treasures.

Nelson leaned forward in his chair. 'The PIAD, with my father's information, which he had discovered in relation to some shady transactions in the bank, after having discovered what had happened, reported it to our top politicians. Had it been revealed at the time, this information could have placed Portugal in a most embarrassing situation with its allies. PIAD quickly rounded up the corrupt officials; a secret trial was held, my father giving evidence at the trial. The public servants were all sentenced to life imprisonment. Some of them just happened to die in prison; we were later told that they died trying to escape. The usual excuse! It was only quite recently, when Portugal joined the EEC, that the last of these men were finally released.

'We believe that the Portuguese gangsters, who organised the whole thing with the aid of some of the local Nazis, travelled on that ship to Brazil with all the gold and the stolen treasures.'

Nelson emptied his glass, which Marçel quickly replenished.

'Yes, my father was aware of your intentions right from the start, and he informed his PIAD superiors of your plans to eliminate the criminals and relieve them of their gold. This was obviously an undercover operation; my father and two other men, whom you employed in the winery, were instructed to report on every move you made. It was decided by the Portuguese government to let you continue your operation as it would, if revealed, counterbalance our government's unwitting involvement in the shipment of Hitler's treasures, thus ensuring the discretion of the British government regarding Portugal's involvement.' Nelson emptied his glass again.

'Also at the time, PIAD considered that the criminals who had organised the shipment of gold out of Portugal would soon realise just what you were up to, and would not be able to resist coming back to Portugal and getting their hands on your gold. PIAD also believed that your department was perfectly capable of quietly eliminating these criminals, thus saving Portugal the task, with all the unnecessary publicity it might have attracted.'

'Okay, Nelson, so what's going on now? And who are these people who seem to want to get rid of your father and now me?' Marçel topped up their glasses again.

'Like my father, Marçel, I am serving my country. After six years in the army in Angola I was posted to the Directorate General of Security, the DGS, which had succeeded the PIDE secret police. My job is to track down criminals, gangsters and anti-state political extremists, the very men who are attacking my family right now. These gangsters are the next generation of the criminals that skipped the country in 1945, my generation in fact.'

By now, Nelson had struggled to regain his composure and continued gravely.

'Five weeks ago my father was approached by two men, who told him that they had just been released from prison after having been convicted in 1947 for their involvement with the Nazi gold shipment—that was such a long time after the Nazi gold shipment had left Porto for Salvador.

'But they had remembered my father because he had given evidence at their trial. They told my father that at the time, they had vowed to kill him when they were finally released from prison. However now, as they had made certain plans for the future, they had decided that my father would work for them instead and his life might possibly be spared.'

'So, this is payback time and your father is the target. Did Alfonso tell them where to go?' Marçel asked impatiently.

'Two weeks later, Monica my daughter, who is only seventeen years old and had just started at the Universidade De Aveiro, went missing. Two days later, my twenty-year-old son, António, went missing at the Universidade De Coimbra. When my father told me how he had been approached by these men, we decided that we had no alternative but to handle this situation ourselves or else Monica and António would be killed; that's if they are not already dead.'

Marçel stood up, stretched himself and sat down again. 'So that's when you decided to contact me. I'm glad you did, Nelson; revenge on an old man—that's sick.'

'For the last weeks, as you can imagine, my wife Bernadette and I have been going crazy. I know that if I inform my superiors, they will charge in regardless and Monica and António will be killed.' Nelson had become quite agitated again.

'Just calm down, Nelson, and take a few deep breaths.'

Marçel gave Nelson several minutes to collect himself.

'So what do you want me to do, Nelson?'

'There is something strange about this. These people knew about your arrival in Aveiro and yet the only person that knew you were coming to Aveiro was the receptionist at the hotel when I made a booking for you, and the head of my department. My father insisted I inform him that you were coming, just in case you might still be on the list of unwanted foreign agents. That of course is ridiculous as it was over fifty years ago.' Nelson had calmed down a little by now and was able to smile a little.

'Yesterday they contacted my father and these people told him he was to tell you to leave Portugal immediately as your life was in great danger. Father found you sitting outside the hotel and instead of warning you off, he arranged for you to meet me at the Petisqueira bar. He is convinced that you are the only person who is able to help us deal with these people.'

'Go on, Nelson.' Marçel smiled inwardly at being asked to help one retired and one active PIDE/DGS agent!

'When I got to the bar, the barman, who I now realise is one of them, told me to quickly drive up to the railway station where you were waiting for me. I waited a while for you at the station but then realised that I had been tricked, so I went back to your hotel to see if you were there, after which I drove around some of the back streets looking for you. I finally returned to the Petisqueira to tackle the barman. He told me he had not seen you, but I knew he was lying. Another man came into the bar and spoke quietly to him. They both disappeared behind the bar and a few minutes later his mother came out and took over. I was about to go on to your hotel when you turned up at the bar.'

'Nelson, have you any idea what these people are planning?' Marçel asked thoughtfully.

'There has been some talk in our department lately about a powerful gang calling themselves the Returned Black Cross Brigade, the RBCB. We understand that they are a very well-organised gang of criminals who control a lot of the criminal activities in Porto as well as several of the northern coastal towns. It has been rumoured that they are planning major robberies somewhere in Porto and in some of the more affluent smaller towns in the area.'

Marçel leaned back in a relaxed position, his hands holding the back of his head. 'This is getting really interesting. You were wise not to call in the DGS at this stage. I'm sure it would sign the death warrant for your children. Nelson—your dad, you and I, have the skills to handle this situation, but it will be dangerous. Alfonso and I are at a dispensable age and you, Nelson, I know, would gladly die for your kids; but let's hope it won't come to that.'

'You are right about the last bit, Marçel. I would certainly die for my two wonderful children.'

Marçel closed his eyes and remained silent for several minutes.

'Nelson, these men must have their own very efficient spy network; possibly someone in your department. We will work together to get your kids back and nail these bastards.' He stood up. 'Do you think you could find me a quiet home to rent, somewhere in the country but not too far from Aveiro?'

'No problem, Marçel, I know of several holiday homes out in the country but not too far from here that you could rent. When do you want it?'

'Ready in two days' time. I will need a live-in housekeeper, mature and discreet of course, and the house will be rented under the name of John Roberts from Dorchester in England.'

'Nelson, I'm going back to Porto; then I will fly to Madrid in Spain. There I will hire a car, change my appearance a little, and drive back to Portugal as John Roberts; I gather nowadays that passports are no longer needed in the EEC. Err … it's getting late. It's time you went home.'

They exchanged mobile phone numbers, 'Try not to worry, Nelson, but we *are* going to need all our wits about us from now on. Is there a discreet person in your department that we can borrow for a few days, who can carry out some surveillance work?'

'That shouldn't be a problem; I have a young assistant called Petra. He would be an ideal person for the job.'

They took the lift down to reception; the street outside the hotel appeared to be deserted. They shook hands and Nelson slipped away.

Chapter 17

Early the following morning Marçel caught the Express Train to Porto, a connecting coach to the airport and a midday flight from Porto to Madrid. By late evening, John Roberts was driving his black VW Golf out of Madrid and heading for the Spanish border, having left the old Marçel behind in Madrid.

Marçel had tracked down the top hair salon in Madrid and had spent a small fortune on a complete transformation. Gone was the old Marçel, in his place—the new image.

John Roberts, the 'gay bachelor', head and beard shaven, a heavy gold necklace, two large gold rings, one on each hand, and dressed in a gaudy decorated T-shirt tucked into knee-length white trousers, displaying his wide decorated leather belt.

Perhaps just a little conspicuous, he thought, but he was now quite unrecognisable as the old Marçel. 'John' would like to have found a Harley Davidson with raised handlebars but decided it more prudent to wait until he returned to Australia.

He stopped for the night at a small motel to the east of Salamanca. After freshening up, Marçel decided to go into the adjacent restaurant for a well-earned meal. He noticed he was getting a few sidelong glances from the clients next to him and soon found he had empty spaces on both sides. He was just finishing his second beer and ready to move into the restaurant when a young blonde man joined him.

'You speak English, sir?'

Marçel gave him a warm smile. 'No, mate, I only speak Australian.'

The blonde male bombshell moved in close with fluttering eyelids. 'I seem to be a bit short of cash; do you think I could share a room with you, just for tonight, dear?' He gave Marçel's arm a little squeeze.

'I'd love to, darling, but my wife went to bed early and anyway, she is not very keen on an *à trois* arrangement.'

The bombshell melted into the now-crowded bar. Marçel was pleased; his disguise was working quite well.

The next morning Marçel drove through Salamanca and by lunchtime he had arrived at Guarda. He decided to divert and take the road to Coimbra. Driving to the top of the hill, he arrived at the very impressive Universidad and after several enquiries, was able to get the lodging address of António Biadassaris.

Marçel drove down through the old town and parked the car by the river. He walked back to the old part of the town up several narrow lanes until he came to a tall drab-looking building. Inside, there was an old iron spiral staircase, which he climbed up to the sixth floor. After the third knock a small dark-haired girl came to the door. It was obvious from her red eyes that the girl had been crying for some time.

'I'm looking for António Biadassaris—I'm a friend of his father's. I'm on holiday in the area and he asked me to look him up.'

'Yes, he lives, or rather lived here, I share this accommodation with him but ... he disappeared almost two weeks ago.'

Marçel moved forward to take her hand but the girl moved back sharply. 'Will you be seeing Nelson; his father?' she asked. 'My name is Simone and I'm a friend of the family.'

Marçel smiled warmly. 'Nice to meet you, Simone, and my name is John and I hope I will be seeing Nelson tomorrow.'

She moved aside to let Marçel pass into the room, which was a typical students' den with books and papers overflowing from the large table and stacked on the floor. The sink was piled up with unwashed dishes. By the window, a computer raised its head above another pile of papers and books. Marçel found an uncluttered rickety chair.

'What exactly happened, Simone?' She cleared a space on the table and sat opposite him; she thought this man looked a bit of a weirdo, but studying his face, she felt that he was someone she could trust.

'António and I were having a coffee at the *café* down by the river. It was about eleven on Sunday morning, the Sunday before last, when a car drew up alongside of us, two men got out; they grabbed António and forced him into the car and then drove off. I immediately reported it to the police. They gave me a funny look and said it was not their business. I realised then it must be the DGS that had taken him away.'

'Why would you think that, Simone?'

She was starting to cry again. 'We have both taken part in peace rallies and lately Antonio has become involved with one of the secret Communist movements that operate from the Universidad.'

Marçel decided not to pursue that matter for now.

'It was white. I think it was a Fiat; it looked a bit on the old side. They were two big burly-looking men; they just lifted António into the car.'

'Cheer up, Simone; I don't think it was the DGS. We are going to find him. Nelson, his grandpa Alfonso and I make a strong team. Alfonso and Nelson have some good friends in the public service. I must go now.' Marçel started for the door, but then turned and took Simone's hand. 'Don't worry and please don't tell anybody apart from Nelson about my visit here today.'

Simone gave him a kiss on the cheek. 'I won't tell. Please find him, John.' She smiled. As Marçel started walking quickly down the stairs she called out, 'I noticed the car had a large dent in the rear-boot as it drove off.'

Once back in his car, Marçel decided to give Nelson a call on his mobile. 'I've found a nice little cottage for you, Marçel—I mean, John—and it's about halfway between Aveiro and Águeda. It's an attractive little house, very private, the garden runs down to the Rio Vouga and you now have a housekeeper. She's already in the house; her name is Maria … yes another one! She is a friend of the family, and has already been shopping for food and I can tell you from experience that she is an excellent cook.' Nelson gave him the address and then rang off.

Marçel took the Auto-Estrada turn-off for Águeda, after which he took the road to Aveiro. Just past the village of Travassó, he turned down a narrow lane until he came to the banks of the Rio Vouga, which was a small river that ran into the large marshlands of the Ria de Aveiro.

Although not a large river, like most rivers it was quite delightful. Marçel followed the track alongside until he came to a lovely old house surrounded by tall trees. He drove through the rusty old gates and arrived at the front door of an attractive-looking house. The studded wooden front door, which was surrounded by climbing roses, opened and a cheerful-looking elderly lady welcomed him into the house.

Maria was in her mid-sixties, medium height, a little overweight, well-groomed grey hair, but her main features were her lovely high shining cheekbones that declared her happy sunny disposition.

The house had been recently renovated. The downstairs was an open-plan design, the kitchen and the eating area-come-family-room taking up all the back of the ground floor, and the front of the house consisted of a large sunny lounge area with French windows that opened onto the long green lawn that ran all the way down to the river.

Maria was a little surprised at Marçel's appearance, but she liked his face and his openness and was immediately charmed by him. She took him upstairs to the two large *ensuite* bedrooms, which also had large French windows that opened onto a wide balcony, giving a splendid view up and down the river.

'I can have a meal ready for you in one hour, *Senhor*, if you wish. I took the liberty to buy in some wine for you, just for tonight, because I am told that you are a wine expert and will want to choose your own wines while you are staying here.'

'And I have been told, Maria, that you are a wonderful cook, so I'm quite sure you will know which wines to serve with your meals. I noticed you have a car outside. Do you live far away from here?'

'Only five minutes, *Senhor*, so it is no problem for me to work late if you need me to at any time.'

'Do you have a mobile phone? We will swap numbers, then I can call you if I need you; I will be coming and going quite a lot while I'm staying here.'

Well dined and well wined, a very tired Marçel decided to turn in early; he would start to track down António and Monica in the morning.

The next morning sitting outside on the patio drinking his coffee, Marçel decided to call Nelson.

'The house is perfect and the housekeeper is a lovely woman, Nelson. It couldn't be more private. By the way, look out for a battered white Fiat—this is our first lead; it has a bad dent in the rear-boot. Can we meet up this morning?'

'Glad you like it, John, Maria is an angel and you will be well looked after. How about ten am at the *Café* Encantro, Rua Homem Cristo?'

'I'll be waiting, Nelson.'

At ten on the dot, Nelson appeared at the door; he looked around the *café* and walked straight past Marçel. He then stopped, turned around, and walked back to where he was sitting.

'John? That's very good. I had to take a second look to make sure it was you.'

Marçel sighed. 'But not quite good enough. Do you have any contacts in the film industry in Porto? I need some false eyebrows and two undetectable stick-on scars for my neck and face.'

'That can be arranged, but you will have to go up to Porto. I will give someone a call and arrange for you to go and have a little face surgery! The white Fiat you mentioned is parked I think in front of the Hotel Arcada. I have instructed one of our men to watch it, and if it drives away, he is to follow it and to call me if it looks like heading out of Aveiro.'

'That's great, Nelson. Try to make an appointment in Porto for two pm today and keep a track on that car. I intend to return to the nightclub tonight, so I hope the disguise will work!'

'You need to get some *'with it'* evening gear; you are facially almost there; and as mutton dressed as lamb you'll certainly pass.'

Marçel enjoyed his fast drive on the Auto-Estrada to Porto in the hired Golf; although it was a bit outrageous, his new image made him feel ten years younger. He pulled over to answer his mobile.

'You are expected at the theatre in Auqusto Rosa Street at two pm, John. My man Petra is following the white Fiat and he's heading for Porto. He will call you when they get to their destination in Porto. Talk to you later.'

'I've just arrived at Porto; the Ponte Do Infante is just ahead. Thanks, Nelson, I'll talk to you tonight.' Marçel checked his map; the theatre was only a short distance from the bridge.

At the theatre, Marçel was taken down to the make-up artist, an elderly gay man called Houray, a name he had acquired in his youth through his over-exuberance when playing marbles in the back streets of Porto. After carefully studying Marçel's face, he created new pencil-line eyebrows and added an old red scar that ran from his left cheek right down to his neck.

'That should be enough, John, provided you don't scrub your face—just wash it gently, these alterations to your face should last at least two weeks.' The elderly make-up artist leaned over and kissed Marçel on the back of his neck. 'I almost fancy you myself now,' he laughed.

Marçel didn't know whether to laugh or hit him.

'That's a really remarkable change. I don't even recognise myself now.' Marçel paid Houray, delighted with the changes to his face, and headed back to the Golf. He was about to open the car door when his mobile phone rang. 'This is Petra; the car I'm following has just crossed the Ponte Do Luis. It looks like we are heading for the Caves do Vinho at Calem.'

Marçel was delighted; it was just down the road from where he was. 'Stay with him, Petra, I'll be with you in five minutes.'

Marçel drove down to the Luis bridge, crossed over the Duro River, and then along the riverside Avenida Diogo Leite. The white Fiat was parked outside the Sandeman's Wine caves. Marçel found a parking spot across the road, locked his car and walked over to the grey Mercedes, parked a little way behind the Fiat.

He bent down to look at the driver, 'Are you *Senhor* Petra?'

The young driver grinned back at him, '*Si, Senhor,* and are you *Senhor* John?'

Marçel jumped in alongside of Petra. 'Why would he stop here, Petra?'

Petra smiled, 'You will see, *Senhor.*'

A few minutes later the driver of the Fiat came out from Sandeman's clutching several bottles of wine. 'It is very difficult to drive past without buying a few bottles of really good wine.' Marçel would bear that in mind, perhaps on his way home.

'He's moving off, Petra; let's see where he goes.'

They followed the Fiat along the Avenue; it turned left up a narrow street. They then followed it up a maze of narrow lanes until it stopped outside a distinctly Moorish-looking white building in the Rue de Floretall. Petra slowed the Mercedes and parked down the lane a discrete distance away. The Fiat's driver parked outside and entered the building through a heavy wooden door.

Petra was looking thoughtful. 'This building is occupied by an important Middle-Eastern wine exporter, which I must say I find a bit strange, when so many of those Arab countries forbid the consumption of alcohol.'

'Do you know if their caves are open to the public like so many of the other wine exporters around here?'

'Definitely not. If it were, there would be cars and people in this street at this time of the day—this street is deserted.'

After two hours, Marçel decided to leave Petra to wait for the man to come out. 'I'm going back to Aveiro, Petra. Stay here until he comes out then just follow him. Find out where he goes, and then report back to Nelson; I'm sure he will return to Aveiro.'

'No problem, *Senhor.* I won't go to sleep.' Petra yawned.

'I'm going to stock up on wines on my way back and then I'll return to Aveiro.'

Marçel started walking down the street in the direction of his car and had just reached the corner when as he glanced back, the heavy door opened abruptly and two men came out both carrying guns. They started firing at the windscreen of the Mercedes. Petra must have fired back as one man was evidently hit and he was dragged into the Fiat by the other man, who got in and drove off.

Marçel hesitated a moment; doors and windows were opening, people were appearing from the houses at the sound of gun shots, and then a police car entered the street from the far end. Marçel melted into the crowd that was forming at his end of the street; moved to the back and watched as an ambulance pulled in behind the police car. One very dead body was removed from the Mercedes and the black plastic bag was taken away.

Marçel turned and walked calmly back to his car; he had lost interest in wine-tasting for the time being.

Shortly after leaving Porto, Marçel pulled over to the side of the road and called Nelson. 'I'm afraid I have some bad news—Petra's dead; shot by the two men who drove off in the white Fiat.'

'We were parked outside of the Mid-Eastern wine company's wine caves, I had left Petra and was heading back to my car. As I glanced back, I saw two men come out, guns blazing. Poor Petra didn't stand a chance, although he did manage to wing one of the thugs.'

'What happened after that, John?'

'They took off in the Fiat before the police arrived. I expect they will be on their way back to Aveiro. I was able to blend into the crowd and I am now on my way back to Aveiro.'

'I'm going to have a lot of explaining to do to my superiors.'

'Well, those thugs have got me really fired up now, Nelson. I think it's time for another visit to the Club. I am pretty sure those bastards didn't get a good look at me in Petra's car, so now it's time to test out my new look.'

'Do you want me to send my men to the Club tonight?'

'Definitely not, Nelson; this is something I can handle alone. I'll call you in the morning. *Até logo.*

Chapter 18

At ten pm wearing an even more colourful shirt over his shiny black, knee-length shorts, Marçel tapped on the Heartbeat Club's door. A face appeared at the grill, the door opened and he slipped into the darkened clubroom.

This time, unlike his previous visit to the club, there were several couples sitting at the tables that were spaced around the dance floor. They were mostly middle-aged men sitting with attractive young girls.

'We don't supply our clients with boys; only girls,' the doorman sneered at Marçel.

'Pity,' he sighed. 'I suppose I'll have to settle for a girl instead.' Marçel pointed at Cleo who was propping up the bar, and talking to the same two gorillas that had tried to attack him when he last visited the club.

'Send that woman over to me. And tell her to bring over a bottle of champagne.'

Marçel strolled over to one of the booths in the darkest part of the dance floor. The red padded seats were set in a half circle around the tables; planters filled with tall green palms divided the booths. He sat down in a corner seat at the back of the booth. A few minutes later, Cleo joined him with the champagne. When Marçel indicated to her to come and sit close to him, he noticed the look of disgust on her face as she stared at him but she hadn't recognised him.

'Don't look so disappointed, babe; the best sounds come out of the oldest fiddles! It's the euros that really count and I have lots of them to spend tonight.'

At the mention of euros, Cleo immediately brightened up. 'You'll need heaps of euros if you want me to play on your fiddle, old man.' She smiled. 'My name's Cleo. What's yours?'

'John. Who were the two men you were talking to at the bar?'

Cleo moved in closer. 'The large fat one is Fredrick the manager and the tall slim one is Joe, his minder. We don't cross Fredrick; he is a dangerous and cruel man especially to us girls.'

'Go over and invite them both to join us, and bring over another two bottles of champagne while you're there. I feel like living a little dangerously tonight, Cleo darling.'

Marçel watched Cleo return to the bar; he noticed her jump forward as fat Fredrick slid his arm down her back. He said something to Joe, who then strode over to John's table.

'Wot yer want, fancy boy?' he said, standing menacingly looking down at Marçel, who realised that he had to create an interest in himself as he needed to make a connection with these people. An idea struck him.

'I'm sure I've seen your friend somewhere in Brazil when I was there some time ago looking for talent. Ask him to come over for a chat. You can tell him that I own much larger clubs than this in Berlin, Paris and London; I'd like to talk shop with him.'

Joe hesitated for a moment but then decided to return to the bar. He came back minutes later. 'Come.' As they crossed the dance floor, Fredrick signalled them to follow him through a door at the side of the bar. As they brushed past Cleo, Marçel touched her thigh and winked at her. She wasn't smiling.

At the end of the passageway past the toilets, the staircase took them to the next level where there were several bedrooms. As they passed the open doors, Marçel noticed several bored-looking girls sitting on the beds, apparently waiting for their next customers.

Fredrick's lush office was at the far end of the passage. The room was dominated by a large carved desk, which stood in front of the blacked-out windows. Sitting in the tall-backed chair behind the desk was a tall powerful man with receding blonde hair; Marçel guessed he was heading for the mid-sixties.

He and Fredrick sat down in the deep comfortable leather armchairs. Joe, standing in the background, quickly opened a bottle of champagne, poured and handed one to the man behind the desk, and then passed glasses of the sparkling liquid to Marçel and Fredrick.

'So, John.' He paused staring thoughtfully at Marçel. 'What brings you to my modest club?' the soft-spoken man behind the desk inquired.

Marçel had a strange feeling he had met this man before: the build, the soft but powerful cultured voice and especially that cruel look in his pale blue eyes.

He realised that was looking at a replica of Karl Schmidt.

But Schmidt had died sixty years ago when his *Stuka* bomber had dived into the mud flats in France. Then as he stared into this man's face, Marçel also saw the likeness to Lolita, Schmidt's wife.

This person had to be Karl Schmidt's son. It had never occurred to him that Schmidt had sired any children.

'Well? Are you going to answer my question, or are you just going to stare at me?'

'I'm sorry; I was just trying to recall where I had seen you before but I just can't remember. So what is your name?'

It was obvious to Marçel; none of these men recognised him as the old man from Australia that they had tried to kill. They had seen him in the distance talking to Alfonso outside the hotel when he had arrived, and later in the club when it would have been too dark for them to have had a close look at him.

Schmidt smiled indulgently. 'I'm Karl Schmidt.'

'I've heard your name mentioned. I must have seen you at some time when I was running my cocaine business in Brazil, many years ago. But now I am living in Europe and involved in the lucrative business of trading in girls; hence my knowledge of the club trade.'

'So what brings you here, John?'

Marçel carefully watched Schmidt's face. 'I have a good selection of girls if you need any. But actually I have heard that a large operation involving the taking of hostages and leading up to a large scale robbery is being organised here in Portugal. Kidnapping, especially young girls, is my speciality.' The only sign that Schmidt gave was a slight narrowing of the eyes.

'You're a bit old for all this aren't you, John?' Schmidt smiled from behind his desk. 'What makes you think I would be involved in such an evil enterprise?' He laughed. 'Joe, fill up this man's glass. No, better still, just show him how we deal with people that know just a little too much.'

Marçel felt the sun burning his face as he slowly came to life. He opened his eyes to see Nelson staring down at him and remembered the first blows to the face and then nothing. 'Oh, God, how's my make-up, Nelson?' He tried to smile; it was painful.

'It's still perfectly intact. The scar down your face looks even more realistic and your false eyebrows haven't moved at all.'

Marçel sat up and looked around. He was sitting on a sandbar that jutted out from the low lying land that ran all along this side of the inland waterway. He was surrounded by water on three sides.

'I don't think they were trying to kill me. They just intended to soften me up and to let me know what to expect if I were to join them and then let them down.'

'A passing fisherman spotted a body lying on this sandbar and reported it to the police. You weren't answering your mobile so I decided to come looking for you. I really thought you were dead, you old fool.'

'I think I have been accepted into the organisation. We might be getting close to finding where they have your kids, Nelson. I'm going back to the club tonight.'

'You'd better stand up, Marçel. Let's see how you are. I'll take you back to your car; at least they have not found that yet. Go home get some rest and talk to me before you go back to the club tonight.'

Marçel had had a difficult day; he realised that Nelson was right; he was a silly old bugger. But in for a penny, in for a pound and at just before midnight, he set off to the Heartbeat Club, having decided not to call Nelson. He parked his car in a side street close to the club, and walked around to the club's back entrance.

The door beneath the red light was open but there was no one about; he stepped inside and mounted the staircase to the bedrooms. Several doors were open, but with no girls in sight. Two doors were closed, evidently busy with customers. The last room next to the manager's office was empty. He cautiously entered and pulled the door behind him, leaving it just open enough for him to hear voices and see if anyone entered or left the office.

Listening carefully, he heard voices coming from the office and then the door slammed. The sounds then became much louder but were muffled. There was a pause, and then the screaming started. The heart-wrenching sound of a woman screaming tore at Marçel; it would stop for a minute and then start again. Marçel guessed one of the girls was being punished for something. There was one long extra loud scream and then silence.

There were more muffled voices and then the office door opened. Through this slightly opened door, Marçel watched Joe carrying a girl over his shoulder, as he passed down the corridor. He decided to follow. The office door was closed as were the other two bedroom doors. He quietly slipped down the stairs and stepped outside to see Joe bundling the girl into the boot of his car.

Marçel waited until Joe got into his car, then wincing painfully, quickly ran back to his own car, which was only a little way down the next street. He drove back to the club just in time to see Joe's car turning left at the end of the street and was able to follow it at a safe distance.

Joe took the highway out of Aveiro which led to the coast; he turned off the highway and headed for Barra which was close to the seaway, the entrance to the Ria de Aveiro. At Barra, Joe turned down an old track leading to a small group of fisherman's huts and a broken-down jetty. In the faint moonlit night, Marçel could see that Joe had parked the car, so he turned off the headlights and carefully drove closer, parking a short distance away.

Joe dragged the girl's body to the end of the short jetty. Marçel, although having not had need of them in quite some time, used his old skills to creep stealthily up behind them, taking full advantage of the dilapidated fisherman's huts to cover his movements.

Marçel watched as Joe pulled out a gun; the girl must still be alive. Joe intended to kill her before pushing her out into what he could see was a fast flowing tide.

Now only a few feet away from them, Marçel launched himself at Joe, who must have heard the click as Marçel's flick knife opened. Joe turned and fired at Marçel who felt a bullet whiz far too close to the top of his head. Marçel's knife entered Joe's throat and Marçel kept pushing until Joe's body went over the end of the jetty and into the fast running tide.

Marçel watched as Joe's head bobbed up and down, before disappearing under the swirling fast running tide. He turned and looked down at the girl to see that it was a very much worse for wear Cleo. He bent down to see if she was still breathing and checked her pulse. He noticed Cleo had a bruise on her forehead but her breathing and pulse appeared normal. There were cigarette burns on her arms and the backs of her hands, which must have accounted for her screams. Bastards.

Marçel decided to take her back to his house. When she had recovered sufficiently, he would be able to question her as to what exactly was going on at the club. In the meantime he had to get her into the car; he had to try and revive her. He realised Cleo must have been drugged, so it could take a while.

Marçel folded his jacket and put in under her head. All he had was his handkerchief, which he took down to the water's edge before carefully wiping her face, placing it on her forehead. He squeezed her hand, being careful to avoid the cigarette burns. Time was slipping by; soon Joe would be missed and his boss would come looking for him.

Marçel was about to attempt to carry her to the car when he saw two frightened eyes staring up at him.

'Time to wake up, sleepy girl. You've had a bad experience, but you are quite safe now. I'm taking you home; we have got to do something about all those burns on your hands.'

Cleo looked down at her hands and let out a yell. 'Oh my God, what have they done to me?' With the realisation came the pain. Cleo started sobbing.

'Try to stand up, Cleo.' Marçel bent down and helped her to stand up. He put his arm around her and carefully walked her over to the car.

'Just spread out on the back seat. We will be back at my house in about thirty minutes.' Cleo didn't respond; Marçel realised that Cleo was completely dazed and traumatised. He drove quickly back to his house, which thankfully was not yet known to the gangsters.

On the way, Marçel used his mobile to call Nelson. 'I've got a damaged girl and I'm taking her back to my house. Do you know of a very discreet doctor you could bring over to my house to treat some minor burns?'

'Do you know the time, Marçel? It's two am.'

'Yes, sorry—we need to get the doctor away from here before daylight. Call me back if you find someone. But definitely not from your department.'

When they arrived back at Marçel's house, Marçel made Cleo comfortable on his sofa and fetched a blanket to keep her warm.

'Tea or coffee, Cleo?' It was the first time he had been able to look at her in full light. Despite her ordeal and apart from a very pale face, the girl was certainly a head-turner. She lay there quietly on the sofa and Marçel saw her endeavouring to come to terms with her ordeal.

'That's a strange question to ask a girl from Brazil. Coffee, of course.' Cleo stared at this strange-looking man. He was certainly not what she had imagined, when she first saw him in the club. He was old, but despite his weird turnout, he was still a very tough and attractive-looking man. He had treated her kindly and with respect. Cleo decided that he was a man she could trust.

Marçel disappeared into the kitchen and returned a few minutes later with two steaming cups of coffee.

'Take these pills with your coffee; they will help with the pain and make you relax a little. A doctor will be coming shortly to tidy up those burns on your hands. My name is Marçel, not John by the way. I have been in disguise for a very good reason.' At four am, Nelson arrived accompanied by a rather no-nonsense-looking female. 'This is Annette, she is our family doctor and not too happy at being called out at this time. But she is also a family friend and is very discreet.'

Annette took Cleo's hands in hers and muttered some Portuguese swear words. 'Nelson, tell her the girl was rescued from a nightclub and will be staying here for a few days.'

Nelson waited until Annette had finished dressing Cleo's burns. They talked for a few minutes and then Annette spoke quietly to the girl in Portuguese. Cleo smiled. '*Obrigardo médico.*'

'The girl must rest quietly; I will come back in two days. She must be careful not to get the burns infected in any way. The poor girl. You did right in calling me, *Senhor*. I realise we must not let anyone know that she is here. Do call me if needed.' She picked up her bag and went quickly out to Nelson's car.

'Thank you, Nelson. When Cleo's ready we will have a little chat; I think she will be very helpful to us.'

Marçel watched as Nelson and the doctor disappeared up the driveway. Cleo was sitting up and looking quite cheerful when he returned to the lounge.

'There is a spare bedroom you can have upstairs. In the morning my housekeeper Maria will arrive; she is a lovely kind lady and will give you a wash if you like. You mustn't get those bandages wet.'

'I am very tired now, Marçel. I need to sleep. Show me the bedroom and the bathroom; I promise I will talk to you tomorrow, if you are a policeman, I'm sure you will find it very interesting.'

Chapter 19

'You know I'm just a common prostitute.'

It was late morning and Cleo, who had immediately been adopted by a very enthusiastic Maria, was stretched out on the sofa having been showered, dressed in Marçel's pyjamas and dressing gown and fed.

'It's just another job, Cleo; it certainly doesn't bother me. Anyway I'm sure you are a *Poule de Lux* and *very* expensive,' Marçel said laughingly.

'My family was very poor; my mother who was quite small was dark skinned and beautiful. My father was an American mining engineer. He raped my mother on his way through our village to his mining camp. My mother became pregnant. But she never saw that American again. When my mother died, I was fifteen years old. Shortly after, some men came and took me and three other girls from our village to work in the city. It turned out to be a brothel and there was no escape for us.'

'That is terrible. Unfortunately it's happening in so many countries around the world today; but how did you get to Portugal and Aveiro?' Marçel was sitting stretched out in a comfortable leather armchair, pleased to be relaxing after all the events of the previous day.

'An elderly schoolteacher, who was a regular client of mine, brought me books. After having sex he would spend time giving me lessons teaching me to read and write. After he left I would study the books. A prostitute really only works at night, so I had lots of time to study during the day.' Cleo stretched herself on the sofa.

'When a client arrived, the girls would all try to grab him, no matter what he was like. I used to hold back and only pushed in when I saw a smart-looking intelligent man I could talk to, but it didn't always work!

'Then one day Karl came into our brothel. He was looking for girls for his very 'upmarket club'. I moved in on him, and when he discovered I spoke fluent Portuguese and could read and write and looked attractive, he came up to my room and I gave him the best sex he could have wished for. Anyway, that's what he said.'

'I can believe that, Cleo. You are a very attractive woman and I'm sure very passionate.'

She gave Marçel a sexy smile. 'Do you want to go to bed with me, Marçel?'

'I think not Cleo; I'm much too old for a pretty girl like you.' He laughed.

'Your age doesn't bother me, Marçel. Maybe some time in the future.' She continued on with her story. 'I got on well in Karl's club and when he decided to buy into the Heartbeat Club here in Portugal, he got me a passport and brought me to Aveiro to help him get the club started.'

'So what's going on, Cleo, and why did they try to kill you?' Marçel leaned forward eagerly.

'I knew Karl was a crook and a drug dealer in Brazil. He was a man who showed no mercy to anyone who tried to cross him. They ended up either badly beaten or killed. But I knew if I stayed with him, one day I would meet the right man, someone with lots of money who would take me away from this disgusting life.'

Cleo looked at Marçel pointedly, with large, now-vulnerable eyes. 'So how about you, Marçel?'

'I wouldn't last a week with a passionate woman like you. Mind you, it would be a nice way to go! Best get back to why you were tortured.'

'I wandered into Karl's office; I was going to ask him for some money to buy some more clothes. Without thinking, I started shuffling the papers around on his desk; I don't even know what I was looking for. Then I heard him talking to someone. He was coming back to his office. I just panicked then. I knew he would punish me for being there. I slipped into the toilet; there was a door in his office, which must have once been a bedroom. I didn't have time to close it properly before Karl came into his office with two other men. I had a glimpse of them as they came past the door. One of them had a beard, and was dressed like an Arab with a white hood on his head.'

'Karl was talking. He was telling them about a truck load of gold that arrived too late for the boat to Brazil. He said the driver, being a Catholic, took the truck to a church close to the river. It sounded like Da Vera Cruz, which was evidently close to where the ship had been loading before it sailed.'

Cleo sat up; Marçel could see she had become stressed. He couldn't help staring at her well-formed breasts, as she leaned forward.

'Karl told the men that the truck driver had been killed in France on his way back to Germany. Only the priests knew about the gold and they were too ashamed to tell anyone about it so the gold remained hidden in coffins in the crypt of the church. When the last priest died, he had been suffering from dementia and he left all his meagre possessions to a down-and-out tramp who he had befriended and who had frequented the church for many years. Amongst the old priest's possessions, there was a box of letters, which the old tramp carefully read. To his amazement, he came across a letter of confession to the Pope, which the old priest had written but had never had the courage to send.'

'That's quite a story, Cleo; so what happened next?' Marçel realised this was quite plausible and could easily have happened.

'The old tramp must have gone to a *café* that night and told one of his friends, hoping that between them they could enter the crypt at night and steal some of the gold. That friend was a friend of a member of the gang that a generation ago had helped to organise the shipment of gold to Brazil and this was how Karl Schmidt in Brazil heard about it. A few days later the tramp's dead body was found in the Duro River.

'I gathered from what Karl was saying to the two men in his office, that word of this gold also found its way to the Vatican, probably via the tramp's friend, who they should have killed but he went into hiding when the tramp was murdered. A search was made and the gold discovered in the old caskets. The Vatican had the crypt sealed off and placed armed guards at the church. They claimed the gold was a gift to the church and was rightfully theirs—in Portugal, no one dared argue with that.' Cleo leaned back on the sofa, trying hard to recall what had been said after that.

'That must have put an end to Karl's plans to steal the gold, Cleo.'

She leaned forward again. 'There was talk of suicide bombing; I think that's what the bearded men were there for. They were to organise the bomb explosions, and Karl said he had a man who was prepared to die. They were going to share the gold. I just can't imagine that.'

'We are talking about a vast sum of money, Cleo; more than you or I could spend in a lifetime.'

'I think they are planning to blow up a bridge at a time when someone important is due to cross it, that is, when he comes to inspect the gold. A second bomb will explode near a church. In the confusion, the gold is to be transferred to a nearby warehouse and then later shipped out of Portugal.'

Cleo bent forward, tears forming in her eyes, holding her clenched hands to her mouth. 'One of the men said he needed to visit the toilet. That's when they found me.' By now, Cleo was visibly shaking as her mind went back to when they dragged her out of the toilet and into the office.

'The two bearded men, I could see they were Arabs, were screaming and showering me with blows to my head and body. Karl shouted to them to stop. He picked up his phone and told Joe to come up to the office. Joe burst into the room, lifted me off the floor and forced me onto an upright chair.'

'Joe pulled my arms around to the back of the chair, while Karl taped my hands together, and then taped my arms to the back of the chair. They taped my legs, to the chair's front legs. I was terrified and quite unable to move.'

Cleo continued angrily, 'That filthy bearded Arab tore open my dress exposing my breasts! I spat in his face and he kicked my chair over backwards. I thought my wrists and my neck were broken; the pain was excruciating. Karl gently moved the Arab aside. 'What were you doing in my office, Cleo?' he asked me. I knew my only way out of this situation was to plead guilty for a lesser crime.' Cleo gave Marçel a weak smile.

'I told Karl that I had gone into his office to steal some money. When I heard them coming to the office I panicked, and hid in the toilet. I told Karl that I had heard voices but had not heard a word of their conversation. He told me to stop lying and tell him what I had heard. That's when Joe started on me. He lit his cigarette and waved it around my face. I pleaded with him not to burn me; then he stubbed out a cigarette on the back of my hand and I screamed with the pain. He carried on burning me with his cigarette; each burn added to the pain; each time I screamed louder. Then Joe taped my mouth so that the girls and their customers couldn't hear my screams. After a while I must have fainted.' Fresh tears coursed freely down Cleo's face.

'Just calm down now, Cleo. You can tell me the rest later.' Marçel knew the agony she must have suffered.

Cleo was quiet for a few moments, reliving the pain of the previous night.

'Not much more to tell, Marçel. After I came to, Karl came out of the toilet. He had been in the toilet listening to the others talking. He came over and stared down at me. 'You're a lying bitch, Cleo.' he said and then turned to Joe. 'Take her away, Joe and get rid of her. You know what to do.' The last thing I remembered was a heavy blow to the back of my head. You know the rest, Marçel.'

Cleo lay back on the sofa and closed her eyes.

Marçel waited patiently for Nelson to pick up his phone. 'Nelson, can you come over this evening please?'

'No problem, Marçel; it will be late, after ten?'

Good, get someone to drop you off a hundred yards beyond my driveway; then come down through the trees to the front of the house. We can't be too careful at the moment, especially with Cleo in the house.'

'You sound nervous, Marçel.'

'Not nervous, Nelson, just cautious. Things are moving fast at the moment. Cheers.'

Maria had insisted on staying overnight in the house while Cleo was recovering. Marçel wondered if she had some notion about protecting the young virgin from a very mature and somewhat oversexed gentleman! But it gave her an excuse to cook them a delicious meal, which they all appreciated after the events of the last few days.

Cleo was lying on her bed. After recalling her life story that day, with all the tragic and cruel events in her life, she was wondering what the future held for her.

She buried her head in her pillow and let the tears flow. Normally she thought she was pretty tough and able to cope with whatever came her way. It was the fact that Marçel and Maria had been so kind to her that had really upset her. No one had ever treated her like this before. Perhaps, she thought, my life is finally turning around and I'm going to find some really good people in this world.

She drifted on; she started to think about Marçel. He was very old but also so caring; he was her knight in shining armour. Could this be love, she thought? If so she would give him everything she had, but then she realised all she had to give was sex, and he'd be much too old for that.

Cleo finally drifted off to sleep.

Pacing the floor in the lounge, being careful not to spill an excellent Port wine on the expensive-looking carpet, Marçel realised just how big an undertaking they were now facing. He and Nelson had to get these thugs off his old friend Alfonso's back. They had to rescue Nelson's two children and he realised that if Nelson informed his boss in the DGS that his children had been kidnapped, they would just blunder in, and knowing what sort of person Karl was, Monica and António would surely die at the hands of these people.

They would have to destroy this Karl junior, the son of the Karl that he had fought against all those years ago. In the end, he had watched as Karl senior's *Stuka* dive-bomber plunged into the mudflats of the Loire River in France. Karl had died in the ball of flame that followed. Now his son would have to be eliminated and his gang, which now seemed to include several Arab bomb experts, must be destroyed.

Despite his age, Marçel knew he was still quite capable of achieving this. But now their first priority was to rescue the children.

The way Marçel saw things at present, Karl had discovered that a whole truck load of gold, hidden in the crypt of a church close to the docks, was part of a large consignment, which Karl's father had believed had been shipped out to Brazil in 1944. The truck had been slightly damaged in an Allied air raid, and had been held up in France. Then it had arrived at the Porto docks on the Douro River, the day after the ship that was taking the gold to Brazil had left. The truck driver, not knowing what to do with the gold and being a good Catholic, took it to the nearest church.

Now all these years later, Karl junior was determined to recover that gold, which today would be worth many millions of dollars and he would take it back to his homeland, Brazil.

To achieve this, it looked to Marçel as if a bomb diversion, to cover the removal of the gold, was being staged with the help of bomb experts from the Middle East. But why had they kidnapped Nelson's children?

Marçel's thoughts were interrupted by a tapping on the lounge window. He opened the sliding door to let Nelson in, who promptly took off his wet shoes, after crossing the rain-soaked lawn. He was breathing heavily, having run all the way from his car.

'The bastards have got Dad!' he gasped. 'Late this afternoon he went missing from the hospital. What do we do now?'

'Just sit down and calm yourself, Nelson. Did anyone see him leave?'

'No no,' he dismissed impatiently. 'The ward sister at the hospital said Dad had received a telephone call, but she was sure no one went into his room. But shortly after his phone call, a porter noticed a pyjama-clad old man leaving the main entrance of the hospital and getting into a white car.'

'One thing I'm sure of, Nelson, they won't be using him in place of your kids and sending them back to you.' Marçel was thoughtful for a while. 'I wonder if they want something from Alfonso, and will use your kids to force him do something for them. This has to be connected to the gold in the church.'

'That's certainly possible, Marçel. Maybe he just wants to use them as hostages in case things go wrong for him when he tries to move the gold.'

'It has to be more than that, Nelson. What exactly is wrong with my old friend?'

'The old man is just worn out. He has cancer of the lungs so he hasn't got long to live ... however, we want to make his last days as comfortable and as happy as possible before he moves on to a better place.'

Marçel paced the floor for a several minutes and then came and stood by Nelson, who was leaning back in the armchair having regained his composure.

'What puzzles me, Nelson, is the Arab connection. I'm sure this Karl and his gang don't need Arabs to put together a bomb for them.'

'I expect it's nothing really,' Nelson continued thoughtfully, 'but the only thing happening in two days' time is that the Pope is sending one of his Cardinals over here to inspect this gold. I expect they are hoping to send it all to Rome one day. It really should all stay in Portugal, but you know how powerful the Catholic Church is in this country.'

'Of course!' Marçel exclaimed. 'That's it, Nelson!'

Marçel walked over to the drinks cabinet and poured out two large glasses of Port and handed one to Nelson before sitting down in the other armchair.

'The Cardinal's entourage has to cross over the Ponte Do Luis to get to the church on the other side of the river where the old docks had been in 1944.'

Marçel was speaking slowly as the picture gradually formed in his mind.

'Nelson my boy, we're dealing with terrorists.' There was a moment of silence as they both realised the implications.

'I think they intend to blow up the bridge just when the Cardinal is driving over it, and they no doubt have a second bomb which will explode outside the church at the same time, enabling them, in the chaos that follows, to remove the gold to a safe place until they are ready to take it out of the country. Your father is being forced to explode that bomb in exchange for the lives of your two children, Nelson.'

'Oh, my God!'

Nelson clutched the sides of the armchair.

'It's true, Dad has no time for the Catholic Church; he has always been more interested in the Muslim faith. He has always said that the church has been 'ripping off' the Portuguese people for hundreds of years, but he's a wily old fox and by no means a walkover as they will soon find out.'

They were both silent for a while.

'He wouldn't just walk out of the hospital and get into their car unless he had some sort of plan. But where the hell have they taken him, Marçel?'

'I've got a pretty good idea, Nelson. Considering the proximity to the church where the gold is, it must be somewhere in the Caves Vinho and also there is the Arab involvement, so it must be where young Petra was murdered by these bastards.'

'Of course. The Rue de Floretall ... that's the obvious place; close by and they could easily hide the gold by concealing it in a tunnel at the end of one of their extensive caves.' His face dropped as he suddenly thought of his two children, also hidden somewhere in those caves.

He realised they might never be found.

Chapter 20

Leaning against the hospital bed, Alfonso's face had contorted; he started to sweat as a wave of pain swept over him. I can't take much more of this, he thought. Why haven't they called me? They told me to check into the hospital. They said it would be much easier for them to collect me when the time arrived.

Earlier that day, when the ward nurse had been busy, he had entered her office and stolen a roll of surgical tape. Later, he went to the toilet and carefully taped his very small mobile phone to the inside of his crotch.

As if to answer him, his bedside phone rang.

'A white car will be outside for you in five minutes. If you keep us waiting, the children will be punished.'

Already wearing his slippers, Alfonso slipped on his overcoat, covering his pyjamas, pulled down his hat over his face, and with no one watching at that moment, walked down the long corridor and out of the front entrance of the hospital.

The white car was waiting at the kerbside with the rear door open. Alfonso lowered himself into the car and then abruptly the door slammed as the car drove way. A puzzled hospital porter, who had observed this occurrence, walked back into the hospital and reported it to a nurse at the reception desk.

Alfonso opened his eyes. He was tied to a chair. A smiling Karl Schmidt was staring down at him. The rough-hewn stone walls, lined with old cobwebbed casks revealed where they had taken him.

'No wine-tasting today, old man.' Karl ran his hands over Alfonso, instinctively searching for hidden weapons. Thinking him only an ineffectual old man; he failed to feel inside Alfonso's crotch and find the mobile phone.

'You know why I'm here, Karl. There's no need to keep me tied up; I'm not likely to go anywhere now. I know what I have to do, so untie me and bring me a good glass of wine.'

Karl smiled at Alfonso as he released him from the chair. 'Where you are going, old man, they don't seek solace in alcohol—they pray to Allah instead.'

'If my grandchildren are here, I would like to see them.'

'That would not be a good idea. However, I will let you hear them. Then you will know they are here.' He was smiling as he locked the heavy door behind him.

A few minutes later, coming from a distance he heard, 'You bastard!' followed by, 'Leave her alone—you dirty pig!' Then silence. There was no mistaking those voices. Monica and Antonio were together and not too far away from him.

Alfonso shuffled around the cellar until he came to a small pile of rubbish, evidently forgotten when the cellar had last been swept. He gently ran his hands through the pile of dust and broken glass until he came across a piece of glass that still had a label stuck to it. He lifted it to the light and read, 'United Arab Wine Merchants.'

It was still very quiet. Alfonso partly unwound the bandage that held his mobile inside of his crotch and quietly dialled Nelson.

Chapter 21

'Cleo did mention that Karl Schmidt was thinking of buying a run-down old property that faced the bridge, with the intention of opening another club.'

'That's not a good place for a club, Marçel. I know the property in question but from there he would be able to look straight down at the bridge. It would be a perfect position for him to run his operation.'

'Unfortunately, Nelson, you can't come along with me. I'm quite sure you are being carefully watched by Schmidt's people and we cannot let them know we are almost onto them.' Nelson looked disappointed.

'I have to change my image again. I'm going back to being an old man. I didn't, except for Cleo, get much response from the fair sex anyway!' Marçel started to chuckle. 'I'll call on Houray, our make-up artist again, Nelson. I want to look just like Alfonso if that's possible. I'll see if I can get a hat like his, and of course a pair of pyjamas, blue I imagine, and a dark overcoat should do the trick.'

Nelson's phone was ringing; he quickly picked it up from the table.

'Son, we are all at the United Arab Wine Caves; you know where they are?'

'Of course, Dad, are you all all right?'

'I move on tomorrow and something bad will happen the next day. When it does, take lots of men to release the children. Don't go near that place before it all happens, but then be ready to move in fast. If you try to call me I'm a dead man so I'm turning off my mobile. God be with you, son.'

Nelson quickly related the brief conversation to Marçel. 'We were right; they are all at the United Arab Wine Caves. He's going to die, Marçel. I'm sure of it. His last words—I've never heard him talk like that before.'

'Go home, Nelson; get some sleep. I will send Maria over to your house to pick up some of your Dad's clothes first thing in the morning. As from tomorrow morning, keep a constant watch on the United Arab Wine Caves. Get a reliable man to help you if possible; that building must be watched for the next forty-eight hours. Be prepared to send in your heavies the day after tomorrow, but they must not go anywhere near the area until some time after the bombs are due to explode. Your father said, "Don't call me". That applies to me as well. I could be with the enemy.'

'Are you absolutely sure you know what you are doing, Marçel?'

'Go home, my friend. Your worries will soon be over. But tomorrow just be ready for anything. Keep your mobile at all times. I may need to call you urgently.'

Marçel believed that Nelson had complete confidence in him. He was not too sure about himself, but with a good plan and sheer bloody determination, he was going to rescue those kids and eliminate the criminals ... God willing.

At first light, Marçel sent Maria to Nelson's house in Aveiro where the old man had been living. Bernadette, Nelson's wife, had collected some of Alfonso's pyjamas, old slippers and a similar overcoat and hat to those he had been wearing when he left the hospital. Bernadette also gave Maria some photos of Alfonso, which she had taken of him recently.

When Maria got back, Marçel changed into Alfonso's pyjamas and slippers, put on the heavy overcoat and pulled the hat low down over his face. They were all a bit short but still wearable. Cleo looked on in amusement. He gave each of the two smirking women a hug and a kiss, jumped into his car and set off for Porto.

On the way he called his new friend, Houray, the make-up man, at the Augusto Rosa Theatre and arranged to meet him at ten-thirty that morning. He had set off in his car for Porto at nine am and arrived on time to be met outside the theatre by Houray, who flung his arms around Marçel, kissing him on both cheeks.

'John, dear boy, I'm in disgrace at present. I got too friendly with the stage manager so we will have to go to my place. Don't worry; I won't make a pass at you. I can only handle one lover at a time! My flat is just around the next corner.'

'You needn't worry, Houray. I wouldn't dream of cutting in on your love life. I have a few other problems to face at present. I need a complete change, back to where I was, but with the appearance of the man in these photos.'

Marçel was amazed at the opulence of Houray's apartment which was so tastefully decorated and containing some very expensive furniture. Perhaps, he thought, a slight case of overkill.

Houray made Marçel sit in front of the mirror at his enormous dressing table. After studying the photos for a few minutes, he set to work.

'It's evident to me, John—'

Marçel interrupted him. 'It's not John now; my real name is Marçel but the person I'm about to impersonate is my good friend Alfonso and he is in deep trouble.'

'So confusing, dear boy. This is relatively easy but you will have to wear a wig. His hair, what's left of it, is quite different to yours and of course you will need that drooping moustache.

After an hour, looking into the mirror, Marçel was amazed to find he really was looking at Alfonso, or at least a very close likeness. The scar and pencil-lined eyebrows had been replaced with shading that accentuated his cheekbones and clever make-up had given him a slightly aquiline nose. The two sideburns, receding grey hair and Alfonso's moustache were perfect.

'I would advise you to keep your friend's hat on all the time as the top of your head is shaped differently to your friend's. Otherwise Marçel-Alfonso, I'm sure you can easily pass as your friend.'

'You really are a genius, Houray; I can't thank you enough.'

'Think nothing of it, dear boy; anyway I don't find *you* nearly as attractive as John. Next time you come to see me I hope your problems will all be over and I'll make you so attractive that the boys, led by myself, will be falling over themselves to get at you.'

Marçel paid Houray and left, feeling that under that gay façade, there was a very unhappy man. But he was certainly a genius at his job.

Parking his car near the riverside, Marçel walked past several very busy restaurants, ignoring the amused glances of people at an old man out for a walk in his pyjamas, and resisted the temptation to sit down at one of the many outside tables and tuck into his favourite dish *bacalhau*, dried cod fish. He took the pedestrian walkway across the Ponte Du Luis. At the end of the bridge the road turned sharply to the right and sloped gently down towards the Caves do Vinho at Calem.

Marçel found he was staring at the old house directly facing the bridge. It was obviously empty and he wondered why it had not been demolished long ago. It must be heritage listed, he thought; the traffic noise and vibrations would make it impossible to live there. Schmidt must have bought it for one purpose alone—to control the diversion, the assassination of a Cardinal, in order to transfer the gold from the church to the wine merchant's caves.

It was an austere three-storey building and looked as if it had been a merchant's house many years ago. Steps led up to the heavily-barred front door and the windows were tall, room height, but not very wide. The outside stonework had been blackened, first by smoke and later by all the emissions from the heavy traffic that passed by this old building. Strangely, it had survived when they built the bridge and inaugurated it in 1886.

Marçel dodged the traffic and crossed the road and walked around to the back of the house. At some stage the area behind the house had been cleared, leaving a large empty parking space. The house had been built on a slope so Marçel had to descend several stone steps to the back door, which was locked so he climbed through a broken window at the side of the door.

As he had expected, the inside of the house had been left to decay many years ago. Looking up, Marçel could see the roof tiles through two lots of broken flooring. There had been four main rooms on the ground floor, what appeared to be a kitchen and a study in the back rooms, a hallway, and in the front of the house, probably a dining room on one side and a reception room on the other.

Marçel quietly climbed the rickety but once-impressive staircase. Surprisingly, except for a large hole in one of the back rooms, the one above the kitchen where Marçel had been able to see the roof tiles, the floors were in reasonable condition. The front room ran the whole length of the house, the full-length windows giving an excellent view of the bridge. It was obvious that someone had been there recently, as there was a table and chairs facing the windows and a portable gas stove with a kettle, cups and coffee and sugar standing on a small table at the back of the room. Marçel noticed two overflowing ashtrays on the table. There must have been several heavy smokers there quite recently. He looked into the two back rooms, the one with the large hole in the floor was quite unusable but the other large back room had a single bed in one corner and a dilapidated old built-in wardrobe taking up one side of the room.

Marçel climbed the small staircase again to the top floor. One side must have been the servant's quarters and the room was quite empty. The other half was evidently a storeroom as there were several old dust-covered crates scattered around the room. On the back wall, there were double doors. Marçel forced one open. Above the outside of the doors the beam extending from the house had an iron wheel attached to it; he realised that this must have been part of an old winch used to haul the merchants' goods up for storage in the loft.

He was looking down at the yard when a large Mercedes van pulled in. Two men jumped out of the van, opened the back doors and dragged out Alfonso. Supported by the two men, Alfonso, who was evidently drugged, staggered across the yard and into the house. Through the cracks in the floorboards, he was able to see Alfonso being brought up the stairs, taken into the back bedroom and helped on to the bed. He recognised Schmidt and Frederick. The two men went into the front room; Marçel could hear Schmidt talking to someone on his mobile but couldn't hear what he was saying.

A few minutes later another car drove into the yard. Marçel, hidden behind a slightly open door, watched as two men, dressed in white and wearing the traditional Arab headdress, headed for the back door, mounting the stairs to where they joined Schmidt and Fredrick in the front room. Marçel, frustrated that he was unable to hear what they were saying, crept back across the storeroom and looked down at the two vehicles parked in the yard; he was unable to read their number plates. While he was looking at the cars, Schmidt and Fredrick came out of the house, jumped into their Mercedes van and drove off.

Marçel felt certain now that the two Arabs had not yet had a close look at Alfonso. He wondered just how he would be able to change places with him.

The solution came quicker than expected.

The two men started to argue loudly; he heard, 'Fetch explosives.' Soon after, they both went down the stairs and out to their car. Marçel quickly descended the stairs.

He couldn't help smiling at the look of astonishment on Alfonso's face.

'What are you doing in my clothes, *Senhor*, or am I just dreaming? Oh, Marçel—is that you?'

'Quickly, old friend; get under the bed, I'm taking your place. As soon as I start shouting and creating a diversion in the front room, get down those stairs and as soon as you get outside, Alfonso, run like hell down the road, where Nelson will be waiting for you.'

Alfonso slipped under the bed and Marçel quickly took his place.

Marçel waited for the light to fade. He could hear the two Arabs talking; he leaned over the bed and whispered to Alfonso. 'How mobile are you, Alfonso? Are you able to slip out quietly and get away?'

'No problem. I'm not nearly as decrepit as I make out. I just hope you know what you are doing, Marçel … you know I was quite prepared to die for the children; I'm dying anyway.'

'Just do what you're told, old friend, and get the hell out of here!'

Marçel slipped out of the bed and stormed into the front room; here goes, he thought.

'How dare you treat one of Allah's chosen men with such contempt!' he yelled. 'Tomorrow I shall be joining him and as one of the chosen, I will tell him of the disrespect that you are showing me today!' He screamed. The two men stared at him open-mouthed.

'What's wrong, oh chosen one?' the older of the two finally asked.

'You are asking me to face Allah with an empty belly!' he thundered. 'I am unwashed, there is no toilet, and I am dressed as an infidel. How can I face him like this?' he screamed.

'Calm down, old man, we have food for you, and in the morning you will be washed and dressed and made ready to meet your maker—our great Allah.'

They handed Marçel a glass of water. He sat down, seemingly exhausted after his long outburst. The younger of the two reached down into a bag. 'I have some food here for you, old man, but first tell us again, true believer, why are you are so determined to give yourself to Allah?' the younger Arab asked.

'There are *many* reasons, young man!' Marçel shouted; he got up and walked to the end of the room so that they were no longer looking out of the window, just in case Alfonso came into their line of vision.

'I wish to gain eternal life and be close to our great Allah. At the same time I wish to save the lives of my two grandchildren who will continue to serve him while on this Earth, and finally I wish to punish those greedy Catholic cardinals who would rob the poor Portuguese people of what is rightfully theirs!' He rejoined them at the table, still shouting. 'Is that not *enough* my friends?' Marçel was wondering if he had given Alfonso enough time to get away.

He sat down, again, appearing to be exhausted. The younger of the two reached down into a bag and handed Marçel a large packet of sandwiches. 'You are a true Moslem, old man; we will help you achieve your hopes tomorrow morning.'

Marçel ate the sandwiches. Within minutes he could feel his head spinning and realised too late that he had been drugged.

The men helped him struggle to the bed in the back room. Stretched out on the bed, he watched the two faces fade into the distance. 'Sleep well, old man.'

Marçel dreamed strange, disjointed dreams … Peter had admonished Marçel but then laughed happily as Gerda swept him into his arms. Mary blushed and gently took his hand in hers and placed it on her warm soft breast …

Gerda? … Where is everyone? Mary? It can't be … you're all …

'We overdid the drug last night. We must handle him carefully if we want to get him ready in time.'

The two faces had reappeared; they were staring down at him and looking quite agitated. Marçel stared back, smiling happily. Marçel shook his head a little to clear the spidery wisps from his mind. 'Good morning boys, I hope you slept as well as I did.' It was broad daylight with the sun shining through the dirty windows. Marçel sat up; he was feeling light-headed and so happy. This was going to be a very special day, a lovely day he decided.

'You have slept too long, old man. It is nine o'clock and you have to be on the bridge by ten. Have you forgotten what you are doing today?'

'No, my friends, today we are going to blow up a bridge and then I'm on my way to meet Allah.' Marçel giggled. It was slowly coming back to him and he remembered the strange feeling he'd experienced before he passed out the night before.

He realised why he was feeling so happy. Apart from relaxing him so that he slept well and was not going to spend the last few hours worrying about his approaching death, the drug was making him light-headed and euphoric, which he realised would last right up to the moment he exploded the bomb.

'What's for breakfast, boys?'

They escorted him into the front room. A basin of water, soap and a towel were ready for him on the small table. 'Where is the razor, I need to shave?'

'Where you are going, old man, they never shave.'

When he had finished, Marçel sat down at the other table. The Arabs placed a mug of coffee and two buttered rolls in front of him. He noticed that the whole time in the house they had been wearing rubber gloves.

Marçel finished the rolls and stood up. 'So when do we start, Brothers?'

'Right now, Alfonso; we are running late, I'm afraid you must stay dressed as an infidel to avoid suspicion while you are standing on the bridge, so let us get this belt around you.'

Marçel shivered slightly as they wrapped the nine-inch-wide belt around him.

There were six silver tubes protruding from tight fitting pockets spaced around the belt, and they were all wired up to one loose, hanging plastic box the size of a small mobile phone.

'You stand on the footpath in the middle of the bridge. You pretend to be looking at all the passing tourist boats, at the same time you will be watching out for a white stretched limousine approaching the bridge. When it appears, wait until it is well onto the bridge, then step forward, you must be holding the activator by then. You wait until the limousine is almost abreast of you; then you press the red button.'

The older Arab took the activator from Marçel, turned a button on the back of the activator ninety degrees and handed it back to Marçel.

'Now put it into your trouser pocket, and don't touch it until you are ready to move up onto the road. You will have to press the red button quite hard to explode the bomb, so it will be quite safe in your pocket.' He put his arms around Marçel, gave him a slight hug, and kissed him on both cheeks. 'Don't worry, Alfonso old man; when you press the button you will feel nothing. In an instant you will find yourself in a far, far better world where all mankind are freed from evil and are forever at peace and we, Alfonso, will be rewarded with so much gold that we will be able to continue our fight for the great cause. May the Great Allah be with you.'

The young Arab helped Marçel into his overcoat and passed him his hat which he pulled down to shade his face; he was ready to go.

'You must go now. There are only fifteen minutes left before the limousine is due to pass over the bridge.'

They helped him down to the front door, at the same time being careful not to reveal themselves while the door was open, and from the downstairs window they watched him carefully as he went down the steps and slowly crossed the road.

'The stupid old man doesn't realise we don't serve the great cause; all this gold will be lining our own pockets. Everything into the car now and the moment the bomb explodes, we drive like crazy down to explode the second bomb and then to the wine caves to wait for the gold.'

Chapter 22

Marçel was standing in the centre of the bridge, leaning on the safety rail looking down at the pleasure boats that were moving up and down the river.

At that moment, he noticed a coach pulling into the side of the road at the end of the bridge, and out of the coach scrambled dozens of excited schoolchildren who soon joined Marçel looking down at the pleasure boats that were moving up and down the river. He checked his watch; five minutes to go. He started to laugh.

Marçel had finally decided on his course of action.

He walked quickly back the way he had come, despite the heavy weight of the explosives around his waist. He mounted the stone steps and pushed open the heavy oak door, climbed the staircase and walked into the large front room.

The two bearded men were standing with their backs to the barred window, and were staring open-mouthed at him. He could see the whole of the bridge through the window and thought it strange that the men should risk standing behind it.

The older of the two pointed his revolver at Marçel, 'What the hell are you doing here? Get back on the bridge! The limousine will be here any minute!'

Marçel withdrew his hand from his pocket. He was holding the activator. 'I thought a change of venue might be appropriate. Pass me your mobile phone, Yassef. Tell me exactly where Nelson's family is being held.'

Yassef was smiling, 'I don't think the old man wants to die after all. You hand me the detonator switch.' He started to move towards Marçel, who began to wave the switch in the air.

'Just try me, Yassef. I still want to die and you know I have terminal cancer. I don't want a slow painful death, so give me that address quickly or else we certainly will miss the cavalcade, and the greedy Cardinals will get away with all that gold.'

'We can't tell you that. We would be betraying our Portuguese colleagues.'

465

It was Marçel's turn to laugh. 'Don't you realise that the moment that bomb explodes your Portuguese colleagues will betray you? They will have your share of the gold, and they stand to gain a hell of a lot more if they can give the CIA *your* names plus a few more of your contacts.'

For a moment Yassef lowered his eyes. 'You will go back onto the bridge?' Marçel nodded. Yassef passed him his mobile. 'You know that if you give me the wrong address, Yassef, you will be damned forever in hell.' He knew Yassef would not take that risk.

'At 87 Rue de Floreletal, the lift will take you to the second floor down. At the end of the cave behind some casks there is a tunnel. I swear before Allah, that is where you will find them.'

Before Yassef had finished speaking, Marçel had dialled a number. 'Nelson, this is Marçel—' He explained to the frantic Nelson exactly where he would find his children. 'You'd better hurry, Nelson, I would give them less than thirty minutes before Schmidt gets to them.'

Nelson sounded happy. 'Don't worry, Marçel, my father is with me and Schmidt and Fredrick are now already safely locked up. Thank you from the bottom of my heart, Marçel.'

'God be with you all, Nelson.' He handed Yassef back his phone.

In the distance they could see the white limousine approaching the bridge.

Marçel thought of the horrors he had seen in his life. He recalled painfully the horrors that had occurred at his own hand.

He was so very tired now ...

Marçel's mind wandered to those that he had loved and lost; remembering with startling clarity the smell of his first lover, Simone's hair and the curve of Mary's soft cheek. He thought of Gerda's passionate lovemaking that had given him a beautiful son, now also long gone ... he wanted more than anything to be with them once more. Above all, Marçel knew in his heart, it was time.

Almost in slow motion, the two men prompted Marçel to move and go quickly to the bridge. Their urging voices seemed to be from far away in the distance, and as if in a dream, Marçel couldn't hear them as he was laughing.

'Right, *you bastards*! It's time for all three of us to meet our maker! This should be interesting; we might all meet up again in *hell*! I doubt your God will be merciful to us.'

Marçel pressed the red button.

Epilogue

May 2006

In a lonely, cold hospital room, the old man sighed deeply, as deeply as his failing body would allow. He thought of the events of last year and although he couldn't open his eyes to see them, knew that his grieving family was gathered around him. That they were alive today was a miracle; one that he was grateful for. His own life had amounted to naught—his achievements small and inconsequential to those of others.

A tear rolled slowly out of one rheumy closed eye as he mourned the loss of his friend who had given his life to save so many.

And with another deep breath in, one which was to be his last, he finally understood why.

'Today is the day, my friend!' he yelled silently and jubilantly. Slowly, as the air escaped his frail body, Alfonso Biadassaris died two weeks shy of his eighty-eighth birthday.

— — —

Also by Richard Le Normand

In 1942 with a Japanese invasion of Australia imminent, a panic decision is made to conceal arms and gold bullion to fund future resistance to the invaders. An officer and his sergeant establish one of these hidden caches on the Myall Lakes but are killed before they record the hiding place. Years later an international criminal inadvertantly discovers this cache. He decides to take the gold out of Australia using a World War II era submarine. A young British army officer is drawn into these events and helps the local police in a race to foil the criminal's plans.